MAY THE FANG BE WITH YOU

JEFFREY POOLE

Jeffrey Poole's Epic Fantasy Books
Bakkian Chronicles:

The Prophecy
Insurrection
Amulet of Aria
Disneyland Debacle (short story)
Winter Wonderland (short story)

Tales of Lentari

Lost City
Something Wyverian This Way Comes
A Portal for Your Thoughts
Thoughts for a Portal
Wizard in the Woods
Close Encounters of the Magical Kind
The Hunt for Red Oskorlisk (short story)
May the Fang be With You (Pirates trilogy #1)
The Hammer is Strong with This One (Pirates #2)
These are Not the Stones You're Looking For (Pirates #3)
Blast from the Past

Dragons of Andela

Harness the Fire
Strike the Spark
Clear the Water

Mysteries by J.M. Poole
The Corgi Case Files Series

18 delightful cozy mystery novels featuring corgi
sleuths, Sherlock and Watson

May the Fang Be With You

Tales of Lentari, Book 7

Jeffrey Poole

Secret Staircase Books

May the Fang Be With You
Published by Secret Staircase Books, an imprint of
Columbine Publishing Group, LLC
PO Box 416, Angel Fire, NM 87710

Book layout and design by Secret Staircase Books
First Secret Staircase paperback edition: August, 2023
First Secret Staircase e-book edition: August, 2023
* * *
Publisher's Cataloging-in-Publication Data

Poole, Jeffrey
May the Fang Be With You / by Jeffrey Poole.
p. cm.
ISBN 978-1649141521 (paperback)
ISBN 978-1649141538 (e-book)

1. Lentari (Fictitious location)—Fiction. 2. Epic fantasy fiction
3. Dragons and mythical creatures—Fiction. 4. Time travel—Fiction.
I. Title

Tales of Lentari : Book 7.
May the Fang Be With You
Poole, Jeffrey, Tales of Lentari epic fantasy series.

BISAC : FICTION / Fantasy/Epic.

813/.54

For Giliane —

You bust your tail on a daily basis, oftentimes starting well before the birds have awoken and finishing long after they've gone to sleep for the night. You make me want to be a better man, and for that, I thank you.

Always & forever, babe.

Acknowledgements

As is the norm with my books, I have a list of people to thank. First and foremost is Giliane, my wife. Her job can have her running easily 16 hours a day, yet she continues to find time in order to sit down and go through my book. Oh, she'll rip it apart, don't get me wrong. But she'll still offer suggestions in order to correct the problem.

My Posse. You people rock! Your willingness to help me get my book prepared for the public continues to astound me. I'm lucky to have you people in my corner. Jason, Toni, Wendy, Debbie, and Krista, just to name a few. And, of course, my mother. She continues to persuade me not to use sentences that are so long that they could easily be their own paragraphs.

And to you, the reader. Thank you very much for purchasing this book and helping support an indie author. It means the world to me.

Now, without further ado, let's get on with the story!

J.

Table of Contents

Prologue

There it is again. You're not looking hard enough. It's there, just above the eastern horizon. I think it's growing larger. It … no, you're looking too far north. Look a hand's breadth to the south. There. Now can you see it?"

"No."

"Come, now, Donovan. I thought you knew how to use the spyglass. You're not even trying to focus. Twist here, and…"

"Leave off, Connal. I know how to work the blasted thing."

The two men were wearing full suits of armor and were en route to the Lentarian capital city of R'Tal, completing the last leg of their daily patrol. Ordinarily, sentries did not report for duty in their finest, but their shift had started just prior to the departure of the king and queen, and they had thereby been ordered to remain as they were for the duration of their shift. Cumbersome, uncomfortable, and extremely heavy, both men were eagerly looking forward to shedding the extra weight at the first opportunity. Now, however, on the final leg of their patrol, they had discovered something. Well, one of them had.

Allegedly.

The Sea of Koralis, on Lentari's eastern shore, stretched for many leagues. Everyone knew that there was nothing worth visiting on the other side of the sea. Rocky, barren, inhospitable land stretched endlessly away in all directions. The few people that were known to live over there were primitive, savage, and—thankfully—devoid of ships and skills necessary to pay Lentari a visit. As far as anyone could remember, no one—including any relative, deceased or otherwise—had ever reported seeing a ship sailing toward them from the east.

Therefore, such a discovery warranted another look.

The first soldier shared a glance with his companion. Both men held their spyglasses tightly against their eyes as they scanned the eastern horizon out over the Sea of Koralis. Gently undulating waves beckoned invitingly. Flocks of kytes could be seen circling overhead as well as resting on the surface. There was no indication that anything was out of the ordinary, except for the simple fact there was a dark spot on the eastern horizon growing steadily closer. The sentries stared at the water. The first man pointed again.

"It's there. I do believe it's coming closer."

"What exactly do you think you see?" the second demanded. "I still don't see anything."

"Your glass isn't even pointed in the right direction."

"It is, too."

Connal sighed and gently twisted his companion until the spyglass was at least facing the right way.

"I still don't see anything."

"I am taking you to see the wizard just as soon as we're off duty."

Donovan turned to his companion and slugged him on his arm. The clang of metal striking metal echoed noisily across the quiet landscape. As a result, the first man's visor was loosened just enough so that it fell down with a loud bang, startling both of them. Connal snapped his visor open with an irritated flick of his fingers.

"There's a reason why the king discontinued the use of fully armored patrols. This damn armor is too noisy. Look, the only reason I mention seeing a wizard is that you want to continue to hold your post for another year, don't you? If so, then you're going to have to go through basic training. Again. If memory serves, you didn't do so well the first time around. You'll never pass the archery drills. How can you expect to hit the targets when you cannot *see* the targets?"

"You will *not* involve that wizard in any way," Donovan contradicted. "The last thing I need to worry about is the possibility of growing an extra set of arms. No way, thank you very much."

"Shardwyn did that only once," the first soldier patiently explained. "And that happened years ago."

"Absolutely not," Donovan vowed. "Would you let him touch your wife, Connal?"

Connal fell silent. Donovan grunted by way of acknowledgment. It was a common belief—shared by many—that the castle wizard should seriously think about retiring. After all, Shardwyn's acolyte had already proven himself countless times and he wasn't even eighteen yet!

"What about the new princess?" Connal asked. "Everyone knows her skills as a healer are unmatched."

"I would never dream of imposing on Kre'Lissa with such a trivial matter."

"But she's a healer," Connal reminded him. "It couldn't hurt to ask, could it?"

"We'll see. I wouldn't have the slightest idea how to ... wait. Wizards be damned, Donovan. I think I see what you're talking about! That! That right there! That looks like a ship!"

"Well, look who just joined the conversation," Connal scowled. "That's what I've been trying to tell you, only I saw that ship nearly ten minutes ago. Without having to use my glass."

"No, you didn't. You only mentioned it less than a minute ago."

"Sight and memory," Connal said, as if he were taking notes to be brought up at a later time. "That's what I need to talk to Kre'Lissa about. On your behalf, of course."

Donovan muttered a curse under his breath. Together, the two guards watched the ship move closer when the ship suddenly veered south.

And accelerated.

"What's going on?" Connal demanded. "How is it doing that?"

"It cannot be a ship," Donovan decided. "Ships are incapable of sailing that fast."

"It's a ship," Connal insisted. "I believe I saw a mast. In fact, I'm certain I saw two."

"It's your imagination. Besides, if there were masts, and that was a ship, then winds that strong would have snapped those masts in half. Like twigs."

"You need to trust me," Connal told his companion. "That is a ship, and it's now speeding south."

Donovan looked down at the suit of armor he was wearing, then over at Connal's. Then his eyes fell on the spyglasses each of them were still holding. A nagging thought had occurred.

"Do you think they could have seen us?"

Connal shrugged. "Perhaps. Why do you ask?"

"Let's just assume what you say is true…"

Connal harrumphed in irritation.

"…and what we see there is a ship. Look at what we're wearing. We were both required to polish our armor for the king and queen's departure yesterday evening."

"And?" Connal prompted.

"And we're out in the morning sun now. You and I both know how easy it is to spot knights. On horseback. On top of which, that ship didn't accelerate until they were within hailing range from the shore. I'm telling you, we've been seen. *They* were watching *us!*"

"And now they're moving away from us," Connal reported. He jammed his glass into its protective leather holder and spurred his mount to attention. "Then that means we need to follow. Hurry!"

The two riders thundered away from the cliffs, intent on heading south just as fast as they could.

"Can you still see it?" Donovan asked, raising his voice to be heard above the thunder of his horse's hooves. "Your eyes are better than mine."

"Aye, I can, but only barely." Connal urged his horse on. "If we don't hurry, we're going to lose them around the promontory!"

Both horses emerged on the top of the narrow strip of land and came to a skidding halt. The edge of the narrow peninsula was only a few feet away and, from their vantage point, they could now see the water nearly a hundred feet below. Connal also noticed that their horses were covered with a fine layer of sweat. He hastily dismounted and urged his companion to do the same. Both men groaned aloud. The ship was gone.

"There's no way it could have lost us," Connal observed. "The ship was traveling fast, aye, but not that fast."

"Then where did it go?" Donovan asked. He gestured at the wide-open expanse of water. "There's nowhere for it to hide. Are you sure it's not out there?"

Connal hurried to his mount and pulled out the spyglass again. He scanned the coast, starting at the base of the peninsula they were standing on and slowly panned south. There was nothing. Nothing but roiling waves and disinterested birds as far as the eye could see.

"What wizardry is this? They've vanished! This must be reported at once."

Donovan turned to his companion with an unreadable expression on his face.

"You want to report this? And say what? We saw a mystery ship appear on the horizon, but when we started to pursue, it disappeared, right from under our noses? I'd just as soon not have to report an unidentified floating object, thank you very much."

Connal shook his head, "No, we must tell someone. We both saw it. The king needs to know."

"Kri'Entu isn't here," Donovan reminded him.

"The king left the prince in charge," Connal said, nodding.

"Very well. We'll tell Kre'Mikal. He'll know what to do."

Chapter 1 — Terra Incognita

Are you sure this is it?" a voice whispered in the darkness. "Dawn is less than an hour away. We were supposed to be anywhere but here long before sunrise, and yet here we are. Still. Without anything to show for it, I might add."

"What does it matter?" a second voice asked. "They can see at night just as well as they can during the day. We'll be exposed no matter how you look at it. I'm tellin' you, Von. This is a bad idea. There's nothing up there but pain and death. We are outnumbered and outmatched. This ain't smart."

"Stop yer frettin', Jino," a gruff voice snapped. "If I want yer opinion, then I'll give it to you. And keep yer damn voice down. Speak out of line again and I'll have yer tongue!"

Several grumbles sounded, but nothing else.

"Rusty, you're the one that led us here," Gruff Voice continued. "You'd best be right about treasure being up there."

"There's treasure all around here," Rusty confirmed, suppressing a sigh. "You can find it on practically every mountaintop in this blasted valley. What do you expect? Dragons are fond of gold, Captain."

"How do we know that you're not leading us to a dragon horde?" a second voice asked.

"Because I can tell the difference, Von," Rusty whispered. "I don't argue with you about which way is north, do I?"

"You have before," Von pointed out.

"Hold your tongue," Rusty ordered, dropping his voice to let it be known this particular subject was over.

"Aye, Q."

"I told you before that only the captain may call me Q."

"I'm sorry, Q, er, Quartermaster."

There was a quiet rustling of clothes as one of their team moved about. Even though it was still fairly dark, Rusty could tell that someone was now standing directly between him and Von. He groaned. He could smell a strong odor of sardines. It didn't take a genius to figure out who it was. Sardines—raw sardines—were the captain's favorite dish.

"Captain Flinn," Rusty acknowledged. "I have it under control."

His captain leaned close, automatically forcing Rusty to take a step back, not from fear but from the smell.

"Be sure that you do," the captain hissed. "Keep them quiet. There be dragons all around us. I, for one, do not want to tangle with the likes o' them."

"Nor do I," Rusty hastily agreed.

"Which of these two mountains be the one we're looking for?" Captain Flinn asked, turning to look at the silhouettes of the two nearby mountains.

Rusty closed his eyes and waited. Within moments, he felt a pull emanate from the larger of the two. He pointed right.

"Both have inordinate amounts of gold within them. However, *that* one has something worth more than all the surrounding nests combined. That has to be what you're looking for."

"Very well. Follow me. We're heading out. We'll conceal ourselves in those trees until we know for certain the nest be empty."

For the next half hour the four men waited, in utter

silence. Each man knew they were doomed if their presence became known, so everything relied on stealth. No one spoke. No one moved, for fear of making a sound.

One of Rusty's job requirements, as quartermaster, was doling out punishment, even though the captain had also been known to administer a little of his own. Flinn had confided with him on their first voyage that he alone liked to be the one administering punishment, but knew that any experienced crew would never board a vessel where one man had too much power. Therefore, the captain had instructed his quartermaster to be mindful of an agreed upon signal, which was Rusty's cue to punish the offending crewmember. In this case, it was the removal of the captain's hat after an altercation. The longer the hat was off his head, the more severe the punishment. Thankfully, the captain's crew had been atypically loyal, and never once questioned his orders. Then again, the simple fact that Flinn had instructed him to divvy up whatever loot they acquired, fairly and evenly amongst the men, dissuaded most disagreements.

Rusty looked at the two men he had personally hand-picked to accompany them. They were becoming restless; fidgety. Thankfully both Von and Jino were experienced sailors and knew better than to disobey orders. Some of the newer crew members—left behind on their ship—would have done something foolish by this point, thus revealing their presence. Hence, the reason they were left behind.

Rusty glanced at the captain. Flinn looked pointedly at him, then at Von, the newest man amongst them, and removed his hat. Understanding, Rusty nodded. He tapped Von's shoulder and silently shook his head. Making eye contact with Jino, he repeated the gesture. They would be staying put, thank you very much.

Rusty detected a new presence on his right. He looked up. Captain Flinn was squatting on the ground beside him. He wordlessly pointed up at the mountain.

All four men looked up. While faint, they could hear something large moving about. Moments later, they saw a large object hurtling to the ground, as though the dragon had forgotten where the edge of its cave was and had simply stepped out into open space. Moments before the huge form would have crashed onto the ground, huge wings snapped open and beat the air. The dragon swooped by overhead and eventually rose into the clouds, disappearing from view.

Von grunted, "Good. The dragon is gone. I can't wait to see what treasure this dragon has. Heh. That is, *had*."

Captain Flinn turned to his pilot and cuffed him on the back on his head. Hard. The captain held a finger to his lips and again pointed at the top of the mountain. Rusty threw a disapproving look toward Von before he turned to look back up at the mountain, too. Did the captain think there were more dragons up there? Since when? Everyone knew dragons were loners. He didn't see any reason why one dragon would live in such close proximity to another.

"The mate, ye blatherin' idiot," the captain hissed, correctly guessing what his first mate was thinking. "We can't do anything until its mate is gone."

"What happens if it doesn't leave?" Von softly asked. "Do you think we could lure it out?"

Captain Flinn grinned lecherously at Von, "Perhaps. With live bait. Either the creature leaves on its own accord or else we kill it. One way or the other, the nest will be devoid of dragons, mark my words."

The three other men turned to look at their captain as though he had sprouted shiny green scales all over his body *and* grown a tail.

"Captain," Jino hesitantly began, "I don't think that's a wise idea. Did you see the dragon that flew over us? It was so big that it could've squashed us flat. The dragons grow large in these parts."

"And how would you know?" Von asked. "It's not like you've seen one of 'em up close before, Jino."

Jino nodded vigorously, "Umm, hello? We just saw one a few minutes ago. I can't speak for the others, but I'm pretty sure we all got a good look at it."

"That dragon was several hundred feet above us," Rusty calmly—but firmly—pointed out. "Let's not get ahead of ourselves, okay?"

"It had a wingspan of at least a hundred feet!" Jino

insisted. "I know I wasn't the only one who saw it. No, this is a bad idea, Captain."

"No one asked you," Captain Flinn snapped. "We're here for one reason only. It's up there. I want it."

"*What* is up there, Captain?" Von asked. "What could be worth the trouble? We passed four different dragon nests on our way here. Dragon gold is there for the taking. What's so special about this cave? What has Q found in that nest?"

"It's the only one that has been recovered in the last century," the captain murmured softly. His eyes had a faraway look to them. "Recovering another, especially for a human, is all but impossible. Therefore, I will have this one."

"Heads up, Captain!" Rusty whispered excitedly. "You called it. There goes another one!"

Everyone looked up in time to see a sleek, dark form streak by overhead. The men silently turned to regard their leader. Captain Flinn fearlessly stood up, scanned the immediate vicinity, and once he had decided it was wyverian free, he beckoned to the others. Once they had gathered at the base of the mountain, Captain Flinn gave each of his three men a crooked smile.

"Well, we're here. We've invaded foreign soil, evaded capture, and snuck into an area infested with dragons. It's time to put this plan into action. What are we, boys?"

"Pirates!" the three men growled, as they raised their clenched fists.

"And what do pirates do?" Captain Flinn continued, making eye contact with each of his men.

"We steal!"

"Damn right we do. Now, you lot be ready to move. Chances are there'll be a dragon or two on our arse when we leave. Methinks I can hold off one, but not for long. We're gonna want to vacate the area as quickly as possible. You boys had better be ready."

"We'll be ready, Captain," Rusty assured him.

The first mate grunted with satisfaction. Never had he served a more cunning—or lucky—captain than Flinn. Rusty still wasn't sure how Flinn had managed to avoid being captured after all these years, but he had a sneaking suspicion it had something to do with Flinn's power. Confronting the captain was out of the question. It was best to keep his nose out of Flinn's business lest it be cut off.

Rusty absentmindedly rubbed his nose. That had been a direct quote from the captain the last time he tried to inquire into the nature of Flinn's secret abilities. Well, he thought, if the captain wanted him to know, then he would have told him by now.

Rusty looked back at his companions and grinned. One thing was certain; he was damn glad he held the rank of quartermaster, of first mate. Holding such a title almost afforded him as much clout as the captain himself. Almost.

Captain Flinn strode purposefully to the base of the mountain. His men looked on as he leaned back to study the distant mountaintop. Before any of them could think about joining him, Captain Flinn held up a hand and signaled them to wait there.

A wind started blowing. Rusty automatically scanned the skies. The last thing any of them needed was to have one of the dragons return to the cave prematurely. He wasn't certain how long the dragons would be out of the nest, but what he did know was that they couldn't waste a moment. The cave was empty. Whatever the captain was going to do, now was the time.

Suddenly the captain was airborne. Having been witness to this particular demonstration before, Rusty watched the other two closely to see how they'd cope with what the captain was doing.

The winds grew stronger.

Captain Flinn now floated several feet off the ground. Rusty heard a cry of amazement from behind him. He knew Flinn's power was responsible for his levitation, only he didn't know exactly how it worked. He caught Flinn staring at him.

"Be ready to move."

Rusty nodded. They would be.

* * *

Captain Flinn rose steadily higher. He glanced down to

see his shipmates rapidly shrink until they were no bigger than specks of sand. He had to make this quick. Like his first mate, he had no idea how long the dragons would be gone. The last thing he wanted was to be discovered by one of the huge, flying lizards when he was hundreds of feet up in the air.

The top of the mountain loomed closer. Flinn scanned the skies. He could only hope that the two dragons he had seen would hunt for some elusive prey on the other side of the kingdom, or wherever else dragons chose to hunt. While he was fairly confident he could hold off the dragon long enough to make his escape, he didn't want to press his luck. After all, this was a dragon's nest and the dragon obviously would know the terrain better than he.

The nest was fairly easy to find, being the only cave on the top half of the mountain. Not only that, he could *smell* it. Dragons had a very peculiar odor, Flinn recalled. Not offensive, but distinctive, like that in a snake's den. One dragon alone was easy enough to detect, provided one knew what to look for. However, this cave held two dragons. He could have found it blind-folded.

As soon as he stepped foot inside the den, he knew he had hit the jackpot. The mouth of the cave had to be thirty feet high and as many feet wide. The domed ceiling was nearly seventy feet high at its highest point and extended at least a hundred feet back, into the heart of the mountain. The walls curved up, suggesting that the cave might have started out as a giant pocket of gas.

There, in the far corner, was the nest. Captain Flinn studied the area where the dragons slept for a few moments. It looked as though the dragons had burrowed down into the floor of the cave, hollowing out a section nearly fifty feet across and twenty feet down. The nest itself was covered in sticks, branches, leaves, and animal hides. Surprisingly, though, there were no signs of animal carcasses anywhere. In fact, he couldn't see any animal remains—be it bone or otherwise—anywhere in the cave.

Flinn paused as his nostrils flared. Wrong. Correct that. His nose had picked up the scent of a rotting carcass, only he couldn't see it anywhere nearby. Before he could ponder that mystery, another discovery surprised him. There was no visible gold in this cave. Where was the dragon's treasure? Where were the pieces of gold stacked so high that they'd cascade down like falling rain? Where were the crowns, the scepters, the chests of jewels?

"It's in here somewhere, foul beasties," Captain Flinn softly muttered. "I know it be here somewhere."

He moved up to the perimeter of the nest and gazed down at the numerous soft pelts that were lining the floor. He spied several small bones in the bottom of the nest and nodded. The remains had been picked clean. His eyes traveled over the rest of the lair.

There was nothing worth stealing. Flinn grunted once, and stepped to the left. There was a vast area on the left side of the cave that needed to be checked. A small part of his brain wasn't surprised that the dragons chose to hide their most prized possession. He just had to find it and do so quickly.

A loud crunch startled him. He looked down, expecting to see a layer of gravel; only smooth stone met his eyes. Stone and ... Flinn stooped to run his fingers over the thick, chalky substance. Whatever it was, it crumbled the moment he had applied his weight to it. What was it? A type of limestone?

He picked up a small piece of the substance, no bigger than a doubloon, and studied it in the palm of his hand. He closed his fist around it and squeezed. The unknown substance cracked noisily and was reduced to tiny particles. Flinn let the remaining pieces trickle through his fingers.

He grunted again. He didn't know what the substance was. He didn't know, and he didn't care. He had more important matters to attend to. First and foremost, he had to find *it*.

Flinn explored the far recesses of the cave and was surprised to discover a tunnel which angled steeply down. It barely looked like it was big enough to pass the smaller of the two dragons. Could this be their hiding spot? Had the dragons hidden *it* down there? There was only one way to find out.

He hurried down the tunnel and was momentarily

rendered speechless. He had found the dragons' horde. Gold, silver, jewelry, and anything else he could have imagined, lay before his eyes. Large chests of coins, huge open jars of pearls, and even several containers of gems larger than anything he had ever seen before sparkled enticingly.

He poked an arm into the heart of the mass of treasure and felt around. Coins clinked noisily as they slid away from him. Cursing, Flinn pulled his arm out and reinserted it in another location a few feet away. Still nothing. He tried several other times before realizing the dragons must not have hidden *it* with the rest of their treasure. Where, then? Where could they have hidden it?

"Too obvious," Flinn muttered. He hurried back up to the top floor of the cave. "It's got to be here, but where? Think, Flinn. Think! If I were a dragon, where would I hide my most prized possession?"

A spark of light drew his eyes back to the nest. Something was there, suspended up on the wall, nearly twenty feet above the nest in the far corner of the cave. The object was shiny enough to reflect light.

Flinn hurried back to the nest and stared up at the item nearly two dozen feet above his head. It was a fang. Or, more precisely, it was a silver fang from the mouth of an incredibly rare red oskorlisk.

The fang had been pressed into the wall, as though it was a stone that had been pressed into soft mortar. Flinn shuddered. He didn't want to think about how much strength it'd take in order to accomplish a feat like that.

Nodding, Flinn backed out of the nest. *That* was what he had come for. *That* was why they were risking detection by the dragons. Possession of that fang was the first step Flinn needed in order to achieve his ultimate goal.

Unlimited power.

A strong wind materialized inside the cave. Instead of picking Flinn up, this wind focused its energy on the silver object and began hammering away on it. The fang refused to move. The winds intensified, resulting in pieces of the nest scattering around the cavern. The animal skin coverings flew out the mouth of the cave.

Now, a full-blown gale was whipping around the confines of the large cave. Flinn remained motionless just inside the nest. He only had eyes for the fang and was eager to claim it as his own.

Bits of stone began flaking off as the jet of air blasted at it with the force of a full-fledged hurricane. With a loud cracking of stone, the fang was finally pried from the wall. The winds died out immediately. The fang fell toward the nest but was caught—one-handed—by Flinn, just before it could strike the ground.

"It's about bloody time!" Flinn happily exclaimed. "Long have I waited for this blasted..."

A small commotion silenced him mid-sentence, a clatter like small rocks falling down a steep hill. An icy chill spread down his spine. He was no longer alone. Something was behind him, of that he was certain. Flinn took a deep breath and turned to look.

A small creature was standing inside the mouth of the cave. It was tiny, compared to a full-sized dragon, probably the size of a juvenile griffin. It was covered in lustrous golden scales and was just folding two small wings against its back when it paused to curiously sniff the air. The creature's head whipped around and Flinn suddenly found himself looking into a set of strikingly green reptilian eyes.

The creature returned his frank stare for a few moments. It tilted its head a few times as if it couldn't figure out what it was looking at. The small creature grunted once and moved deeper into the cave, automatically angling straight toward him.

Flinn stifled a curse and hastily retreated from the nest.

The creature ignored him as it moved past and climbed into the nest. It squealed with delight as it caught sight of the small bones Flinn had noticed earlier, snatching one with a claw. It jammed the bone into its mouth, grunting contentedly. Almost immediately Flinn heard sickeningly loud crunches as the creature made short work of its snack.

"Not good," Flinn muttered, sliding the fang into his belt. It wasn't too difficult to figure out what the creature was, having always wondered what a baby dragon would look like. Now, however, his instincts were screaming to beat a hasty retreat. If the baby was here, that could only mean the mother dragon was on her way back. "Not good at all. I do believe it be time to go. I certainly don't want to be here when your mama…"

An ear-splitting roar rent the air.

"…gets here," Flinn finished. He groaned.

A second form appeared at the cave mouth, only this one was much, much larger. The dragon bared her fangs and roared a challenge. Flinn's eyes narrowed. If it was a challenge she wanted, then it'd be a challenge she received.

The jet of air returned and blasted the dragon square on its chest. Such was the strength of the blast that the mother was knocked clean out of the cave. Flinn hurried toward the mouth, intent on escaping the confines of the nest just as soon as possible. The massive winged reptile roared again. Flinn risked a glance up. The dragon was madly flapping its wings as it attempted to reenter its nest; thankfully, the jet of air was strong enough to keep it at bay.

Flinn sighed. The creature's incessant roaring was giving him a headache. He saw that it had spied him, and was now spitting a steady stream of fire straight at him. The wind, presently preventing any other entries into the nest, shifted, causing the jet of fire to blast harmlessly up into the sky.

More roars ensued. The mother dragon tried again. Once more the fiery breath was redirected, this time blasting harmlessly to the east, away from the mountain. Before a third blast could be lined up, the winds doubled in strength. The struggling wyverian was slowly forced back, away from the cave.

Flinn grinned at the overgrown lizard, gave it a mock salute, and fearlessly stepped off the ledge. He plunged several hundred feet straight down before the blast of air caught him, slowed him, and allowed him to step unhurt onto the ground. His crew was waiting for him, open-mouthed.

"Stow yer questions, lads," Flinn ordered, before any of them could speak.

A distant roar caused his men to all look up at the same time. Flinn looked up, too. The dragon was still trying to unsuccessfully gain entry to its cave. It roared, no doubt angry and worried about her baby, when Flinn heard an answering roar in the distance. He quailed. More dragons were on the way. Mama dragon must have somehow called for help.

"Did you hear that, Captain?" Von nervously asked. "I think there are more…"

"Of course, there are more of 'em on the way!" Rusty interrupted. "Do you really want to just stand around and wait for them to show up? Move, sailor!"

"What's keepin' that one from comin' after us?" one pirate tremulously asked.

"That's not yer concern," Flinn snapped. "We've got what we came for. Back to the *Cadaymas*. Hurry!"

Chapter 2 — King for a Day

Look, it's the same design, the same stones, and the same metal, all attached to the same chain. There can be no doubt about it. He's copying my work."

"Wizards be damned, Rasfin. Clean your spectacles. My pendant does not resemble yours in any way. Ask anyone."

"I fully intend to, Laramas," Rasfin snapped, turning his back on his accuser. "Your Majesty, clearly you can see the similarities, can you not? My competitor lacks, shall we say, artistic imagination. His designs don't sell. Mine do. He copied my work, plain and simple."

"I most certainly have not!" Laramas cried. "Rasfin, everyone knows how much you favor your ale. Might I suggest that you switch to water? It'll make you look less of a fool, trust me."

Rasfin frowned. "Less of a fool?"

"You have no proof, Rasfin," Laramas argued. "Give up this pointless nonsense."

Rasfin suddenly smiled. "I was hoping you'd say that. You

want proof? Here it is." Rasfin retrieved a wadded bundle of felt from within his jacket and carefully unrolled it on the counter before him. "I don't have proof? Allow me to prove otherwise." The felt was unrolled, revealing small pouches sewn onto the surface of the soft fabric. Rasfin slipped a piece of jewelry from within one pocket and held it up. "This is an opal from my own personal mine deep inside the Selekai mountains. Do you see the setting? It has silver wire wrapped helically, with a blue crystal at the top. Now, I draw your attention to this." Rasfin slipped another piece of jewelry out of a different pocket. He held it up for all to see. "I purchased this under disguise from Laramas last week. It..."

"That was stolen from me!" Laramas cried. "I filed a report with the Constable as soon as I discovered the loss!"

"You did no such thing," Rasfin scoffed. "I purchased this with my own gold. I have proof of the transaction." He held both pendants up to one another. Any untrained eyes could see they were a matching set. Then he retrieved a folded slip of parchment from another pouch and waggled it victoriously in front of Laramas' face.

Scared, embarrassed, and now concerned, Laramas turned to the throne and bowed his head.

"Your Majesty, I cannot begin to fathom how this has happened. If you'll only permit me to..."

"Enough," a firm, quiet voice spoke.

The Great Hall fell silent. Everyone turned to the gilded thrones, yet all eyes were only on one. The *substitute* king sat back in his chair and rubbed his temples.

Mikal groaned. How his father, the king, could handle two hours of this nonsense every day, five days a week, was beyond him. Constant bickering. Baseless accusations. One person accusing the other of some trivial matter, day in and day out. How much more was he expected to take before he lost his mind? He eyed the two vendors and kept a neutral expression on his face. This pettiness had to stop. He pointed to the first vendor.

"You. Rasfin, is it?"

Rasfin nodded.

"You claim that this man, Mister ... I'm sorry, what was

your name again?"

"Laramas, Your Majesty."

"Thank you. Rasfin, you claim Laramas stole your work and Laramas insists he has never…"

"But he has, Your Majesty!" Rasfin interrupted.

"I most certainly have not!" Laramas objected.

Mikal held up a hand. Both vendors instantly fell silent.

"Allow me to finish. I need to make certain I understand. Rasfin, you have designed a piece of jewelry. There's no doubt in my mind that Laramas' design has been modeled after your own."

"Hah!" Rasfin triumphantly exclaimed.

"Hold your tongue, Mister Rasfin," Mikal ordered, his voice becoming firm. "Have I given any indication that I need your help?"

Rasfin's head fell. "No, Your Majesty."

"As I was saying," Mikal continued, "there's no doubt in my mind that Laramas is selling Rasfin's design. And, from what the constable has told me, Laramas' shop is selling considerably more than yours. Is that right, Rasfin?"

Rasfin had just sunk down onto a nearby bench when he leapt up, as though he had sat on a nail.

"Your Majesty, it's insulting! If he had any idea just how much…"

"Focus, Mister Rasfin. Answer the question. Is his shop having better luck selling the necklace than your own?"

Laramas' head fell, and he mumbled something.

"Do speak up, Mister Rasfin."

"Aye."

Mikal's attention shifted to the second vendor, who was now studying the floor.

"Now, Mister Laramas. Choose your next words carefully. Did you fashion your own necklace from that of your rival's? And do be mindful of the ramifications should you decide to lie to me."

Laramas' head fell and, after a moment, he nodded. "Aye."

"Finally. We're making progress."

"He has no business selling my designs!" Rasfin protested again. He caught the disapproving look Mikal threw him and bowed his head. "I'm so sorry, Your Majesty. I'll be quiet now."

"Speak out of line again and it's an automatic one-night stay in the dungeon. As you can probably imagine, it wouldn't be pleasant. Do you understand?"

Rasfin hastily nodded.

"Good. Now, as I was saying, Mister Laramas has been selling more of the pendants than you have, but has failed to give credit where credit is due. Here's my judgement. Laramas is hereby ordered to cease and desist the sale of this particular pendant…"

Rasfin gave his rival a broad grin.

"…unless an arrangement can be struck between the two of you."

Both vendors shared a quick look before skeptically turning to the king.

"Aye, you heard me right. It would appear to me that Laramas is the better salesman but Rasfin has the better merchandise. It would make sense that the two of you pool your resources. Each can help the other."

Both of the vendors, Mikal noted, had lifted their chins to look down the nose at the other. Rasfin had already crossed his arms over his chest. Mikal sighed. So much for diplomacy.

"It's your choice. Very well. Mister Laramas, you are hereby ordered to give half the proceeds from every sale of Mister Rasfin's pendant to Mr. Rasfin."

"Only half?" Rasfin sputtered.

"Precisely half," Mikal agreed. "It may be your design, Rasfin, but it was Laramas' skill that sold the necklaces. Since neither of you is willing to work with the other, then I will consider this matter closed. You are both dismissed."

Both jewelers turned to leave. Mikal heard the grumbling start even before they left the Great Hall. His gaze fell upon the empty throne beside him. His new wife, Lissa, was away in Capily, visiting her father. Constable Fensham had wisely asked his daughter for help when an outbreak of some type of skin rash had begun spreading throughout the populace. The village healer had quickly become inundated and asked for assistance.

"Is that it for now?" Mikal asked, as he turned to one of his advisers. "Please don't tell me there are more waiting to be heard."

The elderly adviser nodded.

"That is all of them, Kri'Mikal."

Mikal's eyes narrowed. He still wasn't used to people addressing him as king instead of prince. In ancient Lentarian, adding Kri in front of your name signified the bearer held the highest office a human could hold in Lentari, namely the kingship. The next level down, Kre, signified princes and princesses, which was why it appeared both he and Lissa shared the same title. Kre'Mikal. Kre'Lissa. It was enough to give him a headache.

Mikal had just wearily regained his feet when a commotion sounded from outside. He groaned. Now what?

A guard poked his head into the Great Hall.

"Bredo has escaped!"

Mikal blinked a few times. "Would you care to run that by me again?"

"Bredo — he's the serpent from the moat — has escaped!"

"I know who and what Bredo is," Mikal snapped, growing angry. "How in the name of the Three Sorceresses did our moat monster escape? He's been in that moat for decades!"

The guard hesitated, which prompted Mikal to scowl with irritation.

"Out with it, soldier. What happened?"

"The moat has been drained. While it's being cleaned, the castle foundations are also being repaired. As for Bredo, he, uh…"

"What about him?" Mikal prompted.

"He was removed."

Mikal stared at the guard, waiting for a better explanation. When it became obvious that the soldier wasn't offering any other information, Mikal frowned.

"I grow tired of saying this, so let's try this again. Tell me what has happened, without leaving anything out. You say Bredo had been removed. By whom? Where had he been placed?"

"Uh, Shardwyn said that he could…"

"Oh, no," Mikal moaned. "Tell me he didn't."

"Shardwyn levitated Bredo out of the moat and into a holding cage."

"Sounds harmless thus far," Mikal decided. "So, what happened? How'd he get out?"

"The pen wasn't strong enough to hold a serpent his size," the guard explained further. "Did you know that our moat monster is a relative of the oskorlisk? Those are the serpents the dragons hunt. They can grow…"

"I'm familiar with them," Mikal hastily interrupted.

"Anyway, Shardwyn administered a sleeping potion."

"And it didn't work?" Mikal asked. He motioned to the door and indicated the guard should lead the way.

"Oh, but it did," the soldier contradicted. "Bredo fell asleep almost instantly."

"So, what happened?"

"He, uh, woke up. Early."

"That's just great. Where is Bredo now?"

Right on cue, a series of screams erupted from within the heart of the city. The soldier winced. Mikal groaned.

"He's, er, on the loose in the city."

"Fetch Gareth at once," Mikal commanded. They were going to need someone who had full control of their faculties if they were going to get the ornery serpent back where it belonged.

"Shardwyn's apprentice isn't here," the guard moaned.

Mikal whirled around. "What? Tell me you're joking."

"I'm not. All I know is that he returned to his home to spend some time with his family."

Mikal nodded. He did remember his friend saying something about it being the time of year when his father would shift from shealk—water dragon—to human and spend time at home with his wife. Naturally Gareth hadn't wanted to miss out, so he had been granted a few weeks leave of absence from his duties as Shardwyn's acolyte.

They rounded a corner and almost bowled into a group of armed soldiers. All leapt to attention as they recognized who he was.

"A thousand apologies," the lieutenant hastily offered. "We didn't see you there, Your Majesty."

"Lieutenant Darius!" Mikal exclaimed. "You're just the person I'm looking for."

"I am?"

"I need your help. The moat has been drained."

"*That* must be what I'm smelling," Darius said, more to himself.

Mikal smiled fleetingly. "Aye. It's one of the reasons it was drained. The moat needs to be cleaned. Listen, Shardwyn was responsible for securing Bredo, and he…"

"What did the old fool do now?" Darius grumbled. He suddenly remembered who he was addressing and stifled a curse. "I am so terribly sorry, Your Majesty. As I was saying, how can my men and I help you?"

"We need to get Bredo back into his holding pen."

"And how are we to do that?" Darius asked.

"With live bait," a new voice added.

The group turned to see an approaching adult griffin. Mikal smiled. It was Raben, the griffin liaison. This griffin, Mikal remembered, was also a female.

"Kri'Mikal," Raben said, bowing low. "I offer my assistance."

"I'll gladly take it," Mikal returned. "Thank you. Do you have any suggestions that could help?" Mikal asked.

"The moat serpent is, in essence, a small oskorlisk," the griffin explained. The voice was high and nasal, as were all griffin voices, but at least this time they knew the speaker was a female. "Like any giant serpent, it'll be attracted to prey."

"That's not encouraging," Mikal said. "We don't want him going after the people. I'll give the order to kill him before I allow that to happen."

"Oskorlisks are always hungry," Raben added. "I suggest we lure him out into the open."

"How?" Darius asked.

"With live bait," the griffiness repeated.

"What live bait?" Mikal asked, turning to the griffiness. "What do you have in mind?"

Raben ruffled her feathers and lifted her head high. "Me."

"You?" Mikal and Darius echoed.

"Oskorlisk typically hunt in the water," Raben explained. "They're used to finding prey above their heads. Give the order for all the humans to retire indoors. I will fly above the streets, making lots of noise as I do so. In fact, I'll send for my brothers and sisters. The more griffins circling about, the better. The serpent will be too tempted to resist. He'll then be lured back to the wizard's tower. I assume your wizard will be able to handle him from there?"

"He'd better be," Mikal muttered. He looked at the men that were surrounding him. "Make it happen. Evacuate the streets. Raben, give us about ten minutes and then begin your flight. Give us some type of signal to let us know when you've spotted Bredo."

Raben bowed. "Understood."

Two hours. That was how long it took for three full squadrons of men and half a dozen griffins to lure the cantankerous serpent out from his hiding place. Bredo had coiled up under the foundation of a small one-story cottage and pointedly refused to come out. It wasn't until Raben alighted on the roof of the house did the elusive snake make an appearance.

Characteristic of his species, Bredo's movements were smooth, fluid, and incredibly quick. Raben only narrowly escaped by pretending she was going to jump out of harm's way. If it was possible for the huge serpent to have a surprised look on its face, Bredo would have had one. He had clearly expected the griffin to launch herself into the air, never dreaming that she'd flatten herself on the roof as much as she could.

Bredo hissed angrily the moment he hit the ground. And just like that, Raben led the huge snake back to Shardwyn's tower, where the old wizard was waiting with what he promised was a much stronger sleeping potion. Five minutes later, it was all over.

Mikal thanked the griffins, thanked the men, and hastily retreated before anything else could go wrong.

* * *

An hour later, Mikal was back in the Great Hall, this time listening to a group of vendors request permission to *borrow* one of the kingdom's three galleons moored off the coast of Capily. Apparently, they had decided it would be highly profitable to take groups of people out on the open seas and let them experience what it was like to be a sailor for a few days, but without any of the work. For a hefty fee, of course.

"We could call it *The Erudian Cruises*," one of them said.

Mikal crossed his arms over his chest. "No."

"We'd be renting the galleon from the Crown, of course," another added.

"No."

"We'd only have to retrofit the ship to take on more passengers," the third added. "The cost and work to the ship would be minimal."

"No."

"Is there anything we can do to change your mind?" the first man despondently asked.

"Nothing," Mikal declared. "If you want to offer … what did you call them? Cruises? If you want to offer a cruise to the people of Lentari, then I suggest you use your own ship and leave the Crown's out of it."

Dejected, the men moved off.

"I'll be in the Antechamber," Mikal announced, once he saw that there was no one else waiting to talk to him.

Mikal rose and headed to the Antechamber, his father's enchanted-against-harm private room. He quickly walked to his father's desk, took off the crown he had been wearing, and leaned forward to rest his head on the table.

What a week. What a month, for that matter. He and Lissa had returned from their honeymoon with dire news. They had chosen to visit their southern neighbors, the Straosians, in an attempt to make contact since no communication had been attempted in several decades. What they found had nearly broken his heart.

The country was in dire trouble. Run down roads, crumbling bridges, and bands of outlaws were just some of the obstacles he and Lissa experienced firsthand. Villages were in a severe state of disrepair. Food and fresh water were in short supply.

When Mikal had finally reached Caracal, Straosia's capital city, he was dismayed to see the castle was just as run-down as the rest of the country. King What's-His-Name blamed the state of the economy on a country-wide recession. Mikal had offered assistance, which the Straosians quickly accepted.

Once he and Lissa returned home, and Mikal had filled his parents in on everything he had seen and done, his father immediately called for an emergency meeting with his advisers. It had been decided that an intervention was in order, with or without the Straosian king's consent.

"I do not know how—or why—Straosia has been able to decline so far without anyone taking notice," Kri'Entu had told Mikal the next day. "I am very proud of you, my son, for taking the initiative to travel south. I seem to recall I was against the idea from the beginning."

Mikal grinned. He had been met with resistance from the first moment he had suggested venturing south. Thankfully, he had persisted.

"I remember."

"The Ylanians are our allies," the king continued. "I'm going to extend them the offer of aiding us in aiding the Straosians."

"And what if King Ewam refuses?" Mikal asked.

"Then he refuses. We, however, will not stand idly by while our neighbors suffer."

His father had immediately dispatched a message north, inviting the Ylanians to participate.

"One of our neighbors is floundering," Kri'Entu had privately explained to the Ylanian king. "I will be dispatching aid and I invite you to participate."

Surprisingly, King Ewam had leapt at the chance to help.

"So, what are you going to do?" Mikal asked his father.

"Your mother and I will be going for an extended visit."

"What about your responsibilities here?"

His father smiled at him. "How fortunate for us that I have a suitable substitute to rule in my absence."

Mikal smiled as he remembered feeling all the blood drain out of his face. "Are you sure that's a good idea?"

"Son, you're next in line for the crown. We've been preparing you for this practically your entire life. You'll make a fine king."

Two weeks later he was the acting king. His parents, along with a team of advisers, surveyors, cartographers, blacksmiths, and a variety of other skilled laborers, joined the team from Ylani and sailed south. While not nearly as large as Lentari's, the Ylanian team also consisted of a variety of craftsman and materials, presumably to help restore anything that needed repairs.

"How long will you be gone?" Mikal asked, watching his mother board one of Lentari's huge galleons.

"Long enough to put the kingdom on the right track," his father had told him. "I would say at least a month. Perhaps longer. From what Ewam tells me, the entire government will probably need to be restructured. That sort of thing takes time. Trust me, son. You'll be fine."

The door to the Antechamber opened, breaking Mikal out of his reverie. The guards admitted someone he was finally glad to see. Lissa walked into the room, wearing her traveling clothes and humming to herself. She caught sight of Mikal sitting at the desk, smiled, and danced over to him. Mikal rose to his feet and took his new bride into his arms, hugging her tightly.

"Lissa! I cannot even begin to describe how glad I am to see that you've returned."

Lissa wrapped her arms around him and gave him a fierce hug in return. "My love! I'm so glad to be back!"

"How did it go in Capily? Did you get those skin rash things under control?"

Lissa unfastened her traveling cloak, hung it on a nearby coat rack, and nodded. "At long last, yes. I'm not sure how it got started, or how the infection was spreading from person to person, but Charlin and I finally got it under control."

"Charlin?"

"He's Capily's healer. Did you know he also used to be a teacher of mine when I was in school?"

Mikal shook his head. "I didn't. It's a small world, isn't it?"

"It is. How did it go today? Did you resolve many differences? Oh, I know! There weren't any, were there? You've been lounging around on the throne and were hand fed sliced jansas by the serving girls, weren't you?"

"I wish," Mikal muttered.

"You *want* to be fed sliced fruit by the serving girls?" Lissa carefully asked, frowning slightly.

"No," Mikal said, shaking his head. "Well, anything would be better than the day I've had."

Lissa went sympathetic. "Oh, you poor thing. Did something happen? Did you have to throw someone into the dungeon? I know you've told me several times that you hoped you'd never have to do that."

"Worse. I had to listen to stupid, idiotic, petty arguments."

Lissa took his hand and gave it a few compassionate pats. "Oh, I'm sorry. That had to be tedious. You had to do that all day?"

"Almost. I had to listen to complaints for nearly two hours."

"Two whole hours?" Lissa scoffed. "Please. I had to treat infected people for the last four days."

"For how long each day?" Mikal wanted to know. He knew he was starting to sound like he was whining and was desperately hoping the hours she worked were less than his.

"From dawn to dusk."

"Each day?"

"Yes. We worked as long as we had daylight. It took nearly four days to treat everyone. I should also point out that we treated those who hadn't become infected. Just in case."

"From dawn to dusk. That's..."

"Much longer than two hours," Lissa finished for him. She moved back toward the desk, selected a sidah from the bowl of fruit, and peeled the skin off. "I'm exhausted. But, I'm glad it's done. I don't like to see anyone suffer, especially the people of my own village."

Realizing that Lissa had made his own difficulties pale by comparison, Mikal smiled and decided to skip the rant he had been working on. Lissa was right. He could see that she was tired. He hadn't had lunch yet and was pretty sure Lissa hadn't, either.

"Are you hungry? Would you like some lunch?"

Lissa gave him a warm smile and sank gratefully down onto the closest chair.

"I'd love some, thank you."

While he rang for a guard to deliver a message to the kitchens, Mikal fed more pieces of wood into the fire. Yet again he wished he had a jhorun like his foster father. Steve Miller could set practically anything on fire just by looking at it. His flames were hot enough to melt steel and could even be expelled out of his hands, like jets of water. Steve could also prevent certain things from burning, even if the entire room was engulfed in flames. Steve had defeated the guur horde years ago, not long after they first met. He had even gone back in time to save Sarah, his wife, after she had accidentally fallen into the interdimensional portal that had been discovered near Capily. If only he could have some adventures like that. Instead, he was stuck with his own boring jhorun.

What could his jhorun do? Boost someone *else's* jhorun. He could also break off a small piece of his own jhorun and give it to someone that didn't have one. It wasn't very impressive, no matter how you looked at it.

A mental picture of Sarah's friend, Lia, came to mind. Mikal smiled.

"What are you thinking about?" Lissa asked.

"I was just thinking back to a friend of my Idaho parents. Lia. She didn't have any jhorun when she first arrived here and I was just remembering what jhorun I gave her. It made me smile."

"What jhorun did you end up giving her?" Lissa wanted to know.

There was a knock on the door.

"The ability to juggle," Mikal told her as he rose to his feet. "She could make me laugh and I wanted to give her a unique ability that suited her. So, I, er, thought of jesters and how they made people laugh."

"What did Lia think of the jhorun?" Lissa asked. "Did she like it?"

Mikal shrugged. "Well … perhaps not. I don't think she saw the humor in it. Steve and Sarah did. Well, I know Steve did."

"He would," Lissa mused, stifling a giggle.

Mikal made it to the door and opened it. Three people entered, each holding a large tray. One held drinks and fruit, one held the entrees, and the other held dishes, silverware, cups, and spices.

"I'm still not sure about this," Lissa said later, as she finished her lunch and pushed the plate away from her. "I don't want to get used to someone else taking care of me."

Mikal smiled. "Even if it's me?"

"Are you going to cook for me?" Lissa asked, raising an eyebrow.

Mikal pointed at the rope hanging next to the wall on the left of the desk. "Nope. All I have to do is pull that and presto, lunch is served."

"You do realize that someone has to make all this, right? Someone has to take the dishes away. Someone has to clean everything up. I just don't like knowing that there are people out there who are at my beck and call."

"That's the way it works in the palace," Mikal explained. "It's not like we're forcing them to work. They're getting paid. It's their job."

"So, you're telling me that if I wanted a steak at three in the morning, there'd be someone in the kitchen just waiting for me to place an order?"

Mikal nodded. "Yes. The kitchen is obviously more staffed during the day, but there will always be someone on duty."

"When was the last time any of you ordered something in the middle of the night?"

Mikal shrugged. "It's been a while."

"So, whomever is on duty has to wait in a quiet kitchen until they're given something to do?"

"There's always something to do in the kitchen," Mikal explained. "If they're not making food for my parents, they'll be taking care of the guards who are on patrol. Soldiers use the kitchens at all hours, since there's always someone on patrol."

Relieved, Lissa finally smiled. "Oh. Actually, that makes me feel better. Thank you."

"This castle is never fully asleep," Mikal continued. "There's always someone moving about. Guards, cleaning crews, kitchen staff, and so on. What everyone does is, as far as I'm concerned, as important as everyone else. I don't care if you're sweeping the floors. You're helping to keep the castle running in top form. I appreciate everyone. What? Why are you staring at me like that?"

"You surprise me, Mikal. This is a side of you that I didn't know you had."

Mikal smiled at his wife, took her hand, and kissed it.

"Did you think that I just took all this for granted? The cooking, the cleaning, and the people just *waiting* to do anything I want? That's not me. I'd just as soon do as much as I can on my own."

"You do?" Lissa asked, amazed.

Mikal nodded. "Aye. However, as long as I wear the crown, there are certain things that are expected of me." He looked down at his empty plate and held it up. "Asking for lunch is one of them. I..."

Mikal?

Mikal gasped with surprise and dropped the plate. It made a loud racket as it smacked heavily onto the desk, and the fork and knife catapulted onto the floor. Lissa was on her feet in a flash.

"What is it? Are you all right?"

Mikal held up both hands. "Sorry. I didn't mean to drop the plate. It's just that..."

Mikal, are you there?

Pravara? Is that you?

It is.

Is everything okay?

No.

"What is it?" Lissa repeated. "You've become pale. Are you feeling all right?"

"It's Pravara," Mikal whispered.

Lissa visibly brightened. "Oh. Tell her hello for me and that I hope she's having a great day!"

Mikal shook his head. "She's not, unfortunately."

Lissa's eyes widened, "What's wrong?"

"I don't know."

That's because I haven't told him yet.

Are you sharing with Lissa, too?

No. It's an automatic reaction. I can hear her through your ears.

Then she will not be able to hear you.

I had assumed you will relay what I'm saying.

Is this for her ears, too?

Am I correct to assume that you are presently the acting king of Lentari?

I am.

And that makes your mate…?

Queen.

I thought as much. Therefore, I will trust this matter with her, too.

What's going on?

There's been a theft.

What? Where? Someone stole something from the wyverians?

Aye. From my parents.

Wizards be damned! Someone stole from the Dragon Lord?

Aye. We need to keep that to ourselves for the moment.

What was stolen?

My father wishes to discuss this with you in private. At my parents' cave.

"Oh, snap," Mikal softly muttered, using an expression he had picked up from his former bodyguard's home world.

Lissa took his hand. "Is it bad?"

Mikal turned to his wife and nodded.

When can you be here?

I can be in Verdayn in less than ten minutes. I just need to inform my father's advisers. Then it'll take me an hour or two to reach the valley.

There's no time for that. Can I meet you just outside the village?

Wow. This must really be urgent. Very well. I'll send word to the Constable that a dragon will be touching down on the outskirts of town.

I will be waiting. Mikal?

Yes?
Thank you for coming.
You're welcome, my friend.

* * *

"So, what happened?" Mikal asked, as soon as he and Lissa stepped out of Pravara's huge hands and onto terra firma once more. He looked around the cave she brought them to and whistled. He knew dragon caves could be large, but he never imagined them to be this big. A dozen dragons could easily fit inside.

A large, golden dragon approached and looked down at him. Mikal returned the look and inclined his head. Protocol had to be remembered, regardless of the circumstances. After all, this *was* the Dragon Lord he was addressing and he *was* acting king of Lentari.

"Kahvel. It's good to see you again."

"Kre'Mikal."

"I think you mean, Kri'Mikal," a female voice corrected.

A third dragon, this one an emerald green with bits of black on the edge of her wings, appeared as she climbed out of their nest. She approached the two of them and lowered her neck for a cursory sniff. Pryllan's eyes immediately locked onto Lissa's.

"Hello, Pryllan," Lissa said, giving the large green dragon a friendly smile.

Several seconds of silence passed before Pryllan spoke. "Greetings, young Lissa. I see life has suited you inside the human castle." The green dragon shifted her attention to Mikal. "And I give greetings to you, young Mikal. You make an excellent king."

"Temporary king," Mikal added, offering Pravara's mother a smile. "I look forward to giving my father back the crown."

"Is it not your wish to rule?" Kahvel asked.

Mikal shook his head. "On the contrary, I look forward to being the best king I can be. For Lentari. However, I know that day hasn't arrived yet, so at the moment, I look forward to returning the crown. Tell me, what could have possibly happened that you'd tell Pravara to contact me telepathically to request a meeting? She mentioned something about a theft?"

"Do keep your voice down," Pryllan pleaded. "I just got her to sleep."

"Got *who* to sleep?" Lissa asked, looking around the huge cavern.

"Pylaria. She only hatched a few months ago."

"Oh, that's wonderful, Pryllan!" Lissa exclaimed. "I had forgotten that your new baby hatched. How are you feeling? Is the baby healthy?"

"All is well," Kahvel assured them. "However, the sanctity of this nest is not. It was visited by invaders."

Mikal's eyes shot open. "Invaders? You're kidding! Who would be stupid enough to invade the nest of a dragon? And not just any dragon, but the Dragon Lord himself! Surely there isn't anyone foolish enough to try. Umm, is there?"

"Humans," Kahvel sniffed, raising his head into the air. "A human snuck into our nest."

"To do what?" Lissa wanted to know.

"How did he sneak in here?" Mikal asked, at the same time.

"I will start with your question, young Lissa," Kahvel began. He turned to point a claw back at the nest. "Pryllan's silver fang was stolen, right from over our nest."

"A silver fang?" Mikal repeated, confused. "Why would someone want a silver tooth?"

"This wasn't just any silver fang," Pryllan quietly explained, casting a quick glance back at the nest. "This was the fang that Steve and I took from a red oskorlisk during one of our hunts. It was the first silver oskorlisk fang that had been retrieved in nearly a hundred years."

"So, it's rare," Mikal decided. "I can understand that. But why take the fang? Wouldn't your treasure be more valuable?"

"What do you know of our treasure?" Kahvel growled. "What have you heard?"

Pryllan's long, graceful neck turned until she was looking at her mate. "Kahvel, be at peace. No insult was intended. In fact, they probably don't even know."

"Know what?" Mikal prompted.

"That a human has touched my treasure. Our treasure," Kahvel hastily corrected.

"And that's bad?" Lissa asked, puzzled.

Kahvel nodded. "Aye. It's considered bad luck for a non-wyverian to touch a dragon's horde. And now look what has happened."

Mikal strode past Pravara and leaned out over the lip to the cave. It was over a thousand feet straight down. Mikal turned back to Kahvel.

"Do you have any idea how this guy made it up here? Look at the mountainside. The rock wall is almost as smooth as glass. There's no way a human could have climbed that, unless he knew the two of you were gone from your nest for an extended period of time. Even then, how would he have known?"

"Pryllan was gone from the nest for no more than a quarter of an hour," Kahvel said. "Pylaria was with her and tired more quickly than expected, so she returned to the nest. Pylaria made it inside first. Pryllan arrived next and noticed the scent almost immediately."

"Was the thief still in the nest when you returned?" Lissa asked, turning to Pryllan.

"Aye."

"Did you see what this person looked like?"

Pryllan nodded. "Aye. Short. Black hair. Human facial hair."

"Older than Mikal's father," Kahvel added.

"Did you see him, too?" Mikal asked.

"No. Pryllan relayed an image to me."

Mikal began to pace, a habit he had picked up from his foster father. "Let's think this through. We know the thief was still in the nest when Pryllan returned."

Pryllan fidgeted uncomfortably from leg to leg.

"Correct."

"Is there more than one entrance to this cave?" Mikal asked.

Kahvel, Pryllan, and Pravara all shook their heads.

"No," all three dragons said in unison.

"So, how did the thief make it by you?" Mikal asked, confused. "How did this person escape? You must have been at the mouth of the cave. He shouldn't have had a chance against you."

"The wind," Pryllan recalled. "A wind was blowing in the cave. It pushed at me, preventing me from approaching. I do not know where it came from, but it looked as though it originated from within the nest."

"Which is impossible," Kahvel growled.

"Be that as it may," Pryllan continued, throwing her mate a disapproving look, "I was unable to enter my own nest. Pylaria was already inside. I feared the worst."

"How did the thief escape?" Mikal asked. "Look where we are. There's no way he could have safely made it out of here."

"Yet I watched him step off the edge as we do whenever we leave the nest," Pryllan added.

"You're saying he flew away?" Lissa asked, amazed.

Pryllan shook her head. "I did no such thing. I said this brazen human stepped right off the edge. The winds returned and slowed his descent. I didn't see him land but can only assume that he did so safely."

"Don't you dragons have an amazing sense of smell?" Mikal asked. "How could this human have made it to your valley without any dragon picking up his scent?"

"I have been pondering that," Kahvel admitted.

"And?" Mikal prompted. "Do you have any conclusions?"

"None whatsoever," Kahvel reluctantly admitted. "I do not even have any theories."

"The wind," Lissa murmured, drawing everyone's attention. "The wind is the key. If he was controlling the wind, wouldn't it be possible to mask his scent?"

"Mask his scent with what?" Kahvel demanded. "How could you use the wind to cover up a scent?"

"What if the wind blew in such a way that this human was always upwind, no matter which direction he moved?" Pravara asked from her position near the mouth of the cave. "If the winds blew his scent away from you, would the dragons have noticed? Would that not allow him to approach in stealth?"

The two wyverian parents and both humans were silent as they considered the ramifications of a person who could bend the air to their will.

Mikal quietly approached the nest and pointed up at the jagged hole where the fang had once rested.

"What can you tell me about that fang? Why would it be considered more valuable than your treasure?"

"Many oskorlisk fangs are imbued with power," Kahvel quietly explained. His neck lifted and he gazed wordlessly down into his nest. Nestled inside was a small dragonlet, curled tightly in a ball.

Following his gaze, Mikal and Lissa tiptoed to the edge of the nest and looked down.

"Ohhh…" Lissa quietly exclaimed. "She's precious! And she's all gold, like you, Kahvel. You two are so incredibly lucky!"

Pryllan smiled at them and joined Kahvel at the edge of the nest.

"It took a long time for her to hatch."

"Longer than me?" Pravara added, as she approached the nest.

Pryllan turned to look at her firstborn. "Aye. By three fortnights."

Mikal pointed back at the wall. "You said that the fang has power? Does that mean it has some type of jhorun?"

Kahvel nodded. "Aye. Oskorlisk fangs are precious commodities amongst wyverians. It is said that many of the larger fangs will provide protection to those who possess it."

"Protection?" Mikal asked. "Do you mean to say that the person who holds that fang will be somehow protected from physical harm? They'll become invincible?"

Kahvel shook his head. "Not exactly. Some fangs were said to cause an attacker to miss fatal blows. Others were said to mask one from sight. Essentially, the older the oskorlisk, the more powerful the fang."

"And if it came from the mouth of a red oskorlisk?" Mikal asked. "What then?"

"The last possessor of a silver fang claimed it had made them impervious to attack."

"From any type of attack?" Lissa asked, amazed.

Kahvel nodded. "Aye. My sire. He claimed that he was unable to be harmed, whether the assault was physical or jhorun by nature. I'm told the red oskorlisk that the fang came from was large, suggesting it was old. In the hands of the wrong individual, that fang could be dangerous."

"How did the thief even know you had it?" Mikal demanded. "Not only did he know you guys had it, but knew where to find your cave. Can I assume the location of this nest isn't common knowledge?"

"Only a select few know the location of this nest," Kahvel confirmed.

"And yet this thief not only knew you had the silver fang, but where to find you, is that it?" Mikal shook his head and looked at Lissa with frustration written all over his face. "I just don't get it. There must be something we're missing."

"The fang must be recovered," Kahvel growled. "We can worry about how this thief knew of its existence later. It cannot become known that the Dragon Lord had his most prized possession stolen from under his nose. By a human."

"The fang wasn't yours," Pryllan gently corrected. "It's mine. Steve gave me that fang as a memento of our Hunt."

"I know that, beloved," Kahvel soothingly told his mate. "I am very proud of you for what you accomplished that day. You earned it. The fang is yours. Trust me when I say it *will* be returned."

"As Dragon Lord, your hands are tied," Mikal guessed. "That's why you're asking me for help, isn't it?"

"If I start pursuing this matter, then the details of this theft will become known. I cannot have my wyverians doubting my skills, or my ability to lead. I hereby ask you, Kri'Mikal, for assistance. Will you help me?"

"I wish I could, Kahvel," Mikal began. "However, my parents are out of the country. I am in charge. As such, there's no way I can shirk my responsibilities. Trust me, I wish I could."

Kahvel nodded. "I understand, young Mikal. I would not

suggest you abandon your duties to recover Pryllan's missing fang. I will find another solution."

Lissa suddenly smiled. "May I make a recommendation?"

All three dragons nodded.

"I would contact a certain fire thrower and teleporter. I think they are more than capable of helping you."

Chapter 3 — A Nose for Trouble

Did you have any idea when we first moved here that it'd end up like this? I mean, look at this. With the completion of my parents' house, that'll bring the total number up to ten, I think."

"Ten? Are you sure?"

"Let's count them off, shall we?" An attractive brown-haired woman in her late thirties began ticking off houses on her fingers. "There's ours and the garage…"

"Which you can't count 'cause they were already here," a tall man in his early forties argued.

"…the lodge," the woman continued, ignoring her husband's outburst, "Tristan and Annie's house, the house my parents are planning on moving into, the house your parents have picked out, the house I'm trying to get my grandfather to move into, and the three remaining houses that I have a sneaky suspicion will be filled by the end of the year. That makes ten."

"They just keep multiplying, don't they?" the man mused.

"Wait, what? Did you say the other three are already spoken for? By who?"

"By whom," Sarah Miller corrected. She turned to bat her eyes at her husband.

Steve Miller automatically raised a hand to cover his eyes. "No, don't do that. No batting your eyes at me. Just spill it. Who have you invited?"

"Well, Annie…"

"…already has a house," Steve finished for her. "It's a perfectly adequate house, if you ask me. Paid for free and clear. Why would they need another?"

"Well, house number nine has two extra bedrooms. With the arrival of the twins, Tristan and Annie will have four children. They will need the extra room. I suggested the two of them should take that house."

"And they agreed?"

"Only after I promised there were no current plans for the house."

Steve shrugged. "I have no problems with that. That frees up a house, so there'll still be three vacancies."

"Umm, two. Lia has asked to move in."

At this, Steve frowned. Sarah, watching him closely, smacked him on the arm. Hard.

"What do you have against Lia? She could use a change of scenery, especially since she and Adam separated."

"I thought this little community we built here was for family members only," Steve said.

"You don't think Lia is family?" Sarah countered.

"Fine. That's fine. Whatever. You win. Objection withdrawn."

"Good."

"What about the other two?" Steve asked.

"Well, Lia will take number three, Annie's old house. That leaves numbers eight and ten. I was thinking about leaving number ten as a guest house."

"And number eight?" Steve asked. "What are you not telling me? Who do you want to ask?"

"I haven't asked anyone. In fact, I'm the one who's been asked."

"Okay, you've been asked. By who? Er, whom? I mean … dammit."

"It's okay. Mikal is the one who asked me."

Surprised, Steve turned to his wife and stared at her. "Mikal wants to move here? How would that work? He's slated to be the next king of Lentari."

"He wasn't asking for himself, but for his parents."

Steve's eyebrows shot up. "Whoa, really? His parents want to live here?"

Sarah nodded. "I'm guessing the mall made more of an impression on Ny'Callé than we thought. Mikal actually heard his mother ask what their plans were once he became king. Kri'Entu said that he really didn't know and hasn't given it much thought. Callé said she wouldn't mind visiting the mall again, or seeing some more of our world."

"Well, you can tell Mikal that number 8 has now been officially reserved for Lentarian use only. Wow, I can't imagine having a former king and queen living in one of those houses. We might need to redo a few things in number eight."

"I was already thinking the same thing," Sarah said, as she stepped into the closet.

Peanut, the ever-playful corgi, bounded into the room the moment Steve pulled his shoes out of the closet and let them drop before putting them on. Almost as soon as the corgi trotted into the room, a second creature appeared, and it didn't come close to resembling a corgi. It didn't even resemble a dog. In fact, Steve knew that there wasn't another of its kind anywhere on the planet.

It was a griffin.

They had rescued the little griffin during their last excursion to Lentari. That time around, Sarah had received a distress call from a group of beings who typically hid themselves from the outside world. While there, they met up with old friends, made a few new ones, and ended up keeping a promise.

Little Emerion followed his playmate into the master bedroom and studied Steve as he laced his shoes. The young griffin trilled softly and nuzzled his legs. Steve leaned down to scratch the little griffin on his back, directly between his wings. It was, Steve knew, Emerion's most difficult area to scratch, and therefore, his favorite.

Less than two seconds later, Steve felt another creature nuzzle his legs. Peanut wove herself in and out of his legs, hoping to be noticed. He scratched the corgi behind her ears.

"Don't worry. You two are coming along."

Peanut yipped excitedly. Emerion squawked happily and immediately followed the small dog out of the room and down the stairs. Sarah stepped out of the closet, wearing a winter jacket and a pair of calf-high boots.

"What was that all about?"

"I told Emerion and Peanut that they could go with us outside."

"That explains the bark. And the squawk. Every time Emerion squawks like that I'm reminded of a young parrot."

"Only not as obnoxious," Steve added.

"He's growing so fast, isn't he?" Sarah said, as half an hour later, husband and wife exited the patio door and stepped out into the bright sunshine. While still chilly, as it was wintertime after all, both expressed a desire to go for a walk. "Look at him. He must have put on at least ten pounds since we brought him home."

"The little booger eats well, no doubt about it," Steve agreed. "The people down at the grocery store definitely know we're not vegetarians."

Husband and wife headed for their backyard. Corgi and griffin happily bounded alongside them. Steve pointed at the cobbled "street" they had installed to connect all the houses together.

"It sure is starting to look more and more like a real estate development around here, isn't it?"

Sarah nodded. "Did I tell you that my dad is looking for something to do?"

"Like what?" Steve asked. "What can he do?"

"Well, he's always enjoyed working with wood. I think he'd like to open up some type of shop."

"You mean he wants to go back to work?" Steve asked. He swept his arm in the direction of the houses. "Look at this place. Everything is paid for. The new solar panels we installed even covers everyone's electricity. Is he looking to make some extra money?"

"He's looking for something to do. Maybe he wants to make a few changes to the house he and mom are taking? Then he volunteered to help out with other houses once I told him we really don't have a maintenance crew here."

"I'm not sure I'm comfortable with that," Steve admitted.

"What? Why not?"

"Hoo, boy. How do I put this? Your dad ... well, he's no spring chicken, dear."

Sarah burst out laughing. "You don't have to worry about that. My father likes to be active, to be useful. He knows we don't have anyone here taking care of the place, so he volunteered. It's a wonderful idea. I also think we should build him a place where he can work. After all, we have plenty of room. To be honest, I've lost count of how many acres we own now."

Steve blew out a breath as he considered. "Well, let's see. We originally had a hundred-fifty acres. Then, thanks to our little jaunt through time, everyone thinks our house is haunted and no one wants to build out here."

"And the purchase of those other two parcels?" Sarah teased. "You can't forget about them."

"Of course not. Who was I to argue when the city offered to sell us another four-hundred at rock bottom prices? We have more land than we know what to do with."

"Which is why we should be able to set a small piece aside and set up a few workshops."

"A few?" Steve repeated, confused. "How did we go from one maintenance-type shop to a few?"

"What if someone else wants to do something in their spare time? What if they can find something to do that could actually benefit the rest of us?"

"You're gonna have to give me a 'for instance'," Steve decided as he and Sarah walked up the cobbled street and gazed at the quiet, quaint community they had created.

"Well, as I said, my dad likes to work with wood. Yours likes to work on cars. I would say we build a place for each of them to do what they like to do. I'd also like to mention that

I've heard your father volunteer to check out Lia's car, since it was rattling so badly we could hear her coming for miles."

"He fixed that, didn't he?" Steve asked. "Last week."

Sarah nodded. "Yes. That's my point. It gave him something to do. Let him feel useful."

"Ah. I think I see what you're getting at."

Emerion bounded ahead. Both wings were extended and flapping, but he wasn't generating near enough lift to make it off the ground. Steve noticed Sarah watching the young griffin and grunted.

"Sooner or later he'll become strong enough to start flying."

"I know," Sarah nodded. "I've already told him that he's not allowed to go flying unless we're there with him."

"Do you think he'll mind you?" Steve asked.

"Of course. In his eyes, I'm his mother. You're his father."

"And Peanut?" Steve asked.

"What else? His energetic sister that gets him into trouble."

"You're the one that wanted to go for a walk. Did you have any place you'd like to go?"

"I want to go to the lake," Sarah told him. "I think I have an activity in mind that you'll like."

"Wow! Seriously? What the hell are we waiting for? Move it, woman! Are you sure you don't want to take the ATVs?"

Sarah laughed and swatted his arm.

"It's not what you think, you dork. And yes, I think I would. Provided I get to drive my own."

"Do you want to take Peanut or Emerion?" Steve asked. "You know damn well they aren't going to like us splitting up."

"Let's just see who wants to go with whom."

Five minutes later, two ATVs pulled out of the garage and headed north. Sarah drove her customized purple Polaris. Alone. Steve, following closely in his own customized ATV, glanced in the back seat and groaned. Both corgi and griffin had been buckled in to the seat and both, Steve noted, were having the time of their life. Neither one of them, he recalled, had wasted a moment in deciding which parent they were going to accompany. Although, at least Emerion had taken the time to consider going with Sarah. Maybe a fraction of a second, Steve recalled. He shrugged. He didn't mind.

They arrived at the small lake several miles north of the mansion. It was secluded, private, and well away from any prying eyes. As well as it should be. The Miller Estates extended at least two hundred acres in all directions from this very spot. They had also posted "No Hunting" signs everywhere. Just in case. The last thing either of them wanted was to have someone spot a young griffin gallivanting through the hills and mistake him for something else.

He pulled his ATV next to Sarah's, parked, and unclipped both of his passengers. Both took off like a shot, angling straight for the lake. Steve looked at his wife and grinned.

"I'll put $5 on Peanut."

"No way. Emerion will be the first. And make it $20."

"You're on."

They heard the splash and automatically looked over at the lake. Emerion surfaced, trilling happily. Peanut was barking maniacally as she raced up and down the shore. After a few seconds, Peanut bounded into the water and started swimming straight for the little griffin.

Sarah let out a victorious shout, "Hah! I knew it! Thank you so very much. I'll be sure to collect my winnings when we get home. In the meantime, I hope you brought a towel. You know the rules. Loser gets to dry them off."

"Dammit. Fine. Let them play for a while. So, what did you have in mind out here?"

"When was the last time either of us worked on our jhoruns?"

"What do you mean? We know how our jhorun works. Why would we need to work on it?"

Sarah held up a hand, "No, sorry. That's not what I meant. I'm talking about *practicing*. When was the last time either of us used our jhoruns for something that mattered? And I'm not talking about you lighting the barbecue."

Steve grunted and considered, "Umm, I don't know. Since we came back with Emerion?"

Sarah nodded. "That's right. That was over three months

ago. I've been thinking a lot about this. We should start working with our jhoruns, in order to make sure we are at our top form should the situation ever arise."

"We're not bodyguards anymore," Steve reminded her. "There really isn't a need to stay in top form. Umm, is there?"

"You never know what could happen," Sarah said, leaning against the closest tree, opening her arms. "I'd just as soon be prepared."

"So, what do you have in mind?" Steve asked.

A medium-sized cardboard box appeared in Sarah's arms. She placed the box down on the ground and gestured at it.

"Open that up and you'll see what I have in store for you. Remember, I'm pretty sure you're going to enjoy this."

Steve squatted next to the box, pulled out his pocket knife, and slit the box open. Row after row of orange circular clay targets met his eyes. He looked up at Sarah, who was grinning at him. A smile formed on his face.

"Oh, you are *so* right! Are you thinking what I think you're thinking?"

"These are clay targets that skeet shooters use. I thought they'd be perfect for us. My dad helped pick them out."

"Okay, I know you're referring to me shooting 'em out of the sky," Steve mused, pulling one of the targets from the box. "How does this help you?"

In response, the clay target flew from his hand and sailed out over the open grassland. Once it was nearly a hundred feet away, it suddenly stopped, as if frozen in place. Sarah smiled again at her husband.

"Think you can hit it?"

Steve's hands ignited. "Hell yeah!"

For the next two hours husband and wife practiced. Sarah sent target after target up into the air while Steve effortlessly blasted them from the sky. He watched as three more lifted from the box and were propelled upwards. He fired three blasts, one right after the other, fully expecting to bring them down without any trouble. Surprisingly, all three shots missed when, just before the fireballs could strike the targets, all three targets seemingly jumped out of the way.

"Hey, not fair!" Steve complained. "Inanimate objects

aren't supposed to suddenly jump out of the way."

"How often have you tried to bring something down that wasn't, and I'm sorry to say this, currently alive?"

Steve sobered and frowned, "Never."

"That's my point. Let's step this up. You're going to have to work harder to bring these next ones down."

Steve grinned and cracked his knuckles, "Challenge accepted."

"Are you ready?"

Steve glanced down at his hands. His flames grew brighter. He looked at his wife and nodded.

Half a dozen targets flew out of the box and all took off in various directions. Steve stopped trying to hit the targets with basic blasts of fire and instead, generated 'chasers', which were fireballs created with the sole purpose of bringing down a specific target.

One after the other, the fireballs zipped off, each intent on making contact with its targets. He heard a soft grunt coming from his left. Sarah was now concentrating intently as she tried to keep her targets intact and away from his chasers.

There were several puffs of smoke. Two targets had been eliminated. The remaining clay targets zoomed across the sky even faster, each with a burning ball of fire hot on its tail. Two more disappeared.

The tables were turned again. With only two targets to worry about, hitting them became practically impossible. Sarah was able to jerk her targets out of the way just before the chasers could make contact. In and out, up and down, zig-zagging around trees, rocks, and anything else that Sarah could see.

The chasers chased. The targets eluded. Finally, after nearly five minutes of an intense session of follow-the-leader, one of the two targets was struck. Steve grinned and glanced over at his wife. Sarah, on the other hand, stifled a curse and waved her hand at the target.

The molded piece of clay flipped expertly in the air, just in time to avoid the oncoming strike from the chaser. It instantly swung around to try again, only the target was already halfway across the lake.

The chaser pursued. Just as the fireball cruised out over the lake, at least a hundred gallons of water lifted from the lake's surface and flung itself in the chaser's path. Steve's fireball disappeared with a little more than a small poof.

"Hey, no fair!"

"If I hadn't done that, then we'd still be at it. I don't know about you, but I'm tired. I can actually feel a little bit of a drain on my jhorun. I haven't felt that in a long time."

"Me, too," Steve agreed. "You're right, babe. We needed this. This was a lot of fun."

"Are you going to put that out?"

"Huh?"

Sarah pointed west, where earlier he had blasted several shots in an effort to bring the targets down. On that particular occasion, he had been unsuccessful. Unfortunately, the shots must have hit something because he could see a wisp of dark smoke spiraling up into the sky.

"Damn. I've got it. I'll be right back."

Ten minutes later, Steve emerged from the trees and headed to the lake.

"Everything okay?" Sarah asked.

"Yep. Apparently, I had hit a tree and it, understandably, hadn't liked it one bit. I put it out and made damn certain there wasn't one iota of heat coming from it. Where are Peanut and Emerion?"

Sarah pointed at the shore. Both the corgi and the griffin were reclining on the ground and had been watching the jhorun-enhanced show. Steve headed to their ATVs to pull out the towels they always brought with them.

He was in the midst of drying a wriggling young griffin when Emerion suddenly trilled with alarm. His wings extended and the tiny scruff of fur along his back shot straight up. Peanut rolled to her feet and scanned the area for threats.

"What is it?" Sarah asked, concerned. "What made Emerion do that? Did you rub his feathers the wrong way? I know he's not fond of that."

"No, not that I'm aware of. One minute he was enjoying being dried by a warm towel and the next he started to freak out, like there's a bear or something in the area."

Sarah looked worriedly around the glade.

"Is there?"

"What, a bear? Possible, but I doubt it. Look at Peanut. She hasn't smelled anything, or given us any signs that something is wrong. Whatever is going on, Emerion is the only one who has noticed it."

Sarah squatted and wrapped a protective arm around the young griffin. She gently scratched her fingers along Emerion's back, a move she knew which would typically calm him. The griffin started to relax, but kept turning to look back in the direction of the manor.

Steve noticed where Emerion was looking and glanced at his wife with concern written all over his features.

"Something's wrong. He's looking back at the house. Could he have heard something?"

Sarah looked at Peanut, who curiously returned her stare.

"Possibly. It surprises me that Peanut hasn't really noticed anything. Come on, let's head back."

Sarah teleported the box of targets and her glass of water, back to the house. They loaded up—both corgi and griffin still elected to ride with Steve—and headed back. Once both ATVs had been parked inside one of the stalls inside their exterior garage, they both hurried inside to see if anything had happened.

Nothing.

Steve rushed to his office to check the contents of the special griffin safe. Everything was accounted for: portal keys, jhorun-boosting joriis, the jhorun-charging power crystals, and even the two broken pieces of a certain amulet he avoided touching like the plague. Nothing was missing.

"I'm going to check the library," Steve decided, as he headed for the stairs.

The library was housed on the second floor of their manor and was home to thousands of books. Also inside the manor were the display cases for their Lentarian weapons. Steve, being a collector of medieval weaponry, had swords, shields, crossbows, and even a few dwarven war hammers on display. However, all were right where they were supposed to be.

He trooped back down the stairs.

"There's nothing missing up there. I've checked … is he okay?"

Steve had stopped in the middle of the living room, staring at Emerion. He was still pacing anxiously about, causing Peanut to mimic his actions.

"Something is still bothering him," Sarah told him. She was sitting, cross-legged, in the middle of the floor and was making sure the little griffin didn't wander away. At least not until they could verify there wasn't any danger.

"Why don't you let him go?" Steve suggested. "If he smells—or senses—something in this house, then maybe we ought to let him find it for us."

Emerion looked expectantly at Sarah and gave a victorious squawk.

"Don't you side with him," Sarah warned as she waggled a finger at the griffin. "You're on my side, remember?"

Emerion rubbed up against Sarah's leg before turning to look expectantly toward the kitchen.

"Fine. Do you want to look around? Go ahead. Show us what's bothering you."

Free to move about, Emerion immediately moved toward the kitchen. Steve, Sarah, and Peanut followed from a distance. After a thorough check of the entire kitchen, including floors and any cabinet the young griffin could reach, Emerion moved toward the room Sarah used as an office.

Same as before. Being much smaller, Sarah's office only took a few minutes to check before Emerion gave up and switched to the next room, which happened to be Steve's office. Emerion paused only long enough to look up at the statue of a griffin standing on a pedestal, with one foreleg raised, before moving around the perimeter of the room. The tiny griffin paused again at Steve's desk, trilled softly, and looked back at Steve. Then he trilled a little louder.

"Has he found something?" Sarah asked, poking her head in the room. "I wonder if it … Huh. I wonder if it might have something to do with the large emerald sitting on your desk."

"The large what?" Steve demanded, abandoning his

inspection of one of the four bookcases in the room. His eyes caught sight of the large sparkling green gemstone sitting nonchalantly on his desk, as though it was a paperweight, and widened appreciatively. "Where the hell did that come from?"

"Didn't you tell me you came in here to check the safe?" Sarah asked, perplexed. "Did you see this thing before?"

Steve shook his head, "Er, no. I was more worried about that damn amulet."

Sarah carefully picked up the gem and hefted it in her hand. The jewel was about the size of a baseball—slightly squashed—and sparkled with the radiance of hundreds of facets. Sarah studied the huge gem.

"I don't see any blemishes, or markings, or any type of identification on the stone. And, I'd also say this emerald is at least a thousand carats." Sarah looked over at her husband. His eyes had glazed over and she could swear he was drooling. She nudged his shoulder. "Hey, snap out of it. This isn't ours. We're not keeping it. However, someone left it here for us to find. The question is, who?"

Steve finally found his voice, "That … that…"

Sarah hefted the stone, "Say it with me. It's an emerald."

"That emerald … you think it is a thousand carats?"

"I remember seeing an article on the news a year or two ago that spoke of a tennis ball sized diamond, found in Botswana. This looks like it's not quite the size of a tennis ball, but I'd say it's close. Who do you think would have left this here?"

Steve took the stone and held it up to his eyes. "You're sure it's authentic?"

Sarah shrugged. "I don't see why not."

"Then, wouldn't there be some record of it? Somewhere on the internet, that is?"

"Are you suggesting that this emerald was stolen from some museum and left here? In our house? Search all you want, but I'm fairly certain you won't find any history about that jewel. I don't think it's local."

"Botswana isn't local," Steve pointed out.

"Neither is Lentari," Sarah said. She pointed over at Emerion, who had finally curled up into a ball and was fast asleep. "Think about it. Who is known for having gemstones like this one?"

"The dragons," Steve breathed, amazed. "But…"

"Emerion noticed something was wrong," Sarah reminded him.

"If this is a dragon's jewel, how did they get it here?" Steve demanded.

"Why don't we go find out?" Sarah suggested.

Steve suddenly grunted and held the jewel up for a closer look.

"What?" Sarah prompted.

"Did you notice that this gem is the same color as Pryllan?"

"It's an emerald," Sarah pointed out. "It's green. She's green. No big surprise there."

"What do you want to bet this is from her?" Steve remarked, as he turned the jewel over in his hand. "Or Kahvel. It has to be one of the two. Something's wrong. All right, you win. Let's go find out what… wait. What are we going to do with Peanut and Emerion? We can't leave them here by themselves. Can we call your sister?"

"Annie has two children, with two more on the way," Sarah reminded him. "She can barely find a moment for herself."

"Roger that. Well, umm, how about Lia?"

"She'd work. You get to call her."

"What? Why?"

"It's your suggestion."

"Oh, horse puckey. I know you thought of it first."

"But you're the one who vocalized it," Sarah said, laughing. "Tell her hello for me."

Ten minutes later Steve joined Sarah up in the master bedroom. Sarah had already changed into one of the Lentarian outfits she kept tucked away in her closet. Steve quickly changed into one of his. Corgi and griffin entered the room and both sat, directly in the middle of the doorway, as if trying to prevent them from leaving.

"I'm sorry, Peanut," Sarah soothed, ruffling the fur behind Peanut's ears. "You need to stay here. You, too, Emerion.

Auntie Lia is coming over to take care of you, okay?"

Peanut's ears started to droop. She looked at the two of them and gave them her best attempt at looking forlorn. Emerion let out a quiet, unhappy squawk and sank dejectedly to the floor.

"Oh, come on, you two," Steve scolded. "It's not the end of the world. Our friends are in some type of trouble. We have to go help them, okay?"

The doorbell rang. In a flash, both dog and griffin had reverted back to their usual selves and dashed downstairs. Within moments they could hear Lia's excited peal of laughter.

"They're in good hands, honey," Sarah told him. "We'll be back before you know it."

* * *

"Seems like we were just here," Steve mused, tossing the small bag Sarah had packed onto the bed.

"We *were* just here," Sarah confirmed. "Well, last month, anyway. For Lissa's birthday?"

"Yeah, yeah. I remember."

Steve?

Pryllan? Is that you?

Aye. I am very glad to hear from you. I wasn't sure you would receive my message.

Are you talking about the emerald? Oh, trust me. Message received loud and clear. We brought it with us so we can give it back to you.

"What's going on?" Sarah asked. "You've gone quiet. Is everything... oh. It's Pryllan, isn't it?"

Steve nodded. "Yes. You were right. She sent the emerald."

How did you do that, anyway? How were you able to get something from Lentari to our world? Man alive, if I had known you could have done that, it could have saved us a lot of trouble when we went back in time last year.

I called in a favor.

From who?

A wizard.

Shardwyn? Seriously? You're one brave dragon.

I never said I consulted the elderly human wizard.

Oh. You asked Gareth for help? That's surprising.

I did not consult the young human wizard, either.

What other wizard is there?

The shealk wizard, Balthor.

He's a water dragon. You flew all the way to Capily to talk to him?

No. He's presently in human form, spending time with his human family. Whenever he is on land, he resides in Verdayn. That is a short flight from here. Lord Phaedren owed Kahvel a favor, so now they're even.

"Wow," Steve quietly mouthed.

"What?" Sarah softly asked.

"Gareth's father is the one who managed to get the emerald on my desk. Looks like the shealk lord owed Kahvel a favor."

"I guess that would make them even. Nice."

Does Sarah remember where our cave is? Can she bring you here or do I need to send Pravara?

Hang on. I'll ask.

"Do you remember where their nest is?"

Sarah nodded. "Yes. Does she want us to head over? I can get us there in a blink of an eye."

Yes, she does. She can get us there lickety split.

Lickety split? I'm not familiar with that term.

It means… forget it. We'll be right there, Pryllan.

Thank you.

Sarah took his hand and closed her eyes. Steve did the same and braced for the inevitable jolt Sarah's teleportation jump would cause. Once again, he envied Sarah of her ability. How nice would it be to be able to jump to another location, regardless of distance, by simply closing your eyes and picturing where you wanted to go?

Their house in downtown R'Tal blinked out and was replaced by a large cave. Steve cracked an eye and looked around. Visible outside the cave's mouth was nothing but open sky and an occasional cloud or two. He couldn't see any land anywhere, which wasn't too surprising. He knew the Dragon Lord's private nest was remote and secluded. And at the top of a mountain.

Two adult dragons were present and both of them had

turned to look down at the two of them. At any other time, the presence of a full-sized dragon would have made even the bravest of souls yearn to be somewhere else. These two, thankfully, were friends. A dark forest green dragon approached first and immediately lowered her head to sniff the two humans.

"Hello, Pravara," Sarah said, genuinely pleased to see the dragon. "How have you been?"

Pravara nodded. "I am well, thank you for asking."

Steve raised a hand in greeting, "Hey, Pravara! Still think you're a better shot than me?"

Pravara's golden eyes locked onto Steve's. "Of course. Why would I think otherwise?"

A large gold dragon approached next. Steve bowed at the same time Sarah curtsied.

"Hey there, Kahvel," Steve called out. "It's good to see you, my friend."

"And you," Kahvel returned. "I do wish we were meeting under better circumstances."

"Hello, Kahvel," Sarah said, once the leader of all dragons had looked her way. "I hope we can help fix whatever has happened."

Kahvel nodded. "As do I."

"Where's Pryllan?" Sarah asked.

Kahvel turned to look at the nest in the far corner of the large cave. The three of them moved to the nest while Pravara remained near the mouth of the cave. From their vantage point, neither could see over the lip of the nest. Once they could, Sarah let out an "ooo" of delight.

Pryllan was there, in the depression, curled around the sleeping form of her new baby. The dragonlet, Steve could see, was a sparkling gold color, just like her father. Steve glanced at his wife. Sarah looked as though she was on the verge of climbing down into the nest so she could cuddle the baby.

"She's adorable, Pryllan," Sarah cooed. "You must be so proud. Both of you."

"We are," Pryllan agreed. She gently nudged her baby with the tip of her nose. "Wake up, young one. There are some humans here I'd like you to meet."

The tiny golden snout stirred. Two dark green eyes opened and gazed lovingly up into her mother's eyes. Pryllan nudged her again and pointedly looked up at husband and wife. The baby followed her gaze and finally noticed the two humans standing silently nearby.

"I'd like to introduce Pylaria," Pryllan announced. "Young one, this is Steve and the female is his mate, Sarah. They are friends and can be trusted."

Pylaria turned to give her mother a skeptical look. "More humans? Father said humans are bad."

Steve, Sarah, Pryllan, and Pravara all turned to stare at the Dragon Lord, who shrugged.

"These humans aren't trying to steal from us," Kahvel gently informed his new offspring.

Pylaria slowly climbed out of the nest and approached the two of them. Steve held out a hand and waited for the tiny dragonlet to approach. Only after she gently sniffed his hand did he allow his jhorun to become active.

His hand flamed up.

Surprised, Pylaria jerked her head away, hesitated, and then approached his hand again. She nudged his burning fingers a few times before turning to give her mother a quizzical look. Steve struggled to keep a straight face. He could only imagine the turmoil the little dragon must be feeling after seeing a human's hand go up in flames.

"Steve is a fire thrower," Pryllan patiently explained. "He's the only human who can burn and not be harmed."

"I'm going to hold off on demonstrating my jhorun," Sarah decided. "There's no need to freak her out. Not yet, anyway."

Kahvel chuckled. "Agreed."

"So what has happened, Pryllan?" Steve asked. "Why did you send us that emerald? Speaking of which ... Sarah, did you give it back to them yet?"

Sarah held out an open hand. The emerald materialized on it. She held it up so that Pryllan and Kahvel could see what it was.

"I believe this is yours," Sarah proclaimed, striding

forward to present it to Kahvel. "I'm sure you'll want this back."

"Keep it," Kahvel told her. "It's so miniscule that I'm sure it isn't worth much. If you like it, consider it a gift."

"Isn't worth much?" Sarah stammered. "Are you kidding? This has got to be one of the biggest emeralds I have ever seen!"

"One of these days I will have to show you what a true Lentarian jewel looks like," Kahvel told her. "Jewels that are alive with color. Jewels so bright that they emit their own light. Those are the types of jewels dragons covet. Those are the gemstones that a dragon wants in its collection, not some tiny fragment that somehow found its way into our horde. No, keep it with my thanks."

"It'd be rude to refuse," Steve whispered.

The gem vanished.

"Very well. We thank you for your generosity." Sarah turned toward him and nudged his shoulder. "I'm thinking swimming pool," she whispered. She turned back to Kahvel and smiled. "Now, what can we do for you?"

Kahvel pointed at the stone wall directly above their nest. A closer examination revealed the wall had taken some damage. A small portion of the cavern wall was missing, as though someone had chiseled away at it. Steve ventured as close as he could without climbing into the nest itself. He shrugged. It looked like something had been there, only it had been pried out. What that was, he could only guess.

"I'm very sorry to tell you this," Pryllan hesitantly began, "but the silver fang we acquired during our Hunt has been stolen."

"That big tooth from the red oskorlisk?" Steve asked, puzzled. "Why would anyone want to steal your commemorative snake fang?"

"Because oskorlisk fangs are imbued with power," Kahvel explained. "The older—or larger—the oskorlisk, the more powerful the fang can become."

"I never knew oskorlisk teeth could hold jhorun," Sarah commented. "What sort of power does it possess?"

"It varies," Kahvel answered. "It is said that an oskorlisk

fang can offer protection from a variety of attacks. It is a powerful talisman used to shore up defenses."

Steve's eyes slowly traveled down the wall until it landed on Pryllan.

"So that's why you had it over your nest. You were protecting them. But… protecting them from what? What could possibly threaten a dragon up here?"

"I can protect this cave from any threat known to the wyverians," Kahvel informed them. "However, that is contingent on the threat being something I am familiar with. I am the Dragon Lord. There is always the chance that someone—or some*thing*—would try to find a way to harm my loved ones. The fang helps assure me that my family is safe."

"And that's where you had it?" Steve asked as he pointed at the torn wall above the nest.

"Aye. Embedded into the stone."

"Who knew it was here?" Sarah asked.

"It is known amongst all wyverians that Pryllan and her rider returned successfully with a fang from the mouth of a red oskorlisk. That, however, is news for wyverians only. I do not believe any of them would have spread that information to any outsider."

"Yet someone knew it was there," Steve mused. He started to pace. "This guy, this human that was here… you said he was somehow manipulating the air?"

Pryllan nodded. "There were gusts of wind coming from *inside* this cave. Somehow that human was responsible."

"And apparently the human used the winds to lower himself back to the ground," Kahvel added.

Pravara suddenly thumped her tail. Everyone turned to look at her.

"I am sorry to interrupt, but I just received word from Mikal. He says that he has just heard one of his patrols sighted a ship coming from across the Great Sea yesterday. When it became evident that the ship intended to make contact with the shore, the guards pursued, only the ship vanished and wasn't heard from again."

"And that's remarkable *why*?" Steve asked, puzzled.

"Because no human ship has sailed from across those waters in well over two hundred years," Kahvel announced. "Do you see what this means? Lentari appears to have been invaded."

Chapter 4 — Pirate Power

I bloomin' told ye to watch those turns. Blast it all to hell, Jino. Did I not ask if you could handle the rudder? It'll be at least an hour before we can make repairs and be on our way. I should skin Von alive for allowing you to sit in that seat."

"I'm sorry, Captain," the dark-skinned pirate said, bowing his head in shame.

"He said he could handle it," Von began. "He said he could…"

The sneer vanished from his face seconds later when Flinn glanced his way.

"I don't give a rat's ass if you be sorry," Flinn growled, gritting his teeth in frustration. He looked at the busted boom and shook his head. "As far as I be concerned, ye both busted it. Now, the two of ye get to fix it. Find some wood. Be quick about it."

Jino jumped to the ground, followed immediately by the thin, unkempt Von, and darted back up the hill to disappear into the trees. Watching silently, Rusty groaned. He should have known this mission was going to hit a snag. His instincts had told him that there was no way they'd be able to infiltrate a valley populated by dragons *and* remain undetected. However, the captain had assured them that they'd be safe. So, what had ended up happening? The blasted dragon returned to the nest much sooner than it should have. Thankfully, the captain was true to his word, and held the beast off long enough to escape.

Rusty smiled as he recalled the events after the theft. They had piled back in to the *Cadaymas* and fled the valley as fast as the modified skiff could take them. Thanks to the captain's special touch when it came to manipulating the wind, the special land-bound skiff—built by the captain's own two hands—could travel at speeds far greater than a horse could run. However, when traveling at those speeds, the slightest shift in direction could be detrimental, especially if you weren't paying attention. And that, unfortunately, was what had happened when Jino dozed off on the rudder.

True, it wasn't a typical rudder that you'd find on a boat. Obviously, there wasn't any water to direct so a normal rudder would be useless. However, the captain, in his supreme brilliance, had attached the rudder to the boom, so that one person sitting in the stern of the boat, could effectively steer the unique vessel by himself.

Jino had snoozed his way through a turn, woken up when the entire crew all cried out in alarm, and had yanked the rudder hard to port. The boom had been ripped from the boom jaws as they sideswiped a row of trees. The rudder had broken off from the boom and had been smashed to splinters when it was flung into a nearby boulder. Thankfully, the captain had thrown out the *Cadaymas'* anchor, which was basically just a stout rope tied to a three-pronged grappling hook. It had instantly hooked a tree and brought them to an immediate, if unpleasant, stop.

While the men worked to repair the damage, the captain motioned for the quartermaster to join him in a private meeting.

"I never should have doubted you, Captain," Rusty began,

hoping to steer the conversation away from the predictable berating he knew was forthcoming. "When you told me that you were planning on stealing something from a dragon, I thought you were crazy. However, you insisted from the start that, should we be discovered, you'd be able to handle the dragon. I was wrong to doubt."

"You damn me with faint praise," Captain Flinn grumped. "Enough prattling. We may have what we came for, but I'm sure you'll notice we're nowhere near the *Emberbrand*."

Rusty pointed at the land skiff. "Don't worry, Captain. We'll be off before you know it. The men are working on repairs now. The boom should be fixed within the hour and Jino says he'll have the new rudder ready in plenty of time."

"And if it isn't?"

"It will be. Have faith, Captain."

"It'll be yer hide if it ain't," Flinn grumbled.

Thirty minutes later the skiff was ready. Jino started to head back to his position at the stern of the small vessel when the captain held up a closed fist. Jino came to a reluctant stop.

"Cap'n? Is there something wrong?"

"There'd be something wrong with me, mate, if I let you back in that seat."

"It was an accident, Captain. It'll never happen again."

"Yer damn straight it won't happen again. Von, are ye not the helmsman? Get your arse up here and do your job."

"I can do this," Jino insisted.

"Obviously not well," Flinn added.

Von scurried by Flinn and Jino and quickly took his place. He rested his right hand on the rudder and nervously glanced at the captain while trying not to smirk too much at Jino.

Jino's brow furrowed as he narrowed his eyes. However, he wisely decided to keep his opinion to himself.

Once they were moving, the men started to relax. Spirits were restored. Jokes were tossed about. Several sailors lifted their voice in song and acted like they had consumed too much ale, which they hadn't. Stories were told. Battle scars were compared.

Rusty sighed. From the way the crew was bragging, one would think that they had successfully stolen the fang right out from under the dragon's nose. While it had been sleeping. In broad daylight. They hadn't even made it back to the coast yet and the *Emberbrand.* If Arik was doing his job, their ship would be under full camouflage and should be safe. However, Arik's jhorun needed to recharge, so they could only hope that during the time Arik was asleep, and the boat was visible, no one happened to venture by.

An hour later, the *Cadaymas* emerged from the thick of the forest into bright daylight. Rusty watched the captain shade his eyes and scan the southern horizon. He mimicked the motions and breathed a sigh of relief. There was no one to avoid and no signs of pursuit from the dragons, either. Good. That was very good.

"I wonder what died," Rusty heard one crewman mutter to himself.

Finding the comment curious, the first mate turned to regard the speaker. Alquin, one of the new recruits, was staring up at the sky. Curious, Rusty returned his gaze back to the sky. When he didn't spot anything, he looked back at the sailor and nudged his shoulder.

"What are you staring at? Why would you ask about someone dying?"

"I didn't mean nothin' by it," Alquin mumbled, dropping his eyes back to the ground. "I was jus' wonderin' what them buzzards are lookin' for."

"Buzzards?" Rusty repeated, alarmed. "What buzzards? I see no buzzards."

"That's 'cause you're lookin' in the wrong place. Look behind us. No, too far. There. Look up, above them trees. See 'em now?"

"Your jhorun is enhanced eyesight, isn't it?" Rusty asked.

Alquin nodded. "Aye. What of it?"

"You're seeing something that's much farther away than I can… wait. I think I see what you're looking at. It's… uh, oh. Captain? Captain! I think we've been spotted!"

Captain Flinn scrambled to his feet. He fired off a dangerous look to Von, who instantly gripped the rudder with a steady hand. Flinn produced a spy glass and aimed it at the distant specks growing steadily larger. They weren't buzzards but something larger. Something more reptilian. Rusty groaned. They must have been spotted by the dragons. The captain growled and handed the glass to Rusty. Two seconds later, Rusty was scowling just as much as the captain, his fears confirmed.

"Did ye not assign a lookout?" Flinn snapped, as he pulled Von off the rudder and took his place. The winds picked up. "Did ye not promise me you had recruited the perfect man? Why the bloody hell did he not say something earlier?"

Rusty slipped the spyglass back into its pouch and glared at Alquin, their lookout. Alquin swallowed nervously and dropped below the gunwale, disappearing from sight. Rusty looked up at the approaching wyverians. He didn't need a spyglass to see that they were angling straight for them.

"They're headed this way, Captain. I can see three o' them!"

Captain Flinn pulled the wooden lever situated just inside the skiff on the right of the lone seat in the stern. Rusty nodded. He knew that the wooden handle was attached to a mechanical clamp on the belly of the ship that, when applied, would squeeze the two rear wheels until the craft would come to a stop. The land-bound skiff picked up speed. As one, all the men leaned low, as if they thought that simple act would help them speed away from the encroaching danger.

Just then, the ground exploded directly behind them.

"That was too close!" Von whined as he tried to drop lower inside the small boat. He turned to the captain and frantically clutched at his arm. "You must do somethin', Cap'n! I don' wanna die!"

Flinn knocked Von off his feet, then rubbed his knuckles. The echoing cracks caused his shipmates to flinch.

"Be there anyone else? I will not tolerate cowardice. Should the need arise, and we must fight for our very lives, then I expect each and every single one of you to do just that."

One of the dragons swooped by overhead, but not before it blasted a jet of fire at the rapidly fleeing vessel. Thankfully the *Cadaymas* was moving faster than the dragon had anticipated, and the shot missed. Barely.

A spiraling fireball came out of nowhere and slammed into the skiff with enough destructive firepower to completely incinerate the boat and all its occupants. The blast was also powerful enough to decimate the surrounding trees, reducing them to ash in a matter of moments. However, the *Cadaymas* continued on; the wheeled-craft had survived the dragon encounter without as much as a blemish.

Captain Flinn gave a triumphant shout and pulled the silver fang from his belt, kissing it as he held it up for his crew to see.

"I knew it, boys! I just knew it! Did ye see? We would appear to be immune to dragon fire!"

A large pine tree, complete with an enormous dirt-encased root ball, crashed heavily to the ground, narrowly missing the *Cadaymas*. Captain Flinn cursed loudly and scanned the skies. The wyverians, noticing that their flames were ineffective, were now actively searching for items to throw at them. He and his men silently watched a dragon land several hundred feet behind them, uproot the nearest tree, and return to the air, with the tree clutched in its great claws.

"Lads, we have a problem," Flinn grumbled. He turned to look back at his crew. "Heads up! We're not out of danger yet!"

"What?" Von sputtered. "What are the dragons doing now? You said that your damn snake tooth would protect us from anything, didn't you?"

Captain Flinn gestured angrily at the fallen tree as they carefully passed.

"How do ye expect us to escape when those blasted dragons are throwing things at us? How long do you think it'll take before they figure out all they need to do is to toss a few trees in the road? How will the *Cadaymas* navigate over it? No, shut yer trap. I know the answer. We won't be able to."

"What would you have us do, Captain?" Rusty asked. He was gripping his cutlass tightly in his hand as he stared up at the sky.

"Now you'll see why I was so selective about the men I took with me to this accursed land," Captain Flinn said. "I had a feeling it might come to this. We had to be prepared."

Growing somewhat nervous, Rusty glanced up at the circling dragons as the landbound skiff rattled noisily along the road. The winds were continuing to blow them in the right direction, but that wasn't surprising as he was sure the captain had something to do with it.

Flinn was going to rely on the crew's jhorun? He hesitated a moment as he fought to remember what each man could do. The *Cadaymas* hit a rut in the road and Rusty could have sworn that he felt every tooth rattle in his skull. Worried that someone might have fallen out of the skiff, he quickly glanced around the rapidly moving ship and sighed with relief. Everyone was accounted for and all of them, he noted, were now looking expectantly at the captain.

"Now listen up, ladies. Ye want to get rid of the dragons?"

A chorus of ayes sounded.

"You want to stay safe?"

More ayes.

"Then do as I say. No questions asked. You. Puck, is it?"

A dirty, lean man with skin darkened and weathered by long years spent under the sun, and a full beard that looked as though it had remnants of its owner's last five meals, turned to look at the captain.

"Me?"

"Your name be Puck, right? You're the one I need. Give us some cover. Now!"

"But my jhorun is minor! What do you possibly think I could do?"

"You claim you can affect the very weather, do ye not?"

Puck nodded. "Aye, Captain. However, it is never that much and it never lasts that long."

"We need ground cover, now!"

"But what am I supposed to...?"

Everyone heard the distinctive *schwing* of a sword being drawn.

"All right! All right! I'll try!"

Moments later a thick, albeit small, blanket of fog materialized around the skiff, blocking them from sight. However, little pieces of the small fog bank broke off and dissipated as the *Cadaymas* continued to move. Puck grunted with the effort as he struggled to keep the skiff concealed within the fog.

"How long can ye maintain the fog, sailor?" Captain Flinn asked.

"Maybe… maybe a few minutes more."

"Very well. You. What's your name?"

"Casimir, captain."

"Aye. Casimir, you're next."

"How would my jhorun help us?" Casimir wanted to know.

Flinn pointed up at the faint outlines of the sky barely visible through the fog. Just then a dragon passed by, dangerously close. It was sniffing the air as it tried to locate them in the fog bank.

"Do ye think we be tryin' to avoid a flock of kytes? Use it against them! Hurry!"

"You think I can invoke fear in a dragon?" Casimir skeptically asked. "I don't know, captain."

"You bloody well had better try or I'll personally run you through! In fact, the next person to question my orders *will* be run through, is that understood?"

"Yes, Captain," Casimir stammered fearfully. "I'll try."

The short, chubby man with the bald head closed his eyes and concentrated. Several seconds later they heard one of their wyverian pursuers roar, but this time it sounded different. It had actually sounded more like an exclamation than a full-throated roar of anger.

"Is it working?" Flinn whispered.

Casimir shrugged. "I don' know, Captain. I never tried to scare off anything that big before."

Flinn motioned for everyone to be quiet. Aside from the rattle of the *Cadaymas'* wheels, all was silent. A roar sounded, but it was faint and non-aggressive in nature.

"I think we've lost 'em, Captain!" one man exclaimed as he jumped to his feet. He let out a loud whoop, followed almost immediately by a loud "Ow!"

Rusty had smashed the closest object he could find over the unfortunate man's head, and that was a piece of the former rudder that Jino had saved for some odd reason. The man crumpled to the floor. Damn fool. They needed silence; stealth. Encapsulated inside the fog bank as they were, the last thing they needed was to have someone give away their location. He couldn't take the risk that Grenden might let out a sneeze or a cough next.

A roar sounded in the distance. Unfortunately, it was much closer. A second roar sounded shortly thereafter. Rusty groaned. The damn fool. That was *precisely* what Grenden had done. If he wasn't the ship's surgeon, then he was sure that Flinn would have thrown him over the side.

"I'm gonna hold you responsible," Flinn growled, looking up at the skies.

The mists swirled inside the fog bank and, for a few seconds, a sliver of blue became visible. Five seconds later the fog thickened and the sky disappeared, but not before they saw a dragon zip by overhead. It hadn't found them yet, but unfortunately, it was getting closer.

Captain Flinn singled out another man, one who had yet to speak a single word for the entire voyage.

"You. Ye be one of the cabin boys, are ye not? You're up next."

Two surprised eyes locked onto the captain's. Rusty frowned as he tried to remember what jhorun this recruit had. Ferris. That was the man's name. Rusty glanced at the two boys sitting fearfully at the back of the boat and briefly felt sorry for them. They were both young, looked green around the gills, and were quite possibly the most timid of the entire group. After a few moments, Rusty mentally snapped his fingers. Ferris' jhorun was the ability to render a strong jolt to whatever he touched, like a super-charged stab of static electricity. How did the captain think he'd be able to use that jhorun to his advantage?

"Me?" Ferris's soft, shy voice spoke. "What can I do?"

"Your jhorun. It'd be the ability to shock something, isn't it?"

Ferris gave a slight perceptible nod of his head.

"Aye, but I don't see that that could help you, Captain. Perhaps you meant Pedr? I know his jhorun will…"

"Forget about his jhorun. I'll be needin' it later. It's you

I'm interested in right now, boy."

"I'll do everything I can, Captain. I should tell you that I can't do anything with the dragon unless he gets close enough for me to touch. And even then, I don't know if I would be able to affect a form so large."

Flinn pulled back on the brake lever and waited for the *Cadaymas* to slow to a crawl. He motioned for Von to take over the rudder and nimbly hopped out of the ship, landing lightly on his feet. The captain turned to look back at the ship with an expectant look on his face.

Rusty nudged the trembling boy.

"You best be moving, boy. If the captain wants your help, then you'd best be giving it."

Ferris nodded and jumped over the gunwale, landing next to the captain. From his position aboard the *Cadaymas*, Rusty watched the pair run over to the edge of the trees beside the road. The quartermaster eyed the second cabin boy. Pedr was staring at the empty space on the bench next to him as though he'd never see his friend again. As for Flinn, the captain was now gesturing at various trees. He'd point at one, and then a few seconds later, at a different one. The boy, Ferris, said something to the captain and pointed at a different tree. Captain Flinn nodded. He gave the kid a muffled set of instructions and hurried back to the skiff.

"Be ready," Flinn called back to the tiny ship.

"For what?" Rusty wanted to know.

"You'll see. Wait for it."

Suddenly Rusty felt the hairs on the back of his arms stand straight up. A loud chorus of squawks and chirps sounded from overhead and the skies darkened. Rusty tried to peer through the fog. Kytes! Hundreds and hundreds of small, fluffy kytes were taking to the air!

The mists parted somewhat and they could see Ferris sprinting in their direction.

"Tone it down some, Mister Casimir," the captain quietly ordered.

Two hands suddenly appeared on the edge of the boat. Ferris, struggling mightily, was trying to pull himself over the edge but lacked the upper body strength to do so. Jino leaned over, grabbed the collar of Ferris' shirt, and easily hauled the boy inside.

A sudden gust of wind caught the skiff's single sail and almost snapped the mast in half. The *Cadaymas* leapt down the road, narrowly avoiding several of the uprooted trees the dragons had tried dropping on them. The wind, Rusty dismally noticed, had also blown away their cover.

"What are you doing, Captain?" Rusty frantically hissed. "We've lost our cover! We'll be seen!"

"No, we won't," Flinn contradicted. "Thanks to young mister Ferris here, the dragons are now too busy to notice our retreat."

"Too busy with what?" Rusty wanted to know, feeling more confused than he had ever felt. "What did the boy do?"

"Kytes be sensitive creatures," Flinn casually remarked as he eyed Von at the controls. "They can easily be spooked."

"Ferris gave them a jolt, didn't he?"

"The boy sent the strongest charge he could deliver up the trunk of that tree," Flinn confirmed. "Any kyte perched in its branches just got a jolt."

"Kytes," Rusty said, smiling. "You two were looking for the tree with the most kytes."

"There be no better way to slip away from the dragons' prying eyes than by doing it right under their scaly noses," Flinn chortled. "And how do ye do that? Ye give 'em something else to occupy their time."

The first mate nodded his approval. "A distraction."

"Aye," Captain Flinn confirmed. "It be the only way too … Mister Alquin! Make yer presence known."

Alquin's head popped up from the floor of the skiff, where he had been hiding—shivering—in terror.

"Yes, Captain?"

"Where be the dragons now?"

"I … I…"

"What's your only job, sailor?" Flinn demanded.

"Lookout, Captain."

"How's the view from the ground?"

"Er, not very well, Captain."

"What should you be doin' right this second?"

"Er, lookin'?"

"Precisely. Get your skinny arse up to the bow and get to work."

"Aye, Captain."

Five minutes passed in utter silence. Rusty shared a look with the captain. Flinn, unfortunately, had his hand resting on his cutlass.

"Mister Alquin, report," Rusty snapped.

"No signs of our winged friends, sir."

"Excellent. Mister Von, set a course for…"

"Captain?" Alquin interrupted.

"What?"

"I see somethin' else."

"Blast. Be they dragons?"

"No, Captain. They be, I mean, it looks like people."

"What? Where?"

"Dead ahead, perhaps half a league away."

Captain Flinn held out a hand and waited for someone to slap the spyglass into it.

"I cannot see anything. Out with it. Tell me what ye see."

"Men. On horseback."

A ripple of alarm spread quickly throughout the small vessel.

"Soldiers?" Rusty quietly asked.

Alquin nodded. "Aye. I can see their swords. Oh. I also see archers. It must be several dozen men. Captain, this cannot be good."

"How long before they see us?" Flinn inquired.

"Maybe fifteen minutes. Twenty if we're lucky."

"What are we gonna do, Cap'n?" Von whined. "We can't hope to hide from 'em. Not in *this*."

"Let's ambush 'em," Casimir cackled, as a dagger appeared in each hand. "We have the element of surprise."

"Not in the *Cadaymas* we don't," Rusty corrected. "Captain? What do you want to do?"

"Hmm. We have but a few minutes. Very well. Jino, bring us to a full stop. Rusty, get the men off the boat. We're going to set up camp."

"We're going to *what*?" Rusty demanded. "You cannot be

serious, Captain."

Flinn had already jumped from the boat and was inspecting the forest's edge several hundred feet away.

"Dismantle the *Cadaymas*. Be quick about it! Just like we practiced, back in Aarszan."

Rusty blinked his eyes a few times, shoved his questions and concerns aside, and faced the men. They were staring at the captain as though he had finally lost his mind. Rusty thumped a fist on the side of their skiff.

"You heard the captain! Grenden, you men help Puck take down the sail. Casimir, help Alquin dismantle the mast. Jino, help Von detach the wheels as soon as everyone is out of the boat. Ferris, Pedr, you … you … you two just stay out of the way. Move like you have a purpose, men!"

Fifteen minutes later, the *Cadaymas* now resembled nothing more than piles of planks and various bits of wood. A large tent had been erected, using the skiff's one and only sail, with half of the mast drafted into service as the tent's pole.

Rusty shook his head with amazement. The first time Captain Flinn had demonstrated how easy it was to dismantle the *Cadaymas*, both for storage aboard the *Emberbrand* and to disguise the small skiff should they ever be discovered, he had been amazed. Flabbergasted, even. He hadn't known such a thing could even be possible.

The first mate eyed the sailors, who were busy assembling the last bits of wood into makeshift furniture. Rusty grunted with satisfaction. That was also why the captain had taken a keen interest in anyone who claimed they had experience working as a carpenter, too. In fact, Von, Jino, and Casimir were all skilled wood workers. Three tables, eight chairs, and one bench appeared within minutes. Alquin appeared at his side.

"We are out of time. The soldiers approach!"

"How long?" Rusty demanded, jerking his head up to look in the direction their lookout was pointing.

"Less than a minute."

Rusty hurried to the captain's side. "We have less than a minute, Captain."

Flinn grunted, "Puck, what be the status of that fire?"

"I got it started, Cap'n."

"Good. Relax, boys. The best way to hide from soldiers is out in the open. We will let them pass without incident."

"We ain't gonna attack 'em?" Puck asked.

Flinn shook his head, "No. Not unless we have to. Nothing will bring more soldiers like reports of missing soldiers. We don't want to bring any attention to ourselves. Understand?"

The first rider appeared around the bend. He was wearing a maroon-colored cuirass, gauntlets, and greaves. He had a sword strapped to his hip and a quiver fastened to his back, complete with arrows and a destrung bow. He caught sight of the camp and put two fingers in his mouth. Three short whistles were heard. Nearly thirty more horses rushed around the bend, each with a similarly attired rider. One rider, wearing armor rimmed with gold and a barbute adorned with a plume of white feathers, slowly approached on his horse. He regarded the silent camp for a few moments before he casually pulled off his helmet.

"Identify," the soldier demanded. "State your business."

The men nervously turned to Rusty, just as he turned to look at the captain. He could only hope that Flinn had some type of story ready to give them.

"Speak quickly," the rider demanded. "What is the nature of your business here?"

Flinn slowly got to his feet and smiled at the officer. Rusty frowned. It was the type of smile a thief might give had he been caught admiring a chest of gold. He made a mental note to suggest to the captain he should never try smiling again, but dismissed it. He was friends with the captain, sure, but they weren't that friendly.

"Good day to you, sir," the captain began. "We are but humble travelers. If our camp has inconvenienced you in any way, fear not. We will move it."

The rider's face studied the captain's. He tucked his helmet under his left arm and urged his horse forward. As soon as they were less than a dozen feet away from the captain, the horse was halted.

"I do not know your face. State your business. What are you doing here?"

"We are naught but honest laborers, enjoying the day," Flinn said, adopting as light a tone as Rusty had ever heard.

"You have not answered the question," the rider flatly stated.

"My apologies," Flinn said, keeping a neutral expression on his face as he bowed low. "We are just looking for work. We travel from village to village, acquiring odd jobs here and there."

"What kind of work?" Lead Rider asked.

Rusty glanced at the captain. Flinn, he could tell, was starting to sweat. Not good.

"Why, practically anything! If ye have knives that need sharpening, or a roof that needs mending, then we can certainly do the work at a reasonable price."

The lead rider shook his head, "I don't see any tools. There are no horses to haul those tools. You have no building materials. I do not know what you are, but I do know you are not laborers."

Rusty eyed Flinn. The captain had paled. For the first time ever, it looked as though Flinn was at a loss for words. Clearly the captain did not expect anyone to question his cover story. Rusty swallowed nervously. He eyed the rest of the armed soldiers. They all had their free hands resting on their sword hilts. He then eyed his own men. They, in turn, had their hands behind their backs, hoping to give off the impression of disinterested workers. However, Rusty knew that each one of them were more than likely holding weapons of some sort. If he didn't defuse this situation, and do so quickly, their cover would be blown.

Rusty suddenly smiled. A solution had just presented itself. It wouldn't be easy, and the captain would most certainly not approve, but it would explain their presence here and would, more than likely, satisfy the soldier's curiosity.

"Good day to you, my fine fellow," Rusty exclaimed, raising his voice theatrically. It's all part of the act, he told himself. "You may rest easy, my friend. You are right, of course. You have seen through our ruse."

"And who are you?" the rider demanded.

"Entertainers! Look at us! We clearly have no other skill than to make others laugh at our ineptitude, wouldn't you say?"

The rider grunted once. Rusty smiled. He was off to a good start.

"That all depends," the rider said. "You claim you're entertainers? Where are you coming from? Verdayn?"

Rusty nodded. "Of course. We just, uh, put on a show for the good people of, er, Verdayn, and were so well received that we, um, decided to take our show on the road. We were headed to…" He trailed off. He really didn't know the names of any other village.

"…the castle?" the rider inquired.

Relief flooded into him. Rusty smiled and offered a small bow. His eyes found Flinn's and he inclined his head toward the ground, indicating the captain should bow, too. He watched the captain grit his teeth and reluctantly gave a small bow, too.

"Our plans are supposed to be a surprise, but aye. We are planning on performing at the castle. Forgive me, I am no navigator. The castle lies in this direction, does it not?"

"R'Tal is nearly ten leagues southeast from here, as the kyte flies," the soldier answered, turning to point in the direction they had been heading. "So you've been practicing your show, is that it?"

Rusty nodded again. "That's right. We want to make sure we're at our best for our next performance."

"How about giving us a preview of your act?" the rider casually asked. "I'm sure my men would appreciate the entertainment. We've been riding nearly twelve hours straight. Men, what do you say? Would you like these people to put on a performance?"

There was a chorus of hearty affirmations as the riders collectively cheered their approval. The lead rider turned back to Rusty.

"I am Lieutenant Armund, of the Royal Guard."

"Um, I'm Rusty?"

"You don't sound sure of yourself, man."

"Sorry. I wasn't expecting to, uh, put on a … performance here in the middle of nowhere."

"Well, make with it. Let's see what you can do."

"Of course. Ah, could you give me a few minutes for my, er, fellow entertainers to prepare themselves?"

"I give you ten minutes."

Rusty bowed. "Thank you."

He hurried over to Flinn's side, but before he could say anything, Flinn hooked an arm through his own and pulled him close.

"What in the name of hellfire and damnation have ye done?"

Rusty and the captain hurried back to their tent and motioned for the rest of the men to follow.

"I've bought us some time, Captain."

"By tellin' 'em we're entertainers?" Flinn sputtered. "Are ye daft? I said we had to avoid attention, not draw it to us, you idiotic imbecile!"

"What are we supposed to do, Cap'n?" Von asked, as he grabbed the captain's shoulder to spin him around. "I ain't no damn performer!"

Flinn smacked Von's arm off his shoulder and glared at his subordinate.

"Touch me like that again and ye'll lose that hand at the wrist."

"I'm sorry, Cap'n."

Flinn scowled as he peeked through the tent flaps at the waiting soldiers. He turned to Rusty and crossed his arms over his chest. One by one the rest of the men mimicked their captain.

"What?" Rusty demanded. "I was buying us some time. Surely you cannot be angry with me for that."

"What the blazes would ye have us do?" Flinn demanded.

Rusty hurried over to the tent flap to peer outside. The soldiers had all dismounted and were now sitting on the ground, in semi-circular rows in front of their tent. He held a finger to his lips as he turned around.

"Please, Captain. Keep your voice down. If they suspect we're anything but entertainers, then we're lost. They outnumber us more than four to one."

"Ye don't think I haven't noticed that?" Flinn snapped. "Fine. This be yer performance. What be yer plan?"

Rusty looked back at his men. For the second time, in as many minutes, a solution presented itself. He pointed at the man responsible for losing so much time.

"Jino. You're the best with a knife, right?"

Jino nodded. "I can hold my own. What do you have in mind? What do you want me to do?"

"Can you juggle?"

"Can I what??"

"Can you juggle? Can you toss three knives in the air and catch them, all without hurting yourself?"

Jino shrugged. "I don't know. I've never tried."

Rusty pushed him toward the tent flaps. "Here's your chance. Show them how good you are. Give us some time to come up with something else."

Jino held out a hand.

"What?" Rusty asked.

"I need another knife. I only have two."

Rusty pulled his own dagger from his belt. "Use mine."

Jino disappeared through the flaps. A few moments later they heard muted murmurs of appreciation. Then they heard a round of applause. Curious, Rusty approached the flap and peeked through, as did a number of his companions. Truth be told, the only performer he had ever seen as a child was a court jester. That was where he had first seen multiple objects thrown into the air, but inexplicably, none of the items would ever make it to the ground. Jino had implied he could juggle, only there he was, idly twirling a knife in his hand while he waited for one of the soldiers to set up another target. After much goading by the soldier's companions, the volunteer shrugged, stepped in front of a tree, and set the target—a rounded piece of yellow fruit—on his shoulder.

The soldiers loved it. There were yells, shouts, and quite a few taunts as the men jostled with each other. Rusty even heard a few wagers being cast. He eyed Jino to see how he was holding up. Surprisingly, Jino was all smiles as he watched the antics. As soon as the volunteer stopped moving, Jino flipped the dagger between his fingers, glanced once at the target, and sent the blade on its way. A split second later the men were all roaring their approval as the volunteer stepped away from the tree and wiped fruit juice off his shoulder. The dagger's hilt was still quivering as it held the fruit in place on the tree.

More targets were produced. Jino cast a worried eye at the tent and saw that he was being watched. Rusty nodded his assurance and turned back to the captain.

"We need another act."

"What now?" Von asked. "I can't throw a knife like that."

"What can you do?" Rusty whispered, motioning for everyone to keep their voices down.

"Nothing!" Von whined.

"If ye don't want to be left behind in this blasted land then ye had better find a way to become useful," Flinn muttered.

"His volunteer," Rusty suddenly decided. "Von can be Jino's volunteer."

"In a pig's eye I will," Von grumbled.

Flinn pushed Von toward the tent flaps. "Find ways to challenge Jino. Fetch his knives. Jino be the best knife fighter I've ever seen. Have him prove it."

Scowling mightily, Von disappeared through the flaps.

"What now?" Flinn inquired, completely deferring to Rusty.

"You," Rusty said, turning to Puck. "How much of your jhorun do you have left?"

"Some," Puck answered. "What do you want me to do?"

"Use your jhorun to make Jino mess up. The soldiers want to be entertained. Make 'em laugh."

Puck grinned, "That I can do."

He disappeared through the flaps.

"Ye seem to have this under control," Flinn observed, once he heard the soldiers roar with laughter. Whatever Puck was doing, it was having the desired effect.

"It just came to me," Rusty admitted. He glanced through the flaps. Jino was casting angry, dark looks at Puck, but at least Rusty could tell Jino was having a good time.

"What else have ye up that sleeve?" Flinn asked.

"Jesters."

"What about 'em?" Flinn dangerously inquired. "If ye be suggesting that I should go out there and act like a damn fool, then ye have another thing coming. I will *not* make a fool of myself today or any other day. Be that understood?"

"Think of the fang, Captain. It's just like you said. Hide from our enemy in plain sight, isn't that right?"

"Bugger me. Ye have no idea what's in store for ye later, do ye?"

Rusty grinned, slapped a hand on the captain's back, and pushed him through the flaps.

Chapter 5 — Pirates, Ahoy!

Are you sure? I mean, look at this. There hasn't been any mention of a Lentarian invasion for over a hundred years. Longer, if we take into consideration where the invaders are supposedly from."

"You don't believe Pravara? She got her information straight from Mikal."

Steve sighed and sat back in his chair. He looked around the large chamber and eyed the neat rows of books, the shelves of scrolls and parchment. He looked down the length of the long, white table they were sitting at and saw the disapproving frown of the tiny, withered archivist. Andra Aldwyn had crossed her skinny arms across her chest and was frowning at him.

"Oh, please let me be the one to tell her off," Steve softly mumbled, selecting another book from their stack and skimming through it.

Sarah patted his hand, "She's not a threat. Besides, we can handle her."

"Handle? You can handle me?"

Husband and wife looked up to see the argumentative archivist standing before them. Steve glanced up at the row of skylights above their head and then smiled patronizingly at the old records keeper. He waved his hand, as though he was shooing away a fly.

"Do you mind? You're in my light."

Andra refused to budge.

"Kri'Entu isn't here to save you."

"Do I look like I need to be saved?" Steve said, looking up at the woman with the frizzy white hair.

"I am in charge here," Andra began, clenching her fists in rage. "I will *not* tolerate disrespect. Not in my own Archives."

"We are here by order of the king," Steve coolly replied as he returned his attention to the book he was holding. "You don't want us here? Trust us, lady. I don't want to be here, either. The last thing I want to deal with is a cranky old sourpuss like you."

He heard Sarah suppress a giggle.

Andra strode forward, intent on yanking her precious book out of Steve's hands. The moment her hand made contact on the book, she let out a yelp and jerked her hand back. The book, as well as Steve's hand, had become engulfed in flames. He didn't damage the book, of course, nor did he allow his jhorun to harm the old woman. Tempting as it may have been.

"How dare you use your jhorun to try and frighten me? I'll have you arrested!"

"And we're done with this," Sarah muttered. She turned to the tiny archivist, held out a hand, and watched one of Andra's precious slips of paper extricate itself from her robe pocket to make its way over. She turned back to the table, reached for a bottle of ink and quill, and scribbled a note on a piece of paper.

"What do you think you're doing?" Andra scoffed. "Do you see many guards in here? There's no one to deliver your message this time."

The slip of paper vanished in Sarah's hand.

"Who says I need someone to deliver a message? I can

get my own messages delivered, thank you very much."

"What did you say?" Andra demanded. "Who did you send that message to?"

"Wouldn't you like to know?" Steve snorted, deliberately looking away from the cranky old woman. "Now, if you don't mind, we have a lot of research to do. Would you please go elsewhere and stop blocking my light?"

Andra Alwyn began sputtering with rage.

"How *dare* you treat me like I'm some simpleton? These are my archives. I have full authority here."

"I hope he gets here soon," Steve muttered. "I don't know how much more of this I'm willing to take."

Andra cackled with pleasure.

"I already told you; the king is gone."

"No, Kri'Entu is gone," Sarah clarified, offering her own thin smile to the cranky octogenarian. "There is a pro tem king in place, if memory serves."

"You mean Kre'Mikal," Andra snapped. "I know full well he sits on the throne during his parents' absence."

"Then you'll know that, right now, he's in charge. He's the one who has given us access to this wonderful, cheerful dungeon you have here."

Andra bristled with anger.

"So, go cool your jets elsewhere and leave us in peace. I'm finding it hard to concentrate with you prattling on and on like that."

Andra puffed out her chest and practically expanded to twice her normal size.

"The allowances I give Kri'Entu are in no way extended to his son," the archivist snapped. "The days of you two gallivanting around in here—unsupervised—are over."

"I disagree," a new voice said.

Andra cast her angry glare up at the newcomer and instantly looked contrite. Mikal strode into the Archives, followed closely by Lissa. They were accompanied by four guards.

"Did you, or did you not, receive my order to allow Steve and Sarah Miller complete access to the entire Archives?" Mikal asked in a decidedly neutral tone.

Andra huffed out her chest once more. "I did."

"Did you, or did you not, comprehend the order?" Mikal continued.

"I did."

"Then explain yourself. Why are you harassing them while they are working on a special assignment for me?"

Steve nudged his wife on the shoulder. "I'm really digging this side of Mikal right about now," he whispered.

Sarah held a finger to her lips, "Shush."

"Only Kri'Entu has the authority to allow full access to my Archives."

"No, only the *king* has the authority to grant visitors full access to the Archives. Without interference."

Andra frowned at Mikal. "You are still my student."

"And right now, I am your king," Mikal finished. "Like it, don't like it, I don't care. You will withdraw your petty objections and remove yourself from their presence unless they approach you first, asking for help. Is that understood?"

"That'll be a cold day in Nevir," Steve muttered.

Lissa looked away before the ancient records keeper could notice.

"And if I don't?" Andra challenged.

"Then you'll be relieved of your duties and escorted from the Archives, where I'll assign a replacement in your stead. Further," Mikal added, raising his voice to be heard over Andra's outraged squawk, "should you step foot back inside her without permission, you will be placed into a holding cell. In the dungeon."

"You wouldn't dare. Your father would never allow me to remain in the dungeon. He would release me the instant he returns."

Mikal shrugged. "Possibly. But, it'll also be close to a month before he returns. Maybe longer. If I send you to the dungeon, you'll be there until my father returns. Now, would you care to, as the people of Idaho would say, press your luck?"

Andra's eyes narrowed. With a scowl, she turned away, but not before giving Steve her darkest look. Once order had been restored, Mikal and Lissa joined the two of them at the table.

"I think I'm going to suggest to my father that she retire," Mikal said. He groaned. "I really don't want to throw anyone in the dungeon, but if ever there were a person I'd be willing to look the other way for, it'd be her."

"She is a very intimidating woman," Lissa agreed. "I think this place is her whole life. I think she's just fiercely protective of her records, of her books."

Mikal eyed the titles in the discard stack and leaned forward to see what notes the two of them had made. "Is your research going well? Have you made much progress?"

"Well, right now, I'm looking for anything about the Sea of Koralis," Steve began. "How big the sucker is, how many people have crossed it, what lies over there, and so on."

"What have you found?" Lissa asked.

"Not much. Every reference I find says the same thing: the sea is huge. No one has bothered crossing it for many years."

"Over a hundred fifty," Sarah added, consulting her own notes.

"And what are you searching for?" Lissa asked Sarah.

"I'm trying to find out when was the last time Lentari had been invaded. I'd like to know more about who were the people who last crossed that sea."

"And what have you found out?" Mikal asked. "I must admit, I have no idea, either. I probably slept through a few too many of my history lessons."

"You?" Lissa teased. "Become bored with history? Perish the thought!"

Steve snorted with amusement at the same time Sarah giggled.

"What have you learned about the sea?" Mikal asked. "What's on the other side?"

Nothing but desolate, dreary land as far as the eye can see. The inhabitants are fat, lazy, and lawless.

Steve laughed. When no one else did, he gave a sheepish smile and shrugged. He looked over at Sarah.

"Did you hear that? Did anyone else? Roger that. Just me, then."

Of course, it's just you. Do I typically share my thoughts with other humans?

I know you have before, Pryllan.

True, but the question was, do I typically share my thoughts with anyone other than you?

You got me there. Sorry. Have you ever been to the other side of the sea?

Not many wyverians have.

"What's going on?" Sarah asked. "Did the cat get your tongue? Oh, wait. I'm sorry. Pryllan is talking to you, isn't she?"

Steve nodded. He held up a finger.

Why are you pointing up?

Hmm?

You raised a hand and pointed up.

Oh. No, I didn't. I held up a finger, which in my world, signifies 'wait'. I was letting Sarah know, without saying anything, that I couldn't respond since you were still talking.

Ah.

"What's she saying?" Sarah was asking.

"She was telling me that there's nothing over there but … how did you put it, Pryllan? Desolate?"

Desolate, dreary land as far as the eye can see.

"Desolate, dreary land as far as the eye can see. And before you ask, the answer is no. She's never been there."

Sarah looked straight into Steve's eyes and smiled. "Hello, Pryllan. I have a question for you."

Proceed.

"Go ahead," Steve relayed.

"How long would it take a dragon to fly all the way across the sea?"

I never have, so I am not the one to ask.

Couldn't you ask your Collective?

Steve smiled as he briefly felt a flash of embarrassment wash over his wyverian friend.

I should have thought of that. A moment, if you please. I will inquire.

Don't forget to be discreet.

A valid point. Thank you.

"She's asking the Collective now," Steve softly announced.

"The Collective?" Lissa repeated, confused.

Mikal nodded. "I'm sure I've told you before. It's the gathering of wyverian minds. It's how the dragons talk to one another when they aren't in close proximity to each other."

As the wyverian flies, it would take nearly ten hours. Only the strongest of wyverians have ever attempted it.

"Ten hours," Steve softly whispered. "It takes them ten hours to fly across it. While that's a long flight, I don't think it'd be that impossible to do. Wait a moment."

Is that at your accelerated level of flying or normal, er, casual flying?

That would be at the accelerated rate. If we tried to fly at our normal velocity, then we would deplete our resources long before we reached the other side. Flying at that rate, for that long, means we would have to feed the instant we achieved landfall. Those that have accomplished this have reported nothing but barren rock and gameless land stretching endlessly away in all directions.

"Pryllan says the ten-hour flight would be at her increased pace. If they tried to fly at a normal speed, then they'd exhaust themselves long before they made it to the other side. Sarah, do you remember when Pryllan and I flew all the way from Twin Falls to Coeur d'Alene at that speed?"

"Lia had to have a truckload of meat waiting for Pryllan," Sarah recalled.

Steve nodded. "Right. There'd have to be something similar on the other side. From what I hear, game is scarce over there."

As is fresh water.

"So is the water," Steve added.

"That's horrible," Sarah decided. "No wonder we haven't found any record of anyone sailing across the sea. Do you have any idea how long that must take on a normal boat?"

"Way too long for my reckoning," Steve agreed.

"Ask Pryllan about the people over there," Mikal said. "More specifically, did the dragons encounter anyone? Did they see many cities? Did they fly over many boats?"

Only a few humans, no cities, and no boats.

Steve relayed the information.

"Regardless," Sarah was saying, "there must be cities over there. There must be some type of civilization. Our mystery ship had to have come from somewhere."

"Where did your guards say they saw the ship?" Steve asked.

Mikal looked down at the documents on the table and selected a map of the country. He placed a finger on a point nearly halfway down the eastern coast of Lentari. Steve, Sarah, and Lissa leaned forward for a better look. Mikal had placed his finger on a point just above where the Zylan River fed off the sea and began its westerly trek across the kingdom.

"The guards were on their way back to R'Tal," Mikal explained. "One reported seeing a ship appear on the eastern horizon. They tracked it south, to less than five leagues from the Zylan's headwaters, right about here."

"And how long was it before the guards lost sight of the ship?" Steve asked. "Could the ship have made it up the river? I've seen the Zylan before. That sucker is huge."

Mikal shook his head.

"Whereas a good majority of the river would be deep enough to allow a vessel that size to pass, the headwaters are much too shallow. No, this ship didn't use the river."

Steve grinned, "That's good to know. At least we won't have to search up and down that river. Talk about trying to find a needle in a haystack."

Mikal glanced at Lissa, looked around the quiet wing of the castle they were sitting in, and inclined his head toward the door.

"If you'd like to pick this up in the Antechamber, I'll send for the guards who saw the ship. They might be able to remember something that will help us locate it."

Steve looked down at the open book in front of him, snapped it closed with a loud bang, and pushed back in his chair.

"Sounds like a plan." He held out a hand and pulled Sarah to her feet. "Shall we?"

Once they were in the Antechamber, Mikal sent for the two guards. He took off his father's crown, rubbed his temples, and sighed. Sarah put an arm around the young king's shoulder and gave him a one-armed hug.

"How are you holding up, Mikal? Are you enjoying your time as the king?"

"Let's just say that I'm looking forward to my father's return," Mikal dryly answered. "He makes this look so easy. People respect him."

Steve frowned, "And they don't respect you?"

Mikal sighed, "You saw Andra earlier. She all but accused me of being a phony king with no claim to the throne."

"She was testing you," Lissa soothingly told him. "She's a woman who is used to getting her way. Your father won't allow her any leeway, and neither have you. She didn't like it. She's used to treating you like a pupil. I would say that it's time she learned you're now an adult, and the future king at that."

"Man alive, that lady sure does get under your skin," Steve added.

"Word," Sarah agreed, then giggled as Steve gave her a surprised look. Then he burst out laughing.

"Word? Are you working on your street cred now?"

"That was just for you, dear."

Word? I do not follow.

"You've confused Pryllan," Steve told her. "She doesn't know why you've said that."

"That makes two of us," Mikal admitted.

"Better make that three," Lissa added.

"Let's just say that it was only something I said to make my husband laugh," Sarah explained, giving everyone a smile. "Sorry, Pryllan. I didn't mean to confuse you."

There's no need to apologize. I was just confused.

"She says no worries," Steve told Sarah.

No, I didn't.

I realize that. Sorry. I was just paraphrasing.

Oh.

"What's the matter?" Sarah asked. "You're frowning."

"What? No, sorry. Pryllan was correcting me. She didn't actually say, 'no worries', but she said there wasn't any need to apologize. She was just pointing that out."

And I said that I was confused.

Yeah, yeah, I know.
Well, tell her that.
Fine.
"She was confused."
There, happy?
Actually, I am.

The door opened and two uniformed guards entered. They approached Mikal, saluted, and turned with surprise once they saw who else was in the room.

"You're the fire thrower!" the first soldier exclaimed. "I am Connal."

"Donovan," the second added, also bowing.

"Connal, Donovan, meet Steve Miller and his wife, Sarah. You were correct earlier, Connal. They are my former bodyguards. Steve is a fire elemental while Sarah is a teleporter."

Connal nodded. "I have heard of your jhorun, Fire Thrower. I wish I had one tenth of its power."

Steve grinned, "Thanks, pal. I still think Sarah here has the best jhorun, though."

"What can we do for you?" Donovan asked.

"They are here to look into the mystery ship," Mikal told the guards. "They have a few questions for you."

"It could have just been our imagination," Connal quietly admitted. "We only saw it for a few moments. For all we know, it could be some type of sea serpent."

"You think it could've been an oskorlisk?" Steve asked.

Unlikely. The oskorlisk do not linger at the top of the water. They will only surface if attracted by prey. Ask them how long they saw this ship. Tell them to be specific.

"How long was it visible?" Steve asked. "From the moment one of you saw it until it disappeared from sight. How long?"

Both guards looked at each other.

"I'd say no more than twenty minutes," Connal reported.

There is no way what they saw was an oskorlisk.

"Definitely not a sea serpent," Steve announced.

"How can you be so certain?" Donovan demanded.

Should I let them know that I went on a Hunt with you?

Of course. I'm proud of our accomplishment that day.

You and me both, my friend.

"Because I hunted one of them on the back of a dragon."

Both guards gasped.

"The rumor is true?" Donovan demanded.

Steve proudly puffed out his chest. "And lived to tell the tale. So trust me, the oskorlisk don't like coming to the surface unless they see something they want to eat."

"It *has* to be the ship," Sarah decided. "And it would appear that it's hiding near the mouth of the Zylan River. I say we go find it."

"Thank you, gentlemen," Mikal told the guards. "That will be all."

Both guards nodded and exited the room.

"So how does someone hide a ship large enough to make it across the Sea of Koralis?" Lissa wondered aloud.

Mikal shrugged. "How else? With jhorun."

"Is anyone else worried about people coming from across the sea, with jhorun strong enough to hide a ship in broad daylight?" Sarah asked.

"Let's worry about that later," Steve decided, rising to his feet. "I hereby reckon it be time for us to go find a boat."

Sarah shook her head, "I married a dork."

Steve turned to look at Mikal and Lissa. "If the ship is camouflaged, how will we know when we see it?"

Sarah waved a dismissive hand, "Please. A ship that size? On a beach? I'm sure we'll see it."

* * *

The eastern coast of Lentari formed a gentle arc, stretching from the northeast to the southeast. The Great Sea of Koralis essentially formed the eastern border of Lentari, thereby creating many leagues of shore on which someone could hide a boat. The terrain ranged from heavily forested mountains in the far south to open grasslands in the north, where R'Tal was situated. Stretching for at least a hundred of those leagues were cliffs, rising several hundred feet above the crashing water below.

"I think we can rule out the cliffs," Steve decided.

"I didn't teleport us here to check them out," Sarah reminded him.

"Then why did we stop here?"

"Because we're teleporting by line of sight. I can't just teleport us straight there. Well, I mean, I could, but the whole point of doing a search is to, well, search."

Steve nodded. "Ah. Where to now?"

Sarah pointed south. "We keep heading that way. Mikal told us that those two guards weren't on any cliffs. So that rules this area out. However, I have no idea where the cliffs end, so we have to do this one jump at a time until we're there."

"Got it. Carry on, m'dear."

Nine or ten jumps later, the elevation had gently decreased until they were no more than a dozen or so feet above the water. The river was nowhere in sight, but it also meant they had to be getting close. Steve looked down at the water below their feet. The shoreline reminded him of Oregon and Washington State back home, where nothing but rocks and inhospitable land met their eyes. He looked at Sarah and hooked a thumb at the shoreline.

"There's no way they would have parked their ship anywhere along this. I mean, look at those rocks. They wouldn't risk damaging their ship."

Sarah nodded. "Agreed. We should keep moving south to see if the beach becomes approachable."

It took just three jumps before they noticed the size of the rocks and stones littering the water's edge had begun shrinking. Two mere jumps later brought them to a section of shoreline that had small, rounded, pea-sized gravel scattered all across the water's edge. Sarah knelt down to grab a handful of the small stones.

"They're smooth, like they've been worn down by the water."

"Which makes sense considering our present location," Steve agreed.

"It also means that a boat could easily put to shore here."

"How are we supposed to find it? Obviously, someone is using their jhorun to hide it. We could be looking right at it."

"I've been thinking about that," Sarah said as she slowly stood. "I'm thinking the answer is water displacement."

Steve eyed the coastline. "You're thinking we'll be able to see some type of depression in the water? Like someone is pushing a big glass bowl down into the sea?"

Sarah beamed, "Exactly. I may be wrong, but I just think if we're careful enough, we should be able to see something that looks out of place."

Steve slowly scanned the beach. Gentle waves threatened to soak his boots as the tide slowly came back in. Surprised, Steve stared at the water that was slowly inching higher.

"The tide. That's it! That's how we'll find this thing."

"Come again?" Sarah asked, puzzled.

"The water is slowly rising. That means the ship is going to be rising along with it."

"And how does that help us?" Sarah wanted to know.

"If there's someone out there with jhorun strong enough to mask an entire ship, it means they have to have the ability to make the object look like what's directly behind it, right?"

Sarah shrugged. "I guess so."

"If the object is moving, especially a big object like this ship, then it'll become increasingly difficult to keep the ship hidden. Until the tide finishes its rise, I believe the ship will become slightly visible as the camouflage has to adapt to the changing background."

"You're predicating this on, what, some science show you saw on television?"

Suddenly, Steve looked—and felt—sheepish. "No. Not really. It was, umm, a sci-fi movie."

"Let me guess," Sarah laughed. "It had aliens in it? I'm sorry, I shouldn't make fun of you. I like your theory. Do you really think we might be able to see something?"

"We won't know until we try."

Sarah took his hand. "Then let's hurry. How long does it take for the tide to go in or out?"

Steve shrugged. "Several hours, I think."

"Are you sure? I thought it was faster than that."

"No, there are tons and tons of tables which precisely spell out how long it takes for the tides to come in or out. It depends on location, position of the moon, etc. I had to learn all about it when I got my SCUBA certification. Hey, wait a minute. Before you take us to the next spot, let me do something."

"What are you doing?"

Steve had let go of his wife's hand, stooped to scoop up a large handful of pebbles, and shoved them into his pocket.

"What did you do that for?"

"I'm guessing you can make these things fly out in all directions?"

Sarah nodded. "Yes. Easily. Why? Oh! That's brilliant! Let me get some, too."

She scooped a double handful of the small stones and filled her own pockets.

"This ship might be hidden from view," Sarah began, "but it'll still be there. If the pebbles hit anything, we'll know we've found it."

Steve took a second handful and filled his other pocket. "Ready. Let's go find this thing."

Several hours later they were, by their reckoning, at least thirty leagues farther down the coast. There, visible in the distance, was the beginning of the Zylan River. Steve took five pebbles out of his pocket, eyed Sarah, and flung them up into the air. Each pebble zoomed off in a slightly different direction, all toward the water.

They each heard five distinctive splashes. No ships here. Husband and wife sighed, clasped hands, disappeared, and materialized several hundred feet away. They repeated the process to no avail.

Any luck?

Steve drew to a stop and pulled Sarah with him.

"What is it?"

"It's Pryllan."

"Oh. Tell her hello for me."

Greetings.

"She says hello."

I said, 'greetings'.
Same context. What's up, Pryllan?
I was curious as to your progress. I know Kahvel will ask once he returns to the nest.
Nothing yet.
Has Pravara joined you yet?
Surprised, Steve automatically glanced up at the sky.
Pravara is on her way here? Nice. No, she's not here yet.
"What's going on?" Sarah asked.
"Pryllan says that Pravara is going to be joining us."
We appreciate the extra help.
She volunteered. I know she does not like to see her sire distressed.
When is she due to arrive?
I thought she would be there by now.
"When is Pravara going to join us?" Sarah asked.
"I don't know. Pryllan thinks she should already be here."
"Well, she's not," Sarah pointed out.
"I disagree," a voice said from behind them.
Husband and wife flinched. Steve whirled around to find Pravara resting on the ground and studying them intently. Sarah laughed, shook her head, and turned around.
"Like father, like daughter. Hello, Pravara. How long have you been there?"
"I have been following you now for nearly a quarter hour."
Steve let out a bark of laughter, "Fifteen minutes. You were here for fifteen minutes and we didn't notice you? That's spooky, disheartening, and impressive at the same time."
"I offer my assistance," the dark green dragon said, lifting her head from the ground. "I wish to apprehend those responsible for causing my parents duress."
"Your help is greatly appreciated," Steve told the friendly dragon.
Pravara is here.
I know. She told me earlier. That's why I asked. You really should pay more attention to your surroundings. She says she was there for a quarter hour before she announced her presence.

Yeah, yeah, yeah. I'll get working on that.

He felt Pryllan's laughter before her presence faded from his mind.

"Your mother is a real kick in the pants."

Pravara nodded. "Finally. An expression I am familiar with. Mikal has used those words on more than one occasion. If I recall correctly, it took him a while to explain to me what slang was. Now, how may I be of assistance?"

Steve explained his theory and pointed out the incoming tide. Pravara listened, nodded, and eyed Sarah to see what she thought of this idea. Sarah nodded her encouragement.

"Very well. I will look for any disturbances."

"May I make a suggestion?" Steve asked. He pulled several pieces of gravel from his pocket. "We have these, and have been casting them into the sea. If the ship is out there, disguised, the pebbles should still strike the ship's hull."

"Are you suggesting I carry stones as I fly?" Pravara asked. She looked down at her sleek reptilian form. "I do not believe that would work. I have no pockets."

"But you're flying over water," Sarah reminded the dragon. "If you see anything suspicious, you should be able to splash some water up on it. That ought to let you know if there's something there."

Pravara nodded. "That is an acceptable idea. I will do that. I will be in touch."

Pravara leapt straight up, snapped her wings open, and sailed away.

"Ready for the next jump?" Sarah asked, taking his hand.

"How many jumps have you made today?" Steve asked, growing concerned. "How many more can you make?"

Sarah sighed. "I can feel the drain on my jhorun. I'm nowhere near full power but I still have enough to keep searching."

"I should've brought Mythrin," Steve bemoaned.

"Having your broadsword strapped to your back would have just gotten in the way," Sarah pointed out.

"Maybe," Steve admitted, "but at least we'd have some mimets for you to recharge your jhorun. Are you sure you don't want to jet back to the manor and grab the sword?"

Sarah shook her head. "Men. Always looking to do things the hard way."

Mythrin appeared in her hands. She handed the sword to Steve. Laughing, he strapped the sword to his back, but not before he pulled out one of the special nine-sided crystal discs from a pouch sewn into Mythrin's scabbard.

"Here. Charge up, baby."

Sarah giggled, "You're a dork."

"Yet you married me. You knew what you were getting into."

"You weren't like this before we were married," Sarah countered, throwing her husband a smile.

"You're right. I was worse. Now, feeling better?"

Sarah handed the spent disc back. "Yes. Thank you. You know what? That thing is just going to get in the way. Why don't you let me put it in our cabin? That way it'll be here in case we need it again."

Steve frowned. "But I *like* wearing it."

"It'll just get in the way. Trust me, if you need it, I'll bring it back for you."

Steve unbuckled the sword from his back and reluctantly handed it over. "You promise?"

Sarah sighed. "Very well. I promise. Now, where do you think we should go?"

"We be a' headin' thataway, milady," Steve drawled, pointing south.

What language is that?

Steve burst out laughing.

"What?" Sarah asked, confused.

"Pravara heard me do my John Wayne impersonation and wanted to know what language it was."

"Oh. Pravara, it's called UberNerd. Steve is a master of it."

"Don't tell her that," Steve scolded.

Oobernerd. It must be some unknown dialect of human. Understood. I'll try to remember.

"Nice," Steve grumped. "Thanks, dear. That's gonna be a hard one to explain later."

Sarah flashed him a grin.

Pravara, have you found anything yet?

Only a heretofore unknown language that, apparently, only humans are privy to.

I meant about the missing ship.

Ah. I have not detected a disguised vessel of any sort.

Where are you now?

I am approaching the southern mountains and am about to turn around.

What? Pravara, you're flying way too fast! We have to conduct a much more thorough search if we're to have any hope of finding this mystery ship.

Understood. I will search while flying at a severely decreased velocity.

Thank you.

Thirty minutes later found them three jumps away, exploring a rocky peninsula that extended a dozen or so feet out into the water when Steve pulled Sarah to a stop. He held a finger to his lips and pointed, wordlessly, to the east. They could both see a patch of the open blue water had turned black. The surface of the sea became choppy, as though something was in it, and whatever it might be was thrashing about.

The problem was, Steve knew, that there *was* something there and exactly what it was.

"What is that?" Sarah whispered.

"It's an oskorlisk," Steve breathed. "I don't know what it's doing this close to the surface. Pryllan said they only will appear ... oh, no!"

"What?" Sarah demanded.

"Where's Pravara?"

Pravara? Pravara! Tell me you're okay!

I'm here. What's the matter? I can feel your fear. Why are you concerned?

There's an oskorlisk getting ready to surface about a quarter of a mile from shore. Your mother says they'll only come to the surface if they see something that looks appetizing. I'm just making sure you're okay. I know oskorlisks are quite fond of dragons.

I appreciate your concern. There, I see it now. Fear

not. I am nowhere close.

Where are you now?

Gaining altitude.

I thought you said you were safe. Why are you going higher?

I'm following my father's orders. He was monitoring my progress and overheard your remarks about the oskorlisk. He doesn't want me to take any chances.

Good for him. Kahvel, if you're listening, thanks. I was worried, too.

No, thank you *for thinking of Pravara. I do not want her anywhere near one of those serpents.

That makes two of us.

I will take my leave now, Young One. Stay safe.

Thank you, Father.

The oskorlisk's head broke the surface, but the gigantic snake head was only visible for a few seconds before it quickly disappeared back into the water. A mass of enormous black coils appeared. From their perspective, it looked as though the giant sea serpent had found prey after all, and was wrapping its coils about the hapless victim.

Can you see what it's attacking, Pravara?

No. The serpent is moving too fast.

Just steer clear of it.

I plan to.

"That's an oskorlisk?" Sarah sputtered, turning to smack Steve on his arm. "Look at the size of that thing! You never told me they were that big!"

"I told you the damn thing had me in its mouth," Steve reminded her. "Remember?"

"You most certainly did not," Sarah haughtily returned. "I would have remembered. Trust me on this."

"I didn't tell you? Hmm, I thought I did."

"This conversation is nowhere close to being over," Sarah vowed. "Steve, that thing looks dangerous!"

"That's because it *is* dangerous," Steve confirmed. "It's pretty much the only thing that can take on a dragon and win."

"And Pryllan was okay with putting you in that much danger?"

Steve sighed. "It was for a good cause, okay? We prevailed, we got a fang from the rare red version of that thing, end of story. Kahvel saw that Pryllan and I worked amazingly well as a team. That's why the dragon riders are making a comeback. It's because of that hunt, hon."

"Are you going to go on another one of these hunts?" Sarah cautiously asked.

"Honestly? I sure as hell don't want to. But, if we can't recover the stolen fang, and seeing how important it is to Kahvel to protect his family, I'd be willing."

"We'll have to talk about that."

Steve nodded. "I'd be surprised if you didn't want to talk about it."

"Why is that patch of water black?" Sarah asked.

Steve shrugged. "You know what? I'm really not too sure."

Pheromones.

What?

When an oskorlisk is about to strike, it releases pheromones in an attempt to fool its prey into thinking there is no danger. The pheromones are responsible for changing the color of the water.

You learn something new every day. Hey, do me a favor, would you? Can you bring Sarah into this conversation? It's getting cumbersome relaying everything you say to her.

Of course. Sarah, are you there?

Pravara? Ooo, I like this. Thank you for including me.

It was Steve's idea.

"Pravara was saying that the water turns black when the oskorlisk is ready to strike. The oskorlisk releases pheromones just before it starts its attack."

"I wonder why," Sarah mused.

"It had something to do with fooling the prey into thinking there isn't any danger."

"And the black water wouldn't be a dead giveaway something isn't right?"

"Fish are color blind," Steve pointed out.

"I'm sure that huge snake thing eats other things besides fish."

Steve shrugged. "You've got a point."

Steve?

Yes?

I may have found something.

Really?

Sarah clapped her hands together, "Awesome! What do you see, Pravara? And is it okay I keep talking out loud? It's what I'm used to."

Of course. Five leagues south of your current location, there's a disturbance in the air.

"Disturbance? What kind of disturbance?" Steve asked.

I am reminded of heat waves.

"It's a sunny day, Pravara. Heat waves aren't that unusual."

True, but I only see these heat waves when I approach from the west. When I approach from other directions, I see nothing.

"Where are you now?" Sarah asked.

"Five leagues south from you."

Steve nodded. "Let's go take a look, shall we?"

Five minutes later they were standing on narrow strip of land extending several hundred feet out into the sea. The narrow peninsula sloped steeply down to the water, guaranteeing a nasty tumble should they try and make their way down like a normal person would. Steve tapped Sarah on the shoulder and pointed back toward the land.

"It's supposed to be visible from the west. We need to be over there."

Ten seconds later they were standing on the shore, facing due east. Together, husband and wife watched the gentle undulations of the small waves as they made landfall. Steve grunted. He couldn't see anything out of the ordinary.

Pravara, are you sure we're in the right place? We don't see anything.

The disturbance is slightly to your right, but from your current location, you should still be able to see the shimmering.

"You heard her. We should be able to see something, but I sure as hell don't."

Sarah shaded her eyes and studied the beach. Her eyes widened and she clutched Steve's hand tightly in her own. "I do! I see it! Do you?"

Steve squinted in the direction Sarah was looking. He leaned left, then right. There, visible right at the water's edge, was a light shimmering. The very air itself appeared to be rippling, as if the air had turned to water and someone had dropped in a stone. After a few seconds, the rippling disappeared, only to reappear after a few more moments had passed. Steve anxiously looked at his wife.

"Okay, I see it. So, what the hell am I looking at? That doesn't look like much of a ship to me."

"I can't tell how big it is," Sarah remarked. "Those ripples are really hard to see. Whoever is hiding the ship is doing a really good job."

Sarah slid a hand into her pocket. It was empty. She checked the other. Also empty. She squatted so she could scoop up a handful of sand and pebbles. Throwing the tiny rocks and sand high into the air, she ordered her jhorun to fling the handful at the disturbance.

To Steve, it felt like he was watching one of his favorite science fiction movies, the one where an alien hunter could disguise itself by mimicking its surroundings. The rocks and sand made contact with something and suddenly there were ripples everywhere. An outline of a ship began to form.

Steve whistled with amazement. It looked to be about the same size as the three galleons Lentari had in its fleet of open water ships. So, what was this particular ship doing here? Where was its crew?

Howls and battle cries sounded. The ripples in the disturbance grew more pronounced. From the sounds of things, the crew must have realized they'd been discovered. Steve ignited his hands and placed himself protectively in front of Sarah.

Men began materializing out of thin air. Within moments, a dozen men were glaring angrily at him. In perfect unison, they all drew their swords and advanced, leering evilly at him.

Steve scowled and raised both of his ignited hands. Sword or cutlass, or whatever they chose to call it, these people were brandishing weapons and appeared intent on causing them harm.

"Bad choice, guys!" Steve called out, hoping to talk some sense into the rapidly approaching group of thugs. "Are you sure you want to do this?"

"Would you stop trying to become their friend and do something?" Sarah cried. "I'm about ready to teleport us out of here!"

Steve turned to the armed group of men and blasted out two powerful jets of fire, just over their heads. The invaders suddenly lost all of their aggressiveness and dove to the ground. The air dead went silent. The goons shared a look with one another and then, as one, they all opened their mouths.

Steve rolled his eyes. "Great. Here it comes."

A dozen men screamed like girls. They dropped their weapons, turned tail, and fled back toward the ripples of air.

"What now?" Steve asked, looking around at the unusually empty beach. "They're there. We know they're there. They know that we know that they're there. So if they know that we know that ... hey! Ouch!"

Sarah punched him on the arm. "Would you stop that?"

"What should we do?"

Pravara, where are you?

I am circling high above you. The oskorlisks are still nearby. I am not allowed to venture any closer.

We had a run-in with the crew of the ship.

I know. I watched the encounter. You were more than a match for them.

Wood creaked noisily. A loud scraping began, and grew steadily louder. Husband and wife clapped their hands over their ears.

"What is that?" Sarah asked, raising her voice until she was practically shouting.

Steve pointed at the water. Deep grooves had appeared on the shore. They led straight to the water.

"I think they're leaving! We can't let 'em get away!"

"Can you stop them?"

"How? If I blast my fire at them, there's a better than average chance that I'll end up hurting someone. Or sinking their boat and causing everyone to drown."

Sarah suddenly clutched his arm, "The oskorlisk! It's still out there!"

Steve ran to the water's edge and frantically waved his arm. "Be careful! There's an oskorlisk out there! Big sea serpent! You gotta stay put!"

Just like that, he was looking at the backside of a two-masted sailboat. He saw the name of the boat emblazoned in gold letters on the back of the ship: *Emberbrand*. Contrary to what he had thought earlier, it wasn't nearly as large as the three masted galleons presently moored at Capily, but it was still formidable.

The sails opened, caught the wind, and pushed the ship away from shore even faster than before. The bow suddenly veered south, bringing the starboard side of the vessel directly in line with the shore. Steve gritted his teeth. The ship was trying to make good on their escape.

Both of his hands reignited. Now that he could see what he was looking at, he had no qualms about using his jhorun against the boat. He could easily make only certain parts of the boat burn. Such as the sails, for example.

Steve focused on the largest sail. The center of the sail burst into flames. Several members of the crew cried out in alarm and hurried to extinguish the fire. Steve felt a hand on his shoulder

"Honey, I've got this."

Steve held out an arm, inviting her to take over.

The ship came to a sudden and immediate stop. Steve heard shouts of terror. The men were frightened. Clearly no one had expected to encounter someone who had the strength to bring their ship to a sudden stop. The *Emberbrand* was slowly pulled backward, toward the shore.

"Where would you like it?" Sarah casually asked.

Steve turned to point at the beach. "Right about there will do. See if you can ... watch out!"

Steve ignited his hands and blasted out a huge wall of flames, just in time to incinerate a volley of arrows from the ship. Steve pumped additional jhorun into his wall of fire, hoping it would torch anything the invaders tried to throw their way.

He started hearing thumps, as though doors were being slammed open. Curious, he lessened his flames to see what the crew of the mystery ship was doing. His eyes widened with alarm.

The starboard side of the *Emberbrand* now had seven square holes running in a neat line along the length of the ship. One by one, each of the holes were plugged. With a cannon.

"Sarah…" Steve hesitantly began, turning to look at his wife.

Sarah's eyes widened with shock. She noticed the cannons, too. One of the cannons fired, belching out a plume of white smoke as it launched a cannonball straight at them. One after the other, the other cannons followed suit.

Suddenly the *Emberbrand* drifted loose, released by Sarah as she was forced to deal with deflecting the cannonballs. The crew immediately scrambled to replace the burnt section of sail. The highly efficient crew spent less than ten seconds cutting the burnt fabric out of the primary sail and patching in a new piece. The secondary sail was unfurled, and with both sails at full mast, the ship rapidly fled. However, the men continued to fire arrow after arrow at the two of them as they retreated.

The last thing either of them saw, before the ship disappeared—camouflaged once more—was a black flag. Flapping in the wind, perched high above the tallest mast, was a symbol both husband and wife were very familiar with: a crude skull and crossbones.

Steve turned to his wife with a look of disbelief written all over his face. "They're pirates?"

Chapter 6 — Let's Get Ready to Rumble!

Pirates?" Steve scoffed. "Seriously? Is someone playing a prank on us? Since when have pirates become a problem around here? You and I both know that there have never been any pirates around here. This has gotta be a joke."

"Don't forget where we presently are, dear," Sarah reminded him. "This isn't home, but Lentari. Maybe they *do* have a problem with pirates around here."

"Wouldn't we have heard something about it?" Steve asked. "Pravara? Are you still there?"

Yes.

"Can you contact Mikal and ask him if Lentari has any type of known pirate problem?"

Very well. A moment, if you please.

Sarah shook her head, "The answer is going to be 'no'."

"We won't know for certain until we try."

He says, 'no'. Then he asked why you would ask that

particular question.

"It's because we've identified these invaders as being pirates," Steve answered.

"I told you he'd say no," Sarah said.

"Yep. You called it. Mikal also asked why."

"What did he say? I must've missed it."

Steve shrugged. "You didn't miss a thing. Pravara hasn't answered yet."

I will, as soon as Mikal recovers his composure.

"Recovers his composure?" Steve repeated as he frowned. "What does that mean? What happened?"

Apparently, he was having lunch with his mate…

Husband and wife fell silent as they listened to Pravara relay what she saw and heard.

I asked about pirates … Mikal had just taken a drink of some type of juice when it sounded like he choked. I watched the juice spray over his mate.

Steve stifled a chuckle. "I'll bet Lissa just loved that."

Mikal is responding. He wants to know how you know they're pirates.

"We saw the flag."

A few seconds of silence passed.

"Pravara? Are you still there?"

Yes. I am waiting for Mikal to form a coherent question. He appears to be distressed. Now he is trying to clean up his mess. His mate is less than enthused.

"Poor Mikal," Sarah lamented. "His parents are away and now he has to deal with pirates? How terrible. However, I know he can handle this."

Steve?

"Yeah?"

Something unusual is approaching you.

The two of them turned to look out over the open sea. "Is the ship coming back? Bring it on, baby. I think we can take 'em."

"I'd rather not," Sarah added. "I don't like deflecting cannon fire. What would've happened had I missed one? You could've been hurt. Or killed. I'd rather not go through that again, thank you very much."

The anomaly approaches from the north.

Confused, Steve spun on his heel and looked at the road that ran parallel to the shore. It stretched up to the north, and eventually, Steve knew, would end at the castle. He also knew the southern half of the road terminated near the base of the Selekai Mountains. There was something approaching them on this road? Wasn't it supposed to be enchanted from harm?

He looked at his wife and shrugged helplessly.

"You can see the same thing I can. See anything?"

Sarah slowly rotated in place. She shook her head no.

"Describe it, Pravara. What are we looking for?"

A boat.

"A boat?" Steve turned to the sea. "You said the boat wasn't coming back, didn't you?"

A small boat travels along the land. It is rapidly approaching from the north. In just a few minutes, it will ... That's strange. The boat has become enveloped in a small cloud. It looks and smells like fog. It masks the boat's presence.

"A boat that travels along the land?" Steve repeated, raising an eyebrow. "Is it floating?"

No. The craft has wheels.

"Then it's not a boat," Steve argued.

I also see a sail.

"A sail would definitely indicate a boat of some sort," Sarah agreed. "But on land? That doesn't make any sense."

Dispute my story if you must, but be prepared. It has veered off the road and is now heading southwest.

"The boat isn't coming here after all? I wonder why it changed directions."

"There has to be a reason why," Sarah insisted.

A correction. The boat appears to be still heading toward your location, only now it will approach from the west, not the north.

"If I didn't know any better," Steve began, "I'd say that we've been spotted and whoever is steering that thing is trying to catch us by surprise."

"What do we do?" Sarah asked.

"Be ready to get yourself to safety."

"What about you?"

"I'll be fine. I can handle anything that comes my way."

They heard a commotion coming from the copse of trees to the west. While not nearly as thick as the forest, a small ship could avoid being seen there.

Sure enough, a small fog bank appeared amidst the trees. The fog appeared to be darting behind one clump of trees to the next, as though the low-lying cloud was afraid of being seen. After a few moments, the cloud ventured away from the trees and headed straight toward them. Steve and Sarah watched the fog approach with confused looks on their faces. Sarah held out a hand.

"You'd better give me another mimet. Take one for yourself, too."

"Why?"

"If what Pravara says is true, then we're looking at a *second* camouflaged boat. What are the chances that two hidden boats would appear at the same location?"

Steve muttered a curse, hurriedly slipped two mimets from their holders, and handed one to his wife. He slid the second into a pocket and ignited both hands. Sarah fell silent allowing her jhorun to be replenished by the energy crystal.

"What do you think?" Steve asked as the bank of fog threatened to overtake them in seconds.

"If it's fog," Sarah thoughtfully began, "do you think you could burn it off?"

Shrugging, Steve looked at the approaching anomaly, as Pravara had put it, and waited. He instructed his jhorun to deliver an intense, hot burst of heat as the thing went by, figuring any fog would be immediately burned off. He and Sarah stepped off the road and waited another five seconds before Steve raised his hands and blasted a wall of flames at the silvery mists.

A small, single-masted skiff appeared, lifted off the ground on a set of large, wooden wheels rimmed with a thin layer of rubber. To Steve, it looked as though the boat—for whatever reason—had been placed on top of a stagecoach, flattening it so that only the boat and the wheels were visible. He could see at least ten men in the boat, and none of them looked happy to see them. One man threw a rope, with a crude three-pronged metal hook tied to the end, onto the ground. The hook snagged a nearby boulder and brought the small boat to an instant stop.

Another man immediately jumped over the railing and faced Steve, brandishing a wicked ten-inch curved dagger in each hand. The stranger started running toward him, but just before Steve could blast him, the stranger sailed over him in a neat front flip and landed nearly a dozen feet away. He also felt a stinging sensation on his right arm. A quick check showed that he now had a three-inch gash on his bicep and was losing blood.

Steve clutched his right arm in pain. His left hand ignited, and he prepared to blast the stranger to kingdom come when he noticed his assailant was nowhere to be seen. His eyes narrowed and he groaned. There's no way someone could move that fast. He had to be facing someone with enhanced reflexes.

"Honey, are you hurt?" Sarah asked, rushing to his side. She saw the laceration and cried out in terror. "Omigod! You're bleeding! Did that man do that to you?"

Steve nodded. "Yeah. The dude's quick, so be careful."

Sarah held out a hand. A dingy, tarnished medallion appeared. She tossed it to him just as movement from the south drew their attention. The dark stranger was back, and he was giving them both a lecherous stare.

Sarah frowned. She placed a hand on his arm and gave him a few pats.

"Use the kaormac elixir. Heal your arm. I've got this."

The stranger, overhearing her words, smirked at her. He began running toward her, covering the distance between them at a frightening rate, when suddenly he was lifted into the air. With his feet unable to find purchase on the ground, the stranger's smug smile morphed into a concerned frown. No matter how fast he tried to run, or twist and turn in the air, he couldn't touch the ground. Just like that, their attacker had been rendered harmless. The thug looked imploringly back at the small boat.

"What the blazes are ye doing, Jino?" one man snapped.

"Quit lollygagging around and finish the job!"

"I can't touch the ground! How am I supposed to fight?"

Sarah brought the man in close so she could see him better. The man, Jino, scowled, cursed, and then twisted around in midair. Steve, having healed his arm with the tiny vial of elixir nestled within the medallion, grunted with satisfaction. Shardwyn's gift all those years ago was still as helpful today as it had been then.

He heard a series of angry curses and eyed the strange man still floating several feet off the ground.

"You're damn close to learning what it's like to be a French fry," Steve grumbled. "I have half a mind to … oof!"

A sudden blast of wind knocked Sarah off her feet and slammed her into him. Together, they tumbled to the ground. Jino dropped to the ground and instantly darted off.

Steve tenderly rose to his knees and sat back on his haunches.

"Okay, what the hell hit us? It feels as though I've been hit by a freight train."

"The wind," Sarah moaned, as she painfully rose to a sitting position. "Someone on that boat is controlling the wind. Remember Pryllan's cave? I'd say the thief is aboard that boat."

Pirates began spilling out of the small boat. Jino joined his companions as, together, the nine of them rounded on the husband and wife team still splayed out on the ground. The one who had belittled Jino earlier headed the group.

"And who might you be?" the leader demanded, before shaking his head. "Scratch that. I don't care. You'd be in my way. I don' believe in killin' people just for being in the wrong place at the wrong time, so I'll allow ye to leave, provided ye do so now. Now, *git!*"

"And who might you be, pal?" Steve asked as he slowly regained his feet. He pulled his wife up with him.

"I be Captain Flinn, of the *Emberbrand*. I trust after today, ye won't ever be forgettin' my name again, will ye?"

Steve stretched his back and eyed the pirates that were dangerously eyeing them back.

"My, my, my. Aren't you full of yourself? I guarantee you,

sport, that not only do I not care who you are, I can also take you down a peg or two. You're the captain of that ship that was waiting here? The one that was hidden from view?"

Several men lost their smirks. One by one, the men turned to stare at the captain. Flinn, for that matter, was staring at Steve as though he was certain he was lying.

"Ye cannot know about the ship, or know that it was here. It was hidden!"

"Not very well," Steve casually told the captain. "You really ought to hide it better than that. Tell me something. Do you think it's still down there? I can save you some time. It isn't."

Alarmed, Flinn singled out one of the men. "Alquin! Be he telling the truth? Where be the *Emberbrand*?"

"It's not there, Captain!" Alquin confirmed. "I don't see it anywhere! Where did it go? What are we going to do?"

"Close yer yap, sailor. It has to be here somewhere. They'd never leave us behind."

Steve grinned as he saw a wave of panic spread across the pirates' faces. "What's a-matter, boys? Did you lose your ride?"

"What have you done with her?" Flinn demanded. "I'll boil ye both in oil!"

The strong jet of wind returned and sucker punched Steve in his gut. Sarah hurried over to his side, checked to make sure he was okay, and then turned to the pirate captain. His smug look was back.

"Two can play this game," Sarah muttered.

Her jhorun picked the captain up and tossed him into the water, like the worthless piece of trash she believed him to be. After a few moments, a mini water spout appeared, and dropped Flinn—soaking wet—back onto the ground before them. The captain's eyes were shooting daggers at her.

"I do not know how ye did that," Flinn began, "but I strongly advise ye to…"

"I did it like this," Sarah interrupted, ordering her jhorun to once again dump the arrogant ship captain back into the water.

As before, another waterspout formed and deposited the

dripping captain back onto the ground. Flinn's smug smile had returned. Emboldened, the pirates rallied behind their captain.

"Very well. Ye convinced me. I tried to let ye leave in peace but ye refused." Flinn turned to his small crew. "Dispose of 'em. Make it quick. We need to find the *Emberbrand*."

Steve stepped in front of Sarah and slowly retreated as half a dozen pirates menacingly advanced. He turned to look at his wife. Sarah nodded her readiness.

Steve ceased his retreat, ignited his hands, and blasted a huge wall of flames straight at the pirates. Their attackers, surprised they had again lost their upper hand, turned and fled. Steve grinned and pumped more jhorun into his hands.

"Piece of … whoa!"

A blast of air slammed into his firewall, threatening to extinguish it. Flames were blasted back toward him. Sarah hurried forward to wrap her arms around his waist.

"This guy is starting to piss me off," Steve grunted, struggling to brace himself against the gale force winds pushing back at him.

"There's something about the captain," Sarah agreed as she buried her face in Steve's back. The blasts of air created a swirling vortex of raging fire. "He has a very powerful jhorun. I've never seen anyone who could control the wind like that."

Steve doubled his efforts and forced his flames back from him and his wife. He felt, rather than heard, Flinn's frustrations as it was now the captain who had been forced to take a few steps backward. It was then that he noticed several pirates had broken away from the group and were now quietly trying to approach from the north and south.

He felt a tap on his shoulder.

"You deal with Captain Windbag," Sarah told him. "I've got these guys."

Steve grunted and nodded. He reached a hand into his pocket, snagged the power crystal, and replenished his jhorun. Rejuvenated, and with his jhorun now tingling so strongly that it was starting to hurt, Steve concentrated on his flames. It was time to take things up a notch.

He heard shouts of alarm. The pirates who had been

trying to ambush him suddenly found themselves flying through the air as Sarah's jhorun catapulted each of them into the water. More appeared and tried to rush them. Steve smiled. Let them feel the Wrath of a Pissed-Off Woman.

"The next one of you geniuses who even *thinks* about attacking us is going to find out what it's like to be someone's lunch," Sarah vowed. "I'll drop you right in front of a dragon. I swear it!"

"Speaking of which," Steve muttered, "where's Pravara? We really could use her right about …"

A large fireball raced down from above and slammed into Flinn, knocking him off his feet. The surrounding grass blackened and crumbled into ash. A second fireball smashed into the pirate captain moments later. And then a third.

The power of the dragon's blasts had burnt off all traces of surrounding vegetation. Bare rock peeked through blackened earth while the permeating smell of scorched plants made everyone's eyes water. Steve fanned the air in front of him while he scanned the skies, looking for their wyverian ally.

"I told ye this was worth its weight in gold."

Husband and wife turned to see Flinn pick himself up off the ground and dust himself off. He grinned, slowly spun in place to confirm that he hadn't suffered so much as a scratch, and looked for his companions. One by one, the pirates joined their captain.

"See, boys? Do any of ye question me now? Behold! Not a scratch! Now would someone finally follow my order and deal with these two miscreants?"

They all heard a piercing roar. Steve looked up in time to see Pravara circle about, high above their heads. Her large reptilian form cast a huge shadow upon the ground and caused many fingers to point in her direction. Steve grinned as he saw that Flinn had once more lost his smile as soon as he noticed the dragon circling about overhead.

"Like what you see?" Steve taunted. "That's Pravara. I think she's trying to decide if she'd like you better as 'original' or 'extra crispy'."

What? What does that even mean? I am not familiar

with those terms in that context.

Sorry. Those are terms from my world. I was asking them if they think you'd prefer your food to be raw or cooked.

Oh. I wasn't thinking that.

I know that, Pravara. It was just an expression.

Are you suggesting I should eat the humans? No, thank you. Father says humans give him indigestion.

What?? Are you saying your father has eaten human beings before?

That was a joke. I made it to lessen your discomfort. A word of caution. It appears as though the misfit band of humans is regrouping.

"Are you ready to give up yet?" Steve asked the pirate captain, keeping his hands ignited.

Flinn lifted his cutlass into the air. "We will never surrender, braggart. Besides, ye are outnumbered three to one!"

Steve hooked a thumb at Pravara.

"Don't forget our dragon friend. Did you factor her into your equation? And besides, *you* are the one who's missing a ship. You are the one who doesn't have anywhere to go. How soon do you think it'll be before there are more dragons here? You made a serious mistake, pal. You stole from a dragon. They have a tendency to stick together when one is threatened."

"We will be long gone from this wretched place before that happens," Flinn vowed.

"Six of my brethren have been dispatched," Pravara's cool voice announced as she landed behind Steve. She fixed Flinn with a steely glare. "They will be here within minutes."

"You're running out of time, pal," Steve casually remarked. "I'd give up while you can."

The blast of air appeared out of nowhere. It slammed into Steve and knocked him nearly a dozen feet backwards. He would have taken a nasty tumble had not Pravara extended a wing and arrested his fall by allowing her wing to absorb the impact of the blow. She instantly spat a fireball at Flinn, who remained motionless. The fires bounced harmlessly away, as though it was Steve who had been targeted.

"Ye stupid, blathering, overconfident lizard. Ye cannot

harm me. Have ye not learned that yet?"

Pravara looked imploringly at Steve. "One bite. That's all it would take. It wouldn't be eating him. My father would never know. It's worth a try, isn't it?"

Steve shrugged. "I don't know. Do you want to risk chipping a tooth?"

"Captain!" one of the men suddenly shouted. "Captain! I see the *Emberbrand*!"

Flinn whirled about. "What? Where?"

Steve had been waiting for just such a moment, for when the arrogant pirate captain would be distracted. He clenched his hands and ordered his jhorun to give Flinn a little payback. His jhorun was ready. He only needed the pompous captain to look away.

And he just did.

Steve's hands sprang open. The detonation blasted everything in front of him, knocking every single pirate, including Flinn, onto their respective rears. Pirates were thrown together in a mass jumble of arms and legs. Flinn, buried at the bottom of the pile, started swearing even before the smoke cleared.

"Get off me, ye blasted lardball! Who be sitting on my leg? Get off me this instant!"

"Who is that man, Captain?" Steve heard one man ask. "You told us everyone in this land were spineless weaklings."

The pirates painfully untangled themselves, muttering darkly as they slowly stood. One man, the enhanced fighter, pulled Flinn to his feet.

"Ye throw a wicked punch," Flinn acknowledged to Steve as he wiped the back of a hand against his nose. It came back bloody. "I have never met anyone such as yerself before. Yer power. What is it? I'll tell ye about mine if ye tell me about yers."

"Wouldn't you like to know?" Steve scoffed.

Sarah appeared behind his right shoulder.

"Maybe you should tell him," she softly suggested.

"What? Why in the world would I do that?"

"It would help if we knew more about him."

Pravara's huge snout suddenly dropped down to his eye

level behind his left shoulder.

"Would you be able to trust anything he says?" the dragon softly asked.

Steve noticed Flinn and his pirates were watching him intently. He held up a finger, turned around, and huddled with Sarah and Pravara.

"Are we in agreement? We want to find out more about this guy? So, what do I tell him?"

"What do you mean?" Sarah asked. "You answer his questions and he'll answer yours."

"You are assuming he will speak the truth," Pravara added.

"Should I tell him the truth or make something up?" Steve wanted to know. He looked at Sarah, who shrugged.

"I don't see why you shouldn't tell him the truth."

Steve slowly approached the captain, but pointed at the pirates. More specifically, he pointed at Jino.

"Your goons can all wait back there. Especially Bruce Lee there."

Flinn turned to look at Jino and the rest of his crew. The captain held up a hand, signaling the crew should wait. He stepped forward a few paces. Steve approached, halting a dozen feet from the captain. His nostrils flared. The scent of rotten fish made his eyes water. There was someone who could use a Tic-Tac.

"There wasn't suppos'd to be anyone like ye here," Flinn admitted, lowering his voice. "I realize now that I was given erroneous information."

"Who are you?" Steve asked. "What are you doing here? Why did you take that fang?"

"The reason I want the fang should be obvious," Flinn began. "Ye saw a demonstration of its power, did ye not?"

Steve nodded. "I did. How did you even know the dragons had it? Not only that, how were you able to find it?"

"I have my ways of knowing where the treasure be," Flinn confided. He paced around Steve and cast a wary look at Pravara, who still looked as though she wanted to try chomping him in half. "You are obviously familiar with the fang and what it can do. Why did ye not try and claim it for yerself? I've never met anyone who be friends with the scaly beasties."

"The 'scaly beasties' are wyverians, and they are indeed my friends," Steve stated, growing angry. "Why in the world would I want to take that fang for myself? If I had wanted to do that, then I wouldn't have given it to them in the first place."

"You gave them the fang?" Flinn breathed, amazed. "You're trying to tell me that you hunted the giant sea serpent?"

Steve shrugged. "Yep. That fang was a gift to the dragons, the same dragons that you ended up pissing off. And trust me, buddy. You couldn't have picked a worse dragon to aggravate. I wouldn't want to be you, pal. Hey, don't look so surprised. You asked, I answered. And, for the record, I'm a fire elemental."

Flinn grunted with surprise and finally nodded. "That explains the significance of your power. I've never met another elemental before."

"Another elemental?" Steve repeated. "Are you saying … of course! You're an air elemental, aren't you? That definitely explains that damn wind. I've never met another elemental, either. So, where are you from?"

"Perz."

"Perz? Where's that?"

"It be in the archipelago. *My* archipelago. That's all I'll say on the matter. Now, how did ye find my ship?"

"You did a great job hiding it," Steve admitted. "However, no camouflage is perfect. And that's all *I* will say on the matter."

My brethren are less than two minutes away.

Awesome, Pravara! Thanks for the news!

Flinn was frowning.

"Ye be smilin'? Why would ye be smilin'? Ah. Would it have anything to do with yer pet dragon's friends? Be they close? Mister Alquin! Where be my ship?"

"I can see it over there, Captain," one man was saying. He pointed east, over the open water. "It's nearly half a league from shore. They're near, but not so near as to be discovered or boarded. They're waiting for us! I knew they wouldn't abandon us!"

"Casimir!" Flinn snapped, turning to one of the men huddled nearby. "Ye know what to do. Mister Puck, some atmosphere, please."

A wave of alarm washed over Steve. He heard Sarah gasp and fall to her knees. He instantly ignited his hands and spun in place as he looked for the source of the danger. His instincts were screaming at him to grab Sarah, hop onto Pravara's back, and flee. However, he didn't want to turn his back on an enemy.

"We've got to get out of here!" Sarah cried. "Something is coming. Something bad. We need to leave! Now!"

Pravara was roaring, making conversation difficult. Steve eyed their wyverian friend. Pravara was nervously casting her gaze up at the sky and then back at their immediate surroundings.

Sarah appeared at his side. She grabbed his arm. Then Steve felt the wrenching sensation of being teleported. Suddenly, they were standing beside Pravara. Sarah slapped a hand on Pravara's scaly leg. The beach winked out and what appeared was … the Great Hall. The three of them were now *inside*.

Surprised, Pravara glanced around the room. Unfortunately, her long supple tail had been resting on the ground. As soon as they had arrived, and Pravara had noticed they were now *inside* the castle, she had inadvertently twitched her tail. Tables, chairs, and various other pieces of furniture were flung to the far corners of the room.

A collective gasp of surprise sounded from all directions. Guards jumped to attention, only to start shaking so badly they sounded like a sack of tin cans shaking in a wind storm. Thinking the worst, more soldiers poured into the room, only to slam on the brakes when they discovered themselves faced with their worst nightmare. Indoors. The vast majority of them cursed mightily and sprinted for the exit.

"Okay, okay, I'm starting to calm down," Sarah announced, completely ignoring the frantic guards running all about them. "Oh, that wasn't fun. What was that, anyway?

I haven't felt that scared since you suckered me into riding that roller coaster at Disneyland."

"I'm feeling pretty good now, too," Steve admitted. "That was weird. One second, I was scared sh … um, scared senseless, and the next? I'm fine. I even felt nervous, too. I'd go so far as to say scared. Were you feeling scared, Pravara?"

The dragon nodded. "Aye. I cannot explain it."

"I think we're all feeling a little bit scared," a new voice added.

Mikal appeared, with nearly a dozen guards following close behind him. The newly appointed young king motioned for the guards to wait and looked appreciatively up at the giant dragon. Pravara looked sheepish as she tried to keep from moving.

"There's something that we haven't seen for quite some time," Mikal admitted with a smile. "If I remember correctly, you were the last dragon that the insides of this castle has ever seen. You were also quite a bit smaller at that time, I believe."

Pravara nodded. "I remember. I was playing with the little peanut."

"You were playing with Peanut the Corgi," Steve corrected. "I'm sorry, Mikal. I'm not exactly sure what happened back there. The desire to flee was strong. Something bad was about to happen. Sarah got us out there."

Mikal frowned, "All of you? At the same time? That sounds suspicious."

Sarah also frowned, "It does, doesn't it? As a matter of fact, I stopped being scared the moment we appeared here."

Steve nodded. "Makes sense. You took us away from danger, so why wouldn't the fear go away?"

"The fear?" Sarah repeated. "That's it! Fear! What do you want to bet one of those pirates could make us feel fear? Flinn must have used it as a weapon against us!"

"That two-timing, fish-brained, bottom-feeding scumsicle!" Steve cursed. He snatched up Sarah's hand. "We did exactly what he wanted us to do. We fled, giving him ample opportunity to make his escape. Take us back! Hurry!"

Pravara held out a claw. Steve smiled apologetically at

their former charge. Mikal shook his head and waved them off.

"Go. Be sure to come back here when you're done. I'd love to hear what happened and how Pravara ended up inside the castle."

"You're not angry, are you?" Sarah worriedly asked.

Mikal let out a laugh.

"Of course not. There's never a dull moment whenever you two are around, that's for sure."

They returned to the glade just in time to see the small land skiff pick up speed—thanks to Flinn's jhorun—and sail off the edge of the rocky peninsula. It landed with a splash, and almost immediately, the tiny boat rocketed away from the shore under a wind that could have only been artificially created. Before either of them could say anything, a blast of air slammed into them, causing them to take several steps backward.

"Until we meet again, Fire Thrower!" Flinn called out, tipping several fingers to his hat in a mock salute.

"I can probably pull him back," Sarah mused, as she regained her feet. "He's not out of my range."

"Something tells me that if we try, he'll just hit us with that damn wind again," Steve said. He looked back at Pravara. "Where are your reinforcements? I'd just as soon not have to sink that thing. Not when we know there's an oskorlisk in the area."

Pravara's nose lifted to the sky. "They're close. They arrived when we weren't here, so they automatically headed northwest, back to the valley. I can have them circle about."

"They're on the sea," Sarah mused. She joined her husband and together, watched the small skiff sail east. "Anything we do now could seriously jeopardize the men on that ship."

The air shimmered as the *Emberbrand* appeared. Ropes were lowered. The small skiff was plucked out of the water and secured against the side of the brigantine. The much larger ship turned south and started to move away. Flinn appeared at the stern and gave them another mock salute.

"There will be another time, Fire Thrower!"

"You'd better believe it, pal," Steve called back. After a

moment's hesitation, he cupped his hands around his mouth and offered a warning. "Avoid the black water! There's an oskorlisk in the area!"

Sarah thumped him on the arm. "What did you do that for?"

"What, give him a warning about the oskorlisk? No one deserves to be attacked by a huge snake. Hell, those things are big enough to bite that ship in two. You've heard the expression, 'I wouldn't wish that on my worst enemy'? That's all I was doing."

"You're a nicer person than I am," Sarah muttered. "They hurt you. They could've killed you."

Steve flexed his healed arm, "No harm done. Pravara? Are you okay?"

Pravara joined them at the water's edge. She growled as she watched the pirates sail farther away. Sarah placed a hand on one of Pravara's talons.

"Don't worry. Something tells me this is not even close to being over. We'll get another chance."

"I hope so," Pravara grumbled. "For my mother's sake, I hope so."

Chapter 7 — Unexpected Help

So, I wonder if anyone has heard of Perz," Steve was saying as he and Sarah walked through the castle on their way to the Great Hall. "You'd think it'd be in a history book somewhere."

"I think the question I'd be asking right about now is, can we trust Flinn to tell us the truth?" Sarah countered.

Steve shrugged. "What would he have to lose by not telling us?"

"I just don't see that Flinn character as being the type of person known for truthfulness."

"Why not?" Steve asked. "Is it because he's a pirate?"

"That, and I think he was just telling us what we wanted to hear. He had no reason to tell us where he's from."

Steve snapped his fingers. "Unless ... what if he was counting on us not believing him? Perhaps he just figured we'd chalk up everything he told us as a blatant attempt to regale us with misinformation? Look at his jhorun. We both knew it was powerful and had something to do with the air.

He says that he is an air elemental."

"Do you believe him?" Sarah asked.

"I'm inclined to," Steve admitted. "Look at what we've been told so far. He managed to sneak into the dragon's valley undetected. He somehow managed to go *up* the mountain to gain access to Pryllan's cave. I'm willing to bet Flinn used the same technique to get down the mountain as he did to get up it."

"True," Sarah conceded. "Then we also have to take into consideration that weird land-bound boat they were using. I see now why it had a sail. If Flinn was using his jhorun to supply the wind, logic would suggest he could angle the wind however he saw fit. That means they could go wherever they wanted just as fast, if not faster, than if they were on horses."

"It's a clever way to travel," Steve acknowledged. "And then we have…"

He trailed off as a familiar presence appeared in his mind. He came to a stop, just as they had entered the Great Hall. Sarah tapped his shoulder. Her concerned eyes sought his. Steve patted her hand and mouthed *Pravara*.

Steve?

"Hi, Pravara. What's up?"

You and Sarah need to return to the scene of the battle. Immediately.

Steve's eyes widened in alarm and he inadvertently ignited his hands. "Why? What's happened? Are you okay?"

It would seem, in their haste to flee, the pirates have left behind one of their own.

"Now we're talking!" Steve exclaimed. "We're on our way, Pravara. Wait for us."

"What is it?" Sarah asked. "What's happened?"

"Looks like our buddy Flinn gave the order to retreat too soon. Pravara says they've left a man behind. We need to get back there as soon as possible to get him before the pirates realize their mistake and try to get him back, too."

Sarah slapped a hand over his. The interior of the castle winked out. Suddenly the smell of briny seawater flooded their senses. They could hear the gentle lapping of the water. And, the distinct aroma of burnt vegetation returned.

Pravara touched down next to them. She turned her head to stare at a clump of trees several hundred feet away. Husband and wife turned to study the place where they had first seen the fog bank appear. Had someone fallen out of the boat?

"Who's there?" Steve called out. "Show yourself, pal. We know you're there."

"Just leave me be," a timid voice called back.

"No one is going to hurt you," Sarah said, raising her voice. "Come on out here so that we can talk to you."

"While that monster is out there?" the voice cried. "Absolutely not! It wants to eat me."

"I will if you don't reveal yourself," Pravara added, starting to growl.

"You heard her," Steve said. "She's offering to let you come out in peace. This is Pravara. She's a friend of ours. You can trust her. When she says she won't attack, she means it. However, I wouldn't push your luck. Your pirate buddies have seriously aggravated the situation, thanks to Flinn's theft of that fang. If I were you, I'd really want to get on her good side right about now."

A lone figure reluctantly appeared and stepped away from the trees. Steve narrowed his eyes. The pirate looked to be just a boy. He was short, lean, and looked like he hadn't eaten a proper meal in weeks. What reason would a kid like that have in joining up with Flinn and his gang?

"What's your name?" Sarah gently asked. "Mine is Sarah. This is Steve, and this is Pravara. She's a dragon, not a monster."

The boy swallowed nervously. He timidly approached, but kept his eyes fearfully on Pravara. "I am called Pedr."

"Well, Pedr, it's nice to meet you." Sarah slowly walked up to the boy and offered her hand.

Pedr hesitantly shook it.

"What happened?" Steve asked. "Why aren't you with the rest of your friends?"

"I fell out of the *Cadaymas*. Jino took the turn too hard. Again."

Steve turned to look out at the open water. "Can you tell

if your ship is still out there?"

Pedr shook his head. "The *Emberbrand* could be there, but I do not think so. Alquin would have been the only one of us to spot it if Arik has the ship cloaked, which he should. No, they will be long gone by now. I don't know what I was thinking. I should have listened to my mother."

"Didn't want you to be a pirate?" Sarah guessed.

Pedr nodded. "Aye. Times were tough. They *are* tough. My family needed the gold. To serve on the *Emberbrand* would mean enough gold to keep my family comfortable for the rest of our lives. I couldn't turn that down."

"If you don't mind me asking," Steve began, "can you tell me why Flinn brought you along on this trip? So far, we've seen his air elemental jhorun, that Jino fellow's impressive physical abilities, and the use of fear as a weapon."

Pedr nodded shyly. "Casimir. He can evoke fear in the others. That's how we were able to elude the dragons during our escape."

Sarah held out her hand. "Pedr, would you talk with us? We really need to find out what Flinn wants that fang for."

Pedr shrugged. "I don't mind, only I was not privy to much. I was only a cabin boy. I never heard the captain speak much in my presence."

"But you have heard him speak?" Steve hopefully asked.

The boy nodded. "Aye, I have."

"With your permission, I will take us to R'Tal. I think the king would be interested in joining us when you tell us what you know."

"Why should I betray my crew?" Pedr suddenly asked. "True, they haven't necessarily been that nice to me, but that doesn't mean I should sell them out."

"Let's look at it this way," Steve slowly began as he eyed the boy. "You're now standing in Lentari. You and your friends are responsible for stealing a prized possession from the dragons, who are our allies."

The boy began to fidget uncomfortably from one leg to the other.

"Now," Steve continued, "we can let Pravara here take you back with her to the other dragons…"

"Where they can decide what to do with you," Sarah added.

"…or you can come with us. You need to understand something, pal. You and your friends are the invaders here. I happen to really like Lentari. And, right now, we're willing to help you, but you've got to help us first. So … what's it gonna be?"

Pedr hesitantly looked at Pravara, who was staring straight at him; unblinking.

Lick your chops for me.

What?

You're looking at the boy. You need to make him think that you want to eat him.

But I *don't* want to eat him.

I know that. You know that. He doesn't. So, lick your chops for me.

What are 'chops'?

Oh, for Pete's sake. Run your tongue across your teeth. It'll make him think that you are thinking about what he might taste like.

Ah. Scare tactics. Very well.

Pravara's tongue appeared. Their wyverian friend deliberately flicked her forked tongue straight at Pedr and hesitated for a few moments, as if she was collecting as many scents as possible. She cocked her head, grunted once, and pulled her tongue back into her mouth.

It had the desired effect.

"All right!" the boy exclaimed, rushing to put distance between himself and the dragon. "You win! I'll tell you what you want to know. Please don't let it eat me! I'm all my mother has left."

"You'd better stick close to us," Sarah told the boy. She turned to Pravara and gave her a wink. "If you cooperate, we will be able to protect you."

So you say.

Steve paled. That wasn't Pravara, nor was it her mother, Pryllan. That was…

Kahvel? Is that you?

Aye. You have captured one of the thieves? Excellent. Tell Pravara to return with him. I will conduct my own interrogation.

I'm quite certain we can get more out of him our way. Let us talk to him first. If he refuses to cooperate, then we'll ask for your help. Will that suffice?

No. Is this human from Lentari?

Hoo, boy. Umm, no. He isn't.

Therefore, since the human is not a subject of the human king, this becomes a wyverian matter. That band of humans stole the fang from my nest. He will answer for his actions.

I know he will, my friend. However, this one is just a kid. You'll scare him to death if you try to deal with him by yourself.

Be that as it may...

Trust me, Kahvel. You want justice? We do, too. We're humans, as is the kid. We can get far more information out of him if we allow him to only deal with humans. Besides, I already threatened him with you dragons should he not cooperate.

Very well. You will share with me everything you learn from this human?

I will. That's a promise.

Excellent. I will trust you, friend Steve. Do not let me down.

I won't.

Kahvel's strong mind faded from his own. Steve gasped a sigh of relief and leaned heavily on Pravara.

"What's the matter?" Sarah asked. "Are you okay?"

Steve turned to look up at Pravara. "That was your father. He knows we have young Pedr here. He wants him."

"That cannot be good," Pravara mused. "What did you tell him?"

Steve looked at the teenager and shook his head. "Remember what I said about you guys pissing off the wrong dragons? You stole that fang from the Dragon Lord. He knows we have you. I'm telling you right now, buddy. If you don't come clean with us, it'll probably be the end of the line for you. He wants Pravara to escort you back to the dragon valley."

Pedr shuddered and started crying.

The boy appears to be urinating.

What? Oh, man. Wow. We must have really scared him.

Steve nudged Sarah's shoulder. He looked pointedly at the ground, by Pedr's feet. Or, more specifically, the yellow liquid that was pooling by the teenager's feet. As soon as Sarah noticed that Pedr had inadvertently released his bladder, she went sympathetic.

"That's why it's so very important for you to help us," Sarah gently soothed. "The dragons are angry. They want justice."

"They want to eat me!" Pedr cried. "Why did I come on this wretched journey? Why, oh why did I do it?"

Sarah put her arm around the boy. "Let me take you to the castle. We'll get you cleaned up and then you'll meet the king to tell your story, okay?"

Pedr sniffled loudly and finally nodded. Steve looked up at Pravara. "Would you like us to take you back to the castle?"

Pravara shook her head. "No, thank you. My father has already given me my next task."

"Which is?" Steve prompted.

"To keep searching for the rest of the humans responsible for the theft. I have relayed to him everything that has happened. He believes that if I could find them once before, I could find them again. Therefore, I will search."

"Will you let us know if you find anything?" Steve asked.

Pravara nodded. "Of course. Farewell."

The giant dragon bunched her muscles, crouched low, then sprang straight up. She cleared close to hundred feet before she snapped open her wings and flew away. He turned to Sarah, just in time to see her say something to Pedr. The boy eagerly nodded.

"What's going on?" Steve asked.

"Pedr is embarrassed. We're going to stop by our house and let him change his clothes. You're way bigger than he is, but he's willing to wear baggy pants."

Steve grunted by way of acknowledgement.

Ten minutes later they were back in the Great Hall. Steve stood on Pedr's left while Sarah was on his right. The furniture had been restored, and that which Pravara had accidentally broken had been replaced. Mikal, standing off to the side of the throne, was chatting with several nobles. One of the older men glanced at the three of them and said something to the young king. Mikal glanced over, and indicated he wished to conduct the meeting in the Antechamber. Steve purposely looked straight at Lissa, who was presently addressing a group of school children. He looked at the young girl and then back toward the Antechamber.

Mikal nodded. He whispered something to one of the men he was talking to, pointed at Lissa, and then said something else. The adviser nodded.

"Come on," Steve said, guiding Pedr through the throngs of people. "The king is expecting us."

"That was the king?" Pedr stammered. "He looks to be as young as I am!"

"That's Mikal, crown prince of Lentari. He's filling in for his parents while they're gone. He is the acting king. What he says, goes."

"This is a mistake," Pedr groaned. "This is just a misunderstanding. I really shouldn't be here."

"But you are," Sarah reminded him as they passed the two gilded thrones. "It's either this or you get to explain yourself to the dragons."

Pedr gulped noisily and groaned.

Inside the king's private chamber, they were shown seats by the hearth. Mikal arrived next, followed immediately thereafter by Lissa. Mikal glanced at the cold hearth and then nodded at Steve.

"Would you do the honors?"

Steve lit a hand and shot a jet of flames at the hearth. A roaring fire erupted. Pedr leapt out of his seat. "You really are a fire thrower!"

Steve ignited both hands, generated three chasers, and juggled them.

"I really am. What about Flinn? Is he really an air elemental?"

Pedr sighed and sank down into his chair. After nearly thirty seconds had elapsed, the boy nodded. "He has never admitted it, but we have all seen demonstrations of his power."

Steve suddenly looked over at the acting king and queen

and realized they had not been properly introduced.

"Kri'Mikal, Ny'Lissa, this is Pedr."

"Greetings, Pedr," Mikal acknowledged, once the introductions were done. "Would you care to tell us why you're here? What do you hope to accomplish now that you're in my kingdom?"

"I'd say they already accomplished it," Steve interrupted. "They've got the fang and they managed to escape. They're probably high-tailing it across the water right now."

Pedr was shaking his head. "I may not know what the captain's full plans are," the boy slowly began, "but I do know that the snake fang was only the beginning."

"Meaning the pirates are still in Lentari," Steve said. "Do you have any idea what else Flinn is looking for?"

Pedr sadly shook his head. Sarah thumped Steve across the chest before the teenager could say anything else. Steve massaged his chest.

"Ow! What did you do that for?"

"You interrupted Mikal! He specifically asked Pedr what they had hoped to accomplish while they were in Lentari, not you."

"Oh. Sorry. My bad."

"I wish I knew," Pedr confessed.

"And if you did?" Steve prompted.

Mikal held up a hand. "Hold, please. I think now might be the time to use one of Gareth's wedding presents."

Lissa looked over. "Hmm? Really? Which one?"

"The charm that, for twenty-four hours, will replicate my mother's jhorun."

Lissa smiled and nodded. "It's a good idea."

Sarah tapped Lissa on the shoulder. "Charms?"

"Gareth gave us five different charms for our wedding," Lissa explained. "One for teleportation, one for protection, one for anonymity, one for … oh, my. I think I forgot one."

"There were two for anonymity," Mikal corrected.

Lissa snapped her fingers, "That's right. We've already used one. I remember now. And the final charm? Well, once invoked, everyone in our presence is forced…"

"To speak the truth," Steve finished for her. "Wow.

Gareth made you those charms? That's impressive."

"They may be used only once," Mikal said, pulling two objects from his pocket. They were small, carved figurines. One held a shield, and the other had a hand over its heart. Mikal returned the figurine with the shield to his pocket. He held the other up so that everyone could see it. "I'd say this situation calls for this."

"We should see if we can get Gareth to make a few more of those," Steve said. "Those could be incredibly helpful."

Mikal laughed, "I told him the same thing. Then he told me everything he had to do in order to make them work. Let's just say that, for right now, it's a one-time only gift. He worked very hard to make these."

"Are you sure you want to use one of them now?" Sarah asked.

Mikal nodded. Without a word, he held the figurine up to his eyes, stared at it for a few seconds, then mumbled something incoherent. The small statue flashed once and was gone.

"It's done. It's now working."

"Are you sure?" Lissa asked.

Mikal nodded. He looked pointedly at Steve and inclined his head, indicating he should continue.

"I'm not sure what I had last asked," Steve admitted.

"Mikal had asked Pedr to tell us if he knew what else Flinn had in mind while he was in Lentari."

"Mister Pedr?" Mikal prompted. "Would you answer the question, please?"

"Well, I'd … I'd … I would tell you."

"Have you been telling us the truth?" Steve continued. "Or have you been telling us a pre-determined cover story?"

"I've been telling you the truth," Pedr answered. Moments later, he eyed the four of them speculatively. "What is this? I just tried to tell a lie in the hopes of making all of you think I hadn't been telling the truth and I couldn't."

"Why would you want to lie?" Sarah asked. "You know what the consequences are, don't you? If you fail to tell us everything you know, and you agreed that you would, then you will be transferred from our possession to that of the dragons. Are you sure you want that? I know they're eager to get their talons on you."

Pedr noticeably paled. Sweat trickled down his forehead. He wiped the back of a sleeve across his brow.

"Is it hot in here or is it just me?"

Sarah held the back of a hand to Steve's face. She whipped it away once she felt the heat emanating from her husband. She leaned forward. Yes, Steve was definitely scowling.

"Sorry. That'd be my husband. I'm starting to get the impression he'd rather turn you over to the dragons."

We would like that as well. We are ready to pick him up.

Steve let out a short bark of laughter. "The dragons would like that, too. What do you say, Mikal? The kid wants to lie to us. Let's just give him to the dragons. Let them do whatever they want with him."

Pedr practically leapt out of his chair. "Okay! Okay! I'm sorry! Captain Flinn told us that if we were ever captured, then we had to make certain we didn't disclose his plans."

"Which you were trying to do," Sarah surmised. "Well, let me save you some time. Did you see the king invoke that charm? The small figurine that vanished in a pulse of light? It has enough jhorun imbued in it to force everyone present to tell the truth."

"Oh. You can teleport?"

Sarah nodded. "How else did you think I got all three of us here? If you were to try walking the distance from where we were, to here, then you'd be walking for days."

Steve turned to his wife. "Something has been bugging me. How come you simply didn't teleport that fang out of Flinn's hands? I realize we didn't see it, but that hasn't stopped you from teleporting something you couldn't see before."

Sarah rounded on her husband. "Don't you think I tried? That's the first thing I did as soon as I realized the person responsible for stealing Pryllan's fang had stumbled right up to us. I tried to get an image. I tried to get a sense of where the fang might be. I even knew that the captain must have it on his person, but I still couldn't get my jhorun to touch it. I could only assume it had something to do with the fang itself.

Since it has magical abilities of its own, I'm figuring that had something to do with me being unable to teleport it."

Mikal gave a slight cough. The Antechamber fell silent. Mikal took the crown off his head and rubbed his temples.

"So, Mister Pedr," their former ward began, as he placed the crown on the small table situated on the left of his chair, "what can you tell us about your captain?"

Pedr shrugged. "I only know the legends."

Mikal nodded. "Very well. Legends it is. Let's hear some."

Pedr sat back in his chair and fell silent. After a few moments, the teenager began to speak.

"Everyone in the Seven Kingdoms knows the tales of Captain Flinn and the *Emberbrand*. Never was there a more successful pirate. Ever. It was said that whenever the *Emberbrand* was sighted, and it had targeted a vessel to plunder, you might as well drop anchor and hand over your valuables. In fact, that has happened often."

"I'm surprised your king hasn't tried to capture this pirate captain," Lissa said, drawing everyone's eyes to her own. "Surely your king must have had some way to police the seas, did he not? How would he be able to assure his people that they would be safe?"

"King Weslin has an entire armada at his disposal," Pedr admitted. "However, he has never been able to capture Captain Flinn. Aye, his majesty has come close, but Captain Flinn always managed to escape. Every time. No one knew how."

"He's in a sail boat," Steve muttered. "And he's an air elemental. It's not that difficult to figure out how he kept getting away, not when he has the wind at his beck and call."

Sarah nudged his arm. "Shush. Let him finish."

"Captain Flinn was wealthy. He had more gold than he knew what to do with. And, Flinn was honest."

Steve snorted with derision, earning himself a punch in the arm from Sarah.

"He shared his gold equally amongst his crew. Why else would people be clamoring to join his crew? The captain treated us fairly, split the gold evenly, and always eluded capture. Many of my friends answered the call to join Captain

Flinn's crew. Only my friend, Ferris, and I were chosen. I still do not know why."

"If you don't mind me asking," Steve began, "why do you feel that you *were* chosen? How did you beat out everyone else?"

Pedr gave a rueful laugh.

"Do you know how many times I was asked that very question? I mean, look at me. I'm no swordsman. I cannot fight. My power is insignificant and not very strong. How I would love to be an elemental."

"What power do you have?" Mikal asked, growing concerned. "Perhaps you think it to be insignificant when, in reality, it isn't."

Pedr shook his head. "It really isn't. My power allows me to duplicate a small object, but for no more than a week. The only use I could ever come up with was replicating small bits of food."

"You can do that?" Sarah asked, amazed. "Pedr, that's not only impressive but incredibly useful!"

"No, it isn't," the boy disagreed. "The last thing you want to do is consume food that my power has provided. Remember, the things I can replicate last no longer than a week. Food, however, lasts no more than a day. If you eat the food, then it eventually disappears, leaving you feeling empty. Do you see what I mean? My power has no practical uses whatsoever. Take Ferris. I would love to have his power."

"What can Ferris do?" Sarah softly asked, certain she wasn't going to like the answer.

Pedr was silent for a few moments as he thought of how to best describe his friend's power.

"Ferris could hold up a hand, like this…" Pedr held up a hand and spread his fingers wide, as if he was proving he had five fingers on his hand. "He could make blue sparkles appear between his fingers. I made the mistake of trying to touch one of them."

"What happened?" Lissa nervously asked.

"I was shocked. It really hurt! My hand went numb for hours. My fellow crewmates thought it was hysterical," Pedr ruefully added.

"Sounds like electricity," Sarah decided.

"Has Flinn made this Ferris person use his jhorun against anyone?" Steve anxiously asked.

Pedr nodded. "Aye. Thankfully, only once. The captain made him distract the dragons."

Oh? How so?

Steve chuckled and shook his head.

"What's so funny?" Sarah asked.

"Pravara. She's been eavesdropping."

When you say it like that, it sounds like a bad thing. Ask him. Ask him how the dragons were distracted. Ferris better not have used his jhorun against my parents or I *will* bite him in half as soon as I learn which of the bandits he is. Mark my words.

"Who has been eavesdropping?" Pedr asked, looking around the room as if he expected to see someone lurking in the shadows.

"Pravara. You know who I'm talking about. She wants to know how Ferris distracted her fellow dragons."

"Oh. Just with a bunch of birds. I watched Ferris and Captain Flinn search out the biggest tree with the most birds in it. Ferris sent his power up the tree, which caused all the birds to fly away."

Ah. That must have been what my father was talking about. He kept saying he didn't know what was wrong with the kytes. They were flying erratically about, even colliding with him and each other as he flew back to the nest. The boy's jhorun must have shocked the kytes senseless.

"So where is Perz?" Sarah asked.

Pedr nodded. "The only thing I know about Perz is it's the name of a large archipelago in the southern sea. The captain's private island is rumored to be somewhere in there."

"Do you believe him?" Kri'Mikal asked.

Pedr nodded. "Aye. Rusty, the quartermaster, is also from Perz, as are Arik, Von, and Jino. Everyone knows where the pirates live."

"Then why hasn't the king taken measures to eradicate them?" Mikal asked, perplexed. "If a band of pirates were terrorizing our waters, and harming our citizens, I'd take any and all means necessary to stop them. Especially if I knew where their hideout was."

Pedr's face had gone white. "No. No one knows the Byway but the captain."

"The byway?" Steve repeated, confused. "Why'd you say it like that? What's the significance of it?"

"The Byway is the only way to navigate through Perz without dying," Pedr stated proudly. "It's known only to the captain, the quartermaster, and the navigator. If you try to find your way there without one of those three offering guidance, then you will most assuredly die. Whirlpools, monsters, and booby traps. Captain Flinn made certain that those islands are off limits to anyone but them."

Mikal's eyes had widened with surprise. "And your king accepts this?"

"King Weslin has lost too many men and too many boats in an effort to locate the captain's private island. Our quartermaster, Rusty, said the king was open to the idea of changing the northern border of the Seven Kingdoms so the pirates would no longer be his problem."

"That's twice you've said Seven Kingdoms," Sarah recalled. "What is that? Is that the name of the land where you're from?"

Pedr shrugged. "It's what everyone calls the seven lands. "North, south, east, west, sea, forest, and mountains. Each is considered a separate kingdom, and each is governed by its own people, although several of the kingdoms have more than one."

"More than one what?" Mikal asked.

"Type of people."

"Can you give us an example?" Steve asked.

Pedr shrugged. "There's the west, where humans and sladdi live. Wait, that's not a good example. They have separate cities. Oh! I know. The north! The north is where both humans and fim share the land."

"Fim?" Sarah repeated, puzzled. "Sladdi? I've never heard of either of them."

"That makes two of us," Mikal admitted. "I may not

have been the best student, but I know I never slept through a 'foreign monsters' lesson. Can you tell us anything about them, Mister Pedr? What do they look like?"

"The fim are not like us," Pedr began. "That is to say, they have two legs and two arms." The teenager held a hand near his waist. "From here down, they look like an animal. They don't have feet, but instead have hooves."

Sarah perked up. "Do they have horns?"

Pedr nodded. "Aye. Two spiraled horns that bend around, like this." He drew an imaginary line in the air which started at the top of his forehead and curved back to a point behind his ears.

"Satyrs," Sarah announced. "It sounds like he's describing satyrs. Half men, half goats. They only live in mythology on my home world but, from what I know about them, they typically live in the mountains and the forest."

"The sladdi look like us, but aren't us."

Steve snorted, "That's incredibly helpful."

Pedr made a fist and held it up for everyone to see.

"The sladdi look like us, only they're about this big."

"Small humans?" Steve asked, surprised. "Didn't see that coming."

"Where do they live?" Sarah asked.

"Underground. They build their homes under trees and beneath large boulders."

"Are they intelligent?" Lissa asked, intrigued.

Pedr nodded. "Aye. They have their own city. Melendil. Many stories have been told about the city beneath the ground. Sadly, none of us will ever see it."

Steve looked at Sarah. "So? What's your best guess for that one?"

Sarah shrugged. "Sounds like gnomes."

"You mean with the little red pointed hats? No way."

"Sladdi wear hats," Pedr confirmed. "Only, they're not red."

"It sounds like a really cool kingdom," Mikal breathed. "I would love to visit it someday."

Pedr suddenly stared at Sarah as though he just remembered an important detail.

"Umm, did you say that this isn't your home world? I thought you said you lived here?"

"I do live here," Sarah confirmed, "but only part time. My home world is not anywhere around here."

"How far away is it?" the youth wanted to know.

"It's so far away that, if you tried to walk there, you'd never make it," Steve told the boy. "Not even if you spent your entire lifetime trying."

"Then how did you get here?" Pedr asked, confused.

Steve pointed at Sarah. "Her. Remember her jhorun? Er, her power? She's a teleporter. She can get us practically anywhere in the blink of an eye."

"Could you get all the way to Aarszan?"

"What's in Aarszan?" Steve asked.

Pedr sighed wistfully, "Aarszan is my home. I was working as a cleaning boy at a tavern along the sea when I watched a stranger post a message on the notice board. I saw that the legendary Captain Flinn was looking to hire a new crew. I saw it as an opportunity to help my mother, so I was the first applicant. For reasons that are still unknown to me, the captain chose me."

"Tell us about the captain," Mikal requested, adopting a gentle tone. "What kind of person is he?"

Pedr nodded and sat back in his chair. He closed his eyes and began to speak.

"I can still recall the exact moment when I first met Captain Flinn. He told me … well, not to me personally, but to the roomful of recruits, that he was interested in one final voyage. One man identified himself as the former first mate, and agreed without a moment's thought.

"All the 'regulars', as the captain called them, instantly signed up. Casimir, Jino, Arik, and Grenden all seemed so eager to serve under the captain that it convinced me that I had made the right decision. Any captain that could inspire that much loyalty in his crew was one I wanted to be a part of. However, they needed at least two dozen more before they would risk the open sea. Such was the fame of Captain Flinn, and of the *Emberbrand*, that practically all of Aarszan had answered the advertisement. The first mate, Rusty, left a notice at a waterfront tavern sailors were known to frequent. What they never counted on was the interest. So many people applied that they ended up turning away dozens, if not hundreds of qualified men."

"Were things that bad in … in …" Steve drew a breath and sighed. "I'm sorry. I forgot the name of the city where you're from."

"Aarszan."

"Right. Was there a lot of unemployment in Aarszan?"

"You're asking if there was work?" Pedr shook his head. "Not for someone like me."

"Please continue," Lissa implored.

Pedr shrugged. "I heard Captain Flinn treated his crew so well, so *fairly*, that he split his treasure equally. You have no idea how rare that is."

"What did he promise you?" Mikal asked.

"Captain Flinn insisted there was land on the other side of the Great Sea. He didn't say anything about it being populated, but he did say that the treasure we could find would be worth more than anything he's collected before."

"When did he tell you he was planning on infiltrating the nest of a dragon?" Steve asked.

"About twenty minutes before we arrived in dragon territory. If you're wondering whether or not I was thinking I had made a mistake in joining, then the answer is yes. Most definitely."

"You poor boy," Sarah breathed.

"How could a snake tooth be worth getting yourself being fried to a crisp?" Pedr complained.

Sarah blinked once. "Wait. Are you saying Flinn never told you what the fang was for?"

"He might've revealed his reasoning to Rusty, but he never said anything to me. I just don't get it. From what I hear, Captain Flinn had plenty of gold and silver. His treasure was so vast that each of them could easily retire at any moment and never worry about where their next meal would come from. In fact, once we were at sea, Rusty told us that was precisely what Captain Flinn had done. He had become so wealthy he ended up retiring to his own private island to live out his remaining days in peace and quiet. That was nearly five years ago."

"Something lured him back," Lissa decided. "Maybe he was hired?"

"Other pirate captains tried unsuccessfully to coax him out of retirement," Pedr explained. "Captain Flinn was the most successful pirate of all time. Everyone wanted to learn his secrets. How could he have commanded such loyal respect from the crew? How had he avoided the authorities when capture seemed inevitable?"

"And no one ever figured it out," Steve guessed.

"I have a theory," Lissa began.

Mikal nodded. "You do? Please, share it."

"I've known a lot of people who retired, but then quickly became bored. Retirement? For a pirate? I can only imagine it did not sit well with our Captain Flinn. If he has all the gold he could ever need, then I'm thinking he found something that persuaded him to take up the helm of his ship once more."

"We were a week or so out to sea," Pedr said, growing wistful. "I had long convinced myself that I had made a terrible decision in joining the crew. And, I wasn't the only one. I started hearing whispers. Q overheard…"

Steve looked up. "Q?"

"Yeah. The quartermaster. It's what we call Rusty. Q shared news that convinced every single one of us that we needed to stick by him."

"What was it?" Mikal asked, intrigued by the tale. "What news?"

"A traveler appeared on the captain's doorstep to propose a trade," Pedr said. "He'd give Flinn details about the king of all treasures if the captain would do him one simple favor. This treasure, the traveler had explained, was known only to a select few, and was said to be capable of enabling its possessor to rule over all. He-who-would-not-be-interested had become … interested."

"I feel like I need some popcorn," Steve murmured, which earned him *shush* from Sarah.

"The problem was," Pedr continued, "the visitor spun a

completely false tale. Flinn was able to see through the lies almost immediately, and we all knew what the captain would do to charlatans."

"But it was enough to get Flinn moving," Mikal deduced.

Pedr nodded. "The *Emberbrand*, which hadn't seen open water in years, had to be completely overhauled and made seaworthy once more. It needed supplies. It needed new sails, new masts, and new cannons. And, most importantly, it needed a new crew. And *that* was where I went wrong."

"Please explain yourself, Mr. Pedr," Mikal instructed.

"Captain Flinn was adamant about knowing what powers the crew wielded. He tested everyone. In fact, much more qualified sailors were refused simply because their powers didn't meet the captain's approval. He kept saying they had to be useful."

"You mean, useful to a pirate," Steve scoffed. The teenager sighed and sat back in his chair. "I just want to go home. And now I don't know if I'll ever see it again."

"You will," Sarah vowed.

"What can you tell us about the Seven Kingdoms?" Mikal asked. "I'm sorry. I have to ask. I know my father will want to know. It's not often that we entertain a guest who has information about what land lies across the Great Sea."

"Nothing much happens there," Pedr hesitantly explained. "People are constantly asking about what might be on *this* side of the sea."

"The grass is always greener," Steve laughed. "It sounds like the people over there are just as curious as we are."

Mikal nodded. "It would certainly seem so. Pedr, you've told us about the North. What can you tell us about the South? East? West?"

"The south? That's where my mother lives. That's where Aarszan is. I'm saving up to buy her a house in another kingdom."

"Does anyone live there besides the humans?"

Pedr shook his head. "You can find the fim practically everywhere but the sea, but they aren't as common. The same goes for mavi. You'll find them in all waters, but predominantly in the south. Then again, the mavi can *only* live in the sea, which is why they claim the Sea Kingdom."

Steve cleared his throat. "Could you describe these 'mavi' characters? What do they look like?"

Again, the teenager held a hand next to his waist.

"From here up, they look like you and me, only they don't dress the same. And from here down, they have adapted to the water."

"You said they don't dress like us?" Lissa asked. "Could you explain that?"

Pedr's face reddened noticeably, "They, ah, don't typically wear any clothes. And they have scales—flukes."

"Mer-people!" Sarah exclaimed delightedly. "You're telling us that you have mermaids living in the Seven Kingdoms? Oh, honey. I sooo want to go for a visit!"

"There are both female and male mavi," Pedr confirmed. "However, there are nearly ten females for every male."

"Lucky boogers," Steve whispered to Sarah, who elbowed him in the gut.

"What else? Well, I told you about the Western Kingdom. Humans and sladdi. You know about the North and South. Have I said anything about the East?"

The four of them, Mikal included, shook their heads no.

"It's the largest of the kingdoms, aside from the Sea Kingdom. The East is where most of the humans live."

"Yet you don't live there," Steve mused. "Why is that?"

"My family makes a living on the sea. My father was a fisherman. My mother is a weaver. She mends nets."

"And you?" Sarah prompted. "You mentioned you were employed as a cleaning boy at a tavern. What does that have to do with the sea?"

"Nothing," Pedr scoffed. "Now you know why I jumped at the chance to serve on a ship."

"Can we assume that your Sea Kingdom is peopled by the Mavi?" Mikal asked, attempting to steer the conversation back to what he was desperate to learn.

The teenager nodded. "Aye. No one knows how many there are, nor do they know where their city lies."

"They have a city?" Sarah asked, amazed. She looked at Steve with wistful eyes. "Wouldn't you just love to see how they live?"

"I'd like to know where they go to the bathroom," Steve remarked, eliciting a snort of surprise from Mikal. "I mean, think about it. They obviously do their thing in the water, yet they swim around in it all day. That means they are swimming in their own..."

"Thanks for ruining that mental picture," Sarah groused, interrupting him before he could finish his sentence.

"So, that's all of them, right?" Steve asked. "You've explained all the Kingdoms?"

Except Mountain.

"Except Mountain," Steve repeated Pravara's thought. "Who lives there, Pedr? More humans? Non-humans? Any ideas?"

Pedr noticeably shuddered. "Giegans."

"And what are they?" Sarah quietly asked. "Something tells me that we aren't going to like the answer, are we?"

"It was mistake to allow them to become the seventh," Pedr all but whispered. "If ever a kingdom were to be forced to leave, I pray it'd be that one."

"These giegans are dangerous?" Mikal uneasily asked.

Pedr fearfully nodded his head.

"What do they look like?" Steve asked.

"Just like us?" Sarah guessed.

Pedr nodded again. "Aye. Just like us, only louder. Dirtier. Meaner. Bigger."

Steve's eyebrows shot up. "Bigger? By how much? How big are we talking here?"

Pedr nervously looked around, as though one of the brutes might be listening.

"Giegans are giant beings who live in the northern mountains. They live in isolation, avoiding contact with everyone, including each other."

"Then how could they be considered a kingdom?" Mikal asked, confused. "Who governs those creatures? Who holds them accountable?"

"No one," Pedr answered, shaking his head. "That's the problem. They've grown accustomed to taking what they want. Once they realize we're not as strong as they are, we're doomed."

"The other six kingdoms ought to band together to make sure that doesn't happen," Mikal suggested. "That's what I would do, if I were this Weslin individual. Oh, what I would do to get my hands on a map. My father would have conniptions if I could show him what lay across the sea."

"My entire family has always wondered the same about this side of the Great Sea," Pedr confessed. "I'd like to be able to show them the land I visited."

Mikal turned to look back at his father's desk. He rose to his feet, walked to the desk, and started opening drawers. He pulled out a long tube, uncorked the ends, and slid out a rolled-up parchment. He carefully unrolled the paper and presented it to their guest.

"Here. This is a recently completed map my father commissioned the head cartographer to make. My father wanted something with as much detail as possible, only in a travel-friendly size. Take it. I give it to you as a gift."

"You're giving me a map? Of your kingdom?"

"I'm giving you a map of Lentari," Mikal corrected.

Pedr began a systematic pat down of all his pockets. The teenager sighed heavily once he realized his pockets were empty. "I don't have anything to pay for this."

"It's a gift," Mikal reminded him. "No payment necessary."

The boy caught sight of the king's large, elegant desk and his face lit up with an idea. He pointed at the small bottle of ink and the quill pen.

"May I? I am no artist, and am certainly no map maker, but I can give you an idea of what the Seven Kingdoms looks like."

Mikal held out an arm. "Please. Help yourself. There is parchment in that tray."

Pedr seated himself at the king's desk and began to sketch. Steve and Sarah rose from their seats to watch the map take form. Mikal and Lissa followed close behind.

Immediately apparent were the separate kingdoms. The Eastern Kingdom was easily twice as big as the rest, with the Northern Kingdom being the smallest. Mountain ranges, forests, open prairies, inlets, waterways, and lakes were added.

Steve whistled with appreciation.

"You may claim you're no map maker, kid, but that's pretty damn impressive, if you ask me."

"It's not done to scale," Pedr said with a shrug. "I'd need exact measurements so that I'd know how much to reduce each section."

"Where is the Perz Archipelago located with relation to this map?" Sarah asked.

Pedr tapped a section near the bottom of his map. A series of dots, ranging from tiny specks to thumbnail-sized, were visible just below a string of peninsulas. Some of the narrow strips of land looked as though they extended many leagues out into the water.

"No one knows which one is the captain's private island," Pedr began. "Oh, I ought to add this…"

Pedr retrieved the quill and looked as though he had started to doodle on his map. Starting at the southern tip of land and extending in all directions, Pedr added reefs, huge chunks of stone jutting out from under the water, and several other symbols Steve guessed were more monster-related than geographical.

"Does this have something to do with what you said earlier?" Steve asked. "Where you said Flinn was not concerned about someone finding his island because it'd be too dangerous to find it?"

The Byway, as he called it.

"I think Pedr called it the *Byway*," Sarah said, at the same exact time. "Is this group of islands as large as you've made them out to be?"

Pedr leaned forward to study his sketch. "Yes. No one really knows how many islands are in the Perz Archipelago. Captain Flinn's treasure is somewhere in Perz. Many people have searched for it. Most, I'm told, never see the light of another day. I overheard the captain telling the quartermaster that he cannot wait for the day when Perz becomes the Eighth Kingdom."

Everyone looked up at the boy.

"Flinn wants Perz to become a kingdom?" Sarah asked. "Why?"

"What else?" Pedr sighed. "Fame and glory."

Chapter 8 — Chance of a Lifetime

So, what do you think?" Steve whispered as he and Sarah huddled with Mikal and Lissa on the opposite side of the Antechamber. "I know he's under a truth spell, but no offense to Gareth, can we trust what Pedr is saying? How do we know this isn't all part of Flinn's master plan? 'Oh, whoops! We seemed to have dropped one of our number. Let the enemy capture him so they can question him.' I'm not sure I'm buying it."

Sarah stared at her husband before she burst out in laughter.

"What?" Steve scowled, crossing his arms over his chest. "I'm serious! I'm just saying we need to be careful. As much as I'd like to believe this kid, can we really take the chance?"

"Then let's test it."

Steve raised an eyebrow. "Curiosity piqued. What do you have in mind?"

"We'll ask each other a question that ordinarily we'd say no to."

"I'd never lie to you, babe. Hit me with your best shot."

"Were you ever planning on telling me about how you were inside the mouth of an oskorlisk?"

"Okay, I don't wanna play anymore."

"Answer the question, please."

Steve clamped his mouth shut. He fervently wanted to say absolutely not, and should his mouth open, that's exactly what would come out. Sweat trickled down his forehead as he fought to keep from answering.

"You don't need to say anything," Sarah told him. "Your silence is all the proof I need that you were planning on keeping this under wraps."

Steve took a breath in relief, but in doing so, his mouth opened.

"There's no way in hell I was gonna tell you." His eyes opened wide and he slapped a hand over his mouth. A few seconds later, he groaned. "I'm gonna pay for that later in some subtle way, aren't I?"

"It won't be that subtle," Sarah promised. "Now, are we good? Do you believe it's working now?"

"Don't I get to ask you a question?"

Sarah shook her head. "Nope. I'm not the one who had doubts. Now, back to the problem at hand. What about that map?"

Steve snapped his fingers. "Of course! Good. Thanks for reminding me. The one pirate that we happen to find is capable of drawing a map that would make any cartographer jealous? It's too convenient. There's no way our luck is that good."

"Well, the nice thing about this situation is that it can easily be remedied," Mikal casually added.

Sarah nodded. "That's right. Gareth's gift. If ever there was a time to press someone for more information, now would be it."

Mikal nodded. "I agree."

Steve watched as Mikal looked over at the young pirate and shook his head. Pedr was sitting on a plush armchair on the other side of the Antechamber, nervously looking around the ornate room. Mikal pulled a slip of paper out of his desk, composed a brief message, and handed it to one of the two stationary guards standing silently inside the enchanted room. The guard looked down at the message, bowed, and departed.

"Who'd you send that to?" Steve asked, curious. "You've got something up your sleeve. Spill."

Horrified, Sarah thumped him in his gut. Properly chastened, Steve gave Mikal a sheepish smile. "Umm, sorry? I really shouldn't treat you like a kid."

Mikal shook his head. "It's all right. No offense taken."

"Even though you still are," Steve continued, offering his own smile in return. "At least, not until you can beat me at … um…"

Mikal grinned. "I'll beat you at whatever contest you can dream up, old man."

"Smartass."

Sarah thumped him again. Harder. Mikal smiled fondly at the two of them.

"I'm trying to call in a favor. If it works, I'll let you know. In the meantime, let's go join Pedr. I'd like to get as much information as possible out of him. The *veracity charm*, as Gareth calls it, appears to be quite effective. Let's use that to our advantage."

Steve nodded and took Sarah's hand. Together they walked over to the second, smaller hearth and joined the young pirate. Mikal and Lissa took the remaining two seats on the left. After a few moments, as everyone looked expectantly at one another, Lissa hurriedly got to her feet.

"I have an idea. Hold on for a moment."

"What are you doing?" Mikal asked, as he turned to watch Lissa hurry over to his father's desk.

Lissa snatched the ink bottle, a quill, and a stack of parchment. She hurried back to her chair and pulled a small table over. She placed a few pieces of paper before her, uncorked the ink bottle, and dipped the quill in the ink. She looked up and smiled apologetically.

"Sorry. I thought it might be a good idea to take some notes."

Steve nodded, surprised. It *was* a good idea.

"Let's get started," Mikal said, glancing over at Lissa.

"Now that we can document properly, we'll start from the beginning. What's your name?"

"I already told you."

"This is for the record. I'm doing this because I know my father would do it if he were here. So, if you please, indulge me. Please state your name."

"Pedr."

The soft scratching of Lissa's quill began. Mikal restated the names of the others in the room and asked again where Pedr came from.

"Aarszan. It sounds nice."

Pedr scoffed and shook his head, "It isn't. It's a whole town full of sailors, drunks, and taverns. There are brawls on a nightly basis. I've had to repair broken furniture every single week. And don't get me started on how many piles of vomit I've had to clean. I cannot think of a worse profession than that of a cleaning boy. Why do you think I signed on to become a sailor? It got me away from that filthy hamlet."

"Do you enjoy being a sailor?" Sarah asked.

Steve risked a glance at the young king. Mikal watched Lissa write, and only resumed talking when she looked up at him. She nodded her readiness.

Pedr shrugged. "It has its moments."

"How long have you been a sailor?" Mikal asked.

"Four months now. We've only been to sea for less than a month."

"What else should I ask him?" Mikal casually asked, looking up at Steve, then Sarah.

"Is being the king as cool as it sounds?" Pedr curiously asked.

"No," Mikal snorted. He laughed at the surprised look from Lissa. "If you were wondering whether or not the truth charm was working, then you can consider this your proof. I typically wouldn't have admitted that out loud."

"You're not happy being the king?" Lissa asked, concerned. For the time being, she had stopped writing.

"I'm sure I will be eventually," Mikal told his new wife. "However, my father sprang this on me at the last moment. I feel like I didn't have time to prepare. I'm still nervous."

Lissa smiled warmly at him. "You're doing great. I have faith in you."

"As do we," Sarah added, laying a hand over Mikal's.

"Why did you invoke a magical spell?" Pedr suddenly asked. "You don't believe what I'm saying is the truth? Do you customarily treat visitors like this?"

"Visitors?" Steve scoffed. "You're a pirate, remember? You're the one who invaded our country."

Pedr smiled sheepishly. "That's a fair point."

"We want to believe you, Pedr," Mikal began, as he laid a friendly hand on the young pirate's shoulder. "I want to believe you. We *all* would like to believe you. However, we need to know for certain that you're telling us the truth."

"Of course, I'm telling the truth," Pedr insisted.

"But, how could you convince us of that?" Steve asked. He held up a hand as Pedr took a breath. "No, don't answer that. It was rhetorical. You won't be able to convince total strangers of your sincerity, regardless of how hard you try. That's where the truth charm comes in."

Pedr frowned for a few moments before he finally shrugged.

Mikal nodded. "Excellent. Let's proceed."

"No charm is foolproof," Pedr said, sitting back in his chair. "You still won't know if I'm telling you the truth. You're just going to have to trust me."

"You're suggesting you can fool Gareth's charm?" Mikal slowly grinned. "Now *that* is something I'd like to see."

Pedr cocked his head.

"I'll bet I can. I fool my mother all the time. I told her I had signed on to a fisherman's boat. She has no idea I'm a pirate." Horrified, Pedr slapped a hand over his mouth. "I have no idea why I said that. I didn't mean to."

Mikal smiled again and sat back in his chair. "Were you going to attempt to tell me you were *not* a pirate? Go ahead. Tell me you're a fisherman instead."

Pedr grinned, "Very well. I'm a pirate. Wait, what? What happened?"

"Would you like to try again?"

"Yes. Of course. I shouldn't have any problems telling

you I'm a pirate and not a fisherman."

Steve snickered and Sarah stifled a giggle. Mikal crossed his legs at his ankles and waited.

"What? I did it again, didn't I? Hang on. I can do this. Ask me something else."

"Your name," Lissa softly suggested. "Tell us your name is something besides 'Pedr'. Tell us it's … Steve. That's it. Tell us your name is Steve."

"Sure. It's Pedr. Oh. Umm…"

Steve leaned forward. "I think we can say that we've established the truth charm is working. So, tell us, Pedr. Why did you become a pirate? There's gotta be safer professions in Aarszan than that of being a pirate, right?"

Pedr shrugged. "There are, but nothing that paid well. My mother is all I have. I became a pirate to give my mother a better life."

"Do you like hurting people?" Sarah asked.

"No. I hate it."

"Are you harboring any ill will toward Lentari?" Mikal wanted to know.

"Oh. No, I have no intentions of harming anyone here."

"Are you aware of … of … any other pirates hurting anyone?" Lissa asked.

Pedr shook his head. "No."

"What about the captain?" Lissa continued. "Captain … er, Captain…"

Mikal's new wife looked helplessly around the room. Steve suppressed a smile. Apparently, she had forgotten the captain's name.

"Captain Flinn," Steve quietly supplied.

"Thank you. Pedr, have you witnessed Captain Flinn endangering any Lentarian citizens since he's arrived in our kingdom?"

"No."

"None at all?" Steve asked, impressed. "I wouldn't have called that one."

"Have you witnessed any acts of violence?" Mikal wanted to know.

"No."

"Have you witnessed any acts that you would consider morally wrong?" the pro tem king continued.

"Aye."

"Finally," Sarah said.

Steve waved a hand in exasperation. "Don't leave us hangin', pal. Spill. What did you see?"

"I know Captain Flinn stole a big snake tooth from a dragon cave."

"Besides that," Steve said with a huff.

"No."

Sarah leaned forward. "You're telling us that the only thing Flinn has done, since he's arrived here in Lentari, was stolen an oskorlisk fang?"

"No. I told you; he stole a big snake tooth."

"An oskorlisk *is* a big snake," Steve pointed out. "A big sea snake."

"Oh."

"Why does Flinn want that fang?" Sarah asked. "Can you tell us?"

"I was never told," Pedr answered, shaking his head. "I'm sorry."

"Then we may never know," Mikal groaned.

Steve looked at the king. "Kahvel told us that oskorlisk fangs have power. We watched the fang that Flinn stole repel a full-frontal attack from Pravara. She hit Flinn with at least three shots and yet he didn't suffer a scratch. And we're not talking gentle puffs of fire, but blasts from a full-grown adult dragon."

"I had no idea," Mikal said, amazed.

"Neither did we," Sarah admitted.

"I think we need to find out what Flinn is planning on doing with that fang," Steve decided.

"How would we go about doing that?" Sarah asked.

Steve shrugged and shook his head. He looked over at Mikal. The young king had a pensive look on his face as he mulled over possibilities.

"The captain clearly believes that acquiring the fang will help him obtain his goal of making his home into the eighth kingdom," Mikal began, sounding eerily more like his father than Steve could ever recall. "Pedr, do you believe the acquisition of this fang is the only reason Captain Flinn has come to Lentari?"

"No."

"Oh? Can you expand on that a little?"

"You have to understand," Pedr slowly began. "Before I signed on with the captain, I did my research. I wasn't about to serve under someone until I knew what type of person he was. So, I asked around. I found several former crewmembers."

"Go on," Lissa urged.

"They told me many stories. That was when I started to notice a pattern."

"Don't stop now, pal," Steve added. "Keep going."

"Captain Flinn was very successful in what he did," Pedr continued.

"Meaning piracy," Sarah said.

"Aye. Piracy. Whenever he set his sights on something, he wouldn't hesitate until he acquired it."

"How does that help us now?" Steve asked.

"You didn't let me finish. Once he got the thing he desired, he'd order us to leave. Never once did he get a piece of treasure and then *not* give the order to pull anchor and leave."

"And he hasn't done that?" Steve asked.

"Well, we hadn't made it back to the *Emberbrand* yet," Pedr admitted. "However, I should also point out that there was no rush. No urgency. He only used Casimir to hide the *Cadaymas* when we knew we had been spotted."

"That doesn't sound like someone who was trying to return to his ship as quickly as possible," Sarah decided. "So, are you trying to say that you believe Flinn isn't done in Lentari? He has other objectives in mind?"

Pedr nodded. "Those are my beliefs, aye."

"If we are to assume you're correct," Mikal slowly began, "then what else could he possibly be searching for?"

"I'd say we need to find out," Steve decided.

Mikal nodded, rose to his feet, and returned to his father's desk.

"I agree."

"What are you doing?" Steve good-naturedly asked as he moved to follow.

Sarah hooked his arm through hers as he was passing by and brought him to a sudden stop.

"Would you stop that?" she hissed with frustration. "He's the king now. You shouldn't be staring over his shoulder all the time. If he wanted you to know what he was doing, then he'd tell you."

"Ah. Good point. Sorry."

"Don't apologize to me, apologize to him."

"There's no harm done," Mikal assured them both. "To answer your question, I'm composing a message to Shardwyn. I've asked for his help in this matter."

Steve quietly groaned. He caught Sarah's disapproving frown and threw his face into neutral. The quirky wizard's powers were widely known to be erratic at best.

Five minutes later, Shardwyn appeared, this time in a large puff of white smoke.

"Good afternoon, Your Majesty," Shardwyn said, bowing low. He fanned the air in front of his face, as though someone else had been responsible for the appearance of the smoke. "How may I assist you today?"

"Who is he?" Pedr whispered. Shock and awe were evident in both is tone of voice and his body language.

"That's Shardwyn," Steve whispered back. "He's the castle wizard."

"Should I be concerned?" Pedr quietly asked.

Steve grunted. "I would be."

Mikal rose from the desk and approached the think, elderly man who wore a set of bright orange robes. Steve briefly wondered if the quackpot had a set of robes in every color of the rainbow.

"What do you think you can do in order to help us?" Mikal was saying after he explained what they were after. "Is there some potion you can brew, or some spell you can write, which would point us in the right direction?"

"You were right to come to me, Your Majesty," Shardwyn said, as he sank onto one of the closest arm chairs. "Let me think for a moment."

Steve sidled close to the king. "Are you sure you don't want to ask Gareth about this?"

Mikal leaned forward. "Actually, that's who I sent the first message to," he confided. "The problem is, I don't know if the message will reach him in time. His family's new home is farther out of town than the old one used to be.

"You wrote him a message?" Sarah quietly asked, overhearing the conversation. "Isn't there a faster way to make contact?"

"Like what?" Mikal wanted to know.

Like me.

Surprised, Steve's head lifted and he glanced around the room. No one else was acting as though they had heard the telepathic message.

Pryllan?

No, it's Pravara.

I'm sorry, Pravara. You and your mother sound alike.

Well, we are both wyverian, and she just happens to be my mother, so…

Nice to see everyone has taken their smartass pills today.

I'm not familiar with that term.

Good. Forget I said it. Can you still relay messages to Gareth?

Of course.

Nice. Okay, can you relay to him everything we were just talking about?

You are assuming I was eavesdropping?

We both know you were, my friend. It's what you like to do.

Silence.

Pravara? Are you there?

Aye.

You were eavesdropping, weren't you?

Maybe.

Relax. No one is angry. Please relay what you heard to Gareth. Tell him we could really use his help right about now. If we have to rely on Shardwyn, then I think it's safe to say that we are all doomed.

Very well. A moment, if you please.

Sarah noticed that Steve was staring silently at the ceiling and frowned. "Is everything okay?"

Steve nodded. "Yeah. I'm waiting to see what Gareth has to say."

Mikal perked up. "You're in mental contact with Gareth?"

"No, but Pravara is."

Mikal groaned and shook his head. "Of course! Pravara! I completely forgot about her."

Steve?

Yes? Were you able to reach Gareth?

I spoke with his father first. Balthor is a very powerful wizard. He was shielding his son from any unwelcome contact. I explained to him who I was, and that we had met before. I told him I had a message to relay to his son. He permitted me to speak with the young human wizard.

And?

Gareth is willing to help. He said to tell you that he'll be there in just a few moments.

That's awesome, Pravara. Thank you for your help.

You're welcome.

Will you continue to eavesdrop?

Of course. I find it highly entertaining.

"Gareth is on his way," Steve happily informed the room. Mikal nodded, pleased.

Surprised, Shardwyn looked up from his chair. "My apprentice is returning? Early? Whatever for? I'm sure I can solve this dilemma, Your Majesty."

Prepared for just such a response, Mikal nodded coolly. "Actually, Shardwyn, this is such an important matter that I feel we'll need as much help as possible. There's an unknown threat to Lentari. I, for one, would welcome all the help I can get."

Shardwyn nodded. "Agreed. You will make a fine king someday, young master Mikal."

"He *is* the king today," Steve said, under his breath. "And he's a perfectly fine king."

Mikal held out a closed fist. Steve bumped it with his own as soon as Shardwyn looked away. Overhearing Steve's compliment, Lissa smiled at him.

"How long did he say it would take him to get here?"

Sarah asked.

Steve shrugged. "He didn't say. I would think…"

He trailed off as he suddenly raised his left arm and stared at it, as though he believed he was now staring at a stranger's arm. Alarmed, Sarah rushed to his side. She quickly ran a hand over the skin of his arm, checking for injuries.

"What is it? Are you all right?" Sarah asked.

"The hair on my arm is sticking straight up. Whoa. Both arms are now doing the same thing. What the hell is going on? Look, yours are, too."

There was a flash of bright light and the very air crackled with energy. A small white sphere of pure energy, no bigger than a basketball, appeared several feet away. It rapidly expanded until it had a diameter of ten feet before disappearing in another brilliant burst of light.

Steve blinked his eyes a few times, trying to clear away the spots dancing before his vision. "That was bright. I'll be seeing spots for quite some time. Sarah, are you okay? Is everyone else okay?"

"We're good," Sarah informed him. Her vision cleared. "Gareth! That was quite an entrance!"

The lanky teenage boy grinned at them as he rose from the crouch his unique method of travel had apparently required.

"Lady Sarah. Sir Steve. Hello, everyone. So, what's so important? What do you need me for?"

Steve turned to point at Pedr, who was now standing and backing nervously away.

"That's Pedr."

Gareth nodded at the boy who was a few years older than he was. "Greetings. I didn't see you over there. Look, there's no need to be alarmed. Traveling by energy may look scary, but it's perfectly safe as long as you take all proper precautions."

Steve grinned. "Traveling by energy? Kid, you never cease to amaze me."

"You brought me here to make a friend? Couldn't this have waited? My father and I were going to go flying."

"Pedr is from Aarszan," Sarah explained. "His home is the Seven Kingdoms, on the *other* side of the Sea of Koralis."

Gareth stared at her for a few moments before his brow furrowed and he cocked his head.

"You heard that right," Steve confirmed. "Pedr is not from around here."

"How'd he get here?" Gareth asked. "I always heard there wasn't anything but barbarians and savages on the other side of the sea."

"That's what we were told, too," Pedr said, hesitantly approaching. "Lawlessness, few people, greenless countryside. Nothing I've been told was accurate."

"How can I help?" Gareth asked, turning to Mikal. He caught sight of Shardwyn, facing the small hearth on the other side of the room, and frowned. His voice dropped to a whisper. "What's he doing?"

"He says he's working on something that will be able to help us," Mikal quietly answered.

"What do you need help with?" Gareth wanted to know. "I'll see if I can do it before he blows something up."

"We need to figure out what Pedr's companions are up to," Sarah told the young wizard, filling in the details. "We believe Flinn hasn't left Lentari yet, which means he's out there, looking for something else. We need to know what."

Gareth looked at the older boy. "Your companions have stolen an oskorlisk fang? Wait. Does that mean you're a pirate?"

Pedr groaned. "*Former* pirate. I've just decided to resign. Contrary to the popular saying, a pirate's life is *not* for me."

"What can I do?" Gareth asked.

"The best way to learn about what Flinn is up to is to learn about the man himself," Mikal decided. "I think we need to pay his homeland a visit."

Gareth's eyes widened with surprise.

"Discreetly, of course."

"I could teleport us straight there," Sarah said, "only I don't have any picture to reference."

"I'm not sure how I fit in here," Gareth admitted.

"Can you come up with something to help Sarah get one of her visions?" Steve asked. "It certainly beats spending weeks crossing the sea when she can do it in the blink of an eye."

Gareth sat in the closest chair, leaned back, and closed his eyes.

"I'll see what I can do. Lady Sarah, refresh my memory. Tell me what you need to make your jhorun work."

"If I can picture it, I can teleport there. However, the bad news is that I can't teleport to somewhere that I haven't seen before."

"But you've done it once before," Steve reminded her. "Back when Rhenyon wanted to go to Ylani? You looked at a simple sketch and was able to create one of your safe zones. What about Pedr's map? Can you get anything off of that?"

Mikal handed the map to Sarah. She stared at the lines and symbols for a few moments before she closed her eyes. Five minutes later she conceded defeat.

"I just can't picture anything. It isn't working."

Gareth rose to his feet and began pacing. "I might be able to redirect a small portal. That would at least give us something to work with."

Steve automatically shook his head. "That won't work. You're good, Gareth, but not that good. If you're suggesting that you might be able to change a portal's destination, like a Gatekeeper, then you'd need the strength of at least three Gatekeepers, and you only have one."

"Who?" Gareth asked. "I know you're not talking about me. I may be able to replicate some of a Gatekeeper's jhorun, but I suspect I wouldn't nearly be strong enough."

Steve tapped his chest. "Me. My Lentarian ancestors were Gatekeepers. Turns out I have part of that jhorun in me."

"You learn something new every day," Gareth remarked. "Very well. No modifying a portal. Let's see. Hey, what about just using Pedr? I've never experimented on a human before, but I'm sure I could come up with ..."

"Absolutely not!" Pedr cried, as he jerked backward so hard he tripped and landed on a nearby chair. "No experiments! No way!"

"You won't feel a thing," Gareth promised.

Sarah held up a hand. "Gareth, he said no. We certainly don't need any more ... *accidents* in here. Pedr? We'll find another way."

Gareth sighed. "Well, we could … wait! I've got it! You need to be able to see where you're going, right?"

Sarah nodded. "Right."

"I think I have a way to be able to do that. The only thing I have to figure out is how to share the images with everyone else."

"How do you plan on getting a picture of the Seven Kingdoms?" Steve wanted to know.

"I'm going to use a 'familiar'."

"A what?" Mikal, Steve, Sarah, and Pedr repeated.

"A *familiar*. It's where I temporarily borrow a creature's senses, including sights, sound, smell, and anything else that might be helpful to me."

"You're going to look through the eyes of a creature that's currently living in the Seven Kingdoms?" Steve repeated, amazed and impressed. "How in the hell do you know how to do that? You know what? Scratch that. I don't want to know. You're the man, kid."

It was too late. Gareth had heard the request and was already launching a detailed description on how his spell would work. Husband and wife gave a collective groan.

"It shouldn't be too difficult," Gareth was saying. "I just have to take the images, amplify them, and share them with everyone else. Let's see. A multi-layer spell should do the trick. The first layer will be a locator spell. I'll instruct it to find a creature that's easily familiarized. The second layer will be to temporarily gain control over the creature's faculties. The third layer will more than likely have to translate the images into something I can fathom. And finally, the fourth layer will have to allow me to share the visions with whomever would like to see them."

"Er, how long will that take?" Mikal hesitantly asked. "Or are you going to tell me jthat you've already created it?"

Gareth sank down into the closest chair and closed his eyes. His mouth was moving, only no one could hear anything. Gareth, it would seem, was already hard at work crafting the spell he had envisioned. Mikal smiled, noticed there was a small, crystal paperweight on the desk, and decided their young wizard friend could use it to hold the spell.

"What's he doing?" Pedr quietly asked.

"Did you hear him talk about that spell he needed to create?" Steve asked, eliciting a nod from the young former pirate. "He's creating it now."

"I must admit," a new voice added, "that I wish I could create spells as easily as he can. I only ask that you never tell him I said that."

Husband and wife looked up, saw who had wandered over, and shared a grin with each other. Evidently Shardwyn was curious.

"Did he say what type of spell he wanted to create?" the old wizard inquired.

Mikal nodded. "Aye. It's another one of his multi-layer spells."

Shardwyn sighed wistfully, "I really need to practice my multi-layer spell crafting. Do you know how many layers he plans on using?"

Sarah nodded. "Four. Locator, something to take control of the familiar, something to translate what the familiar sees into something he can understand, and then a layer to allow him to share what he sees with the rest of us."

"I was going to ask about that," Steve recalled. "Layer three. Why would he need to translate what he's seeing? What does that even mean?"

"How well do you remember your biology class from school?" Sarah asked as she turned to her husband. "I don't know exactly what went on in your class, but my teacher taught us about the many ways animals and insects see our world. You know, the multi-faceted vision a fly can see in, the eight eyes that spiders have will create a completely different image, and even dogs."

"What about dogs?" Mikal asked, curious.

"Well, they don't see color. Their world is nothing but black, white, and shades of gray."

Steve was nodding, "Ah. I get it. He probably doesn't know what he's going to find, so he has to be ready. Wow. Those spells sound complex. I sure do hope he doesn't take too long."

"Finished," Gareth announced. He noticed the paperweight Mikal was holding out to him and nodded appreciatively. The crystal glowed briefly as the young wizard imbued his spell within the small object. "All right. Who's ready to see what's on the other side of the sea?"

"We all are," Sarah assured him.

Gareth looked down at the crystal, drew an invisible symbol in the air, and closed his eyes. The crystal paperweight began to glow once more. A few moments later, Gareth frowned and shook his head. Several seconds later, he frowned again.

"Is everything okay?" Steve asked. "What's with the frown? Is something not working the way you had planned?"

"The first two familiars my spell targeted returned such foreign imagery that my spell couldn't translate them into something I could use," Gareth explained, keeping his eyes closed. "I'd love to know what creatures they were, but I'm not going to worry about that now. So, before my spell can fracture apart, I told it to search for another subject. It has to be … wait." The young wizard closed his eyes. "I think this will work. Aye. I think this will work nicely."

"What do you see?" Mikal eagerly asked.

"A vision I can relate to," Gareth answered, keeping his eyes closed. "I see waves crashing against the shore. Huge broken chunks of stone litter the water's edge. From my vantage point, it looks as though my familiar is some creature living under a rock, near—or perhaps *in*—the sea. I … pincers? My hands are pincers. Huh. I guess my spell found some type of crustacean."

"Could it be a crab?" Sarah suggested.

"Well, if you're a crab, then does that mean you can make it leave the rock and look around?" Steve wanted to know.

"I'm doing that right now," Gareth relayed. "I can feel the crab's resistance. It is reluctant to venture that far away from the rocks. I can only assume there are predators nearby."

"How can I see what you're seeing?" Sarah asked. "I'd love to create a safe zone."

Gareth held up his right arm and pushed his sleeve up, baring his skin.

"Physical contact. The image will be shared with anyone

in direct physical contact with me."

Sarah approached first. She gently laid a hand on the boy's arm. When nothing happened, Sarah gave the arm a gentle shake.

"Gareth? Is there something I need to be doing?"

"Hmm? Oh. Sorry. Close your eyes. Allow your eyes to unfocus. The vision should come once your mind isn't thinking about anything else."

Steve snorted and, once he noticed Sarah had fired a dangerous look his way, slapped a hand over his mouth.

"Allergies."

"Uh huh. Keep it up, Glitter Boy."

"You and that damn glitter," Steve grumbled.

Sarah closed her eyes, took several calming breaths, and visibly relaxed. After a few moments, her eyebrows lifted, surprised. Ten seconds later, she was smiling.

"Do you see something?" Steve asked.

Sarah nodded. "Yes. I see exactly what Gareth described. I'm looking at the surface of a rock." She swayed to her right. "The crab is walking. This is weird. It's walking sideways!"

"Well, it's a crab," Steve reminded her. "They have a tendency to do that. Gareth, how many people can you accommodate? Could I see it, too?"

Keeping his eyes closed, Gareth nodded. "Of course. Grab my arm and close your eyes. Empty your mind. You'll see what the crab sees, too."

The corners of Sarah's mouth turned upwards in the beginning of a smile.

"Steve has to empty his mind? Well, that shouldn't be too…"

"Hey!" Steve exclaimed. "Play nice, woman!"

Sarah giggled. Just as Steve made physical contact with Gareth's arm, he noticed Mikal, Lissa, and (at Mikal's insistence) Pedr. They were slowly approaching. Steve closed his eyes and ordered himself to relax. An image instantly formed. It was just as Gareth had described. He was sitting on a rock, basking in the warm sunshine. A large segmented leg, capped with a huge pincer, appeared in the vision. It waved in the air a few times before disappearing from sight.

"This is incredible," Mikal breathed. "Gareth, you are truly amazing."

"May I join you?"

Steve cracked an eye and saw that Shardwyn was standing before them. With everyone in the room leaning forward to lay a hand on Gareth's exposed arm, no part of his skin was left for the elderly wizard to grasp.

"Gareth, could you roll up your other sleeve?" Steve quietly asked. "No, don't open your eyes. Can Shardwyn do it for you? I think he'd like to see the vision, too."

Gareth's left arm lifted. He nodded. "Go ahead, Shardwyn."

"Truly remarkable," the resident wizard was saying after he had made contact with Gareth's left arm. "Truly remarkable, indeed. Do we have any idea where this is?"

"Pedr?" Mikal asked. "Are you seeing this, too?"

"Aye," came the young pirate's voice. "This looks like the shore of the Western Kingdom, overlooking the great sea. Those stones? They could be from the Cliffs of Gehd."

"Lady Sarah?" Gareth asked. "Is this acceptable? Can you use this image to teleport here?"

Sarah nodded, forgetting that no one could see her. "Without a doubt. Provided this is across the Sea of Koralis then this will do nicely. This is all I needed, Gareth. Thank you."

The image vanished. As one, everyone opened their eyes.

"What?" Pedr demanded. "Just like that, you can teleport there? All the way across the Great Sea? That's impossible!"

"Now that we know you can do it," Mikal began, ignoring Pedr's outburst, "we need to talk about who is going. Obviously, Sarah and Steve. Pedr, would you accompany them? Your knowledge about your homeland would be invaluable."

"You're offering me a chance to go home and you're asking if I'll accept?" Pedr stammered. "Of course, I will!"

"Who else?" Mikal wondered aloud, drumming his fingers on the arm rest of his chair. "I really should send someone who can speak for the crown should the need arise. As much as I'd like to go, I have a feeling it would be frowned upon."

The young king returned to the desk, hastily composed a message, and handed it to a nearby guard. "See to it they report here at once."

The guard nodded and quietly exited the Antechamber.

"Do you have someone in mind?" Steve asked.

Mikal nodded. "Aye. Two men, and you're familiar with both."

Ten minutes later, the door opened and two soldiers entered. Husband and wife both broke out into smiles. Steve strode forward to clasp the arm of the tall soldier in the lead.

"Pheron! It's good to see you, buddy."

"Sir Steve. Lady Sarah. Just like old times."

"And Darius!" Steve continued, grasping the younger man's hand to give it an enthusiastic shake. "It's good to see you, too."

"I'm honored I was chosen," Darius told the assembled group. He bowed in Mikal's direction. "I hear we're undertaking a journey? May I ask where we're heading?"

Pheron turned to look at his subordinate. "Does it matter, Lieutenant?"

"Not at all, Captain."

"You're accompanying Steve and Sarah as they investigate the Seven Kingdoms," Mikal informed the two men.

Darius frowned, certain he had misheard. "I'm sorry, but will you say that again? Where are we going?"

"To the land of the Seven Kingdoms," Mikal repeated.

Surprised, Pheron turned to Mikal and raised an eyebrow. "That's a new one on me, Your Majesty. Is that up north, in Ylani? Or is it south, in Straosia?"

"Neither," Mikal answered, with a grin. "You're looking in the wrong direction. It's to the east. The Seven Kingdoms can be found on the *other* side of the Sea of Koralis."

"And, er, how are we getting there?" Pheron hesitantly asked. "I wasn't aware of any ships on our eastern shore that could make a journey that long."

Steve pointed at Sarah. "We're taking the Express. Sarah will get us there in her usual fashion."

Darius reluctantly raised a hand, "I seem to recall that Lady Sarah had to have visited the destination first. How is she able to see where she's going? No one has been over there before."

"I have," Pedr contradicted. "It's my home."

"I didn't think anyone lived over there, Captain," Darius exclaimed.

Pheron nodded. "That makes two of us, Lieutenant. Well, when do we depart?"

"There's no time like the present," Steve quipped. He took Sarah's hand. "Any idea how long we'll be gone?"

Sarah shrugged. "It doesn't matter. I can get us back here at any time. But, just to be safe, you'd better start charging up some mimets."

"I'd like to go."

Everyone turned to Gareth.

"I thought you'd want to get back to your father," Mikal told his friend. "I know his time is limited in human form. How long does he have before he has to change back to a water dragon?"

"A week. I have some time. I've already asked for my father's permission. He gave it. He could tell that I really want to go."

"You already asked for your father's permission?" Steve asked, confused. "How could you have possibly known that we'd end up going over there?"

"I didn't," Gareth said. He tapped the side of his head. "I asked him, up here, just a few moments ago. He gave me his blessing."

"Why do you want to come along?" Steve asked. "This isn't going to be especially fun, you know."

"Are you kidding? You're going someplace new! How cool is that? Besides, you might need my help."

"I'm sure as hell not gonna turn down the help of a wizard," Steve remarked, turning back to Mikal. "However, this is your call."

Mikal shared a look with Lissa, smiled, shrugged, and faced his young friend.

"Keep them safe, Gareth."

Gareth let out a whoop and hurried over to slap his hand on top of Sarah's and Steve's. The three of them waited for

Pedr, Pheron and Darius to add their hands. Once everyone was in physical contact with one another, Sarah brought up a mental picture of her newest safe zone and gave the order.

The six of them vanished.

Chapter 9 — A Brave, New World

An inhospitable, blustery, bleak shoreline appeared before them. Large broken slabs of solid granite lay like giant discarded dominoes all up and down the water's edge. What the crab had failed to see, Steve realized as he slowly looked around, was that the land's edge was nearly a hundred feet above their heads. As if they thought the landscape wasn't bad enough, completing the unwelcome first impression of the Seven Kingdoms was a jagged cliff wall extending as far as the eye could see in both directions.

"Looks downright homey, doesn't it?" Steve grumped.

"I'm freezing," Sarah complained. "My hands are cold. I can't seem to get warm."

Steve approached her from behind, laid a hand on either of her shoulders, and gently applied his jhorun.

"Is anyone else cold?" he asked, turning to look at his companions. "No? Alrighty then. Don't say I never offer you guys anything."

Once he was certain his wife was no longer in discomfort, Steve turned to regard their surroundings. He caught sight of Pedr looking longingly at the jagged pieces of stone littering the shore and motioned him over.

"Do you recognize this place? Is this the Seven Kingdoms?"

Pedr shrugged. "I think so."

Steve rounded on the young pirate. "You think so? *You think so?* Come on, man. You can do better than that."

"I'm sorry. This looks like the Cliffs of Gehd, and those rocks could be the Fallen Graves, but I'm not certain. I've never seen either of them in person before."

"Didn't you say this was your home?" Darius muttered.

"Have you seen everything there is to see in your home kingdom?" Pedr countered, leaning around Steve to look at the lieutenant. "I'm willing to wager there are places that you have undoubtedly heard about but have failed to see. Am I correct?"

"Point taken," Darius acknowledged. "Any ideas where we go from here?"

Steve turned to point at the top of the cliffs.

"I'd say we go up there. We'll have a better vantage point from a higher elevation. Then, hopefully, Pedr might see something he'll recognize."

Sarah nodded. "Sounds like a plan. Everyone ready? Deep breath."

The group of six appeared at the top of the cliffs. The stony ground was laced with deep cracks and for the most part, was as flat as a pancake. As a result, a brisk east wind was blowing.

Sarah tucked an errant strand of hair behind her ear, only to have it dislodged seconds later. She pulled the elastic band from her hair and hastily rebraided it. Once she was sure her hair would not be flung back in her face, Sarah studied the landscape. She peered down into the depths of the nearest crack.

"I wonder what made these. Look. They're everywhere. Pedr, do you know anything about this area? What happened up here? What could have caused the ground to crack apart like this?"

Pedr held up his hands and shrugged. "I'm sorry. I do not know."

"Gareth?" Sarah prompted. "Do you have any idea what caused this?"

Their wizard friend dropped down into a squat and studied the deep fissure. He placed a hand on the ground, closed his eyes, and softly chanted. After a few moments, he looked up at his companions.

"There are no traces of jhorun here. I sense nothing untoward. If I were to venture a guess, then I'd say these cracks were caused by some type of geological process."

Steve shaded his eyes and slowly spun in place. "Any idea which way to go? Where's the closest village, Pedr? Which direction?"

Pedr turned and pointed roughly southeast. "Although I've never been there, and if these are the Cliffs of Gehd, then I know Miron will be that way. Can you take us all the way there?"

"Teleporting without a safe zone is limited to line-of-sight jumps," Sarah explained. She pointed southeast. "I don't see anything to reference, so I'm just going to pick us all up and drop us as far as I can see. I'm hoping that, sooner or later, we'll see something that looks like a village. For now, right about *there* will do."

Once everyone was again clasping their hands together, Sarah teleported all six of them as far southeast as she dared. Once the slight feeling of nausea passed, Steve dared to open his eyes and look around. The same featureless—cracked— stony ground lay in all directions as far as the eye could see. Just as before, the rock covered ground was riddled with thin spider web cracks and huge jagged crevasses that they'd have to jump over if they wanted to cross. Thankfully, Sarah's jhorun made it unnecessary.

"Wow," Steve commented, turning to look behind them. "You can't even see the water from here. How far did you take us?"

Sarah shrugged. "I'm really not sure. As far as I thought

we could go. Safely, that is. How far that is, well, I'm not sure."

"How many more times can you teleport us before your jhorun will be drained?" Pheron asked, concerned. "I'd rather not risk the possibility of becoming stranded out here if we don't have to."

Sarah nodded. "I couldn't agree more. I'm fine for right now. Let's keep going, shall we?"

Four jumps later the rocky terrain started to undergo a slight change. Vegetation appeared in the form of tiny, scraggly shrubs dotting the landscape, offering scant protection from the elements. Several jumps after that, the shrubs were replaced by knee-high plants with large leaves. The stone-covered ground was starting to fade, almost as if the stones themselves were sinking into the ground. Grass appeared two jumps later and the stones had all but disappeared.

Pedr appeared by Sarah's side and pointed off in the distance, in the same direction they had been heading. The ground had started to swell upward, forming the base of either an extremely large hill or a small mountain. Sarah teleported them a final time, bringing them to the first copse of trees they had seen since arriving in the Seven Kingdoms. These trees, Steve noticed, reminded him of the umbrella acacia trees typically found in African savannas, only smaller, no more than eight feet tall, at their highest points. However, it was more than adequate to provide cover as the six visitors covertly studied the village.

Sunk into the very surface of the hillside, Steve saw, were row after row of houses, cottages, and all manner of domiciles. It was as if the city planners decided they didn't want a boring city laid out on a flat plain, but rather wanted a challenge. Therefore, the entire village had been built at an angle, starting at the base of the hill and reaching nearly halfway up.

They could see villagers going about various activities. Some were driving livestock up narrow, winding roads in an effort to pen the strange squat animals inside caves cut into the hillside. Others were gathered in small groups, no doubt talking about that day's activities. A large band of children could be seen playing in the lower streets, kicking a ball from one team of kids to the other.

"This is not what I was expecting," Steve whispered to the others. "There's nothing wrong with these people. They aren't the savages we were told that live here."

"And why would they be?" Pedr countered. "There's nothing wrong with the people here. In fact, we have been told over and over that there wasn't anything on the other side of the sea, either. Nothing worthwhile, that is. Er, no offense."

Pheron grinned and waved a hand dismissively. "None taken. Well, now that we're here, what do we do? We're here to learn more about this pirate captain, right? How do you suppose we go about doing that?"

"By finding his hideout," Steve decided, earning a nod of approval from his wife. "You want to know about this guy's weakness? Well, it's arrogance. He thinks he's untouchable. And you know what? Maybe he has been untouchable. However, that comes to a screeching halt right now. We find his hideout, we learn what we can, and then we catch Captain Windbag in the act."

Darius nodded. "I would say we have a plan. Where do … what? What's wrong with him?"

Everyone turned to look at Pedr. The young pirate had an ashen look on his face and was slowly backing away from them. Pheron deliberately moved so that he was standing behind him, effectively blocking his retreat.

"Is there something the matter?" the tall captain casually inquired. "If you think our plan is a bad idea, then now would be the time to say so."

"Your plan will never work," Pedr stated. He looked imploringly at each member of the group. "Do you have any idea how famous Captain Flinn is? Do you know how many people have searched for his hideaway? Do you have any idea how many people were never heard from again?"

Steve cracked a smile, "Based on your facial expressions, I'm guessing all of them?"

Pedr nodded vehemently. "Yes. Every single person who tried searching for the treasure never saw the light of day again."

"Do we know what happened to them?" Sarah asked, growing uneasy.

"Killed by pirates, killed by monsters, or who knows what else is waiting out there? The point is, unless you find—and follow—the Byway, risking an open water excursion to find Captain Flinn's lair is nothing short of guaranteeing your own death."

Steve recalled the smug look on the pirate captain's face during their encounter. There was someone who was used to winning. There was someone who truly thought they could get away with anything. In fact, Flinn was *banking* on no one being stupid enough to try and track him down.

Well, as Sarah had repeatedly observed, Steve had just enough of an ornery streak in him to try and prove Flinn wrong. They were going to track this pirate down and find the lair that no one else could find. They were going to figure out why Flinn had chosen to cross the great sea when he did, and then they were going to use that information to capture him once and for all.

The only problem was, he had no idea how they were going to pull any of it off.

Right about then, Steve let out a low whistle. Something had just walked into his line of sight and … better make that a couple of somethings … he had promptly lost his train of thought. He stared at the creature and remembered what Pedr had said about them. Above the waist, they looked human—except for the horns—but below the waist? That was another story.

It had to be one of the fim, Steve decided, the creature that looked like a cross between a man and a goat. With the exception of the tightly spiraled horns protruding from their foreheads, the fim could easily pass for a human. Provided they were standing behind a counter.

Nearly a dozen of the sprightly fellows skipped merrily down one of the winding roads. They could hear laughter, friendly banter, and the occasional greetings as they passed other villagers. This was a town where both humans and fim lived peacefully together. In fact, they watched a small band of fim, near the bottom streets of the town, join up with a similarly sized group of humans, and together, entered the nearest tavern.

"It makes my heart glad to see humans and satyrs living together," Sarah sighed wistfully.

"And why wouldn't we?" a new voice curiously asked.

Steve, Sarah, Pheron, Darius, Gareth, and Pedr all whirled around. A small, middle-aged fim was standing behind them, clasping his thin hands behind his back. He was wearing a dark blue tunic, had a short, dark brown beard, and a full head of equally short brown hair. The fim was even wearing a pair of golden spectacles and was peering at them as though they were the ones who were out of place. The fim took a few steps toward them, leaned close, and sniffed the air. He slowly walked around the six of them, stopping periodically to sample the air. As he neared Steve, his eyes widened and he cocked his head.

"You smell like fire, my good sir. Why would that be?"

Steve shot his wife a nervous look.

"Umm ... are you friendly?"

The fim stared incredulously at them for a few moments before throwing back his head and letting out an enormous bellow of laughter.

"Am I friendly? Am *I* friendly? What a silly thing to ask, my good man. Why, of course I am! I am Titus, professional reveler, master of merrymaking, and expert consumer of ale. As a matter of fact, I am headed to my favorite tavern now. Although, if the truth were to be told, any open tavern is my favorite. You must join me for a drink! I insist!"

"You don't even know us," Steve protested, amused by this turn of events, "and you're inviting us to join you for a drink?"

"And why not? Drinking is never meant to be done alone. Besides, I appreciate all my human brothers. And sisters. No offense, milady."

Titus bowed as he looked at Sarah. Sarah looked imploringly at Pedr and inclined her head toward the half man half goat creature. Pedr nodded and stepped forth.

"Good morning," the young pirate began. "We're travelers, hailing all the way from..."

"Morning?" Titus sputtered good-naturedly. "Good morning, you say?" The fim's curly head angled up to study the sky. "It's nowhere near morning, young lad. It's well past midday. Do you even know what time it is?"

"Erm, do you?" Pedr hesitantly asked.

The fim stared at the young pirate for a few moments before bursting out in laughter. The half man creature laughed so hard that tears were running down his cheeks. He slapped a friendly hand on Pedr's back.

"Of *course,* I do! It's time for a drink! I'm parched! Now, will we be needin' a table for seven or will you doom me to an afternoon of boredom and solitude?"

"I'm not sure that's a good idea," Steve hesitantly began. "You see, we're…"

"Not from around here," Titus interrupted, offering all of them a wide smile. "I can tell. Now, let's try again, shall we? Would you like to accompany me to my favorite tavern and have a friendly drink or would you like me to alert the Magistrate and tell him I've discovered a group of people who are clearly not from around here? I'm sure he'd be more than happy to hear what I have to say. So, what will it be?"

Steve clapped his hands together and gave the strange being the friendliest smile he could come up with.

"You know what? I think we could all use something to drink. Who knows, Titus? Maybe we could even persuade you to help us out."

Titus suddenly appeared on Steve's right and squeezed past Pheron. The fim draped an arm around each of their shoulders, only it was a stretch for the poor creature. Titus couldn't have been more than five-foot-three, where Steve and Pheron were over six feet tall.

"My friends, if you buy, then I'll personally tell you where my brothers hide their gold."

Pheron's eyebrows shot up. "You've got yourself a deal. The first round is on me. Or the crown," the captain quietly added, eliciting a giggle from Sarah. "'Speak for the Crown', he said. Well, I plan on drinking."

"Drinking for the Crown," Darius chortled.

"But, I'm not old enough to drink," Gareth protested

quietly to Sarah. "And ale tastes awful. Why would I want to drink that?"

Sarah leaned forward and tapped Gareth on the shoulder, "I couldn't agree more. It tastes terrible."

Pheron grinned at the young wizard, "And how would you know that?"

Gareth stared at the floor. "Ummm…"

"It's no problem," Pheron assured the teen. "I'll do the drinking for the both of us."

Ten minutes later, the seven of them were sitting down inside one of the many taverns lining the busy hillside street. Steve and Pheron had decided to push two tables together after noticing the tavern was nearly deserted.

"What can you tell us about this village?" Pheron asked, as soon as they were all seated. "Are the villagers predominantly farmers? Craftsman? Fishermen?"

"Fishermen?" Titus repeated, puzzled. "There's nowhere to fish around these parts. The Endless Sea is a seven-day journey west, and even then, I'm told the fishing isn't that good. The fish are tiny, tasteless, and are practically impossible to catch. Oh! Dear me! Were you referring to the river? My apologies. However, no one really makes a living fishing the river."

"You have a river running through town and no one fishes it?" Darius asked, bewildered. "What do you use it for? Bathing?"

"The river is how we ship our goods to the entire Seven Kingdoms. You can't see it from here, I'm sorry to say. The eastern side of town, namely the oldest part of the village, was built around that river. That was the birthplace of our fair village."

"Does it have a name?" Darius asked.

"The village? Of course, it does. Miron."

Darius shook his head. "No. What I meant was, does the river have a name?"

The fim nodded. "Oh. Of course."

Gareth blinked his eyes a few times and eyed the others. He hesitantly held up a hand.

"Did he already say it and I missed it, or had I dozed off

and didn't know it?"

Titus turned to Gareth and held out a hand, as though they were meeting for the first time.

"I'm sorry. I didn't see you there. What is your name, young man?"

"Gareth. We've already met. Earlier? Outside the village? Do you remember?"

"Nonsense. I would've remembered such a strong face, wouldn't I? Fear not, my young friend. It's always fun to make new friends, don't you think?"

Gareth frowned, studying the fim's face, "Out of curiosity, how many of my companions do you remember?"

Titus turned and gave a visible start. "More new friends! How spectacular! Would you care to join me for a drink?"

"I'm getting a strong feeling of déjà vu right about now," Steve quietly murmured, nudging Sarah on her shoulder. "How about you?"

Titus noticed Sarah standing quietly near her husband and his eyes lit up with recognition. "Ah! Miss Sarah! It's so nice to see you again!"

"Hello, Titus," Sarah hesitantly began. "It's nice to see you, too. Again."

Titus grinned and spread his arms wide, intent on throwing them around Sarah and encompassing her in a huge bear hug. Frowning, Steve stepped in front of his wife and stared down at the fim. Much to Steve's chagrin, he noticed Titus' eyes were closed. Still thinking he was going to be embracing Sarah, Titus wrapped his arms around Steve's waist and held on tight.

"Okay, you horny little twit, I think that's far enough."

"Eh?" Titus broke away and glanced up at Steve with surprised eyes. "Oh, I'm terribly sorry. I thought you were someone else. In fact, I see her now. If you'll excuse me."

The fim tried again to embrace Sarah. He lined her up in his sights, closed his eyes, and lunged forward again. Sarah quickly checked the surrounding environment, saw that no one was watching, and teleported herself out of harm's way. At the same time, Steve felt himself being teleported, only to appear once more in the path of the over-affectionate fim.

"What can I do to him?" Steve asked, after the fim had once more encompassed him in a hug. He looked over at Sarah, who was giggling. "This isn't funny. I was trying to protect you, remember?"

"There's something odd going on here," Pheron observed. "He was perfectly coherent earlier. Now he's forgotten who we are?"

"But not Sarah," Steve added.

He looked down at the satyr and suddenly grinned. An idea had just formed. Steve ordered his jhorun to release a quick burst of heat all throughout his body. As expected, Titus released him, as though the satyr had suddenly discovered he had been holding a red-hot bar of steel. The fim suddenly leaned close, sniffed, and then regarded Steve with a quizzical expression.

"You smell like fire and soot."

"You said that to me already," Steve reminded the fim. "Earlier? When we were all outside?"

"Did I now? How peculiar. I don't remember any of that."

About to take a gulp of his ale, Pheron suddenly sniffed the contents. His nose wrinkled. He caught Darius' arm as the young lieutenant also prepared to sample the ale and shook his head no.

"What kind of ale did you say this was?" Pheron asked.

"The best," Titus belched, taking another deep draught of ale. "I need another!"

"Perhaps something else?" Steve idly asked. He had caught the look of alarm from Pheron after the tall captain had been ready to take a drink from his tankard.

"Do they have wine here?" Sarah asked. "I'd love a glass of Zinfandel, but in case they don't have that, any type of red wine will do."

Titus suddenly squealed with delight and rounded on Sarah. "Wine? Do you love wine? How wonderful! Miron is known for its wine, milady! Allow me to fetch you a bottle."

"What's going on?" Steve whispered, the moment the fim left for the bar. "Why did he forget us? Is there something in the ale?"

"There's either something in the ale or else the ale itself has that effect on fim. Pedr, do you have any idea what happened to Titus?"

Pedr nodded and shrugged. "Fim could never hold their ale. One drink is all it takes to get them drunk."

"Is it only ale or will wine have the same effect?" Steve asked, watching Titus argue with the barkeep.

"Beer, ale, wine, it doesn't matter. If it has alcohol in it, it has the same effect."

Steve shook his head. "Let me venture a guess. This happens to all fim, doesn't it?"

Pedr nodded. "Aye. They love their ale, no doubt about it. However, there's never any harm done, and the fim have plenty of gold, so it's never a problem."

"So, they're lousy drunks," Sarah decided. "That's just great. Hon? Would you … I mean, could you…"

"…make sure he keeps his distance?" Steve finished for her. He nodded. "Absolutely."

Titus returned to their tables and plunked not one, or two, but three bottles of wine down. He gave them all a victorious grin and indicated the bottles. He grabbed the closest, bit down on the cork, and pulled it out with his teeth. Instead of spitting the cork out, Titus elected to chew on it, like a stick of chewing gum.

"Now, who would like some?" The fim turned to Sarah and held the bottle up questioningly. "Milady? You said you'd like some wine? You'll find none finer than these!"

"Um, er, is Miron known for its wines?" Steve hesitantly asked.

Titus nodded. He grabbed the closest tankard and discarded the last dregs of ale onto the ground, like unwanted trash. He then filled it full to the brim—emptying nearly half the bottle—and slid it over to Sarah.

"Are you a connoisseur of wine?" Sarah asked as she eyed the dark ruby liquid swirling about in her tankard. "What do you know about this one?"

Titus opened his mouth to answer and hesitated. Still holding the bottle, he rotated it until a label appeared. He squinted at the neat scrawl on the label before shrugging.

"All wines are good here. My friends, everyone knows this is where you come for wine. If there were a land called Bliss, then this would be it."

"Do you make wine here?" Pheron asked.

Titus nodded proudly, "Of course. It's what we fim are known for. We make the kingdom's finest wines, using fruit cultivated by our own hands."

"Is that what you do, Titus?" Sarah asked. "Are you a winemaker?"

"Oh, heavens no," the fim exclaimed, pushing his glasses up to the bridge of his nose. "I find work to be too tedious. I avoid it whenever I can."

"Of course, you do," Steve mumbled. Sarah overheard and gave him a conspiratorial wink.

"So, if this village is known for its wine," Sarah began as she hesitantly took a sip. Her eyes bulged, her nose crinkled, and when she was sure Titus wasn't watching, she spat the wine onto the ground.

Both Lentarian soldiers were grinning at her. Pheron took a cautious sip from the mug Titus had poured for him. Grinning, and smacking his lips, he drained half of his mug in one sitting.

"It's quite tasty," the captain decided. He looked at Sarah and shrugged. "It might be a little stronger than you're used to."

"A little bit?" Sarah wheezed. Her eyes were watering. "That's the understatement of the century."

Pheron took a second draught and polished off the remaining wine. He set the empty tankard on the table and smiled when Sarah quickly took his empty tankard and replaced it with her full one. She held the empty mug in her hands to make sure that there wouldn't be any chance Titus would refill it. Then she watched Gareth slowly slide his tankard over to Darius, who readily accepted it.

"Fim wine has always been strong," Titus exclaimed, overhearing parts of the conversation. "What could be better? We produce bottles of wine that will get you intoxicated in half the time as regular wine. That is efficiency at its finest. Do you need a refill, milady?"

Sarah shook her head no, "I've still got plenty. Thanks."

"So, you're telling us fim wine is stronger?" Steve slowly asked. "Is that a good thing?"

Titus nodded. "Of course. Everyone wants our wine. It's what we use to barter with. Neighboring villages supply us with everything we need, provided we keep them stocked with wine."

"How many neighboring villages are there?" Darius asked.

Pheron grunted with approval as he polished off his second mug of fim-created wine. Titus paused with his tankard halfway to his mouth. He cocked his head as he thought.

"Oh, let's see. There's Argoth to the north. Haradur is south, but is a journey that would take many days. Then there's…"

"We could really use that map," Pheron reminded their host. "Do you think you could get your hands on one for us?"

"A map?" Titus repeated, fixing the tall human with a stare. The fim's eyes appeared unfocused. "You want a map? That's easy."

Titus trailed off as he leaned back in his chair. The problem, Steve noted, was that the poor fellow continued to tip backwards. His chair fell over with a loud crash. His resonating snores echoed noisily inside the tavern.

"Hey! Hey, you lot!"

The six companions sitting at the two joined tables looked over. The barkeep was waving an arm at them. Or, more specifically, at Titus.

"Just tip him back up. Happens to 'im all the bleedin' time."

"Do you know him?" Steve asked as he got to his feet. He nodded at Pheron. "How often does this happen?"

"Ev'ry time he comes in," the barkeep answered. "Am surprised. He usually passes out long before this. Must be a record."

Pheron and Steve gently lifted the snoring satyr's chair until it was sitting upright once more. Titus' head lolled forward. The fim slumped over. His head was due to make a hard landing at the table when, inexplicably, his head stopped several inches before contact. Surprised, Steve looked over at Sarah. Her eyes were narrowed.

A large metal bucket of water was unceremoniously plopped down on their table. The barkeep appeared by Titus' side. He gripped the bucket, eyed the swirling water within, and started lifting. Sarah's eyes widened. She hastily lowered the fim's head until it was resting on the table then quickly scooted her chair back.

The bucket was upended over Titus' head. Water sloshed down over the table, effectively clearing it of any glasses and mugs. The fim squealed with surprise, leapt backward out of his chair, and stared suspiciously at the people staring back at him. Water continued to drip off his soaked tunic as the satyr stared from face to face.

"In the name of all that is good and sacred, what did you do that for?"

"You dozed off," Steve told the fim. "You started snoring in the middle of our conversation."

"I did? What were we talking about?"

"We were talking about how to get a map."

"Oh, yes. A map." Titus scratched the back of his head. "Why, exactly? What do you need a map for?"

"We're going in circles," Steve quietly grumbled as he looked at Sarah.

"We'd like to learn the lay of the land," Sarah told the fim and she placed a reassuring hand on her husband's.

"I could hit him with a truth spell," Gareth softly suggested. He reached into a pocket to pull out a leather pouch. He held it up and showed Sarah. "I've got my bag of spells, so to speak. I never leave home without it."

Sarah shook her head, held a finger to her lips, and gently pushed Gareth's arm under the table, where no one could see what he was holding.

"Are you feeling better?" Steve asked the fim as Titus shook himself off, like a dog coming out of a pool of water.

"I'm sober now," Titus complained as he held his head with his hands. "I wouldn't wish that experience on anyone. Barkeep, another round!"

Steve caught the barkeep's eye and shook his head. The owner of the bar nodded sagely. A pitcher of water was filled and placed on their table.

"This must be the weakest ale I've ever tasted," Titus grumbled, as soon as Steve poured him a glass.

"Give it some time," Sarah assured him. "I'm pretty sure this ale takes a while to kick in."

Titus groaned and sat back in his chair. He eyed the six of them and shook his head.

"So, where are you six from? I know you're not from around here. Not only can I smell ash and soot on you, my good fellow," Titus said, pointing at Steve, "but I also smell … I smell … something. I don't know what it is. There are a number of scents about your person that I cannot identify. Whether or not that is a good thing, I haven't decided."

Pheron glanced once at Steve and looked around the mostly deserted bar. A few other patrons had come in since they had, but not one of them had given them the slightest bit of attention. Several noisy conversations kept steadily increasing in volume as each person tried to make themselves heard over the others. Steve shrugged. They wouldn't have to worry about being overheard in here.

Pheron nodded. He mouthed *more water* to the barkeep and held up the empty pitcher. As soon as Titus' tankard was full, Sarah leaned forward to rest her elbows on the badly scarred table and took a deep breath.

"We're travelers. We come from, er, we come from the … Eastern Kingdom. Yes, that's right. The Eastern Kingdom. My husband and I, along with our, uh, sons, Gareth and Pedr, and hmm, my cousin, Darius, are simply exploring the kingdom. We decided to tour the countryside since we were tired of hearing inaccurate information about this wonderful place and wanted to see it for ourselves."

"And what about your large friend here?" Titus mischievously asked, turning to Pheron. "What about *him*? What familial relationship would you have me believe him to be? Your father?"

"Her father?" Pheron sputtered. He turned to Steve with a less than enthusiastic smile on his face. "Please. I don't look that old, do I? Why couldn't I be a cousin?"

Steve grinned and elected to stay quiet. Pheron grunted irritably and drained his tankard. Titus leaned forward to fix Sarah with a stare.

"Do humor me, milady, and tell me why you're really here. You cannot expect me to believe your silly story about wanting to explore the West. No one wants to explore out here 'cause everything there is to see has all been thoroughly charted before."

"What do you know of Captain Flinn?" Steve suddenly asked, drawing a gasp of alarm from Sarah.

Titus' eyes narrowed and his face hardened. "I know he's not someone to be reckoned with. No one does. Do not tangle with the Pirates of Perz, my friend. To do so would seal your fate."

"You asked why we're here," Steve said, shrugging. "He's why."

"What can you tell us about him?" Sarah asked.

Titus ignored Sarah's question and, instead, stared at Steve.

"What business could you possibly have with Captain Flinn?"

"Only that we need to know more about him. What can you tell us?"

Titus sighed, leaned back in his chair, and reached for his tankard. Looking down into its contents, he frowned. He poured a little of the liquid into a cupped hand.

"If I didn't know any better, I'd say this was water."

"It's your imagination," Steve assured the fim. "Now, what were you saying about Flinn?"

"Flinn is the captain of the *Emberbrand*," Titus wistfully began. "That ship has been the scourge of the Seven Kingdoms for years. No one has ever found him. Have you seen him?"

Steve nodded. "You could say that."

"How close were you?"

Steve shrugged. "Pretty close."

"Did you know he's a Wind Talker?"

Steve nodded. "If that means he can control the winds,

then yes. I'm aware."

"That is the secret to his success," the fim told him, dropping his voice to a confidential whisper.

"Where does he live?" Sarah asked. "Do you know?"

Titus shook his head. "No, only that he lives on a private island. I should also say the location of that island is no mystery. It's hidden within the Perz Archipelagos. Do you have any idea how many islands we are talking about?"

Steve shrugged. "No. Do you?"

"No one does," Titus argued. "That's the point. On top of which, Captain Flinn is way too clever to leave his island unprotected. You can rest assured he has placed fiendishly clever devices all over the island, protecting what's his."

Steve looked at Pedr.

"That's what you meant when you said Byway, wasn't it?"

Pedr nodded. Titus shook himself, as though he had been doused with water again, and snatched up his tankard. He took several large swallows before he speculatively eyed the contents once more.

"By all the Gods, this is water. It must be. Why in the world would someone consume water when wine is readily available? Bah. Wretched stuff. Now, where was I? Oh, yes. We were talking about the abominable Captain Flinn. Rest assured, my friends. You needn't worry about him. Thankfully, the *Emberbrand* and her crew retired from piracy years ago. No one has seen him in near five years. Leave the captain in peace and, hopefully, he'll do the same for you."

Sarah stiffened and sat up straight as a board.

"Wait. You said Flinn is retired?"

Titus nodded. "Aye. For several years now. What of it?"

"What if he's not?" Steve asked. "What would cause him to come out of retirement?"

"Your words trouble me, my friend," Titus admitted. "Captain Flinn is back at the helm of the *Emberbrand*? What dreadful news. Has he found something? Has he finally found a way?"

"Has he found something?" Steve repeated. "Clarify that, pal. What do you mean?"

"Captain Flinn wants the Perz Archipelagos to be

recognized as the next kingdom."

"Whatever for?" Pheron asked.

The fim shrugged. "What else? More power. As you may have imagined, the Council of Elders rejected his proposal. In fact, they said they'd never approve such an outlandish request. Can you imagine? If an eighth kingdom were to be created, as Captain Flinn suggests, then it would throw the entire land into chaos."

Titus started to bring his tankard up to his lips when he sniffed disdainfully at the liquid within and returned the mug to the table.

"How bad would it be if Flinn were to somehow force the Council's hand?" Pheron asked. "What if Flinn *did* find a way to get what he wanted? What would happen?"

"The Seven Kingdoms would erupt in war," Titus sadly answered. "Could you just imagine what type of message that would send to the people? You know very well that Captain Flinn would appoint himself as Lord Magistrate over the eighth kingdom. Pirates with power. Why, the very notion scares me senseless."

"Because Steve can be just as ornery as Flinn," Sarah told the speechless fim, "Let's put that aside for now. Yes, we've met the captain. Yes, we've fought with the captain. He's got some formidable power at his disposal, no doubt about it. You want to know what we're doing here, Titus? We're trying to find a way to stop him. We need to know what he's doing and what he's looking for. Will you help us?"

Titus looked down at his tankard, groaned, and held it out to Sarah. "You will have my cooperation if—and only if—you fill this with something besides water. Something *good.* Do that for me and then aye, I will help you. I have no love for piracy, either."

Pheron looked pointedly at Darius, who nodded and rose to his feet. He retrieved Titus' mug and headed for the bar.

"Shouldn't we inform the Magistrate about our suspicions?" Pheron pointedly asked.

Titus cast a nervous glance around the tavern. "Captain Flinn has spies everywhere. They could be listening to us right now."

"This needs to stay quiet," Steve told the fim. "And this needs to stay between us, for reasons we can't disclose at the moment. So, zip your lip about it, pal."

"I have a question," Gareth said, breaking the silence while everyone waited for Titus' mug to be filled. "Something managed to pull this captain fellow out of hiding. I wonder if I could come up with something that might tell us what that was?"

"Could you?" Sarah asked as she turned to the wizard. "Seriously? That'd be incredibly helpful."

Gareth shrugged. "It couldn't hurt to try, right?"

"Hello, I don't think we've met."

Everyone turned to Titus. He was holding an arm out to Gareth. Steve shared a look with Sarah.

"I wonder if they have coffee over here. That'd sober him up."

"Titus has agreed to help us," Sarah argued. "If he wants to drink himself silly, let him. As long as he's on our side, I'm inclined to let him."

Darius returned to the table and held the mug out to Titus, who cautiously accepted. A wide smile appeared on his face as he warily sniffed the contents. He eagerly gulped down the ale, belched loudly, and eyed the six of them at the table.

"If he forgets any of us again," Sarah began, "then I'll personally drop him in the nearest body of water."

"What did you give him?" Steve asked.

Darius shrugged. "I left it up to the barkeep. Clearly, he knows Titus here. Perhaps I should have asked the barkeep to give him something that wasn't as strong?"

"There's nothing to be done now," Pheron observed. "Mister Titus? Are you still with us?"

Titus hiccupped, "Of course. I have nowhere else to be, my fine fellow. What was your name again?"

Steve groaned.

"Titus. Focus. That's Pheron. You've met him before. Several times, in fact. Gareth, maybe you should try to come up with something. If we're to keep Titus cooperating with us, then we're going to need a way to keep him coherent."

"I've written spells to make people forget things," Gareth chuckled, "but never one to keep the memories inside someone's head. This'll be a first for me. I'll get on it."

"Are you a Spellcaster, young master?" Titus enthusiastically asked.

Gareth shrugged. "I can hold my own."

"We need that map," Pheron reiterated as he looked at the fim. "The success of this mission is critical. Can you get us one? As detailed as possible, please."

"What's in it for me?" Titus asked.

Pheron pointed at the bar. He held up a leather pouch and jingled it enticingly in front of the fim.

"Get us what you need and I'll put twenty gold pieces down in your name so you'll be able to drink to your heart's content."

Titus' eyes widened appreciably.

"Be back here in less than ten minutes and I'll increase that to 50 gold pieces," Pheron added, opening his money pouch to count the coins inside.

"Well, why didn't you say so before? We have a deal!"

The fim pushed away from the table and *sprinted* out the door.

"We could have saved ourselves a whole lot of time if we had just done that to start with," Sarah commented.

Steve shrugged. "Live and learn. The next time we have to deal with one of them, then we'll know what to do."

"Are we to search for Perz, then?" Darius eagerly asked.

Pheron shook his head, "We will save that for another trip. I think it's clear that we need adequate time to plan. It'll be too dangerous to attempt without knowing what we're up against."

"You might want to reconsider that," Pedr said.

As one, everyone at the table turned to look at the young pirate.

"While I do not know what has caused the captain to end his retirement, I can tell you that he's devoting all his resources to this mission. I overheard him say that, at the moment, there's no one left on his island."

"How did you come by this information?" Pheron

immediately asked. His voice had dropped and had become firm. "Tell us everything."

"There isn't much to tell," Pedr admitted. "I overheard Captain Flinn tell the quartermaster that, once the *Emberbrand* had put to sea, all of his safeguards had been activated. Even the servants had been ordered to leave, not to return until the *Emberbrand* did. Granted, I don't know the captain that well, but from what I hear, he never orders his servants away."

"Where are these servants now?" Steve eagerly asked.

"The only thing I know about them is that they live elsewhere on the Perz Archipelagos. I have no idea where."

"We need to find one of these servants," Gareth quietly mused. "If we do, I can make him talk. I may not have my spell book with me, but I can certainly make a veracity charm without it."

"Then that's our plan," Steve said, nodding his head. "We find one of these servants and get him, or her, to talk."

"I have heard of the captain talking about someone named Stockley," Pedr added. "I think he might be a personal servant of his. If that's true, I'd make him your target. Chances are, he'd be the best person to ask about what the captain is up to."

"I wonder where this Stockley is now," Steve wondered aloud.

Pedr shrugged helplessly, "I honestly have no idea. I've never been to the captain's private island. Not many have, from what I hear. I always assumed Stockley lived there on the island with him."

"And yet Flinn sent him away," Steve mused thoughtfully. "That would suggest that he knew he was going to be gone for a long time. More than likely, he sent this Stockley person home."

"To somewhere on the archipelagos," Sarah added with a sigh. "That doesn't help us much."

"Sure, it does," Steve disagreed. "I'd say we found our stool pigeon. We just have to…"

Steve?

Whoa! Pryllan? Is that you?"

Hardly. It's Pravara.

Oh. Sorry. You two sounded alike. Wow, I didn't think you'd be able to reach me all the way out here.

Where are you?

We're in the Seven Kingdoms.

I'm not familiar with that name.

It's…

Steve? Can we table that for another time? Wherever you are, you must come to me now.

What? Why? What's the matter?

I have picked up the trail of the thieving humans.

You found Captain Flinn? That's fantastic, Pravara! Nicely done! Where is he?

They are near the human settlement of Verdayn.

What? That doesn't make any sense. That would suggest that they've backtracked and are now headed back toward you. I would've thought they'd want to keep as far away as possible from you dragons.

I believe they are looking for something.

What? Can you tell?

I do not know what they search for. Steve, if you choose not to intercept them, then I will. I do not know how long they will remain in this area, but as soon as my father receives word from Mikal, he will order the attack.

You're waiting on word from Mikal? For what?

No wyverian will attack a human, regardless of the circumstances, unless the Dragon Lord notifies— and receives permission—from the human king. At the present moment, Mikal holds that position. Those are my father's orders.

Understood. We're heading back.

I would hurry if I were you. I do not know what they were doing, but whatever it was, they appear to have finished.

"Crap," Steve softly swore. "Sarah, we need to get back."

Their entire party looked surprised. Pheron, detecting the note of alarm on Steve's face, leapt to his feet, prompting Darius to do the same. Sarah slowly stood up.

"What is it? What's happened?"

"That was Pravara. She's found Flinn." He hurriedly summed up what Pravara had told him. "Whatever they're looking for, we need to find it first, especially since it sounds like the dragons are itching to take them out."

"Oh, that can't be good," Sarah groaned. "We need to stop them before they're discovered."

Pheron nodded. "Agreed."

Steve held up a hand, "Who? The dragons or the pirates?"

"Both," Sarah answered.

At that moment, Titus returned, holding a tightly rolled scroll. He held it up triumphantly over his head and trotted back to their table, his sides heaving from exertion.

"A map of the Seven Kingdoms, as requested. Now, have you started my tab yet?"

Chapter 10 — Round Two

But I wanted to stay behind! I wouldn't have been any trouble. I told you before, you can trust me. You can all trust me. I don't want to be a pirate anymore."

"Your position has been duly noted," Pheron told the young *former* pirate. "However, I still cannot allow you to run amuck in your homeland, not when you know all the details of our operation." When Pedr began to protest, the captain laid a friendly arm on his shoulder. "Look. No one appreciates your input more than I. Your insight has been invaluable. However, until we can figure out what Captain Flinn is up to, we continue to need your help. Do you understand?"

Pedr nodded miserably.

"I'll return you home just as soon as all of this is over and done with," Sarah promised. "No boat rides necessary. Now that I've been over there, I can drop you directly in Miron, if you'd like."

"Miron is not my home," Pedr mumbled, rubbing his eyes.

"But it's across the sea," Steve pointed out, growing irritated. "Look, kid. You came to this country uninvited. Your companions are wreaking havoc throughout the countryside. At the moment, you have gained a favorable foothold with the Lentarian king. Don't blow it. Continue to help us out and we'll do the same, agreed?"

Pedr sighed. "Very well. Where are we now?"

Steve pointed at the large structure directly behind them. "That's the castle. We're back in R'Tal, the capital. You've been here before, remember?"

"I still find it difficult to believe that you can transport us over that great of a distance," Pedr said as he turned back to Sarah. "You make traversing the Endless Sea something as trivial as snapping your fingers. Your gift is truly remarkable. I would love to have an ability that was one-tenth as strong as yours."

"You and everybody else," Steve laughed. His chuckle died off as he looked at his wife. "You look beat. Do you need another mimet?"

"You can keep charging up my jhorun as much as you'd like," Sarah said, as she yawned. "It doesn't do anything about restoring my physical energy. I feel like I've been run over by a steam roller."

"We'll go easy on you," Steve promised. "Can you handle another jump or two? We need to get to Verdayn. Otherwise, I'll have to call for some wyverian assistance."

Sarah took the nine-sided smoke-colored crystal disk Steve was holding out to her. She replenished her jhorun, stretched her back, and handed the spent disk back. After a few moments, she nodded her head.

"I'm not out of it yet. There are a few jumps still left in me. Now, who is going to Verdayn?"

"I hate to say this," Steve began, before anyone could respond, "but the fewer the better."

Captain Pheron stepped forward, "I'd like to go, Lady Sarah."

Darius mimicked him, "And I, Lady Sarah."

Husband and wife looked over at Gareth.

"Oh, I plan on going, but I can get there myself."

Steve clapped a hand on the young wizard's back.

"Good man, Gareth. We'll see you up there, okay? Let's meet up at the Constable's office."

"I'll be waiting," Gareth assured him.

The four of them watched as Gareth drew an imaginary symbol in the air, chanted a few lines of verse, and then vanished from sight. Sarah nudged Steve on the shoulder and gave him a coy smile.

"Admit it. You like him."

"I definitely like him better than the first time we met," Steve admitted. "He's growing on me."

Sarah held her arm out. "Okay, everyone. We're now boarding the Verdayn Express at Gate 1. Whoever's going with me, grab on."

Pheron and Darius laid their hands on top of hers. Steve leaned in and slapped his hand over Darius.' Pedr approached and carefully laid his hand on top of everyone else's. Steve then eyed his wife and nodded their readiness.

The hustle and bustle of the castle was replaced by a scene of quiet tranquility. Tall, majestic pine trees stretched nearly a hundred feet into the air. A few chirps from unseen birds and the soft buzzing of insects were the only things they could hear. Looking about, they could see a quiet community nestled amongst the trunks of hundreds of trees. A cobblestone road snaked through the trees, connecting the various buildings they could see together. Three-hundred feet away the street joined a second, and then a third, before branching off in different directions.

Steve inhaled loudly and grinned. "Man, I love that smell."

"What smell?" Darius asked.

"Trees. Pine needles. Fresh, open air. I wouldn't trade it for anything."

"You make it sound as though clean air is a scarcity in your home world," Pheron observed.

"Believe it or not, it can be," Sarah added. "Thankfully, our home, er, village is located in a forest, much like this one. I think that's why Steve and I love Verdayn so much. It reminds us of Coeur d'Alene."

The sound of a door opening caused the five of them

to turn around. Gareth emerged from the building directly behind them, which happened to be the Constable's office. He sauntered down the steps and nodded at them.

"It is very pretty here," Gareth agreed, having overheard Steve's comment. "I grew up around here. This is my home village."

"You're lucky," Pedr told the teenager. "I grew up in Aarszan. There are very few trees there. The only scarcity there would be the greenery."

"Where is Aarszan located?" Sarah asked. "Which kingdom was it, Southern?"

"Aye. My village is located on the southern shore of the Southern Kingdom."

"Convenient," Steve mused. "Although, one would think your home village would be swimming in trees and grass if it were that close to the sea."

"Shush," Sarah said, holding a finger to her lips.

"Where are we going now?" Darius asked. "Where are the pirates?"

"Good question," Steve said. "Just a second. I'll ask."

Pravara?

Steve?

Yes. It's me. We're in Verdayn. Where are you?

At the southern tip of our valley. The pirates, as your companion called them, are just inside the forest. I can see them peering intently out at the valley floor.

Can I borrow your eyes? I need to see where you're at.

Of course. I just opened my senses. Can you see anything?

Yep. You're airborne, aren't you? Jeez. How high are you?

High enough where I haven't been observed.

Look down. I can't quite tell where ... wait. Yeah, okay. I know what you're looking at. I should've known. Flinn and his merry men are in the same place we were when we first laid eyes on the valley. They'll be easy enough to spot. I wonder what the hell they're up to.

Isn't it obvious? I believe they're looking for a dwarf door.

What? Are you sure?

Why else would they risk returning to our valley?

We're on our way.

"Get us to the valley," Steve instructed as soon as he opened his eyes. "Flinn and his gang are just inside the trees, looking north, toward Lake Raehón. Pravara thinks they're looking for a dwarf door."

"What in the world is going on?" Sarah demanded, bewildered. "How do these people even know the dwarves are up there, let alone where to find them? There's definitely something we're missing here."

Steve ignited his hands and quickly extinguished them. "Well, what do you say we go ask them? In person?"

The five companions clasped hands. The forest disappeared, replaced by a scene of a picturesque valley. Mountains ringed the small valley in all directions but the south. Huge, rounded boulders dotted the landscape, as if a giant passed through the area holding a double handful of the stones and spilled some as he wandered through the area.

The five of them quickly ducked behind the closest boulders. Steve peered out from behind his. He glanced over his shoulder at a group of three boulders that were nearly a dozen feet away. One of them, he knew, was the doorway leading down into the dwarven realm.

Ah. I see you now. You just appeared behind one of the large stones, did you not?

Yep. That's me. Do you see the others?

One moment. Aye. I see Lady Sarah behind the boulder to your right, while Gareth and another human male are behind two boulders a dozen feet behind you.

What are the pirates doing now?

They are still watching the area.

Any idea what they're searching for?

Dragons, I presume. They appear to be arguing amongst themselves.

Man, would I love to hear what they're saying.

Just a moment.

I'm sorry, what?

Voices suddenly filled his head, voices which weren't his. One voice stood out among the others. Steve grunted with surprise. Pravara had apparently shared her impressive auditory capabilities with him, too.

"I don't like waiting out here like this," one voice was complaining. "What if we're seen? I never dreamed we'd be back here, Captain."

"Can we not go now?" a second voice asked. "I don't care what the quartermaster says is out there. Nothing is worth being fried to a crisp."

"If Rusty says it's out there, then we'll find it," a third voice grumbled. The first two voices fell silent.

Out on the valley floor, hiding behind one of the huge boulders, Steve's eyes widened with recognition. That last voice, he noted with surprise, was none other than Captain Flinn himself. If he was there, that meant the fang was there, too. It was time to show those thieving pirates that they weren't the only ones who were wielding considerable power.

How many dragons are in the area?

Sixteen.

Yikes. That's a lot. Are they all hidden?

Of course.

Would you please inform them that we're out here, too? I don't want any of them to attack us.

You are well known to us. You and Sarah. Fear not. They would never attack you or your companions. Nevertheless, I did inform them that you were planning on engaging the thieves. You are, aren't you?

Without a doubt. Tell the others to remain hidden, no matter what they see. I want the pirates to come to us.

Your instructions have been relayed. No one will move without your consent.

Nice. I'm really enjoying my phenomenal cosmic power over you guys.

I'm not familiar with that phrase.

Forget it. It was a bad joke. Look. Here they come!

The first pirate appeared at the edge of the forest. It was the same pirate he had faced earlier, the one with the heightened reflexes. Ah. There was Captain Windbag, standing beside Mr. Steroids.

Are they saying anything? I don't see their mouths moving.

No one is talking. They're barely moving. I think

they're ready to … aye. There they go. Be ready.

Steve twisted in place and found Sarah watching him from her position behind the neighboring rock. He held a finger to his lips, pointed south, and mouthed, *they're coming*. Sarah nodded, nudged Pedr, and quietly passed on the message. Steve then caught Gareth's eyes. He frantically pointed back at the pirates. The young wizard nodded. He held up a handful of small stones and nodded his readiness. Curious as to what Gareth was planning on doing with a bunch of pebbles, Steve took a deep breath and readied himself.

Steve, wait!

What? What is it? Pravara, we only have about fifteen seconds before they reach us. Thankfully they're not running too hard.

This isn't Pravara. It's Pryllan.

Oh. Sorry. Damn, you two sound a lot alike.

Several of the invaders have broken off and are now circling west. They are in that strange land contraption. I believe the humans are using the wind to make the craft travel fast.

I thought Flinn was one of the pirates who were running toward us. How could he be in two places at the same time?

Steve? This is Pravara. The one that was giving orders left with several others. Half of their party are headed toward you. The other half is retreating in the strange land ship.

We can handle the pirates, guys. There's nothing to worry about. Pravara, perhaps you should follow Flinn and the others? We need to know…

I am already having them followed.

Kahvel? Is that you? What are you … hold on. Let me deal with these guys first.

The first group of pirates skidded to a halt as Steve and the others appeared. He didn't waste any time. His hands ignited and he blasted a wall of flames straight at the pirates. He grinned as he heard vulgar exclamations. The pirates reversed course.

"Steve! Watch out!"

Gareth's warning had him jerking his head up. The young wizard was pointing frantically to the east. By the time he looked in that direction, nothing was there. Gareth chanted a few lines of some unknown language and then paused, as if he had forgotten the last part of the spell.

Jino seemingly materialized out of thin air. He was brandishing a long, curved knife in either hand and menacingly approached Gareth, who much to his credit, stepped in front of Sarah. However, Gareth suddenly smiled and flung the handful of pebbles into the air. One, thankfully, bounced harmlessly off of Jino's chest.

The pirate scoffed as he watched the small stones fall abruptly to the ground.

"Rocks? You throw little rocks at me? Is that the best you can do?"

Gareth smiled, produced a small clear bottle, and uncorked it. He held it up and spun in place, so that everyone could see what he held.

"And what is *that* supposed to do?" Jino sneered.

Gareth tossed the bottle to Sarah.

"Be ready," he instructed, ignoring Jino.

Then it happened. Jino started to shrink, eliciting a cry of alarm from the pirate. Smaller and smaller he shrank, until he was no bigger than an ordinary grasshopper.

Gareth signaled Sarah and pointed at the bottle.

"Would you do the honors, milady?"

Sarah giggled, "Why, I'd be delighted, good sir."

Jino's tiny form slowly rose off the ground. While the pirate continued to spew high-pitched rants at her, she held the cork in one hand and then placed the open bottle directly below Jino with the other. After a few moments, Sarah carefully allowed Jino's minuscule form to enter the bottle. She tapped the cork back into place and looked thoughtfully at the tiny, enraged figure in his glass prison.

"He's not going to run out of air, is he?" Sarah worriedly asked as she turned to Gareth. "Will he be safe?"

"As long as he's in that bottle, aye. He will be."

Steve watched the rest of the pirates. They had witnessed Jino's capture and were now understandably hesitant. Steve blasted another wall of flames at the group of thieves. Smiling, he watched the band of pirates scatter. Every single one of them, Steve noted with satisfaction, had turned tail and were running as fast as their legs could carry them.

Sarah held out the small bottle as Steve approached.

"Would you hold on to this thing for me? I don't like knowing I'm carrying around another person."

Steve nodded. "Gladly."

He left his hand ignited and reached for the bottle, knowing full well that Jino's eyes had widened and he was now frantically dancing as he tried to get someone—anyone's—attention. Just before contact was made, Steve pulled back his jhorun and allowed his hand to poof out. He brought the bottle up to his face and he eyed the terrified pirate inside his glass prison.

"You might want to remember something about me," Steve casually began. His eyes dropped to his empty left hand. Moments later it ignited. "I don't have to be in physical contact to make something burn. Do you catch my meaning?"

Jino's head nodded frantically.

"Good. Remember that and you might just stay alive. If I so much as get the idea that you're trying to escape, then one of two things are going to happen. Either I'll heat that bottle so damn hot that you're liable to turn into a piece of popcorn, or else I'll turn you over to the dragons. I'm sure they'd love to have you. For dinner."

Jino gasped with alarm. He was mouthing something, but Steve couldn't make anything out. He shrugged and was about to put the bottle in his pocket when he hesitated.

"Maybe I shouldn't. Might be a bit rough on him."

Pheron held out his hand, "Give him here. I will take possession of our prisoner."

The bottle switched hands. Moments later, it was tucked inside a pouch on the captain's belt. If they listened long enough, they could make out tiny, muffled *clinks* as Jino apparently hammered against the glass in frustration.

"Don't worry," Gareth assured Pheron. "I've spelled that bottle against breaking. It could survive a fall from the highest cliff, so it'll most definitely withstand anything that pirate can do in order to break out. The only way out is to remove the cork, and that can happen only if I abolish the containment spell I put in place."

Steve?

Kahvel? Sorry. I got tied up dealing with these guys. Not to worry. We have them on the run. We have even taken a...

Please get to my nest as quickly as possible. I am too far away and won't arrive in time. Hurry!

What's going on?

Pryllan says that the same human who was in the nest before has returned. He is using the wind to travel up the mountain. He'll arrive at the nest in only a matter of moments.

But Pryllan is there! He may be strong but he's no match for her. What would possess him to return to the nest? I know there's no way he's feeling remorseful and is planning on returning the fang.

I believe he seeks leverage against me.

Leverage? With Pryllan? What in the world could he possibly do?

Pylaria. If he gets his hands on my offspring, then he knows he'll have the leverage to pressure me into doing things I ordinarily would never do.

"Pheron, are you and Darius good here? Sarah and I have to go. Like, right *now*."

"What do we...?" Sarah began.

"We're good," Pheron assured him. "Sir Steve, Lady Sarah, go. Return for us when you can."

"Sarah, take us to Pryllan's nest. Hurry!"

Sarah's eyes had widened with alarm. Her mouth opened, then was quickly closed. She grabbed Steve's hand and they both vanished.

Pryllan's nest materialized. The first thing they heard was Pryllan's vicious growl. She was at the mouth of the cave, pacing back and forth in front of the entrance. Then they heard the roar of the wind from outside. It looked as though Pryllan was trying to leave, but the winds were pushing her back inside the nest. Little Pylaria had dropped as low to the ground as she could. Her scared eyes swung around to land on the two of them. The tiny dragon's nose lifted.

"Mother! Humans!"

"I know, young one," Pryllan snapped, as she continued to pace. She spat another fireball, directed farther down the mountain, and then ducked as the relentless wind pushed her fireball back toward her. "I'm trying to keep them from approaching."

"No, mother. There are humans here, in our nest."

Pryllan's head whipped around, fangs bared. She saw who was standing inside her nest and visibly relaxed. She looked back out the mouth of her cave and looked down.

"The human nears. I cannot prevent his approach. I will *not* allow him to take Pylaria!"

"Where's he at, Pryllan?" Steve asked, igniting his hands. "How far away?"

"At his current speed, he will be here in less than twenty seconds."

Go! Get out now! Take Pylaria with you!

Steve visibly jumped as Kahvel's powerful thought spoke in his mind. Pryllan shook her head and had bared her fangs again.

"Kahvel is speaking to Pryllan," Steve quietly relayed. "And he's allowing me to hear."

I am allowing you to hear because I am hoping you will be able to defend my family!

Count on it, my friend. In fact, I have an idea.

"Sarah? Get them out of here! Hurry!"

"What about you?" his wife wanted to know. "I will not leave you defenseless against that pirate."

"I can handle myself," Steve assured her. "Now get out of here! Our twenty seconds are up!"

Sarah slapped a hand on Pryllan's side and then leaned forward to place a hand on the tip of Pylaria's tail. All three vanished. Steve turned to look around the empty cave and noticed that the winds had picked up in strength. He hurriedly ducked behind one of several strange rock formations inside the cave.

Captain Windbag had arrived.

* * *

"Well, well. This is a surprise. And whom do we have here?"

Sheer exhaustion was threatening to close Sarah's eyes. She teetered precariously as she took a step toward Mikal's voice. She knew they were inside the Great Hall, but thanks to that last jump, and the simple fact she had just teleported two dragons with her, she could barely open her eyes more than a crack. She would have stumbled and fallen if not for Pryllan's quick thinking. The huge green dragon whipped her tail around to offer it as support, which Sarah gratefully accepted. She clung to the tail like a life preserver.

"Mikal, look!" a female voice was saying. Sarah couldn't open her eyes, but she knew it was Lissa. "It's a baby dragon! How precious! It's Pryllan. Mikal! Look! It's Lady Sarah! Something's wrong!"

If the throne room wasn't already in chaos with the appearance of two dragons in their midst, it certainly became so now. A mad rush of people descended upon Sarah, all while trying to give Pryllan a wide berth. Pryllan, for the most part, knew the mass of people was trying to aid Sarah, and the one way she could help was by holding as still as possible.

Someone appeared by Sarah's side and gently held her arm.

"Sarah?" Mikal's voice asked. "Are you all right?"

The last of her strength left her. She was able to take a single step before she collapsed. A few moments later she was quietly snoring.

"I believe she is well," Pryllan's strong voice announced, bringing the activity level of the Great Hall to an absolute standstill. "She has overtaxed her jhorun. I believe she just needs to rest."

"What happened?" Mikal wanted to know, growing angry. "Who did this to her? Was it those pirates?"

Pryllan nodded. "Aye. She was trying to protect us. She teleported us from my nest to here. I must apologize. I do believe only Lady Sarah is capable of extracting me from this chamber."

"Why would you want to leave your nest?" Lissa asked. "Aren't you the safest there?"

"The same human who stole the fang in the first place was returning."

"Why?" Mikal demanded.

"It is Kahvel's belief that the pirates wanted to capture Pylaria, in order to win his obedience."

"No wonder she teleported you here," Lissa mused. "Can we get you anything? Are you hungry?"

"I am fine," Pryllan announced, "but perhaps you could bring some water for Pylaria?"

"We're on it," Mikal assured the adult dragon. He motioned a few of the guards over and quickly explained what they needed. "Where's Steve? Is he all right?"

"He chose to remain behind," Pryllan gravely said. "It was a decision I am not happy with."

"Father made us come here," a timid voice added.

"Mikal, Lissa, I'd like to present Pylaria. Little one, these two are the human king and queen of Lentari."

The tiny, golden dragon peeked her head around Pryllan's leg. She eyed the humans and didn't say a word. Pryllan gave her a slight nudge.

"They're friends, Pylaria. You may say hello to them."

"Hello," the tiny dragonlet squeaked. Pylaria immediately whisked her head out of sight and tried to remain concealed behind her mother's body.

"Is there any way we can help Sir Steve?" Lissa asked as she turned to Mikal. "There must be something we can do."

"The best thing we can do right now is allow Sarah to rest. Lissa, would you see to it she's taken to a chamber and not disturbed?"

Lissa nodded. "Of course."

Mikal's face turned grim as he returned his attention to the large green dragon.

"Now, what can you tell me about those pirates?"

* * *

Back inside Pryllan and Kahvel's nest, Steve watched Captain Flinn poking around the nest. The winds had lessened somewhat inside the cave, but outside it sounded like a category 5 hurricane.

The man's arrogance annoyed him greatly. From his

hiding point, Steve watched the captain stride around the cave as though he owned the place. Steve's brow furrowed with annoyance. He was personally looking forward to wiping that smug grin off of Flinn's face.

"Come out, come out wherever you are, dragon. I know you're in here. Somewhere. It pains me to admit it, ye scaly beastie, but I do need your help. I need time to search this valley, and I aim to search this valley without fear of being attacked by other dragons, and I'll be borrowing that young 'un I saw earlier."

Steve's eyes narrowed. If this fool didn't shut up, soon, he was inclined to release every bit of jhorun he had and direct the flames at that smug captain.

"There aren't that many places to hide, dragon. Make it easy on yourself. Come out now and … you?!"

Steve had stepped out and was resting a hip on the rock formation.

"Me. You're looking for a dragon? Well, they're both safe, so you can stop looking."

"What have ye done with them? They could not have slipped away undetected. I was watching this cave the entire time!"

"Yet neither one is here, and I am. What does that tell you?"

The winds returned, swirling this way and that throughout the cave. The roar of the air became so loud that Steve briefly thought he'd rupture an eardrum inside the cave. Then he blinked in amazement as the churning winds appeared to have twisted itself into an actual fist. Not waiting to find out, Steve dropped to his knees and rolled out of the way, just as the Air Fist impacted the rock pillar he had been leaning against.

Cracks formed throughout the pillar, but the rock formation managed to hold its form. The blast of air then twisted around the stone pillar and zeroed in on him again. Once more Steve was forced to dive for cover as the jet of air smashed into the stone surface of the cave.

Steve grunted, rolled to his feet, and ignited both hands. He blasted a super-heated jet of fire straight at Flinn, who sneered and used his own jhorun to blast it harmlessly away. However, Flinn's sneer quickly melted off his face as he saw not one, or two, but three additional fire jets rapidly approaching.

The blasts of fire zoomed around obstacles and abruptly changed course to avoid the air jets intent on snuffing them out. It was Flinn's turn to dance out of the way as he was forced to flee. Sensing he had the upper hand, Steve doubled his efforts. Within moments the entire cave was amass with swirling chasers and blasts of fire. Catching sight of the arrogant captain as he ducked behind a ridge of stone, Steve hurried forward to slap both hands on the nearest rock wall.

Let's heat this sucker up, he ordered his jhorun. *Come on, monkey. It's time to dance!*

Flinn began to bellow with anger. The captain cried out in pain as he inadvertently brushed by a mound of stone and briefly laid a hand down to steady himself. He whipped his hand off the smoldering rocks and glared angrily about the cave.

"That's fairly impressive, Hot Shot. You'd make a fine pirate. I don't suppose ye could be tempted to lead a life of piracy?"

A jet of fire came spiraling out of nowhere and blasted the tri-cornered black hat off of Flinn's head. The red feather, which had been proudly displayed at the top of the hat for years, shriveled and burned.

"Now ye've done it, miscreant," Flinn growled. "That be my favorite hat. You have been a thorn in my side long enough. It's time for ye to feel the full wrath of my power!"

"Get over it, Captain Windbag," Steve sneered. "What do you think you could possibly do to me? Go on. Hit me with your best shot."

The cave trembled as a tremendous gust of wind suddenly appeared. It carried so much debris and miscellaneous detritus within it that the overall shape of the gust could be seen. It writhed and coiled around the cave, looking very much like a living being. It was searching for him. He quickly retrieved several mimets and clutched them tightly in each hand.

"There ye be, ye damn fool."

Steve straightened and looked behind him. Both he and Flinn were now standing in the open, only Steve had his back to the cave entrance. Flinn gave a sudden lunge as the winds intensified and then punched forward, intent on slamming into him with the force of a diesel locomotive.

Having replenished his jhorun only moments before, Steve was ready. He blasted out jets of his own. Fire and Air slammed into each other and were each bounced back to their creators. Flinn was practically knocked off his feet while Steve was startled to see that he was now standing in a raging inferno. Every ounce of fire he could generate was thrown back in his face since Flinn's air jets were of equal strength.

Fortunately, that also meant that Flinn wasn't having much luck, either. He could see the pirate captain gesturing frantically, no doubt ordering his jhorun to try and force him back a few paces. After a few minutes of relentless blasting from either side, Steve finally saw something that made him smile.

Flinn was sweating.

Whether from exertion, or from the ambient temperature, Flinn now had several beads of sweat trickling down his forehead. The pirate captain wasn't making any leeway in this battle, either. No matter how hard either of them tried, neither could gain the upper hand on the other.

Steve?

Kahvel?

Are you well? Where are you?

I'm still in your nest. This jerk is hitting me with everything he's got. Then again, I'm doing the same. I hate to say it, but it looks as though we might be evenly matched. Neither one of us are having much luck with the other.

I have dispatched every dragon in the area. They will come to your aid. The first should be arriving in just a few moments.

I really hate to say this, my friend, but you'd better hurry. I'm doing my damnedest to gain the advantage, but the truth is, I'm throwing everything I've got at him and it isn't doing a damn bit of good.

And my nest?

Umm, anything that isn't fireproof is gonna be a total goner. I'm sorry.

I was referring to my treasure.

Oh. I know he hasn't touched it because I haven't let him out of my sight.

Good.

If only I could… Whoa! Crap! Crapcrapcrap!

What is it? Are you in danger?

If you consider falling to my death dangerous, then yeah. I'm in danger. Damn! I let my guard down. How he knew to hit me the moment I wasn't watching is beyond me. Man, this isn't good!

I can see you. I am too far away to render assistance.

I thought there was supposed to be over a dozen dragons in the area. Where the hell are they?

Use your flames. You need to slow your descent until one of us arrives.

And how the hell am I supposed to do that?

I told you. Use your fire. Let the strength of your flames arrest your descent.

Steve was silent as he stared at his hands. He cast a quick glance at the ground rushing up at him from below. Thankfully, Kahvel's cave had been over two thousand feet up the side of a mountain. By his estimation, he had about seven seconds left before he'd strike the ground.

He held his arms out, palms open, and blasted everything he had straight down. His body instantly flipped a hundred-eighty degrees as the rapid deceleration tipped him over until he was looking up at the sky. His arms dropped to his sides and he blasted out more flames, being careful to keep his palms facing down. He noticed the jets of fire were dangerously close to his left leg and, without thinking about the repercussions, automatically shut off the flames coming from his left hand.

The sudden loss of balance resulted in him being propelled upward in a tight spiral. His remaining lit hand tried to overcompensate by expelling even more flames. However, the only result was an even tighter spiral and higher-pitched screams.

Why did you extinguish one of your appendages? You

need both in order to maintain balance.

You think? This is worse than a roller coaster. I don't know how Iron Man does it. I think I'm gonna throw up.

Ignite your other hand. Hurry! You had managed to gain altitude until you started spinning out of control. There, you're only a few dozen feet from the ground. You should be able to ... stop waving your arms. The only thing that has accomplished was to resume your spinning.

Ooo, somebody stop this thing. I want to get off. You try to steer using two jets of fire. It ain't easy. Trust me. Are you close? Can you just put me out of my misery?

Rhamalli has almost reached you. He ... Rhamalli! Change course! I see the human who stole the fang. He has already returned to the ground. Stop him at all costs!

Wait, what? What about me? If somebody doesn't stop me spinning, then I'm going to be sick! Trust me, it won't be pretty!

What was that? Oh. Start reducing your flames, Steve. You're less than twenty meters from the ground. Now ten. There. You should be able to feel the earth under your feet.

I do. Thanks. Now, where is that...?

A fireball struck the ground less than fifty feet away. A cloud of dirt and pulverized stone rose into the air. Then a second blast struck. And a third. Within moments, fireballs were streaking across the sky to strike the ground less than a hundred feet from where he was standing.

Steve looked up. Kahvel had clearly spread the word about the pirates' location to the Collective. And, from the looks of things, every dragon in the area happened to be tuned into their telepathic joining of minds. He almost felt sorry for the pirates.

Almost.

Another blast of fire detonated uncomfortably close. It was definitely time to get moving. He could only hope the unsettling feeling of nausea would soon pass. No more flying for him, thank you very much.

He noticed Captain Flinn was defiantly standing in front of at least six pirates. He was gesturing to the air, evidently instructing his jhorun to direct the dragon fire well away from them. For the most part, Flinn was doing an admirable job, Steve reluctantly admitted. The dragons had yet to score anything close to a hit. But, for the first time, he could tell that Flinn appeared to be tiring. The shots were starting to inch closer to the small band of pirates.

Something approaches from the south.

What was that?

A mechanical contraption is approaching your location.

A mechanical ... wait. Does it look like a boat, only on land?

Aye.

That's the rest of the pirates. Flinn must be hoping to use that ship to escape!

Not if I can help it.

Right there with you, pal.

"The *Cadaymas* approaches!" Steve heard one pirate exclaim.

"It's about bloody time, Alquin!" Flinn snapped. "Signal Rusty to pick us up. Be quick about it!"

"But captain, what about the dragons?" another voice asked.

"What about 'em? I'm holding 'em off, no thanks to the likes of you vermin. Get the *Cadaymas* over here. Now!"

Kahvel, tell me your dragons can stop that funky ship.

They're trying. No one seems to be able to hit it. I can see that I have to, once again, institute mandatory target practice. It'll be a cold day in Nevir before I allow a repeat of this shoddy performance.

What if the fang is on that ship?

Oh. I hadn't considered that.

The land bound craft appeared and rapidly closed the distance. Steve could see that Flinn had his hands full trying to make certain none of them were fried to a crisp. The small boat on wheels pulled alongside the pirates, but didn't come to a stop.

"Stop the blasted thing!" one pirate whined as he tried to sprint after the boat. "I cannot run that fast! Don't leave me behind!"

The rest of the pirates abandoned their cover and tore off after the ship. One by one they flung themselves up and over the gunwale. Bemused, Steve turned to look back at the captain. He had yet to break cover, and seemed unconcerned about joining his companions.

Intent on bringing the small ship to a halt, Steve generated a chaser and threw it. The speeding fireball slammed into the side of the *Cadaymas* but bounced harmlessly away. Steve groaned. Well, that confirmed the location of the fang. Flinn had left it on the boat. Well, he might not be able to damage it, but he could certainly bring it to a stop.

He generated another chaser. This time he threw it at a nearby tree. It smashed into the trunk, causing the tree to shudder. The trunk was hit by a second chaser, and then a third.

An excellent idea! Brothers! Sisters! Stop that ship! We might not be able to harm it but we can prevent it from leaving!

Two dozen fireballs were suddenly speeding toward the ship. Massive trunks were obliterated as the dragons targeted all the surrounding trees. In less than ten seconds, there was nowhere for the *Cadaymas* to flee. All possible escape avenues had been blocked.

Pirates began jumping overboard as though they were on the open sea and their ship had begun sinking. Nearly a dozen different men ran in a dozen different directions, each scurrying to conceal themselves as quickly as they could. Steve sprinted over to the small ship, hoping against hope that the fleeing pirates had forgotten to take the fang.

Speaking of pirates…

Steve skidded to a halt. He cast a quick glance back at the pirate captain and stifled a curse. Now that the dragons had focused their attention on decimating as many of the surrounding trees as possible, no one had bothered to keep an eye on Flinn. The cunning pirate captain had disappeared!

Where the hell did he go?

Who?

Captain Flinn! The human in charge of the pirates! One minute he was facing a losing battle as he tried to stave off being fried to a crisp, and the next, he slips away unseen. That is one smart pain in the ass.

What now?

Take prisoners. Someone has gotta know what Flinn's plans are.

Agreed.

However, by the time Steve had reached the *Cadaymas*, the pirates had vanished without a trace. Kahvel gave the order to thoroughly search the area while Steve climbed into the small ship. A quick check of the floorboards gave him a welcoming surprise.

"Kahvel! I've got the fang! Those idiots must've dropped it when they fled!"

Chapter 11 — Ace in the Hole

Those idiots must've thought we dropped it. Do they really think so little of us, Captain? One of us must've grabbed it. There's no way any of us would've left it behind. All right, mates. Someone's got it. Turn out your pockets. Check everywhere. Von, the last time I saw the fang, it was by you. You had to have seen it, and therefore taken it. Where's it at now? What have you done with it?"

"Don't look at me!" Von cried. "I never saw the blasted thing. I was too busy following orders. We were told to abandon ship. That's exactly what I did."

"Who was sitting next to you?" Rusty snapped. "They must've seen the fang and taken it."

"It be clear as the skies above," Flinn muttered darkly as he rose to his feet. "One of you idiots left it in the *Cadaymas*. That means *they* have it now."

"You don't know that for sure," Rusty began. "It could've…"

"Do ye see it anywhere?" Flinn snapped. "Think one of

the men be hidin' it? My crew be loyal. I trust all o' them. They would never dare to keep the likes of that fang from me. I would know it. No, the fang be lost, and that vexes me greatly."

"Perhaps if we…"

"SILENCE! If ye so much as utter another word then I'll personally cut yer tongue out of yer mouth and feed it to the fishes!" Glaring angrily around his band of men, the captain clasped his hands behind his back and started to pace. Every pirate he passed hastily dropped their eyes to the ground to study some insignificant object. "The only job the lot of ye had was to protect that fang. Were my orders unclear?"

"No, sir!" the men echoed together.

"Did ye think I wanted the likes o' them to reclaim that fang?"

"No, sir!" the men shouted.

"Did ye think that… wait. What the blazes? One, two, three, four, five… Where's the quartermaster? Rusty? Get over here!"

Rusty hurried over, "Captain?"

Flinn motioned at the row of pirates standing stiffly at attention.

"Arithmetic may not be my area of expertise, but do we—or do we not—have a smaller crew?"

"Excuse me?? You're suggesting we're missing some crew? Who?"

"You tell me. We had more men than this. Who are we missing? Wait. Blast it to the Heavens and back. We've lost our best fighter. Where be Jino?"

"Jino went with you after we split into two groups, Captain."

The unmistakable sound of steel being drawn silenced all chatter.

"Ye best not be insinuating that I be responsible for his absence, mate. I'll gut ye like a fish. Don't think I won't do it."

"Apologies, Captain. I simply meant that I thought he was with you, so I never noticed he was gone."

"And how are your powers of observation, quartermaster?"

Rusty nodded proudly, "Second to none, Captain. Why, nothing escapes my notice. My men are my top priority. Why?"

"Is that so? Tell me. How many cabin boys are we suppos'd to have?"

"Two, Captain," Rusty immediately answered.

"Well, there's one of 'em. Ferris, his name be. Where be the other? When be the last time ye clapped eyes on 'im?"

The quartermaster's mouth dropped open with surprise. He hurriedly counted the members of their group. Rusty groaned.

"Where's Pedr?" Rusty snapped. "Who was the last to see him?"

Casimir slowly raised a hand, "During the first battle with the fire man, methinks."

Flinn's eyes widened with surprise. "That be *hours* ago! Surely someone has seen 'im after that! Speak up. Puck? Von? Ferris? Anyone?"

The men quietly shook their heads. Captain Flinn growled with frustration. His pacing resumed.

"Very well. We have to assume that Pedr has fallen into enemy hands. He…"

"Should we go after him?" Rusty hesitantly asked.

"Nah. Young Mister Pedr has already accomplished the task I needed him for. Right now, we have more important matters to worry about. First and foremost, we need to get that blasted fang back."

"Why, Captain?" Rusty asked. "Aye, we all saw a demonstration of its power during the battle with the dragons. The fang essentially rendered the dragons harmless. From the air, that is. I'm sorry to ask this, and if I'm out of line, just say so, but why do you want it so much? Why do we have to get it back?"

Flinn didn't bat an eye.

"You're out of line. The only thing ye need to know is that we must get it back. And we will, mark my words. Now, we be a long way from the sea and the *Emberbrand*. Find a secluded spot and we'll make camp. Send some of the men out to hunt and fetch water. I'll make sure no one finds us."

Flinn turned away as he heard his first mate start to give orders. What needed to be done now required some privacy. He wasn't about to let anyone know about his most prized possession. If anyone knew he had it, then he was certain there'd be talk of a mutiny with every member of the crew fighting to the death to gain possession of it. More than anything, what Flinn wanted now was to be able to secure the thing back in his desk aboard the *Emberbrand,* only thanks to their present predicament, that wouldn't be happening any time soon.

Flinn scowled, chose a spot far enough away from the rest of the men, and paced.

It was worth a fortune. He knew he shouldn't have taken it off the ship. It would've been much safer in the special desk he had created just to protect it. However, they were in a foreign land with untold dangers coming at them from all sides. Who could have imagined that they'd meet some foreigner with the power to control fire? As far as he was concerned, the stranger's power rivaled his own, only he had to be certain never to admit that out loud.

His hand settled on the lump inside his jacket pocket. He grimaced as he recalled retrieving it from its hiding place the moment land had first been sighted. He had retreated to the Captain's Quarters in the bow of the ship, locking the door securely behind him. Once the door was fastened, he situated himself behind his desk and again made sure he wasn't being watched. He dug at the base of his neck until his fingers slid under a thin silver chain. Pulling the chain up revealed a small, one-inch golden key swinging at the end. Flinn took the key, twisted one of the small wooden carvings on the surface of his desk counter clockwise, and inserted the key into the tiny, newly revealed keyhole.

A panel popped loose near his right knee, as though the craftsman who had created the desk had used glue to hold the panel in place and the adhesive was starting to fail. Flinn carefully pried the wooden compartment out of the desk. Whoever had crafted the desk had done a superb job in making sure the wooden box fit snugly within the desk.

Again, making sure no one was watching, he reverently

laid the narrow box on the desk and opened it. Nestled within the satin-lined interior lay something wrapped in soft leather. Placing the wrapped bundle on the desk, Flinn began peeling back layers of leather until the item had been completely uncovered. Underneath the coverings was an ordinary looking knife, just as he had ordered from the blacksmith back on Perz. The logic was, should the knife ever be discovered, he could simply claim it was a valued family heirloom.

From the tip of the blade to the end of the pommel, the dagger measured seven inches long. The handle was tightly wrapped black metal wire, only it had seen better days. The blade had a few nicks and blemishes, but for the most part, was polished to a shine. The pommel was nondescript and made of pewter. All in all, the weapon was fairly unremarkable, which was the whole point. What was remarkable? The pommel. It was hollow. Tucked safely inside the dagger's hollow handle was another key. This key unlocked the second, much larger compartment also hidden with the desk.

Flinn twisted the butt of the pommel loose and allowed the small key to drop into his hand. He rolled up the navigational charts that were spread out on top of his desk and traced a finger over one of the many etchings that had been carved onto the desk's surface. The carving's mouth opened, revealing another keyhole.

The far-left corner of the desk's surface shifted upwards by several inches. This time, it wasn't a panel that had popped loose but the latch that held a hidden door securely in place.

It was one of the four Alchos Stones.

The large, palm-sized glittering sapphire was oval shaped, polished to a mirror shine, and had a seven-point asterism just off center. It was small enough to fit in the palm of his hand but too large to be able to wrap his hand around it. The first time he had seen the stone was when he and his crew had taken one of the Northern Kingdom's prized galleons nearly ten years ago. While laden with expensive fabrics and exotic spices, the ship's hold had also contained a small crate which didn't have a lid. It was covered with carvings, knobs, dials, and buttons, which could be pressed, twisted, poked, or prodded. The head of a fim, the tail of a mavi. Each time he found one of the hidden buttons, it would cause several of other already pressed buttons to pop back up.

It was then that he realized the small crate must have been some type of puzzle box. The correct combination of pressed buttons, and presumably twisted dials, would allow the crate to open. However, the entire crate was *covered* in carvings, figurines, protrusions; finding the right combination that would open the crate would be practically impossible. However, six months of poking and prodding would pass before his luck would finally prevail. There, in the privacy of the Captain's Quarters, his luck held, and after a few furtive button presses, the chest finally opened. Inside the box was the stone. Who it had belonged to, or how the previous owner had acquired it, didn't matter. It was his now.

It had taken Flinn nearly a full year of careful research to learn what the stone was, and how to best use it to his advantage. He had been surprised to learn the stone had even been given a name: *the Essence of the Sea.* According to a scholar who was three sheets to the wind, it had once belonged to someone by the name of 'Aeus', whoever that was, and that the stone was one of the four mythical Alchos Stones. None of that would make any sense until his quartermaster, of all people, informed him what the definition of 'Alchos' was. In the archaic tongue, Rusty had quietly explained, belying a keen intellect for a pirate, 'Alchos' translated to 'ancient'.

Apparently, back when the world was young, there were four beings. The Alchos, or Ancients as everyone called them, presided over the elements. Earth, Air, Fire, and Water. Aeus turned out to be the Water Guardian. The sparkling blue gemstone he had blindly stumbled across just so happened to be the good luck charm that Aeus himself had allegedly carried around. What's more, it was said that the stone would bestow upon whomever carried it a powerful gift: invisibility. Anything he touched, or anyone in physical contact with him while he was holding the stone, would become completely invisible.

Eager to see if the other three Ancients also carried around charms of their own, and what powers each possessed, Flinn visited scores of Archives and spent many pieces of gold getting multitudes of scholars intoxicated. In disguise, of course. Who in their right mind would share their knowledge or secrets with a nefarious pirate?

His diligence eventually paid off.

Much later, nearly three years after first discovering the blue Alchos Stone, and after visiting what must have been at least two dozen different archives, Flinn learned that yes, each of the Ancients carried a stone. He learned that the Earth Ancient had been a prankster, and had something that would allow him to change his form to any living creature. The Air Ancient held a stone which granted its possessor the power of flight. And the Fire Ancient…

Flinn gritted his teeth.

The Fire Ancient had a stone which could render its holder impervious to attack. Yes, the oskorlisk fang had some power in that department, but it was nothing compared to the awesome power of Fire's stone. To possess one of the stones was unheard of, especially since all the stones had been lost to time. But, thanks to his good luck, one of the powerful stones had quite literally fallen into his lap. And … he knew there were more out there.

He had to find them.

Let the crew think he wanted to make the Perz Archipelagos into the Eighth Kingdom. It would distract the men from what was really important, which was the search for more of the stones. And, thanks to the strange visitor who had appeared on his doorstep last year, he had been given his first lead on where to find the next stone.

"Great power lies across the Endless Sea," the stranger had said. "Not even they realize what they have. You will find what you seek there."

Flinn knew immediately what the stranger was talking about. It was another Alchos Stone. It had to be! But which one? Then again, did it matter?

Fast forward to the present. Here he was, pacing across land belonging to the kingdom across the sea. Was all this effort worth it? Should he be risking his crew just so he could find another Alchos Stone that was rumored to be here somewhere?

Flinn grunted with frustration. He palmed the smooth blue stone as he paced and hefted it appraisingly. A sapphire of this size could easily quadruple the total amount of gold he had pillaged throughout his entire career as a pirate. He could simply sell off the gem, or else have it cut down to smaller jewels, and sell the pieces off individually, indubitably earning himself far more than he could have should he choose to leave the gem intact.

He angrily shook his head and dismissed the thought. Absolutely not. He wouldn't dream of harming *the Essence of the Sea*. For all he knew, if he so much as *scratched* the stone, then it might render it inert. He had already used the powers of the stone several times since achieving landfall in order to escape the dragon valley. Thanks to the power of the stone, and his ability to command the winds, he could waltz into practically any situation *undetected* and no one would be the wiser. But, what if he had two of the stones? What if this wretched foreign kingdom actually held one of the other Alchos Stones?

Flinn gave his head an exasperated shake. It was something that was too irresistible to pass up. He had to know, one way or the other, if the dark stranger spoke the truth.

Therefore, he had pulled the *Emberbrand* out of dry-dock, patched her up, and persuaded his old crew to follow him a final time. Then again, it hadn't taken much convincing. The mention of caves flowing with gold was all it had taken to get every member of his old crew to sign away a year of their lives.

Flinn sighed, returned the gem to the large inside pocket of his coat, and continued to pace. He thought of his crew and frowned. He had taken good care of his men and saw to it that each of them earned their fair share. After all, loyalty was not something to question out in the middle of the sea. He had to know that each and every member of the crew was loyal, to the death. How did something like that get accomplished? By fairness. By respect. Don't give the men a reason to question their orders. If they knew that following him across the Endless Sea could possibly result in a huge pile of gold for each of them, then that's all they would need to know.

Flinn felt the weight of the gem inside his coat and felt a pang of guilt. No one knew he had it, let alone what it could do, or how much it was worth. However, he was aware that several members of the crew knew he had something he was hiding, something he was unwilling to reveal to the men. Therefore, he pretended he had jhorun-infused charms which he had obtained at great personal expense. Charms, Flinn had explained, that could be useful in the right situations.

For example, after they had been pinned down by the dragons following their ill-fated attempt to dragonnap the infant, Flinn had ordered his men to clasp hands, like they were a group of school children. It was also necessary to tell a few white lies, such as one of the charms he carried would hide them (which was the truth) while another would see to it no wyverian would be able to pick up their scent (also a truth, although his jhorun had been responsible for that, not the sapphire).

The loss of the *Cadaymas* had not been part of the plan. Damn that fire thrower! How had he managed to find them in the valley? No one should have been able to guess where they were, yet these foreigners did. It seemed like every time he turned around, the fire thrower was there, challenging his authority and making him look like a horse's ass.

The final straw, unfortunately, was the loss of the fang. He had threatened each of the crew with death itself should it fall into the wrong hands. Naturally, that was exactly what had happened. The men were too concerned with saving their own skins.

Compounding his problems was the loss of Jino and Pedr. Their absences vexed him much more than the crew would ever know. Jino was the best fighter on the ship. His jhorun gave him preternatural speed, making him more than a match for anyone. So, what had happened to him? Had he run up against the fire thrower? Perhaps one of the fire thrower's companions also held great power. How, then, were they expected to deal with such a situation? His own power over the wind had been unable to drive the fire thrower back, when thus far, every other opponent he had ever faced had been forced to flee.

Not this time.

And then there was Pedr. Thank the Gods the boy had already accomplished the task he had set out for him. However, what if he needed him again? Should he risk exposure by trying to recover him?

Flinn grunted and resumed pacing. At least it had looked as though the fire thrower had been just as unsuccessful as he had been when it came to trying to drive him off. It would seem that the two of them were evenly matched. And it made sense, too. He was a Wind Talker—an Air Elemental—while the stranger was a Fire Thrower—Fire Elemental. Two Elementals, both powerful in their own way, yet neither could gain the advantage over the other.

Flinn scowled. He'd have to consider his options. He didn't like knowing that someone out there had a jhorun as strong as his own. Every fight he had ever been in, and every skirmish he had participated in, had always ended quickly. He had never been bested. He never had to flee.

Until today.

His carefully laid plans were starting to unravel. He needed that fang in order to continue his search for the second Alchos Stone. Without it, he would have to constantly check the skies for potential attackers. He would have to wonder if the authorities on this side of the Endless Sea were anywhere near as adept as the kings and queens from the Seven Kingdoms. If they were, then he was more than likely in for a difficult time. While the possibility of capture never crossed his mind, the right circumstances could force his men into a full-fledged retreat.

Again.

"I *will* get that fang back, fire thrower," Flinn muttered darkly under his breath. "I did not come all this way to fail now. Mark my words."

"I will consider them marked, Captain," a voice said.

Flinn stopped pacing; anger clouded his features. "Quartermaster, I assume ye have a good reason for this?"

Rusty nodded. "I do, Captain. I couldn't help overhearing that you were planning on retrieving the fang."

"That be a good way to lose an ear, mate," Flinn growled, stepping up close to his first mate.

"What is so blasted important about that fang, Captain?" Rusty sputtered. "You're risking everything on a big snake tooth! Why?"

In less time than it takes to blink an eye, Flinn's cutlass found its way into his hand. The captain rested the point on Rusty's chest.

"I will not have ye questioning my methods, quartermaster. The only thing ye need to know is that we need to get the fang back. Now, whether we…"

"Captain!" a new voice shouted.

"Blimey!" Flinn exclaimed with disgust. "The next scallywag who be interruptin' me will…"

"I'm sorry, Captain," Alquin exclaimed, interrupting him for a second time. "I thought you'd want to know this as soon as possible."

"This had better be good, Alquin," Flinn grumbled. "What do ye want?"

"The fire thrower! He's…"

"What about 'im?" Flinn demanded, cutting off Alquin's strangled reply.

"He's…"

"Well?" Flinn prompted, after the hapless crewman trailed off. "Out with it. What about 'im?"

"I just saw him!"

Flinn promptly forgot about his anger at his crewmen and immediately straightened.

"Where? He cannot have followed us. That be impossible!"

"He hasn't," Alquin confirmed. "However, I just saw him. He rides on the back of a dragon."

Flinn's eyebrows shot straight up, "Indeed? Our fire thrower be full of tricks. A dragon rider, eh? He originally told me he be friends with the scaly beasties. I didn't believe him. Hmm."

"Which way was he heading?" Rusty asked. "We have to assume he has the fang. We need to follow him."

"The dragon flew off, heading southeast."

"They be returning to the castle," Flinn mused

thoughtfully. "We need to get there first."

"The *Cadaymas* has been destroyed, Captain," Alquin nervously reported. "I saw the dragons burn it to the ground."

"Damn those monstrous freaks," Rusty swore. He looked at Flinn and shrugged helplessly. "What do we do now, Captain?"

"Gather everyone. We make for that village we saw earlier. They must have some way to keep in touch with the castle. We need to learn how and figure out how to get a message to the *Emberbrand*."

"They wouldn't have wandered far," Rusty agreed. "Arik has to recharge his power, or else the ship will be visible at all times of the day, not just the night. Trust me, Captain. They will stay within sight of the shoreline."

Thirty minutes later, Flinn and his motley band of men were peering at the quiet village of Verdayn from the safety of the forest. People had gathered in the village square and were having some type of festival. Musicians were playing a variety of instruments and at least several dozen villagers could be seen dancing in rows of four. Flinn held a finger to his lips and pointed at a line of nearby cottages. Nearly half a dozen of the small, thatched roof homes had clothing drying on lines behind the houses.

"Fetch the clothing," Flinn quietly ordered. "The more we blend in, the less likely we raise any alarms. Go."

Von, Alquin, and Casimir slipped out of the woods and quickly relieved the homes of their drying clothes. The pirates each dumped a double armful of the clothes in a pile back in the safety of the forest and picked through the selections with disgust.

Von held up a green tunic and a pair of worn, brown trousers.

"Seriously, Captain? I wouldn't be caught dead in this."

Von took one look at the captain's expression and immediately started to change, which prompted the others as well. Even the captain reluctantly began unbuttoning his frock coat. Sashes, bandanas, baldrics, and knee-high leather boots started to pile up.

"We're coming back for our things, right?" Rusty

hopefully asked. He was now wearing a white long sleeve shirt, dark brown trousers, and thick-soled leather shoes. He found a thick black cord in one of the vest pockets and held it up inquiringly.

"I believe it's used to hold the vest in place," Casimir informed him. "Look. There are holes on either side here."

"Hide our things," Flinn instructed.

He was now wearing a dull gray tunic that fell halfway to his knees. He had found a beige belt and had wrapped it around his midsection, tying it securely in place. His pants were also beige, and appeared to be either skin tight or else too small for him. Completing the picture was a brown traveling cloak, held together by a pewter brooch. Not finding any shoes that fit him, he elected to keep his dark leather boots.

"I do not wish to wear this outfit any longer than necessary."

There was of chorus of *here, here* from the men.

"What now?" Rusty wanted to know.

Flinn singled out one building, larger than the rest. "We start there. There be people going in and out of that building all day. That may be where we find the Mayor's office."

Not a Mayor, but the Constable in charge was easily persuaded by a dagger to the throat.

Flinn turned to the men crowded into the constable's office and held up a glittering crystal key.

"We've struck it rich, lads. They've got a portal."

There was a chorus of ooo's and aaah's. Flinn noticed one of the men was frowning. Casimir noticed he was being watched and hesitantly raised a hand.

"Er, Captain? How do we know what's waiting for us on the other side? How do we know we're not walking into a trap?"

Flinn gazed appreciatively at Casimir and made a mental note to add a few extra pieces of gold to his stash during their next payout. He turned back to the Constable, now gagged and tied up. Flinn gave a sharp tug to the gag and held his dagger to the man's throat.

"Scream for help and it'll be the last sound ye hear. Now, what be waiting for us on the other side of that portal?"

"It's … it's connected to the portal room in the castle," the Constable nervously answered. He eyed the sharp blade near his throat and swallowed. "The portal room is adjacent to the Great Hall, where the king and queen can be found."

"That's too close," Rusty grumbled. "Unless the portal is used on a frequent basis?"

Flinn turned back to his prisoner. He gave the dagger a menacing shake. The prisoner paled.

"The Kri'yans are the only ones allowed to use the portals. That is, unless there's a dire emergency. If you activate the portal, they'll undoubtedly hear it from the Great Hall."

"It's a chance we have to take," Flinn decided. He heard gasps of surprise and turned to see his men curiously regarding him. "They have the fang, lads. We need it back, plain and simple. We be going to the castle. Hide your weapons. We don't want to risk setting off any alarms."

"What's the plan, Captain?" Rusty asked.

"All we have to do is get outside. I have the advantage outside, whereas the fire thrower has the advantage inside. We have to assume he's either already there or on his way."

Flinn looked down at the key he was holding. Following the constable's instructions, he activated the portal and eyed his men.

"Remember. Keep yer eyes down. Ye don' want to attract attention to yerself. If we are forced to separate, go outside and head to the water. Everyone understand?"

Heads were nodding. Flinn suddenly cocked his head. He could hear a soft musical chiming. He also noticed he wasn't the only one. His men were eyeing each other, no doubt wondering if the portal's chime was normal behavior.

"What do we do with him?" Von asked, looking back at the constable. He was the last to step through the portal. "Should I gut 'im so he can't raise no alarm?"

Flinn waved a dismissive hand. "Forget 'im. He's not important. Get over here. Now!"

Von hurried across, just as the portal faded out. They were now in a darkened, quiet room. Three of the men were pushing some type of heavy fabric out of the way to allow the rest of their group to enter the room. Flinn turned to look back at the portal. The men let the heavy covering fall back into place. It was a tapestry. Apparently, the king and queen had been using it to conceal the portal itself. Flinn pointed at the only entrance to the room and motioned for several of his men to cover it.

"Be ready. Remember. Keep yer heads down. Head outside."

"What if we get lost?" Von whined. "What if we can't find our way outside?"

"Yer jhorun be the ability to know which way is north, right?"

"Aye, Captain."

"Good. As ye have always been, yer the compass. Get us lost, Von, and I'll personally make ye walk the plank *with* one of those blasted sea serpents directly under us. Do ye catch my meaning?"

Von hastily nodded. "Aye, Captain."

"Good. Here we go. Von, take the lead."

The door opened and the men hurriedly exited the quiet chamber. What they found themselves faced with, however, could only be described as their worst nightmare.

They were indeed in the Great Hall. That was immediately apparent, as each of them could see the two gilded thrones. Thankfully, the royals weren't there. However, none of that really mattered because sitting directly in the middle of the Great Hall was a creature so large that it easily dwarfed every other being present.

It was a dragon.

Movement caught his attention. Something was moving near the large green dragon's left foreleg. Flinn's eyes widened with shock. It was the same baby dragon he and his men had tried to abduct earlier in the day. That could only mean…

The huge green dragon gave an audible sniff. The long serpentine neck twisted until those horribly long fangs were oriented on their small group. Two reptilian eyes locked onto his. A look of surprise slowly passed over the dragon's face.

"You."

There was a long, pregnant pause. Then absolute chaos ensued. The mother dragon roared a challenge and bared her teeth. The baby scooted behind its mother and peered fearfully at him from behind the mother's tail. Furniture, suits of armor, and even the paintings on the walls were swept aside as the huge dragon tried to position itself to attack.

"Pryllan," he heard a woman's voice say. "What is it? What's the matter?"

"The human thief is here. He's there, along with nearly a dozen other humans. I didn't smell them a moment ago. They must have just arrived."

"From the portal room?"

Now Flinn saw her. The speaker was an attractive girl with long brown hair, wearing an elegant green dress that stretched all the way to the floor. The woman looked straight at him.

"Him? Are you sure?"

Flinn didn't waste any time. Drastic times called for drastic measures.

"Hostages! Take hostages or we'll never get out of here alive!" He pointed at the woman. "Someone grab her. She looks like she could be a noble. Hurry!"

Two pirates materialized next to the girl and pinned her arms behind her back. The mother dragon's long neck twisted again. It was looking directly at the girl and her captors.

"Release her or I'll burn you to a crisp."

The girl was instantly placed between the dragon and the pirates.

"Not without harming her, ye won't," Flinn haughtily disagreed. "We're leaving here. Cooperate and ye might just get yer queen back alive. Cross us, and ye'll be picking up pieces of her all across this pretty castle. Do I make myself clear?"

The dragon started growling.

"What's going on here? Lissa! What have they... who are you? What do you want?"

Flinn turned to see a young man not much older than Pedr appear in their midst. He was dressed in a dark leather tunic, matching trousers, and a white fur-lined floor length robe. Flinn smiled. This had to be the king, but he was so young!

"Ye cannot be the king. If I had but known this land was governed by mere children, then I would have started my search many years ago."

Surprisingly, the young man bowed. "You must be the pirate captain. I am Kri'Mikal, king of Lentari. You're Captain Flinn of the *Emberbrand*, I presume?"

Flinn's mouth dropped open. How in the world did this young boy know who he was? Were his exploits so well known that they had somehow traveled across the Endless Sea?

"Ye have the advantage," Flinn admitted. He pointed to his two men who were holding the girl hostage. "I take it she is yer queen?"

"That would be Ny'Lissa, my wife and queen. Kindly release her."

"I will do no such thing, boy."

"What do you want?"

"I want to leave."

"Then leave, but do me the favor of leaving my wife behind. Unharmed."

Flinn leered at the young king. "And if I don't?"

The boy's face hardened. "Then you will find out that we're not nearly as harmless as you might think."

Flinn frowned. In the blink of an eye, the young man had gone from an inconsequential kid to a protective king who was essentially *daring* him to try something stupid. He and his men started edging toward the main hallway. He had noticed enough soldiers and servants coming and going from this hallway to determine it had to be the quickest way out. He did a quick head count and, satisfied all his men were accounted for, slowly backed away from the angry dragon and the unsettling young monarch.

"They're trying to surround us!" Rusty suddenly exclaimed.

Flinn turned. Dozens of soldiers were blocking their escape. Flinn pulled out his dagger and held it up to their captive's throat.

"Clear the way, boy."

"My name is Mikal."

"Fine. Clear the way, Mikal. Ye don' want to be testing my

patience today."

"And if I clear the way? Will you let her go?"

"Once we're safely outside, ye may have her back."

"Captain!" Rusty quietly hissed. "What are you doing? We're gonna need her to…"

"Hold yer tongue," Flinn snapped. He turned back to the young king. "Ye keep crowding me, who knows … I would not want anything to happen to yer lovely wife now, would I?"

"Allow them to leave."

One soldier, a tall man wearing a maroon tunic underneath his leather armor, drew his sword. "Your Majesty, I cannot simply allow this miscreant to…"

"Captain Pheron. You will step aside. Now."

The tall man scowled, lowered his weapon, and indicated the rest of the men to do the same. He and his men stepped to either end of the hallway, creating an empty aisle down the center of the hall. Flinn and his men backed slowly down this aisle, pausing only to verify that no one was trying to ambush them when they came to a juncture of halls. Flinn also noticed the boy king was keeping pace with them, and keeping completely cool about it.

Flinn scowled again. This mere boy was getting on his nerves. He was too calm, too collected. If all the people who lived in this land were of his caliber, then this mission wouldn't be as easy as he was led to believe.

"Take the doorway to your left," the young king instructed. "You'll find the bailey just through there. Then you'll want to head west, toward the western guardhouse. They'll allow you through and you can be on your way."

Alquin was closest to the doorway. He glanced through and nodded at Flinn. Apparently, the young king was speaking the truth. They slowly crept through the doorway until they were standing—blinking profusely in the bright daylight—in the castle's bailey. Strange. He looked up at the sky. The sun was hiding behind the clouds. He could have sworn the sun had been out. Whatever. It didn't matter, because there, just as the king had instructed, was the gatehouse and their ticket out of the castle.

"Mister Flynn. I would say that I have followed all of your demands, have I not?"

Flinn turned to see that the young king had followed him outside, including four squads of fully armored soldiers.

He nodded. "I would."

"Uphold your end of the arrangement. Release my wife."

"Methinks I will hold on to her for a bit longer."

A frown appeared on the king's face.

"That wasn't part of the arrangement."

"I be altering the terms of our arrangement," Flinn coolly replied. "I have my men to look out for."

"And you're doing an admirable job," the king smugly replied.

"What's that supposed to mean?" Flinn demanded. His hackles were raised. What did this kid know that he didn't?

"Have you, perhaps, done a recent head count?"

Alarmed, Flinn pulled Rusty close. "Check everyone. Make sure the men are all accounted for."

"Right away, Captain. There's Von. And Alquin. And … and…"

"And what?"

"Are you a few men short?" Mikal nonchalantly asked. "You seem to be missing a few."

"Who are we missing?" Flinn whispered to his quartermaster. "Tell me he be bluffing."

"He's not bluffing," Rusty groaned. "We're missing Casimir and Puck."

"I thought they were right behind us!"

"They *were* right behind us," Rusty insisted. He turned to the young king, who was standing nearly twenty feet away with his hands clasped behind his back.

There was another flash of light. Flinn automatically glanced up at the sky. It was still clouded. He frowned. Something wasn't right.

"I propose a trade," Mikal began. "I will return your men, and you will return my wife. Do we have an accord?"

"And if I don't?" Flinn asked, knowing full well he was provoking the foreign king.

"Then your men will continue to disappear right from

under your noses."

Flinn shared a look with his first mate. Rusty glanced behind him and was dismayed to see that Von was now missing. He nudged the captain and quietly reported his findings.

"Von was just here," the captain snapped. "All right. Enough of this. Return my men or I'll level this whole damn castle."

"You're good, Captain Windbag," a new voice said, "but you're not that good. You know it and I know it."

Flinn whirled around. It was the fire thrower. He was casually leaning up against the portcullis in the western gate. Movement in his peripheral vision had him lifting his eyes to look over the castle's outer wall. A second dragon, this one even darker than the dragon trapped inside the castle, was now peering at him from over the castle wall. It opened its mouth and roared a challenge.

"Easy, Pravara," the fire thrower soothed. "You'll have your chance. Right now we need to focus on getting Lissa away from those creeps."

Flinn smiled. So, they did value the girl's life. Good. That meant the advantage had returned to him.

"You're good, Fire Thrower. I will give credit where credit is due. However, I have the upper hand here. I be the one giving orders. Not you, and certainly not the boy."

"You really ought to listen to the boy," the fire elemental casually remarked. "It'll make your life a lot more bearable if you do."

"Release her," Mikal repeated.

"First, tell me how ye have managed to incarcerate my men."

Mikal raised his eyes skyward. "Gareth? Come on out. I think Captain Flinn would like to say hello."

A boy appeared, sitting on the outer wall right next to the dragon. He looked even younger than the king! What was it with this kingdom, anyway? Where were the men?

"Gareth, this is Captain Windbag," the Fire Thrower began. "Captain Windbag, meet Gareth, hands down the strongest, most powerful wizard you'll ever encounter."

Flinn growled as his fists clenched with rage. A huge blast of air encircled the castle, ripping banners and pennants out of their holders. He directed the air jet at the castle's keep and watched with satisfaction as every window in the castle imploded.

Gareth drew a few invisible symbols in the air, chanted a few lines of verse, and then fell silent. An odd, crinkling noise sounded from behind the pirates. Flinn turned, amazed to see that every single window in the castle had been properly restored.

"Very well. Release my men. Allow us to board my ship and we will be gone. Agree to that and I will allow the girl to go."

"It's a trap, Captain," Rusty whispered in his ear. "Ye cannot trust them."

"Ye just spit in my ear, mate. Do that again I'll cut off yer tongue."

"We have an accord," Mikal replied. "Now release my wife."

"Do I look daft to ye? Absolutely not. Ye will release my men first."

Mikal glanced at the Fire Thrower, who nodded, and then looked up at the boy wizard still sitting on the wall.

"Very well. Gareth, bring his men out. That way they can see for themselves that they're perfectly safe."

"Even…"

Mikal shook his head. "No. Release the men that you just captured."

"I want Jino released, too," Flinn suddenly added. "Ye have no right to hold him prisoner."

"Who is Jino?" Mikal asked.

The Fire Thrower reached into a pocket and extricated a small glass bottle. He held it up for everyone to see. Inside was a tiny figure who hammered helplessly against the glass.

Flinn stared at the glass vial. "Ye expect me to believe Jino is in there?"

The Fire Thrower slowly walked over to the small group of pirates. "Don't do anything stupid, guys. You don't want my hands flaming up while I'm holding this, do you?"

Flinn squinted as he stared at the glass bottle. Sure enough, he could see Jino's tiny form inside, angrily shouting and pounding at the glass confines of his prison. Impressed, Flinn looked at the irksome stranger.

"How the blazes did ye pull that off, Fire Thrower?"

"It's Steve."

"What?"

"That's my name. Steve."

"Why would I care what your name be?"

"It's easier than saying, Fire Thrower all the time."

"Whatever. How did ye pull it off?"

"I didn't. Gareth did."

"Ah. The wizard. Very well. Hand 'im over."

Steve held out the bottle and waited for Flinn to take it.

"How do I release him?"

Steve glanced back at Gareth.

"Everything is spelled on the bottle," the young wizard explained. "The act of opening the bottle will nullify the spells I used one by one."

"And the rest of my crew?"

Gareth closed his eyes and chanted. Puck, Casimir, and Von appeared, but frozen in place, unable to move a muscle. Their eyes were still moving, though, staring at their captain, pleading for him to get them released.

"What's wrong with 'em?" Flinn demanded. "Why are they not moving?"

"It's a new incapacitation spell I've developed," Gareth excitedly began. "You see, I instructed my spell to completely immobilize the body, but leave the…"

"Gareth," Mikal interrupted, drawing the wizard's attention. "Focus, please. Release his men."

"Oh. Sorry. Sure, just a moment."

Several seconds later, all three men gave visible jerks as control of their own bodies were returned to them. They hurried to Flinn's side and peered nervously about, as if afraid they would be paralyzed at any time. Flinn heard Mikal clear his throat.

"Captain Flinn, I expect you to uphold your end of the accord. I've released your men. Now, release my wife."

"Ye will have her only when we are safe on our ship."

The pirates backed slowly away from the throngs of people and edged closer to the waterfront.

"Mister Alquin, do ye see the *Emberbrand*?"

"Not yet, Captain."

"But I do," a new voice added.

Flinn turned to look up at the second dragon. It was alarmingly close. The dragon turned to point at a spot of water nearly three hundred feet from shore.

"The human vessel is there."

"And how the blazes do ye know that, ye overgrown lizard?" Flinn snapped. "Ye cannot possibly tell me ye can see the ship while it is disguised."

"Who do you think found your ship the first time?" the dragon sarcastically responded.

"I don't like it here," Von whined. "Captain, let's go."

"I give the order to go. Mister Alquin, do ye see the ship yet?"

"Aye, Captain. It's there, just as the dragon described."

"Well, what are ye waiting for? Flag 'em down. Get 'em over here, now!"

Ten minutes later, the illusion was lifted and the entirety of Flinn's ship was revealed. It was a two-masted brigantine, complete with rows of cannon holes on either side of the ship. It beached itself on the sandy shore and waited for the pirates to climb aboard.

Flinn noticed both of the fire thrower's hands had ignited. He grunted once, gave the girl he was holding a violent shove forward, and turned to sprint to the ship. Once aboard, he reached inside his jacket, wrapped his hand around the Alchos stone, and then slapped his other hand on the gunwale.

The entire ship, and everything on it, vanished.

Chapter 12 — Air vs. Fire

No, I do not see it this time," Pravara reluctantly admitted. "I cannot see it, nor can I smell it. I do not even see any evidence of displaced water. Either it has completely vanished or the method of concealment has changed."

"So, you're telling us you've lost them?" Steve demanded, rounding on the tall green dragon. "I thought nothing could match a dragon's eyesight."

"That's true," Pravara admitted, giving her head a slight nod.

Steve hurried forward, intent on climbing onto Pravara's back. "Fine. We'll do this the hard way. Come on. They've gotta be out there somewhere."

"If they are," Pravara began, "then they have properly concealed themselves this time. I can see no traces anywhere. If you were to ask me to fly out there, over the water, then I'd have to refuse. The only way I can think of to effectively search for the missing vessel would be to fly as low as possible, and I wouldn't want to run the risk of flying into the vessel.

Plus, I have no desire to be that close to the surface of the water."

Agreed.

Pravara immediately looked up.

"What is it?" Steve cautiously asked. "Do you hear something?"

Pravara's great head nodded. "Aye. My father. He agreed with my assessment of the situation. Until the ship's location is known, I wouldn't risk flying out over the open water, especially when a human air elemental is out there. My father overheard and agreed with me."

Kahvel? Do you have any idea how those pirates are able to hide themselves?

I would imagine jhorun has something to do with it.

It used to. That's how Pravara found them the first time. She can't see them now, yet they must be out there somewhere.

I would agree. However, there is a more pressing matter that concerns me.

Oh? What's that?

My mate is presently stuck inside the human castle, without any possibility of escape.

Oh, snap! I forgot about Pryllan! Is she okay?

Aye, although she would like to remove herself from the confines of the castle. Where is your mate? Where is Sarah?

That's a damn good question. I haven't had a chance to look for her yet. I can only assume she's passed out somewhere, due to her jhorun becoming completely exhausted.

Could we, perhaps, awaken her so that Pryllan can finally be …?

What? What is it? Why'd you trail off like that?

Steve?

Yes?

Your patience is about to be tested.

Umm, okay. Why'd you say that?

It would appear as if your pirate friends have not left the area, as you have surmised.

The pirates are back? Where? I can't see them anywhere. Neither does Pravara.

You are looking too close to the shore. Cast your eyes

northeast. It would appear the ship has unmasked itself.

Steve shaded his eyes and looked east. Sure enough, there was a tiny speck on the horizon that was growing steadily larger. He could see that the sails were unfurled and noticed the winds were (unsurprisingly) blowing from the east. If Flinn didn't slow down, then they were going to unquestionably beach themselves on the shore. He frowned as a chilling thought washed over him. What if that was the plan? Then again, why in the world would the pirates return? Why wouldn't they simply flee?

Steve hurriedly glanced up and down the shore. Thankfully, Pheron and his soldiers had also noticed the ship's approach and were in the process of forming ranks. They had retreated several dozen feet away from the water's edge and were carefully watching the *Emberbrand* as it approached.

Fifty feet from shore, the anchor dropped.

The bow of the *Emberbrand* was yanked downward as the anchor caught. The ship began to drift, bringing the starboard side of the ship parallel to the shore. One by one, the small, square ports snapped open.

"That can't be good," Steve groaned miserably.

What is it? What is happening?

You saw the pirate ship return. Can't you see what it's doing now?

I see many smaller windows opening. I fail to see the significance.

They're cannon ports. That damn ship is about to open fire on us! All it has to do is wait a few more seconds and we're all going to be sitting ducks.

Pravara! Seek shelter! Steve, I would advise you do to the same!

Pravara leapt up, snapped her wings open, and disappeared from sight.

"Mikal!" Steve called, as he hurried to his former charge's side. "Get inside! It's about to get ugly!"

"Agreed!" a voice shouted. Steve saw that Pheron was hurrying over, too. "Seek shelter at once, Your Majesty. We can handle this. After all, we have Sir Steve fighting alongside us. We cannot lose!"

"Your faith is admirable, pal," Steve remarked. "I can

only hope it isn't misplaced. Mikal, do me a favor. Go check on Sarah, okay? If she's up to it, I could really use her out here."

"I will have Lissa see about waking her," Mikal promised.

A dozen guards suddenly surrounded the young king and whisked him away to the safety of the castle.

"How do you want to handle this?" Steve asked, as he ignited his hands.

"Do you think you could sink the ship?" Pheron asked.

Steve nodded. "It'd be my luck that half the men on that damn ship would drown. I can't have that on my conscience."

"I should think that the ability to swim would be an occupational requirement," Pheron muttered.

"You would think so, as would I. We should … look out!"

The deafening roar of the cannons effectively silenced all conversations. Steve watched, mesmerized, as various parts of the shoreline erupted, sending bits of pulverized stone and sand hundreds of feet into the air. His ears had begun ringing, making it difficult to concentrate.

A solitary blast of fire suddenly sped by—over his head—to slam into the pirate vessel. It had to be from Pravara! However, the jet of fire veered into the water at the last minute, leaving the brigantine unscathed. Steve gritted his teeth. Flinn must've deflected the shot.

I am uncertain as to what happened. I have never missed before in my life. Ever.

Pravara? Is that you?

Aye.

Don't feel bad about missing. It wasn't you. Captain Windbag is on that ship. He's using his jhorun to deflect your shots. I have a feeling he's gonna be able to block anything you throw at it.

Ah. Very well, what do we do now?

I'm open to suggestions.

I have called for aid. My father says that three of my brethren will be here in less than ten minutes. Perhaps if all of us attack the vessel at the same time, then maybe there's a chance one of us will score a hit? The human windbag could not possibly be able to defend the vessel from multiple attacks, could he?

Human windbag. Oh, Pravara. I love it. You said ten minutes? I seriously don't think we're gonna last longer than five, Pravara. Those cannons are brutal. I don't want anyone to get hurt. I'm going to have to advise Pheron to retreat.

Agreed. You will not place yourself in danger, young one.

Father, I will not leave. I will not abandon my friends.

Pravara, do not make me order you.

Then don't.

If you don't…

Pravara, look out! They've spotted you!

Steve, protect my daughter.

I'm on it, buddy. Pravara? Do you see me? Can you come get me?

I see you. I dare not risk landing, not when you're that close to the water.

Well, I don't know how else to … wait. It isn't the smartest move on the planet, but I have an idea that will get me away from the water. I'll propel myself straight up using the Iron Man trick your dad taught me. I'll be really hard to miss. Just follow the screams.

I will.

Steve stood as straight as a board and held his arms at his sides. He extended his hands, palms facing down. He took a deep breath and held it, just before he blasted out what he hoped were fire jets of equal strength.

They weren't.

One hand wasn't as strong as the other. Why that was, he didn't have a clue. The only thing that mattered to him now was the simple fact that he was executing a perfect corkscrew as he jetted up into the air. Just as he had predicted, he had let out a terrified shout that, unfortunately, was nearly two full octaves higher than his normal speaking voice.

Expel even amounts of jhorun from your appendages and you will not spin as you rise.

Thanks, Captain Obvious. Let's face it, using one's fire to push one's self off the ground, through one's hands, is a dumb idea, no matter who you are.

Pravara swooped out of nowhere, snatched Steve from the air, and stretched her foreleg back to place him as close to her back as possible.

"You will have to climb the rest of the way. That's as far as I can reach."

"It's close enough. Thanks. Now, we need to … whoa! Hang on! I've got this one!"

An errant cannonball was careening straight toward them. A hastily thrown chaser was enough to trigger the gunpowder within the hurtling metal projectile. The cannonball exploded long before it could make contact with either of them.

Steve grunted irritably. How the people of the Seven Kingdoms had the knowledge to create gunpowder, and the people of Lentari didn't, was beyond him. Clearly their technological development had strayed significantly from one another.

"How is it a metal ball can explode?" Pravara asked, as if reading his thoughts.

Steve snorted. Well, maybe she had been doing just that.

"I believe I can answer that question. Cannonballs are either one of two types. Most of the times they are simply solid metal objects. Trust me, if you put enough *oomph* behind one of those things, and it's fired at you, then it will do some serious damage should it make contact. However, the people of my world learned that, if they make a hollow cannonball and fill it with gunpowder, then it can do even more damage when it strikes its target."

"What can we do about it?"

Steve shrugged. "Well, I can hit them with chasers. The problem is, I don't know how long I could keep it up. Plus, I couldn't guarantee that I'd be able to get them all. Besides, I wouldn't put it past Flinn to use cannonballs to keep me distracted and out of the way. Do you know who we really need right now? Sarah."

"Why do you say that?" Pravara asked. Her left wing dropped, sending her banking north.

"She'd have a much better time being able to deflect these things. We really need to make certain that they don't fire their cannons again. If they learn that the Lentarians do not have similar cannons to return their fire, then it's a sure bet the castle is going to be destroyed. It would be a one-sided battle."

Cannon fire rang out from below. Pravara's wing dipped even further, bringing her sharply around. Sure enough, the *Emberbrand* had fired again, only this time it was targeting the nearby castle. Huge chunks of stone and masonry were ripped from the outer walls.

The castle's alarm bell began tolling. Streams of soldiers, both on horseback and on foot, flowed out of the castle and headed toward the ship. Pheron, however, brought them up short.

"Only five of the seven cannons have fired! Seek cover!"

Scores of horses and men spread out along the beach, seeking refuge behind anything large enough—or sturdy enough—to protect them. High above their heads, circling helplessly, were dragon and rider. Steve scowled with frustration.

"They are sitting ducks down there, Pravara! We need to do something!"

"My blasts are ineffective against that human," Pravara bitterly growled. "What can we do?"

Steve rose to his feet, gripped one of Pravara's spinal plates for support, and ignited his hand.

"Let's just see how good this guy is. We're going to attack together. I want to see if Captain Windbag can handle both of us at the same time. Ready? One, two … three!"

Steve ignited the largest chaser he could and targeted the ship. He sent the flaming ball of fire trailing after Pravara's shot. Not waiting for either of the blasts of fire to score a hit, Steve fired off a second. Then a third. Pravara matched him blast for blast.

Thus far, after nearly a dozen hits, the ship had remained untouched. Blasts of air had appeared out of nowhere and effortlessly swatted aside the incoming shots. Unfortunately, the act of deflecting two shots was apparently just as easy as it was for the one. The pirates, fearing for their lives once they saw that they were being attacked by a dragon, began recovering their wits. Realizing their captain had thus far been able to protect them, they began taunting both dragon and rider with a flurry of insults.

Suddenly, three additional blasts joined Steve and

Pravara's and, together, all five shots streaked toward the ship. The *Emberbrand* shuddered under the assault. Turning to see who had been responsible for the additional blasts, Steve whooped aloud. Kahvel's reinforcements had arrived.

A familiar striking red dragon with purple-flanged wings streaked by them at frightening speed. Rhamalli pulled out of his dive at the last minute and returned to the air. He had forgotten that Pheron was one of the newly appointed dragon riders.

Movement from down below attracted his attention. Steve leaned out over Pravara's side to watch the ship. The anchor it had dropped before had been pulled back up. The *Emberbrand* was now pointed west and was moving steadily closer to shore. What was it doing?

"Something's up, Pravara. They've switched tactics. Observe. All seven of the ship's sails have been unfurled. The wind is picking up, which means Flinn is using his jhorun to speed things along."

"Whatever for?" the dragon inquired.

"I'd say he plans on beaching the ship on the shore. Why, I'm not sure."

Whatever they're doing, a new voice mentally added, *it doesn't matter. We must clear the area.*

Who is this? Steve demanded. *Who is speaking?*

Sir Steve, it is I. Captain Pheron.

Oh. I don't think I've ever talked to you this way before.

Rhamalli thought it'd be best to include me as we try to figure out what the brigand is doing.

Steve nodded thoughtfully. *Okay, I can get on board with that. Well? What do we do?*

Observe for now. Behold. The ship approaches the shore.

A few moments later, they heard the telltale sound of creaking wood as the large brigantine was pushed halfway out of the water. The blustery winds immediately died down. From their vantage point, Steve watched as the pirates scurried over their vessel, like ants swarming over a piece of discarded candy. Oddly enough, it looked as though they were taking down the sails just as fast as they could. Then…

Steve, what's wrong? Why do you make that face?

Steve's face had gone slack. His mouth opened, but unsure what to say, he had closed it again. He wordlessly pointed at the *Emberbrand*.

What is happening? Kahvel's voice demanded. **What do you see? Steve? Pravara? Speak!**

The vessel. It's … it's … changing!

I do not follow, Steve. Changing? How so?

Er, the ship has dropped its sails. The masts look like they're being absorbed back into the ship. How it's doing that, I don't know. And … I'll be damned. Pravara? Do you see it? Do you see what's happening to the bow?

Aye, I do.

Well, I don't. Someone—and I don't care who—must tell me what is happening. Anyone?

Kahvel, two panels have opened near the base of the ship. More of the pirates are coming out of them. Now something else is coming out. It looks … well, it looks like mechanical legs, like the ship suddenly decided it wanted to prop itself up.

Legs? On a sailing vessel? That makes no sense.

Look, man. I know. I'm the one watching it happen. I haven't the foggiest idea what it's … wait. Wait! I know what it's doing now! Those things coming out of the ship are pushing it up. It's making the ship level.

Level? What is the advantage of making a ship level?

I can only assume that it's going to try and use something else against us. Something that requires the ship to remain stationery and level.

And that would be, what? Pheron mentally asked.

Far below the dragons, the *Emberbrand*'s twin masts finished retracting into the bowels of the ship until only the two crow's nests were visible. The crew was seen scurrying across the surface of the ship, opening other compartments to drag items out, and hastily attach them to the tops of what used to be the two masts.

Steve frowned as he, along with Pravara, Rhamalli, and Pheron, circled about nearly two hundred feet above the ship. The pirates were up to something, but what? If only he could see what they were doing.

You could just ask me.

Oh, snap. I forgot that we're linked telepathically. I'm sorry,

Pravara. I need to watch my thoughts.

You freely share your thoughts with my mother, correct?

Yes, that's correct.

Why should I be any different?

Because … because … hmm. I don't know. I guess I didn't want to impose on you.

There is no imposition. You wish to see what the humans are doing on the ship? Very well. Allow me to show you.

Thanks, Pravara. I guess I should've asked.

Steve closed his eyes and took several deep, calming breaths. He emptied his mind, but not before the corners of his mouth turned upwards in the beginning of a smile. Sarah would definitely have a comment about that.

Sarah. Steve shook his head and pushed his concern aside. Wherever his wife was, he fervently hoped she had rested enough to recover use of her jhorun. He was confident she'd be able to deflect cannon fire just as easily as Flinn could deflect dragon blasts.

An image formed. It was the *Emberbrand,* lying motionless half out of the water. The vision shifted to look at the ship's forecastle. The image magnified, as if he had hit the zoom button on a camera. Now he had a perfect view of what the pirate crew was doing.

What he saw did not make him happy.

It looked as though the pirates were attaching various implements to the two crow's nests that were still visible on the ship's surface. In fact, it had started to look like the pirates were assembling some type of weapon. Weapons, *plural.* The men stepped aside and Steve's eyes widened.

He was right. Both crow's nests had been transformed into strange looking guns. The two guns were now slowly rotating until they were pointing at the groups of Lentarian soldiers that had engaged the pirates who had jumped off the ship. Whatever type of weapons they were, it couldn't be a good thing. He had to put a stop to it before they fired.

Pravara? Did you catch any of that?

Aye. I am in total agreement. However, how do we

**stop them? What should we do? Every shot I fire has
been diverted to the sea.**

As has mine.

*Steve? This is Captain Pheron. We need to alert my men. Rhamalli
and I will continue to keep the pirate captain occupied. What I need you
to do is to warn the men. Can you do that?*

In answer to the question, Steve generated a chaser and
hurled it straight down. The speeding fireball detonated upon
impact, less than a dozen feet from the closest Lentarian
guard. The soldier looked up, confused. Steve, waiting for the
soldier to make eye contact, immediately pointed at the ship.

"DANGER!" he shouted. "GET AWAY FROM THE
SHIP!"

The soldier's eyes widened with surprise as he noticed
the two guns slowly swiveling their way. The guard shouted
a warning. Before the soldiers could move out of the way,
however, the first gun reached its target and fired.

The ground in front of the largest group of Lentarian
soldiers exploded. A white, hissing noise could be heard, and
then a light fog seemingly appeared. Within moments, the
soldiers dropped to the ground, unconscious.

What the hell was that?

It must be some type of sleeping potion.

*Why would they put them to sleep? They wouldn't want to do that
unless… Holy cow. Pravara, I think they want to take them prisoner!
We can't let that happen!*

A stiff westerly breeze appeared. Steve stifled a curse.
Captain Windbag was in fine form, it would seem. When
would he run out of jhorun?

As Pravara descended, and Steve prepared to come to
the aid of the helpless Lentarian guards, an errant gust of
wind suddenly had Pravara flapping her wings like mad.
Concerned, Steve snuffed out his flames and gripped several
nearby scales to steady himself.

Damn that wind. Had Flinn spotted them? Or had the
winds picked up on their own accord?

A nagging thought occurred. The wind. Could the wind
recharge Flinn's jhorun much like how fire could recharge
his?

An interesting notion. If you, a human fire elemental, can recharge your jhorun by being in contact with your element, then I would think a human air elemental could do the same with his.

Thanks, Kahvel. I have been wondering about that. So, that's gotta be how he's doing it. The sneaky devil has been recharging his jhorun from the very air around us. I'm both impressed and dismayed at the same time.

A concealed door opened in the bow of the ship, almost directly between the two 'leg holes'. More pirates streamed out, angling straight for the unconscious soldiers. Faint wisps of white smoke could still be seen lingering around the soldiers' inert forms.

We need to do something and we need to do it now! Come on, Pravara! Go faster!

Steve, I believe you are the answer.

What? How?

Awaken the sleeping humans.

And how, pray tell, do I do that?

Do you see the mists from the sleeping potion?

Yeah. What about it?

Burn it off. I believe that mist is remnants from the potion. Remove the mists and allow the humans to awaken.

Oh. That makes sense. Okay, I'll give that a shot. What about the other gun?

What about it?

What's it doing?

It has finished turning. It has not fired. Yet.

Kahvel, it's aimed at the castle! We need to stop it from firing!

Back on the *Emberbrand*, their luck ran out. The second strange gun had stopped moving, selected its target, and fired. A strange elongated projectile flew out of the gun's barrel and punched through the castle's outer stone wall as though it were made of paper. Then Steve heard several more crashes as, evidently, the projectile had kept going. Finally, nearly twenty seconds later, they heard a distant explosion.

That projectile made it all the way to the other side of the castle! How is that possible?

I don't know what they're loading into that gun, or how they're managing it, but I do know this: we can't let that thing fire again. I feel sick to my stomach. Look how much damage that thing created! What if there were people in the way? They wouldn't stand a chance!

Steve, do as my father suggests. Awaken the human soldiers. They must not allow themselves to be captured.

With a look of grim resolution, Steve nodded. His hands curled into fists and ignited. He targeted the white wispy vapors he could see just above the ground and ordered his jhorun to flash burn the area. However, remembering that he didn't want any human casualties on his hands, he modified the order to target everything one foot above the ground and higher.

Both hands tingled. He raised both palms, aimed them away from Pravara and the men still actively fighting the pirates, and blasted a huge jet of flames from both hands. A wall of fire appeared. It sped away from dragon and rider and then dropped like a rock, speeding toward the unconscious men.

Those pirates who were unlucky enough to be in the way cried out in pain and leapt away from the Lentarian soldiers. Nearly a dozen pirates, sporting fresh sunburns, dropped to the ground and rolled around, attempting to extinguish flames they didn't realize *weren't* there. They angrily got to their feet but gasped with surprise when they noticed the Lentarian soldiers hastily rising.

Weapons were recovered and with a whoop, the soldiers lit into the pirates with the gusto of freshly rested men. Steve watched, mesmerized, as the soldiers easily gained the upper hand over the pirates. The hidden door on the bow of the ship closed with a loud bang, forcing the fleeing pirates to scramble up rope ladders on the side of the *Emberbrand*.

Just then, a wave of fear washed through Steve. He instantly cursed and was about ready to tell Pravara to evacuate the area when he hesitated. The intense bout of fear was exactly the same as he had felt before.

He felt Pravara start to turn.

No! Don't turn! Stay where you are. One of those damn pirates is using his jhorun against us!

It is very effective.

I know it is. Hang in there. Don't pay it any attention.

Easier said than done. If they ... do you see that? A fog bank is forming.

I see it. I think I know what's happening. The soldiers are better fighters than the pirates. We know it and they know it. Flinn must be using every trick at his disposal in order to turn the tide. If that fog bank is allowed to form, then that will give the pirates the edge. Take me down. I'll deal with the fog.

What should I do?

You, Rhamalli, and the others need to keep targeting the ship. Keep Captain Windbag busy. Can you do that for me?

With pleasure.

Steve hopped to the ground just as soon as Pravara touched down. The moment he did, the huge dragon was off again. Whatever she had planned, he could trust her to follow through with it. His business was with the pirates and forcing them to leave.

The fog continued to coalesce. At the rate it was thickening, Steve guessed he had less than ten seconds before he wouldn't be able to see more than a few feet ahead of him. He grinned. This was something he could deal with. A fog bank was composed of tiny drops of water. Water had the tendency to disappear whenever fire put in an appearance, so this ought to be easy.

He thought back to what he remembered seeing from his perch on Pravara's back. The shore extended north to south, with the width of the beach being nearly fifty feet at the widest. The ship had been pushed up, almost halfway out of the water. He could see pirates everywhere. However, there were also Lentarian soldiers down there. Could he launch a wall of flames and burn anything that wasn't Lentarian by nature?

Steve frowned. He didn't want to hurt the pirates, either, no matter how much they tried to convince him otherwise. Perhaps he could order his jhorun to burn everything and leave the humans alone? It was worth a try.

Steve interlaced his fingers and pushed them away, cracking his knuckles. He eyed the thickening fog, gave *strict* orders for his jhorun to leave both pirates and soldiers alone, and curled his hands into fists. He implored his jhorun a final time to leave the humans unharmed, and then allowed his hands to spring open, full expecting to see another wall of flames burst forth.

Apparently, his jhorun had other plans.

Anyone familiar with Steve's power would know that, under dire circumstances, his jhorun would seemingly take matters into their own hands and act accordingly. It usually resulted in detonations capable of collapsing large hills, or blasting out windows. This time around, the tiniest of sparks appeared directly in front of him.

Steve groaned, closed his eyes, and braced for the worst.

A highly powerful concussive blast of superheated air, which rapidly expanded in all directions, appeared. The fog bank disappeared, exposing a single oak tree large enough to conceal a pirate. As it so happened, one pirate happened to be using it for that very purpose. The pirate in question had been leaning around the base of the trunk to watch the proceedings. Steve and the pirate locked eyes with each other.

A chaser formed in Steve's outstretched hand. He eyed the pirate and gave the trembling man a two-fingered salute.

"This is the part where you start running, pal."

"Puck, get back here on the double!" a man bellowed from the beached ship. "He's mine!"

The pirate didn't have to think twice. He sprinted from his hiding place and ran toward the ship. The burning fireball poofed out in Steve's hand as he watched another pirate jump over the gunwale and casually walk toward him, as though he had nothing better to do with his time.

Slowly, as though he were savoring the image he was presenting, the approaching pirate drew his cutlass. "I owe you a lot of pain, mate. You're about to feel what it's like to be gutted, like a fish."

Steve's eyes narrowed. It was the pirate that Gareth had shrunk and bottled. That meant…

The approaching pirate suddenly broke out into a sprint. Moving impossibly fast, he approached at an impressive rate. Steve groaned as his memory returned to him. This was Jino, the pirate with superhuman reflexes. More than likely, this was not going to end well.

Jino's form zipped by him, presenting nothing more than a swift blur of motion. A stinging sensation appeared on his right arm. Steve glanced down and saw blood dripping onto the sandy beach. He gripped his arm and glared at Jino, who had appeared a comfortable distance away.

"You've been a pain in our side for long enough, mate," Jino sneered from a safe distance. "Think you can hit me with one of your fireballs, mate? Give it your best shot."

Anger coursed through his veins. Damn, punk-ass pirate. There was no way he was going to allow some...

Jino squawked with surprise as he suddenly rose into the air. He hung there, at least five feet off the ground, for just a few moments before he gave another cry of surprise as he began to move. Jino began circling in the air, picking up speed, as though a giant was holding him by his boot and was whipping him through the air, like a cowboy twirling a lasso. After the fourth revolution, the invisible force holding Jino released him, allowing him to fly through the air, on a direct course to ... the sea. Jino's head surfaced. He cursed and started to swim back to the shore. The same invisible force that had plucked him off the ground returned and pushed him several hundred feet out to sea, forcing Jino to let out a cry of dismay.

Equally surprised, Steve refrained from launching the chaser he had created. What magic was this? It had looked like some invisible hand had just plucked Jino off the ground and *flung* him out to sea. Whoever it was had just earned themselves a fruit basket for Christmas.

"Keep it up, Paco. I'll push your sorry butt so far out to sea that you'll develop gills before you see land again."

Steve's face broke out into a grin. He knew that voice anywhere. It was Sarah! She was finally awake! He saw his wife slowly walking toward him with a frown on her face.

"All I wanted to do was to take a nap and look what happens. This place went straight to hell."

"Damn glad to see you, babe!"

"Are you hurt?"

"Mr. Steroids over there got me again. On my arm. I really don't know how bad it is. It stings like crazy, that's for sure."

Steve remained motionless while his wife inspected his arm.

"It doesn't look too bad. Use your shirt to make a tourniquet. Hurry, will you? It looks like Pheron's soldiers could use a hand."

Steve tore off a section of his tunic, ripped it into several thin strips, and wrapped it tightly around his arm. Satisfied the wound had stopped dripping blood—for now, anyway—Steve returned his attention to the pirates. Nearly two dozen of the unruly brutes were still fighting the soldiers, striving like mad to drive them away and, presumably, into the sea. However, the soldiers were trained fighters. They knew the area. They had the upper hand, not the pirates. What was the result?

The pirates were slowly forced back to the *Emberbrand*.

"How's Pryllan? Were you able to get her out of the castle?"

Sarah nodded. "I had to replenish my jhorun with another mimet, but yes. I didn't take her all the way back. Pryllan didn't want to overtax my jhorun, so she and her baby are flying back to their nest. Kahvel sent nearly a dozen dragons to escort them home."

"Good."

"I'm so tired of fighting," Sarah idly commented, as she selected a pirate in her line of sight. She used her jhorun to effortlessly lift the hapless man and fling him out into the water, like she was returning a fish to the sea. "One little, two little, three little pirates…"

Steve ducked as a pair of cursing pirates sailed over his head. Twin splashes announced their forced introduction to the sea. As Sarah continued to sing, more and more pirates found themselves picked up and flung into the water, as though they weighed no more than a feather.

A blast of air brought Sarah's song to an abrupt end. The jet originated from the ship—unsurprisingly—and slammed into Sarah, knocking her a full five feet backward and onto her rump. A drop of blood trickled from her nose.

"That shut ye up, didn' it?"

Flinn was standing on the *Emberbrand*'s prow, with a booted foot up on the bowsprit.

Steve knelt down by his wife and laid a hand on her shoulder.

"Stay down."

Sarah was about to scramble to her feet when she noticed Steve's hand had turned an ugly, mottled red.

Steve rose to his feet and eyed the pirate captain. "Do you enjoy picking on women? Okay, if that's the way you want to play it, let's do this."

"Ye don' stand a chance against me, fire thrower."

"You took the words right out of my mouth, you overweight, long-winded, pompous windbag."

Several of the nearby pirates snickered, but just as quickly fell silent. Flinn gave a broad smile, opened his arms wide, and bowed.

"How did ye say it, mate? 'Hit me with yer best shot'? Very well. Let's see what ye got. If it's anything more than…"

Flames exploded up from the ground and quickly surrounded the pirate ship. In the blink of an eye, it appeared as though the *Emberbrand* had lost the battle. The deck became engulfed in flames. Tendrils of fire snaked under doors, down stairs, and sought out every nook and cranny the ship had to offer.

Flinn let out a bellow of rage and used his own jhorun to push the ship off the beach and back out to the open sea. Once there, he created small funnel clouds to splash sea water all over the ship, effectively dousing the flames. However, before the pirate captain could launch an attack of his own, the ship was hit with another blast of fire, only this time the attack didn't come from the ground. It had come from the air.

Steve didn't waste any time. He followed Pravara's shot with one of his own. Then another. The more he flung, the more enraged he became. Steve continued to let chaser after chaser slam into various parts of the ship, effectively keeping Flinn too occupied with putting out the fires to do much of anything else. He also noticed that the pirates Sarah had flung into the water were now swimming toward the ship. He could even see several of them pull themselves over the gunwale and run to the aid of the captain. In fact, there was Mr. Steroids himself climbing up a rope ladder.

Flinn was gesturing angrily. While he couldn't quite make out what the captain was saying, he knew it had something to do with putting out the fires. Presumably, Flinn needed to free himself up so he could go on the offensive rather than use his jhorun only to put out the flames.

Suddenly, the two masts rose back into the air. The crow nests guns were long gone, having been rapidly dismantled by the pirates. Sails were unfurled, and the ship was just starting to inch away when Steve noticed something in the water that made his blood run cold. A small patch of jet-black water had appeared on the surface and was growing steadily larger.

Shocked, Steve glanced back at the shore. They had to be less than fifty feet away from solid land. There was no way one of them would venture this close, would they?

Steve ran to the water's edge and waved his arms. "Flinn! Heads up! Danger!"

Flinn appeared on the prow once more. He glared angrily at Steve before noticing that his foe was pointing at the water.

"Yes! Look! Look at the water, you nimrod! Get the hell outta there! Now!"

Flinn looked down at the large patch of black water and gasped. Steve could tell right away that the pirate captain knew immediately what the problem was. The tide of the battle had turned, no doubt about it. However, it wasn't to either of their advantage. Their fight, unfortunately, had attracted the largest predator to ever call Lentari home.

The waters directly behind the bow of the *Emberbrand* erupted, as if someone had detonated a bomb below the surface. Something large, dark, and moving insanely fast, breached the surface of the water. The creature leapt over the bobbing brigantine, clearing the tallest mast by at least a dozen feet.

Steve, with his mouth open in shock, turned to look nervously at Sarah. Her look said it all. The pirates were doomed.

A gigantic serpentine head rose out of the water. This one, Steve noted with surprise, wasn't black, or even red. It was violet colored, heavily scaled, and far and away the biggest oskorlisk he had ever seen. The huge snake head immediately oriented on the *Emberbrand*. It flicked its tongue out in rapid succession, as if deciding where it should strike first.

Steve squinted at the huge snake. From what he could remember from the time he had gone on the Hunt with Pryllan, the oskorlisk shouldn't have had any eyes. Well, unsurprisingly, he had been wrong. This particular giant serpent *did* have eyes, only they were so tiny that the oskorlisk clearly had to use other means for locating its prey. Yes, that had to be it. The eyes looked as though they were solid white. That had to be why the huge serpents developed their ability to seek out heat signatures. He remembered that, during their hunt, he and Pryllan had discovered the giant serpent was able to track them just by reading their body heat.

Steve heard several cries of alarm, followed almost immediately by frantic splashing. Both Steve and the huge snake looked. Steve groaned. There were still pirates in the water! If they didn't get out of there, then they were going to become nothing more than an afternoon snack for the oskorlisk.

The serpent's huge coils appeared. It wrapped several of them around the ship, as if to be certain it wouldn't escape, and then it focused on the disturbances coming from the surface of the water. It brought its head down within a dozen feet of the first pirate, as if wondering whether prey that small was worth the effort. With a flick of its tongue, the great jaws opened and it prepared to strike.

Just then, a fireball slammed into the snake's head. While nowhere near powerful enough to cause any damage, it did have the effect of getting the great serpent's attention. The oskorlisk hissed with annoyance and turned to identify what was responsible for the blast.

"Over here, you overgrown set of luggage!" Steve shouted, waving his arms. "You're looking for who did it? Wanna know what hit you? That was me!"

The oskorlisk hissed angrily as it turned away from Steve,

deciding there was more appealing prey to be found in the water. Steve watched the giant scaled snout quest about as it presumably searched for more of the pirates. Steve generated two more chasers and sent them careening east before having them circle about and strike the oskorlisk from the opposite direction. As expected, the huge serpent abandoned its search and whipped its head east. Steve also noticed that the pirates had stopped swimming toward their ship to watch the speeding fireballs.

"Are you friggin' kidding me? Guys! What the hell are you doing? Flinn? Come on, man! I'm trying to buy you some time! Get your men out of the water! I'll try to keep this thing busy. You save your men! Hurry!"

A look of surprise appeared on Flinn's face. He hesitated only a moment before whipping gale force winds into existence. The swirling jets of air became a funnel cloud and started plucking members of his crew from the water.

After the sixth chaser had slammed into the oskorlisk, each from a different direction, Steve decided it was time for some wyverian assistance. He had finally made himself a big enough pain in the butt for the oskorlisk to take notice, and unfortunately, a rapid relocation was required. Pravara, much to her father's chagrin, pulled him off the beach before the oskorlisk could venture any closer to land.

Steve had been trying to make the oskorlisk ignore the remaining pirates in the water and, instead, focus on him. However, his plan had worked too well. Without realizing it, Steve had mistimed his last shot and had thrown the chaser just as the huge snout had oriented on him. Oskorlisks might not have been the sharpest tool in the shed, but even it could figure out the small biped with the flaming appendages was the one responsible for the majority of the attacks.

The oskorlisk swam closer. Steve swallowed nervously. Pravara had swooped in so fast that the great serpent didn't notice he was no longer on the beach. Steve had a feeling that history was about to be made in Lentari. For the first time ever, an oskorlisk appeared as though it was about to venture up onto dry land. Just as the great serpent arrived at the beach, a blur of motion caught its attention. The heavily scaled snout immediately lifted as its primary prey had been scented.

Curious as to what had distracted the oskorlisk, Steve turned in time to see Rhamalli and Pheron execute a second dive, and then a third. Dragon and rider had courageously offered themselves up as bait to lure the oskorlisk back to the sea, while Pravara had rushed to retrieve Steve.

"Where is Sarah?" Pravara inquired. "I do not see her anywhere."

"She's teleporting the soldiers off the beach," Steve explained. "I watched her teleport at least half a dozen soldiers, one at a time. I just hope she doesn't over-exhaust herself again."

"What are your plans for the oskorlisk?" Pravara nervously asked. "I don't think I've ever seen one this close up before."

And I hope you never have to again, young one.

Father, I know I went against your wishes, but…

No. There is no need for explanations. Your loyalty to your friends is commendable.

We need to drive that oskorlisk off. Kahvel, do you have any ideas?

This is how you protect my daughter? By riding her into battle with a great serpent?

Umm…

I will address that later. Rhamalli, take Kaden and Shalen. You three are some of the best fliers I have ever seen. Impress me. Lure the serpent away from land.

And if we're unable to lure it?

Who is that? Steve quietly asked.

Be silent. That is Rhamalli, Pravara whispered in his mind.

You are wyverians. It is an oskorlisk. No great serpent can resist a wyverian, let alone three. It will pursue.

Acknowledged. Kaden? Shalen? Follow my lead.

Steve?

Yes?

Will you aid Pravara and continue to attack that serpent? Distract it, in any fashion you can.

You got it.

Do not get anywhere close to that creature. Either of you. This foe is beyond any of us. Is that understood?

Yep. Come on, Pravara. Let's see if we can go piss off the mother of all snakes, okay?

Pravara executed a tight left turn and headed west. The oskorlisk had removed one of the two coils wrapped around the *Emberbrand*, but it was still clearly unwilling to let the ship go. Rhamalli and the other two dragons were nothing more than blurs of color as they swooped, dived, and ducked in their attempt to get the oskorlisk's attention.

Steve retrieved a mimet, replenished his tiring jhorun, and generated as many chasers as he could. Three dozen blazing fireballs, in three rows of twelve each, were now pacing them as they flew overhead. Steve pointed at the huge snake far below them.

"That's our target. Those things seem to be attracted to fire and bright objects, so let's see what you guys can do."

Thirty-six identical balls of fire sped off. Some collided with the serpent's scaly hide while others zoomed precariously in front of its snout, presenting an appealing snack. The oskorlisk hissed, reared back, and then lunged forward, snapping up a full third of the chasers before Steve could call them back.

The oskorlisk's head disappeared into the depths of the churning water, only to reappear on the other side of the ship. The oskorlisk's head was angled up, as if it had detected an aerial assailant. Its mouth opened and Steve could see something dripping from its two primary fangs, whether excess water or venom, he didn't know. Now that he thought about it, he didn't want to know.

"Pravara, where are the other dragons? Look at the oskorlisk. It looks like it smells something."

"No one is near," Pravara assured him.

Steve suddenly smiled. An idea had just presented itself. He heard his own words come back to him.

Those things seem to be attracted to fire and bright objects…

Steve glanced down at his hands. He was willing to wager

he could create a chaser large enough to attract the giant serpent's attention, only he didn't think he could make the fireball that size move fast enough to lure the oskorlisk away. He caught sight of Flinn as he appeared on the deck of his ship. Captain Flinn was gently moving his arms in a series of various gestures, no doubt doing what he had to do in order to control the wind.

"Drop me on the ship, Pravara."

"Excuse me? I will admit that I am in no way an expert on human affairs, but I cannot help but think that is a bad idea."

"There's no way I can drive that thing off by myself. The captain and I are going to have to work together, whether he likes it or not. If push comes to shove, and it looks like I'm in danger, I'll do my Iron Man thing again and shoot myself straight up. Then it'll be up to you to catch me before I end up becoming lunch for that oskorlisk."

"What would Sarah say?" Pravara inquired.

"You and I already know what she'd say."

"So, what are you going to do?" the dragon coyly asked.

"You're still going to drop me on that ship."

"I believe that's a bad idea. What if you need to vacate the ship as quickly as possible, and you launch yourself up so high I cannot find you?"

"It'll be easy. All you'll have to do is follow the screams. Listen, I'll take the heat for this. Do it, Pravara. Drop me on that deck there near the back."

Pravara waited until the oskorlisk was looking the other way before she swooped in low and deposited her rider on the quarterdeck. Steve quickly rolled to his feet and ignited his hands as a warning to the pirates who were rapidly approaching. He lifted both arms in the universal sign of 'I surrender', but kept both of his hands lit.

"Chill out, guys. I come in peace. I need to talk to Captain Flinn. Now."

No one said anything.

"For Pete's sakes, guys. Do you want to get eaten by the oskorlisk? Someone find me the damn captain!"

"How about I deliver him your head?" one voice hissed.

Steve turned to see Jino approach. The pirate had pulled

his cutlass from his belt and was about ready to attack when a third voice brought him up sharp.

"Stow that weapon and stand down, mate," Flinn snapped. The captain stepped down from the forecastle and regarded Steve curiously. "Ye got mettle comin' onboard my ship without permission, fire thrower."

"We have a common problem."

"The sea serpent, aye. I noticed."

"We're gonna have to work together, pal, whether either of us likes it or not."

"What do ye have in mind?"

"Ever play baseball?"

"No."

"Hmm. Okay, listen. I'll generate a fireball, one that won't be going out any time soon. I'll also make the sucker as big as I can get it. Now, I'm going to need you and your wind to propel that thing as far as you can, and as fast as you can get it. I'm guessing the oskorlisk will pursue it."

"Why should I trust the likes of you?" Flinn demanded. "Ye have been a pain in my side for quite some time now."

"I'm not asking you to trust me," Steve told the pirate, fighting valiantly to keep the exasperation out of his voice. "However, if we don't do something, and do it, like, right *now*, then we're all gonna become lunch to that huge snake. I have no plans on becoming someone's dinner. I'd like to think that you don't, either. Would you agree?"

Flinn's head gave a perceptible nod.

"Good. Do you think you could make the wind push my chaser far out to sea? And we're talking fast. We have to make it look like the chaser is fleeing the scene. I'll wager the oskorlisk will take off after it. What do you say?"

"Aye, I can do that."

"Good."

"However…"

"What?" Steve demanded.

"Nothing be changed, fire thrower. This does not make us friends. You are still my enemy."

Steve shrugged. "I can live with that. As much as I don't like you, either, I can't have your death on my hands.

Or any of your crew. Speaking of which, are all your people accounted for?"

"Quartermaster," Flinn snapped, "have ye taken a head count? Is everyone here? We cannot allow anyone to … Jino, so help me, if ye don' drop that sword and return to yer post, then I'll personally feed the likes of ye to the serpent. Be that understood?"

Jino dropped the weapon and stalked away. Rusty appeared next, looking contrite. His eyes dropped to the deck and stayed there.

"I have, Captain. I am ashamed to say we are still one man down. Er, it's the same person we discussed before. Nobody can recall when they saw him last and he has yet to turn up."

Steve rushed to the side of the ship and anxiously peered into the water. "You're missing someone? Damn. He's gotta be out in the water somewhere."

Flinn appeared by his side. He slowly shook his head. "No, if he be the one I think he is, then methinks we lost him somewhere south of that accursed dragon valley. He be dragon fodder by now."

Steve shook his head, "I seriously doubt it. Don't worry, I'll let the king know. If he's out there, then we'll find him."

"Why are ye doin' this? Why help us out?"

Steve hooked a thumb at the oskorlisk. "Whatever you're doing here, whatever your reasons are for being here, no one deserves to meet up with one of those."

"Ye warned us about black water earlier. I figure ye were warnin' us about that, right?"

Steve nodded. "That's right. Now, get ready."

Flinn nodded and raised his hands. A huge gust of air materialized over the water next to the *Emberbrand* but opposite the oskorlisk. The captain nodded his readiness.

Steve closed his eyes, clenched his fists, and then created a chaser. He cupped the blazing fireball with his hands and slowly pulled them apart, channeling more of his jhorun into his hands as he did so. As a result, the chaser grew in size.

The chaser grew larger and larger. First it was the size of a softball. Then it grew to twice the size of a basketball. After a few moments the chaser had expanded to the size of a bean bag chair.

The oskorlisk's head suddenly spun around, and just like that, Steve and the captain were looking at the business end of the oskorlisk.

"Time's up, mate," Flinn muttered softly.

"I'm almost there," Steve reported. "Just a few more seconds."

Up until this time, the writhing mass of compressed air that Flinn had summoned was slowly rotating in place. The huge jet of air had essentially twisted itself around so that it was starting to form another funnel cloud. At the flick of the captain's wrist, the funnel unwound itself and snapped forward, impacting the oskorlisk's head just as it lunged forward.

The mammoth snake was disoriented long enough for Steve to finish creating the largest chaser he had ever made. It was now the size of a small automobile and—understandably—was taking its toll on his jhorun. He had to release it soon or else, contrary to what he had bragged to the captain, the huge flaming fireball would drain all of his jhorun in less than a few minutes.

"Okay, batter up! Flinn, hit it with your best shot!"

Flinn made a gesture with both of his arms akin to pushing a heavy weight off his chest. The howling winds surged forward and impacted the fireball with enough force that Steve actually thought he heard the crack of a bat. The fireball soared out to sea, followed closely by a strong gust of wind to make certain the chaser kept moving. The oskorlisk's head whipped around to follow the course taken by the chaser. Whether in anger or in anticipation, the great serpent hissed, flicked its tongue in rapid succession, and released the final coil it had looped around the *Emberbrand*.

The oskorlisk whipped its massive body through the water so fast that the resulting waves threatened to tip over the brigantine. Steve, Flinn, and the pirates were flung about as they tried to keep from getting thrown off the ship. Once the waves subsided, and the ship stopped bobbing about, Steve released his death grip of the gunwale to look out to sea, toward the eastern horizon. Chaser and oskorlisk had disappeared from sight.

Steve groaned and stretched his back, "All things considered, it could have been worse."

"Aye," Flinn agreed, nodding his head. "It could've."

"What are you… hey!"

Steve was cut off as a powerful blast of air knocked him off the ship and into the water.

"As I said, fire thrower," Flinn said, leaning over the gunwale to stare at him, "it changes nothing. I cannot allow ye to interfere with my plans anymore. Should we cross paths again, it will be yer last."

Steve coughed up water and stared angrily up at the ship. The sails had been unfurled and the ship was picking up speed. A second figure appeared by the captain and smirked at him.

It was Jino.

The pirate reached inside his tunic and tugged something loose. He held it up for everyone to see. Steve groaned while the rest of the crew whooped with approval.

It was the oskorlisk fang.

Steve's eyes widened. His hands flew to his belt, where he had stashed the snake tooth. Sure enough, it was gone. Then he thought of the brief skirmish he had with the pirate, where he had received the cut on his arm. Jino must have seen the fang and took it upon himself to steal it back.

Satisfied that Steve had seen the reclaimed fang, Captain Flinn turned on his heel and strode toward the aft of the ship. The winds immediately strengthened and began pushing the *Emberbrand* further away from shore. A few moments later, the vessel shimmered and disappeared from view. However, since Pravara had located the disguised vessel before, and had told him what to look for, he could see that the *Emberbrand* was still there, slowly sailing away. Whatever technique Flinn had used to hide his ship—when Pravara had been unable to detect it—hadn't been used this time.

Pravara? Can you come get me? We need to follow Flinn and that ship. I can see him, but only when he's up close. If he gets too far away, then we're gonna lose him.

I'm on my way.

Once he was securely seated on Pravara's back, Steve

pointed southwest. "They went that way. Hurry. There's no way I'm letting that dillhole out of my sight."

Let them be for now. Do not pursue.

Dragon and human both hesitated and shared a look with each other.

Pravara, you heard that, right?

Aye.

Why would your father want us to stop?

That's wasn't my ...

Kahvel, that's a bad idea. I don't know what type of jhorun Flinn is using to hide his ship, but it's not perfect. The closer we are to the ship, the easier it is to see.

I am not the aerial king.

You're not the aerial king? Whoa, wait. You're not Kahvel? Then who is this? And who refers to the Dragon Lord as Aerial King, anyway? No one, that's who.

"I have heard it before," Pravara quietly admitted, switching to her normal speaking voice.

Surprised, Steve leaned over Pravara's side to look at her distant head.

"You have? When? Where?"

"I'm trying to recall. I was with Mikal. And Gareth."

"When?"

"Within the last year. I could probably deduce the identity with a few guesses. Why they're telepathically communicating with us now remains a mystery."

Because I am not physically there. I am near the settlement humans call Capily.

Who are you? Steve demanded. *Why haven't you identified yourself yet?*

You're a shealk, aren't you? Pravara asked, growing cautious. **You *must* be. What business do the water dragons have here?**

I have been monitoring. Your situation has escalated. We have learned what the human bandits are after.

"I know who this is," Pravara whispered excitedly to Steve. "It must be Lord Phaedren, of the shealk!"

Right species, wrong shealk. We have met before, youngling. I am Balthor.

Chapter 13 — The Alchos Stones

Confused, Steve looked down at Pravara just as she bent her neck to look back at him. That was Balthor? Steve remembered meeting the shealk wizard at Mikal and Lissa's wedding earlier in the year. Gareth's father had been polite, even cordial. He had enabled the attending shealk to be able to converse with the rest of the wedding guests by creating a communication spell. Balthor, it would seem, was just as powerful as Gareth, if not more so. He had been monitoring the situation? Why would the normally timid water dragons express interest with human affairs? There had to be something they were missing.

"I think you ought to land, Pravara. Something's up. I do believe the shealk know something we do not."

"Agreed."

Balthor? Are you still with me?

Only for a moment longer. I am on my way.

You're on your way? To where? Here?

Aye.

Can you at least tell me what's going on?

The shealk wizard's voice had fallen silent. Steve glanced at Pravara, who shook her head, indicating she didn't hear him anymore, either. Steve shrugged and pointed at the ground far below.

"If I wasn't curious before, I sure as hell am now. We'd better land."

"Agreed."

Once they were back on dry land, Steve noticed Sarah rushing toward him. His wife caught the look of concern on his face and frowned. She instantly vanished and then reappeared beside him.

"What's the matter? Why aren't you smiling? You should be happy! The pirates are gone!"

Steve pulled up his shirt to expose his belt. "They got the damn fang. I had it tucked in my belt, but just before they left, Mr. Steroids held it up so that I could see it. He must have snagged it when he got close enough to cut my arm."

"Mr. Steroids?"

"That's the pirate who's clearly doped up on something. He's the one who moves so fast that you can't see him."

"Ah. That's not playing fair, is it?" Sarah decided. "I'm surprised you aren't heading out after them."

Steve pointed at the still form of Pravara, lying quietly nearby. "We were ready to head out when we were warned off."

A look of surprise crept over Sarah's face. "You were warned off? By who?"

"Balthor. Do you remember him?"

Sarah nodded. "Gareth's father, right?"

"Right. He advised us to let him go and that he had something to tell us."

"I wonder what that means," Sarah mused.

"Tell her what the shealk wizard said next," Pravara instructed, lifting her neck off the ground so that she could turn her head.

"Right. He said that they had learned what the pirates are looking for. I got the impression that it wasn't good."

"As did I," Pravara agreed.

"He's on his way," Steve added.

The look of surprise on Sarah's face was priceless. "Balthor is on his way? Here? Wow. I hope this isn't as bad as it sounds."

"Where's Gareth?" Steve asked, taking a step backwards to scan the area. "I haven't seen him in a while."

"He was helping me evacuate the soldiers, but now that you mention it, I haven't seen him around, either."

Just then, nearly fifty feet out to sea due east, the surface of the water erupted, as though someone had let off an underwater explosion. Flocks of brightly colored kytes abandoned their perches out of nearby trees and took to the air, squawking loudly. A few moments later, they collectively flew south.

Steve's eyes narrowed. What had caused the disruption in the water? Whatever it was, it had been significant enough to persuade the small red birds to seek their perches elsewhere.

He felt a light tap on his shoulder. Sarah silently pointed to the same section of water that had exploded. The surface had just returned to its calm, pristine state when a small patch of water looked as though it was starting to boil. After nearly ten seconds passed, two dragon heads rose steadily out of the water on long, sleek necks. One was jet black while the other was several shades of blue. The blue head had a pair of slightly curved horns whereas the black one did not. Also, the blue head was much larger than the black head.

Steve grinned. They were the shealk! Well, Balthor had said that he was on his way. One of these two had to be Gareth's father.

The large blue head turned to look straight at him, as if it had sensed his thoughts. It nodded once, shimmered, and then vanished. Moments later, a tall human about the same age as he was, complete with graying hair, appeared by his side. He bowed at the two of them and then held out a hand to Steve.

"I remember you, Fire Thrower. I am Balthor. It's a pleasure to see you again. And you, Miss Sarah."

Sarah curtsied and offered the newcomer a smile. "Hello, Balthor. We remember you, too. What are you doing out here?

How did you possibly get all the way from Capily to here?"

"Why, the same as you would, Miss Sarah. Teleporting may not be my specialty, but I can still manage it from time to time."

"Well, that explains what happened in the water," Steve murmured.

I do not wish to lose sight of the pirate vessel. I will return to the air.

Both Steve and Balthor glanced over at the immobile dragon. Steve nodded once. Within moments, Pravara had launched herself straight up and had disappeared into the endless blue sky.

Gareth appeared next as he stumbled up the beach, soaking wet, in the same clothes he had been in earlier. His lips started to move as he softly chanted. Several seconds later, he was smoothing the wrinkles out of his dry clothes.

Balthor looked at his son, noted the bedraggled look he was presenting, and gently shook his head. "Remember, son. I told you to cast the impervious spell just before your arrival, lest your clothes become wet."

"Are we too late?" Gareth finally asked. "Have the pirates already left?"

It was Steve's turn to scowl. "Yes, although not before those scumbags were able to steal the fang back from me. I was about ready to go out after them when your father suggested I hold off."

"You really need to hear what he has to say," Gareth said, turning serious. "I don't know how that pirate captain knew to come here, but I can guarantee you he's not going to leave any time soon. Not without a second stone, that is."

"A what?" Steve asked, confused. He turned to Sarah, who shrugged.

"A *stone*," Gareth slowly repeated.

"What kind of stone?" Sarah asked.

"A special one," Gareth cryptically answered.

"Do not tease them, son," Balthor scolded. "You did not know of their existence, either. I had to tell you what they were and what they were capable of."

"Spoilsport," Gareth muttered.

"These stones," Balthor began, "are very powerful. They can quite literally…"

"Hold on a second," Steve interrupted, bringing his hands up into a time-out gesture. "I think Mikal really needs to hear this."

"Where is he now?" Gareth asked, looking around.

Sarah turned and pointed at the imposing castle behind them. "When the pirates attacked, he was escorted inside."

"And is my son correct?" Balthor asked. "Mikal is now the king?"

Steve nodded. "During Kri'Entu's absence, yes. His parents should be back in a few weeks."

The four of them started up the embankment and headed toward the castle. A loud, piercing whistle caused everyone to look back toward the beach. Pheron had collected his men together and, after leaving nearly half a squadron behind to secure the beach should the pirates be foolish enough to return, fell into step behind them. As they walked, Balthor continued to pepper them with questions.

"Do we know where this human bandit is from?"

Steve nodded. "Yes. He's from across the sea, some place called *The Seven Kingdoms*."

"Yes, yes, I know that," Balthor said, waving a dismissive hand. "I was hoping you could be more specific."

"Perz," Sarah said, after a moment's pause. "He told Steve that he was from a place called Perz."

Balthor scowled. "The Perz Archipelagos. I should have known. That's where I found *him*. This is starting to make sense now."

"What is?" Steve asked, rounding on the shealk-wizard-in-human-form. "It's where you found *who*?"

"I will explain everything in the castle. It's a rather long story, and I would prefer to say it just the one time."

"Maybe a teeny tiny clue?" Steve pressed. "Come on, something juicy must've dragged you all the way out here. Give us a hint!"

Sarah smacked him on the arm. "Honey, he just said that he wants to wait until we're all together. Wait for Mikal. Sheesh!"

He looked up in time to see Gareth share a smile with his father. Steve guessed—correctly—that Gareth must have peppered his father with all kinds of questions, too. Balthor said they were looking for a stone? A stone with magical powers? Steve groaned. As if they didn't have enough problems to worry about.

Once they were inside the castle, Pheron ushered them straight to the Antechamber. Mikal didn't need any introduction to Gareth's father, having met him late the previous year when he and Pravara had been transformed to shealk themselves. Temporarily, of course. He and Pravara had accompanied Gareth on a mission to deal with a jhorun-consuming monster that had been threatening the kingdom.

"Now," Balthor began, taking a seat near the hearth, "the reason I dissuaded Steve and Pravara from pursuing the human bandits was because we recently learned that an Alchos Stone has come into the humans' possession."

"And just what *is* an Alchos Stone?" Mikal asked, leaning forward. He clasped one of Lissa's hands tightly in his own before he turned to the others. "Does anyone know?"

"I haven't," Steve admitted.

"Neither have I," Sarah added.

Steve looked at the semi-circle of chairs and the people that were present. Sarah had mentioned she didn't know. From the looks of things, neither did anyone else. Gareth was the only one who was smiling, and that was only because his father had obviously clued him in.

"The Alchos Stones," Balthor breathed, leaning back in his chair. "Where do I start?"

"I'd start with Usol," Gareth suggested, drawing gasps of astonishment from both Steve and Sarah.

"You would start with *who*?" Lissa curiously asked. "That's a name I am not familiar with."

"Who is Usol?" Pheron asked at the same time.

Balthor looked straight at Steve and smiled, "Perhaps *you* would like to inform everyone about Usol? I hear you are quite familiar with his name."

"He's the Earth Guardian," Steve solemnly answered, once everyone was looking his way. "We had a run in with him earlier in the year. Trust me when I say he's someone you really don't want to mess with."

"When was this, Sir Steve?" Pheron asked.

"This was back when we adopted Emerion."

The captain nodded. "Ah. The young griffin. I do remember that now."

Balthor also nodded. "I had forgotten about the infant griffin. Son, you had a hand in the griffin's adoption, did you not?"

Gareth nodded. "I suppose you could say that. I helped point her in the right direction."

"Continuing on," the shealk wizard said as he offered his son a smile, "the Alchos Stones each belonged to one of the four Alchos, or Ancients. There was Oros, who was Creator of Fire; Eion, Master of the Winds; Aeus, Protector of Water; and, finally, there's Usol, Guardian of Earth."

Steve sat forward, interested. "So, these stone thingamajigs, they were carried around by these ancient beings? As what, lucky charms?"

Balthor shrugged. "It's hard to say with any amount of certainty. What I can tell you is that each of the four stones, being in such close proximity to the Ancient Ones for so long, became imbued with some of their immense power. As a result, the stones became highly coveted, but—unsurprisingly—were lost to time."

"Do we know what abilities each of the stones possessed?" Mikal asked. "And what would happen if a human were to find one of these stones?"

"A human has already found a stone," Balthor corrected. "The *Essence of the Sea* has been located. And used."

"The stones have names?" Sarah asked.

"How did Flinn get his hands on one of those stones?" Sarah asked.

"Isn't it obvious?" Steve scoffed. "He stole it. How else would a pirate captain get his hands on a rock like that?"

"They are called Alchos Stones," Balthor explained, "and they look nothing like ordinary rocks."

Steve shrugged. "Okay, I'll bite. What do they look like?"

"Imagine, if you will, a sparkling blue sapphire slightly

larger than your closed fist," Balthor answered. He held up his hands and touched his fingertips together, forming an O. "The *Essence* is about this big."

"Do we know what this stone does?" Mikal asked again.

"Aeus loved his element," Balthor explained. "He was also the most mistrustful of the Ancients. As a result, he spent the vast majority of his time hidden in the depths of the deepest ocean. In fact, it is said that he slumbers to this day, hidden somewhere on the floor of the Erudian."

Has the shealk ever searched for him?

"Pravara has a question," Steve began, holding up a hand. He briefly glanced skyward to see if he could see his wyverian friend, but could not. "She wants to know..."

"...whether or not we have ever searched for Aeus," Balthor interrupted. "I know. I heard her, too."

You heard me? How is this possible? The only one I am sharing my senses with is Steve!

"You have very powerful thoughts, young Pravara," Balthor said, as he looked directly at Steve. "I'm surprised more people are not able to hear the thoughts of the wyverians."

Are you implying I *think* too loud?

Steve snickered loudly.

"Aeus' stone," Balthor continued, ignoring Pravara's question, "is rumored to grant its owner the power of deception."

"Deception?" Steve repeated, frowning. "I don't like the sounds of that."

"Would you let him tell the story?" Sarah asked, growing exasperated. "I know you have questions, dear, but Mikal is the king. Let him ask the questions."

Steve smiled sheepishly, "Sorry, Mikal. I'll shut up now."

Mikal gave his former bodyguard a smile and shook his head, indicating he wasn't upset.

Balthor nodded appreciatively. "In case anyone was wondering about what a stone imbued with the power of deception could do, I was hoping to answer that question personally. You see, I had laboriously researched the *Essence of the Sea* for centuries. In the last couple of years, I managed to track down the last reported resting place of Aeus' stone when…"

The transformed shealk wizard trailed off and sighed. His head slowly fell. Steve opened his mouth but immediately closed it when Sarah nudged him. Mikal was poised to ask a question when Lissa did the same to him. She quickly shook her head no. In a collective silence, they waited. After a few minutes of silence, the shealk wizard spoke again.

"I should have realized that it would only be a matter of time before someone else became aware of the Stones' existence. The presence of the pirates here in Lentari is our fault. If it wasn't for us, no one else would have ever located a stone. The Alchos Stones would have fallen from memory. As it happens, the humans were told."

"What?" Mikal sputtered. "You're saying that … My apologies. Do continue."

"One of my research assistants slipped away, transformed himself into a human, and ventured to the surface. I do not know the specifics, nor do I know everything that transpired during the visit. The only thing I can tell you is that a transformed shealk will leave a trail of jhorun that can be read by the right individual. I was able to follow his trail to a group of islands the indigenous people called the Perz Archipelago. How my assistant found his way to a notorious human pirate is beyond me. I have been struggling to find a common link between Mephlas and your pirate captain, but thus far, I've been unsuccessful. If there's a reason, I've been unable to locate it."

"Do you have any theories?" Lissa quietly asked.

Balthor scowled and shook his head, "Mephlas, I'm sorry to say, was a prankster. I can only assume he thought it would be great fun to watch humans quarrel over the stone, much like how younglings would fight over a rare shell."

"This is your apprentice we're talking about?" Steve asked. A moment later, his eyes widened as he noticed Sarah's disapproving frown. "Sorry. I can't seem to keep my trap shut. Balthor, please continue."

"Mephlas was my *former* apprentice," Balthor clarified. "He was relieved of his duties the instant I learned of his transgressions. Now, where was I? Oh, yes. The Alchos Stones. You're probably wondering how I knew to find them. It took me over two hundred years of research to determine that a human nobleman, living in the Seven Kingdoms, had the stone in his own private collection."

"And do we know how *he* acquired it?" Mikal asked as a frown appeared on his face.

Balthor nodded. "Aye, I have a theory. Pardon my assumption, and I will offer my most heartfelt apologies if I offend anyone, but it can only be through illegal means. Fortunately, once I learned the human nobleman had it, I created spells to monitor the stone's location at all times. I wanted to know if the stone was ever moved. And that, unfortunately, was my undoing."

"Why?" Mikal asked. "What happened?"

"Mephlas was present when my spell was triggered. The stone was on the move for the first time in nearly fifty years. In my excitement, I cast another spell to see where the stone was heading and in what manner it was getting there."

"And?" Mikal prompted, after Balthor had fallen silent.

"For whatever reason, the *Essence* was placed onto a sailing vessel and sent to another human settlement. The vessel fell to a band of human bandits. The rest is, as they say, history."

I wonder how Flinn figured out how to use it? Steve silently thought to himself.

Would you like me to ask?

Pravara? I forgot you were still monitoring. Would you?

A few seconds later, Mikal's head lifted, and suddenly the young king was looking straight at Steve. The corners of his mouth turned upwards with the beginnings of a smile.

"Do you have any idea how Flinn figured out how to use the Stone?" Mikal asked.

Balthor shrugged. "Unknown. The only thing I knew was that the stone had disappeared and I couldn't find it, no matter how hard I tried. I had to wait for the *Essence* to reveal itself."

"I take it the stone finally did?" Mikal asked.

"Aye."

"How long ago?"

"Less than an hour," Balthor confirmed.

Steve snapped his fingers and grinned. He sat up straight in his chair. "So, Flinn has this stone and is obviously using it. That's why we couldn't see the ship when it vanished!"

I was able to see the ship.

Not the second time, remember?

True.

Still, it's worth mentioning.

"Pravara said that she was able to see the ship," Balthor relayed, picking up the thought.

"That would suggest a pirate was hiding the ship the first time using nothing more than his jhorun," Gareth said, as he decided his father wanted to include him in the conversation. "The second time it happened must have been when Flinn used the stone."

"I'd like to know how Mephlas knew where to find Flinn," Sarah mused. "Of all the humans he could have told, he chose a pirate?"

"We will never know why Mephlas chose a human bandit, milady," Balthor sadly told her. "I do not know how Mephlas initiated contact with the pirate, but I do know the trail ended at Perz."

"This Mephlas dude must've either overheard you or else learned about the location of the stone," Steve guessed. "Then he told Flinn where to find the *Essence* thingy."

Balthor shook his head, "Not quite. By this time, it is my belief that Flinn, as you call him, already had the *Essence* in his possession. I personally believe..." The shealk wizard paused and cleared his throat, as if he was having difficulty continuing. After a few more moments had passed, Balthor continued. "I'm fairly certain if Mephlas overheard my report to Lord Phaedren, then he also must've heard me tell him about the suspected known location of a second Stone. I believe he passed *that* information to the human bandits."

"You're certain?" Mikal repeated, frowning. "Why don't you confront this assistant of yours and find out for sure? You're a wizard, Balthor. Couldn't you write some type of truth spell?"

Balthor clasped his hands together and let them fall onto

his lap. "I would if I could."

"What happened?" Lissa gently asked. "What happened? Where is this Mephlas now?"

"I found what was left of him, buried on Perz."

Sarah clapped her hands over her mouth. A split second later, Lissa did the same. Steve whistled loudly and looked around the room to see what the others' reactions were.

"Flinn killed him? That scum-sucking, bottom-feeding, low-life piece of…"

Sarah thumped him in his ribs, bringing him up short, but not before a quizzical look appeared on her face.

"How do we know Flinn is the one who killed him? How do we know Mephlas wasn't killed by something on the island? Pedr told us that there are all kinds of protections in place whenever Flinn ventures away from his private island."

Steve shrugged. It was a good question. The only person who knew the answer to that would be Flinn, himself, and he was quite certain the ornery pirate captain wouldn't be volunteering any information. At least, not any time soon. Speaking of Pedr…

"Where is our young stool pigeon?" Steve asked. "I haven't seen him in a while. Is he okay?"

"He was feeling sick," Lissa explained. "I gave him an elixir to calm his nerves, but it worked a little too well. It knocked him out. He's sleeping off the effects as we speak."

"Under guard," Mikal quietly added.

"Who is this Pedr?" Balthor wanted to know.

"He is one of Flinn's men," Mikal answered.

"Ah. Very well. To answer your question about Mephlas' untimely death, I can only assume this human pirate was directly responsible."

"Why have you waited so long before saying anything?" Mikal demanded. "Didn't you say anything to the Constable there? Er, the Magistrate? Wouldn't that have been the prudent thing to do?"

"And tell them what?" Balthor countered. "That a shealk, temporarily disguised as a human, passed along information which could result in the location of one of the Alchos Stones?"

"So, what did you do?" Steve asked.

"I waited. I had my shealk watch that tiny island for nearly five years before I decided nothing was going to happen."

"Obviously, Flinn had the *Essence*," Steve guessed. "How'd he do it? Why did he wait so long before he did anything about it? Did he suspect that he was being watched?"

"This human is clever," Balthor admitted as he shook his head in exasperation. "I can only postulate that he waited until he was ready to set his actions in motion."

Mikal held up both of his hands in a universal 'wait' gesture. "Just a moment. That covers the how and why Flinn has one of these Alchos Stones. However, now I need some clarification about something Gareth said earlier."

"And that would be…?" Gareth asked.

"You said Flinn wasn't going to leave here until they have a second stone. Is your father suggesting…" Mikal trailed off and turned to the impassive shealk wizard. "Are you suggesting a second stone is somewhere here in Lentari?"

Balthor nodded, as did Gareth. "I am, aye."

"Where?" Steve asked. "If so, then we need to find this damn thing before he does."

"I couldn't agree more," Mikal muttered.

"How do you know another Alchos Stone is somewhere in Lentari?" Sarah asked.

"Because I was close to discovering its final location," Balthor explained. "Several heavily modified locator spells both indicated that a second stone lies somewhere within your borders. Sadly, Mephlas was in the room at the time I reported my findings to Lord Phaedren. I never dreamed that my assistant would take what he learned and pass it on to the humans. So, as you can see, the presence of Flinn and his band of pirates was a direct result of my careless handling of sensitive information."

Be that as it may, now that everyone knows why Flinn is here, what do we do about it?

Steve looked at Balthor. "Did you catch that? Pravara asked…"

"Yes, I heard," Balthor answered. "The Fire Thrower is right. We must find this second stone before Flinn can get his hands on it."

How does the oskorlisk fang fit into this scenario?
Steve nodded. "Good question, Pravara."
Thanks.

"Pravara asked why the pirates stole the fang."

Balthor sighed heavily and ran his hands through his graying hair. "Don't you see? Flinn must think he needs the fang in order to successfully locate the second stone."

"And that helps us how?" Steve asked.

Balthor thought for a moment, "Well, we'd have to ask ourselves where the Stone could be hiding that it would require the use of an oskorlisk fang in order to retrieve it."

An oskorlisk fang only offers some modicum of protection. We've already seen this fang's power at work. Are you suggesting there is some other use for the fang that we are not aware of?

Balthor relayed the question so that everyone present could hear both the question *and* the answer.

"Not at all. The fangs of the great sea serpent have long been known to offer its possessor protection from physical attacks, be they jhorun or non-jhorun in nature."

"Again, how does that help us?" Steve asked, exasperated.

"That's something we're going to have to figure out," Sarah answered as she patted her husband's hand.

"I'm having a hard time believing that one of these Stones is hiding in Lentari and we are just now hearing about this for the first time," Mikal admitted. "I just wish there was a way to validate this."

"And if there is?" Lissa quietly asked. She was smiling at her husband.

Mikal's face drained of color. "No. Absolutely not. I want nothing more to do with her."

"What is going on?" Gareth quietly asked Steve. "Why has Mikal's face become so pale?"

"Because I'm pretty sure Lissa is suggesting Mikal should ask the head of the Archives for some help."

Gareth, Steve, and Pheron all shuddered.

"I wouldn't want to do that," Pheron quietly admitted.

"I wouldn't, either," Steve added. "And even if I wanted to, it'd be a cold day in, well, Nevir, before she'd willingly help me. That old lady hates my guts."

"That's because you're never nice to her," Sarah pointed out.

"And you are?" Steve countered. "Don't try and make me out to be the bad guy. You like her just as much as I do."

Sarah pretended she couldn't hear him and, instead, focused on Mikal. He was scowling, pacing, and having a quiet argument with his new queen. Several minutes later, Mikal groaned and accepted defeat. He scribbled something on a piece of paper, handed it to a nearby guard, and sighed the moment the message left.

"That had to be hard," Steve quietly told his young friend.

"You have no idea," Mikal softly muttered.

Ten minutes later, an elderly, frizzy haired woman wearing a white robe with purple butterflies on it was standing before them. She had her customary frown plastered on her face and had her hands on her hips. The grouchy octogenarian slowly surveyed the group gathered in the Antechamber and smirked.

"Why am I here?"

"Of course, you mean, *why am I here, Your Majesty?*" Pheron quickly corrected. "You are addressing your king, Miss Alwyn."

"One would think the head of the Archives would know all about proper protocol," Steve quietly quipped.

Sarah elbowed him in the gut. The frown on Andra Alwyn's face deepened, but thankfully, she elected to keep her mouth closed. Her angry black eyes briefly landed on Steve's before her nose lifted and she completely ignored him.

"What can I do for you?" Andra slowly asked. A few seconds later, she deliberately gave Mikal a small bow and added, "Your Majesty."

"The Alchos Stones," Mikal began. "What do you know about them?"

"The *what* stones?" Andra asked, with what could only be forced innocence.

"Miss Alwyn," Lissa suddenly interjected, as she slowly

rose to her feet. "I know you heard the question, yet you seek to belittle my husband at every opportunity. That ends now. I assume you enjoy your work in the Archives?"

Andra bristled with annoyance, "Of course."

"And I presume you wish to retain your position?"

The ambient temperature in the Antechamber seemingly dropped by several degrees. Steve's eyes widened as he noticed Mikal give his normally shy wife an appraising stare. To his credit, he didn't say anything.

"I do," Andra answered, with a frown.

"Then I suggest you act like it. Should you continue to demonstrate your, shall we say, loss of hearing, or indicate your mental faculties are beginning to fail, then you will be replaced."

Andra took a deep breath, no doubt to voice her displeasure. At the same time, Steve, Pheron, and even Mikal let out a small groan. There was no way Andra was going to allow herself to be insulted in such a manner.

"He—or she—who holds the position of Archivist has to be one of the most respected members of this court," Lissa continued, before Andra could speak. "The Archivist is responsible for the entire kingdom's history, its culture, and the proper cataloging of all its printed material. Only the sharpest, most intelligent minds could hope to tackle such formidable duties, wouldn't you agree?"

Oddly enough, Andra was no longer scowling, but smiling. "I would."

Lissa smiled, "Excellent. I cannot begin to tell you how much of a headache it would be if we had to try and find someone with all the same qualifications as those you currently possess. I'd much rather have you continue to oversee our Archives."

"As would I, Ny'Lissa."

Steve's eyebrows shot up. Andra had addressed Lissa by her title? And she wasn't scowling? What magic was this? A quick check around the room confirmed that every male present, including the guards stationed around the room, was gaping at the tiny Archivist as though she had just sprouted a second head.

"What's going on?" Steve whispered to Sarah. "Why is she suddenly being nice? It's creeping me out."

"Right with you there, Paco," Sarah quietly added.

Andra smiled at Lissa and gave her an honest-to-goodness curtsy. "You ask about the Alchos Stones? What would you like to know?"

Lissa turned to Mikal and held up an arm, encouraging him to take over the questioning.

"We need to know everything you know," Mikal began. "How many there are, what they look like, and where they can be found."

"As well as what they can do," Steve hastily added.

Andra spun on her heel until she was facing Steve. She gave him an unreadable expression before turning back to Mikal.

"Not much is known about the Alchos Stones," the frizzy-haired records keeper began. "There were four of them, no more, no less. Each of them was rumored to be a large gemstone. Which gemstones they allegedly were, I cannot say with any certainty. As for where they could be found, well, I'm sorry to say, they have become lost to time."

"Do you have any idea what these Stones were capable of?" Mikal asked. "I think *that* is what we're most anxious to learn."

Andra was silent as she thought for a bit. "Maybe one of my titles could help with that. Please excuse me for a moment. I will fetch it."

Belying her age, the frizzled old woman nimbly hurried out of the Antechamber and disappeared from sight as she all but sprinted down the hallway. The moment the Antechamber's door swung shut, Steve rounded on Sarah. He hooked a thumb back at the door.

"What the hell just happened here? Since when can she pull off a Jekyll and Hyde?"

"Pull a what?" Mikal asked, confused.

"It's a saying from our world," Sarah explained. "When someone's behavior changes that drastically, and you're inclined to think you're dealing with a completely different person, then a reference to Dr. Jekyll and Mr. Hyde is made."

"For the record," Steve added, "Jekyll and Hyde are the same person."

"Well, I'd like to hear about her sudden change of heart, too," Mikal admitted. He deliberately looked at his wife. "What did you do? I didn't see her eat or drink anything."

Lissa blinked a few times as she stared at Mikal. "What are you talking about? Of course, she didn't eat or drink anything."

Mikal nodded. "I know. No one saw her eat or drink anything, but clearly you slipped her something."

"Slipped her something?" Lissa repeated, confused. "I'm not sure what that means."

"It's another saying from my world," Steve clarified. "It means, given your background in local plants, Mikal thinks you've given something to Miss Congeniality, and that's why she's playing nice."

Lissa paused. A smile appeared on her face and she broke out in giggles before she was able to compose herself. She slowly shook her head.

"It occurred to me that our Archivist was just simply craving praise; attention. What could it hurt to give her a little respect?"

"Well, it worked," Sarah observed. "Good job, Lissa. Way to analyze the situation!"

Just then, the Antechamber banged open, revealing the return of Andra Alwyn. This time, she was toting a book nearly half as large as herself, and nearly three times thicker than anything Steve or Sarah had ever seen. It looked as though it weighed as much as she did.

Mikal caught Pheron's eyes and nodded toward the huge book. The captain nodded once, strode forward, and then held out a hand. Surprisingly, Andra bowed formally and surrendered the book. Steve's eyes narrowed.

"Okay, what's going on? She's never this nice."

"Just play along and don't say anything," Sarah whispered in his ear. "I don't know what she's playing at, either, but you do have to admit that she's cooperating. That's gotta be a step in the right direction. You'd better be on your best behavior, buddy boy."

Steve shrugged and slipped his hands into his pockets.

Andra indicated a nearby table where she wanted her book to be placed. Sarah used her jhorun to lift the small piece of furniture from the other end of the room and place it directly in front of the elderly records keeper. Andra nodded her thanks. At that moment, Steve began quietly humming the theme song to *Twilight Zone*. That is, until Sarah thumped him on his arm.

"This is *The Living Realm*. Only five copies have ever been printed. This is the only known copy to remain intact." Andra watched as Captain Pheron reverently placed the book on the table and stepped away. She slipped on a pair of white velvet gloves and carefully opened the thick leather volume. Andra began gently turning the thin, vellum pages when, after a few minutes, she stopped and thoughtfully tapped the page she was reading. "Ah. Here it is. I knew I remembered something about those stones. It is written here that the Four Alchos each carried a symbol of their power."

"You said they were lucky charms," Steve whispered to Balthor.

"No, that's what *you* called them," the shealk wizard quietly argued.

Sarah tapped each of them on their arm, "Shush. Let Andra finish."

"Thank you, dear," Andra said, all without looking up from her book.

Steve eyed his wife and shook his head. It was almost too much for his addled brain to process. How was it that a simple scolding from Lissa, of all people, would suddenly turn the sour Archivist pleasant?

"The book speaks briefly of the Stones, stating that each, as you surmised, had a power unto their own. I thought there might be ... here it is. Now, listen carefully. This is important. Each of the four Stones, long since carried around by their respective owners, absorbed some of their host's power."

Andra spent the next several minutes carefully flipping pages, evidently intent on searching for something specific. Once she found what she was looking for, she uncharacteristically motioned everyone over. She looked at the passage she had found and tapped her bony finger on it. It was clearly a rudimentary sketch of four simple objects.

"I do believe this is the only known illustration of the Alchos Stones," Andra proudly reported. "I came across this years ago and thought nothing more of it, passing it off as an elaborate bedtime story for children."

Steve leaned forward to study the drawing. Each of the four stones appeared to be different shapes. He realized he was in no way a gemologist, but even he could recognize basic, rudimentary gemstone cuts. What he was looking at didn't resemble a jewel by any definition of the word.

All four of the "stones" looked nothing like gemstones. At least, in Steve's opinion, they didn't. One looked as though it might have originally resembled a cube, but only if that cube had been somewhat squished. Or melted. Then another looked like a misshapen sphere, with Steve deciding it looked more elliptical than spherical. A third shape didn't have any real form whatsoever, aside from looking like a random object with ruffled edges, almost like a seashell. The final object was the only one that looked remotely recognizable, shaped like a pyramid.

"Did you really think they'd look like something you or I would recognize?" Sarah quietly asked, as if she had sensed his thoughts.

"I know I heard the word gemstone," Steve argued. "Those don't look anything like gems to me."

"You do know that uncut gemstones look nothing like the finished product, don't you?" Sarah reminded him.

Steve sighed. "Okay. Point to you."

"Are these their true shapes?" Mikal asked. He looked at Lissa, who shrugged. "Can you tell us anything else about them?"

Andra flipped through the next several pages and stopped a few minutes later. Her eyes rapidly skimmed the neat hand-written script as she read through the text. After a few moments she straightened.

"There are only passing references. Rumors."

"At this point, we'll take rumors," Steve told her.

"Agreed," Captain Pheron added.

"I have a list here of what the author thought were the four abilities the Stones possessed. How accurate it is, and which stone each ability belonged to, is unknown."

Mikal nodded. "Understood. Please proceed, Miss Alwyn."

"There are only four words here. They are: flight, deception, protection, and change."

"Change?" Pheron repeated, puzzled. "What type of ability is that?"

"We won't know unless we have a chance to study the stone itself," Balthor answered.

Andra turned at the sound of a new voice and suddenly found herself face to face with the transformed shealk wizard. After a few moments, the tiny records keeper again surprised them all by giving Balthor a curtsy and a very rare smile.

"I do not believe we have met," Andra all but stammered. "And you are?"

"You may call me 'Balthor', dear lady. You may know my son, Gareth."

Andra Alwyn's eyes flew open. She looked briefly at Gareth before returning her gaze to Balthor.

"If he's your son, then that makes you … that is to say, you're a…"

"…a water dragon," Balthor finished for her. "Aye, I was born a shealk."

"A water dragon," Andra breathed, amazed. "I'm conversing with a shifted water dragon. I, er, um … it's a pleasure to meet you."

"Okay, what is happening here?" Steve demanded. "Andra, what is it with you? Since when have you become so polite? You're freakin' the hell outta me. Stop it, would you?"

For the first time ever, Andra Alwyn, official Lentarian Archivist and sworn enemy of the Nohrin, offered Steve a sly smile.

"You mentioned deception," Sarah said, offering the elderly records keeper a smile of her own. "Balthor identified the stone Flinn has as having the power of deception. There's one we can cross off the list."

"You are familiar with the Alchos Stones?" Andra asked

as she turned back to the mysterious stranger.

Balthor nodded. "I am. I have spent many years studying them."

"Indeed? I do not suppose you would be interested in telling me what you know of them? I would be most appreciative of the inclusion of that information into our Archives."

"Why, I would be delighted, Miss Alwyn."

Everyone present heard it: the giggle of an excited school girl, and there was no mistaking where it came from.

"I think I'm going to be sick," Gareth quietly muttered.

Steve let out a short bark of laughter and quickly converted it into a coughing fit after Sarah shot him a dirty look.

"Miss Alwyn," Balthor began, giving his own son an equally scathing look, "is there any mention of what would happen if a human were to come into possession of one of these stones?"

Andra returned to the huge book and flipped a few more pages.

"The only reference I've seen that addresses what would happen should a human come into contact with one of the stones gives a single word reply: corruption."

"That might explain why Flinn is so bent on finding more of these stones," Steve added. "It's kinda like those potato chips. You can't eat just the one."

Sarah shook her head, "Dork. Quit thinking with your stomach and focus on the problem at hand. Flinn seems to think that another Alchos Stone is hidden in Lentari."

"That's because there *is* another stone in Lentari," Balthor corrected. "If I can read the signs that a Stone is here, then so can someone else. It'll just be a matter of time before someone finds it, and if Flinn happens to be collecting jhorun-empowered artifacts, then you'd better believe that he has an idea where to look."

"Was your apprentice privy to the same information as you?" Mikal asked with a tired sigh.

Balthor sadly nodded.

"Swell," Steve grumbled. "Well, what are we supposed to

do about it?"

"Isn't it obvious?" Gareth asked in a dumbfounded voice, as though he couldn't believe his ears. The young wizard turned to each person present and stared at them as though they had all sprouted scales. "I've said it before and I'll say it again: we find that second stone before Flinn does!"

Chapter 14 — Inconceivable!

That's not what I said, son," Balthor corrected, giving Gareth a stern glare. "I told you earlier we need to prevent that second stone from falling into Flinn's hands at all costs."

"And what better way to do that than by finding it ourselves?" Gareth argued. "Flinn already has an advantage over us by possessing one of these stones. The way to counteract that is have one of our own, too."

Steve cleared his throat, "You have to admit, Gareth has a point. Flinn has a powerful tool at his disposal. The only way we're going to be able to fight something like that is with a Stone of our own."

"Or else get that fang back," Sarah quipped.

The room fell silent as everyone turned to look at the most powerful teleporter Lentari has ever seen.

"Think about it," Sarah urged. "Flinn clearly thinks he needs the power of that fang to find the second Alchos Stone. Well, if we can steal it back, then logic suggests he won't be able to get the Stone. No fang, no Stone. Everyone is happy."

"Except he'll still have the *Essence*," Balthor reminded him.

"True," Steve groaned. "Damn. Sarah, couldn't you just teleport that thing here? I mean, you've teleported much larger items than that stone a lot farther before. Couldn't you just wiggle your nose and make it appear?"

"One more reference about that nose wiggling thing on *Bewitched* and you're going to be taking an impromptu dip in the moat."

Steve grinned at his wife, shoved both hands into his pockets, and took several healthy steps away.

"Besides, don't you think I've tried? I couldn't even teleport the fang back here. What makes you think I'd have any better luck with an all-powerful Stone? No amount of … Hon, I'm a teleporter. There's no distance you can move away from me which will render you safe."

"Couldn't you at least give it a try?" Steve persisted. "You never know. You just might surprise yourself."

"I *have* tried. Over and over, since I first learned Flinn had the *Essence*."

"Allow me to venture a guess," Balthor began. "You're unable to visualize anything to teleport?"

Sarah nodded. "Correct. I can't bring up a picture of either the fang or the Stone. Apparently, my jhorun doesn't want to touch jhorun-infused objects."

"That's a crock," Steve grumbled.

"What was that?" Sarah asked. Her voice had dropped to dangerous levels, causing every male in the room to take a few steps backward. "Would you care to say that again?"

Steve held his hands up in what he hoped was a harmless and soothing manner. "All I'm trying to say is, you've teleported magical objects before. All without any problems, if memory serves."

"What magical items?" Sarah wanted to know.

"Do you remember that Ylanian wizard, what's-his-name? You teleported his magical cup when he wasn't looking."

"Thaden," Sarah quietly murmured. She shrugged and eventually nodded. "Very well, I concede the point. I do remember sneaking that cup away from him. However,

I think the problem here is that these objects are far more powerful than that goblet of his."

"I think this is exciting."

The group collectively turned to the young queen.

"Think about it," Lissa began. "We've just been presented the opportunity to locate and protect a powerful talisman. Is an Alchos Stone here? Is it somewhere else? Either way, our choice is clear. We have to search for this Stone."

"And if it isn't here?" Mikal prompted.

"Then we'll rest better knowing we did everything we could to help Balthor search for the Stone."

"And if it is?" Steve prompted. "What do we do with it?"

"That's easy," Gareth answered. "We find out which stone it is and learn how to use it. I believe *that* will be the key to defeating Flinn. We beat him at his own game."

"In the meantime," Mikal announced, "we have to recover that fang. If the pirates lose the fang, they lose the ability to retrieve this second stone. Provided it's actually here."

"It's here," Gareth assured him. "My father says so."

"And when we find it?" Steve asked.

"We return it to its rightful owners," Mikal answered. "The wyverians."

Actually, it belongs to my mother.

"Pravara just reminded me that it belongs to her mother," Steve relayed.

Mikal nodded. "Of course. I'm sorry, Pravara. You know what I mean. Now, how do we accomplish this?"

"We find the pirates," Pheron stated, his face becoming firm. "We take this snake fang back."

"And how do we find the pirates?" Sarah wanted to know.

"We find the second Alchos Stone," Balthor answered. "My son and I will work on identifying its final resting place. I was close to discovering it before. With my son's help, it shouldn't be a problem. Steve, you and Sarah concentrate on getting that fang back."

Steve nodded and ignited both of his hands. His hands clenched into fists and blazed brightly. Noticing that people were starting to inch away from him, he flicked his hands out. "It would be my pleasure.

May I recommend that you and Sarah get started? I have located the pirate vessel.

You have? That's wonderful news, Pravara!

If truth be known, it was actually my grandfather who located the ship. He has been mentoring me in an attempt to sharpen my visual acuities.

Your grandfather?

Aye. Caradoc. He is widely regarded as having the best eyesight amongst all wyverians.

"What's going on?" Sarah whispered. "Is Pravara saying something to you?"

"She's telling me her grandfather helped her find Flinn's ship. I guess he's the best dragon to ask for help when you're searching for something."

"Where are they at?"

Where are the pirates?

They have anchored on the river, within sight of the human village of Donlari.

"They're close to Donlari," Steve quietly reported. "What they're doing that far inland on the Zylan River, I don't know."

"The pirates sailed their ship that far west on the river?" Pheron asked, amazed. "I didn't think a ship that size would be able to navigate those waters."

"Well, it clearly can," Steve said. "We need to get over there, pronto."

Pheron immediately motioned for one of the guards standing silently nearby. "Send word to Lieutenant Darius. I want three squadrons assembled and ready to move out in fifteen minutes. We will be accompanying the Nohrin to Donlari." The guard bowed and hurriedly left. Pheron turned to Mikal and held out a hand. "I will require the Donlari portal key, Your Majesty."

A look of surprise swept over Mikal's face. "The portal keys? I don't have the keys. My father keeps them in his safe."

"That safe?" Steve asked, pointing at the false wall behind Kri'Entu's desk.

Mikal's cheeks reddened. "I cannot open my father's safe."

"How will you know until you try?" Sarah gently asked.

"Because I *have* tried," Mikal whispered as his face turned bright red. "When Lissa and I first started seeing each other, I tried secretly accessing my father's safe—several times—to no avail. It responds to him and him alone."

"You're the king now," Steve reminded him. "Maybe your dad left hidden instruction within the safe. Remember the safe back in my office? It used to belong to my grandparents. I was able to open it, and I think that was only because I was a direct relative to him. Besides, this is your father we're talking about, Mikal. He's the King of Preparedness. He *must* have left a way for you to access the safe, should the need arise."

Mikal stood. "Very well, I'll try. I can only hope you're right."

He approached the wall directly behind the large desk, singled out one of the nearly identical stones comprising the wall itself, and gently pushed. A loud click sounded, followed immediately by a rough grinding noise. The wall recessed inward and then slid into a hidden panel, revealing a very familiar sight.

Nestled within the alcove was an identical version of the griffin safe Steve had sitting inside his personal office back home. The safe was essentially a statue of a griffin, seated on a thick stone pedestal. Steve knew that if the safe recognized an authorized person, then there would be an audible chiming. Then, once that person was close enough, the statue of the griffin would raise its right front foreleg, revealing a recessed button. That button would unlock the front of the pedestal, revealing the hidden compartment within.

Sure enough, as soon as Mikal stepped foot in front of the safe, the chiming began. A collective sigh of relief echoed around the room. Steve, however, was all smiles.

"See? I told you it'd work. When will you people learn to stop questioning me and just assume I always know what I'm talking about?"

Sarah snorted, eliciting several snickers from around the room. She hesitantly raised a hand.

"I'd like to weigh in here."

Steve laughed, gently pushing his wife's arm down, "Nope. Nuh-uh. Absolutely not. I do not believe I have requested any comments from the Peanut Gallery today, thank you very much."

"What's going on?" Steve heard Lissa whisper.

"I've seen this before," Mikal quietly answered. "Steve is getting ready to go on a trip."

"A trip? To where?"

"Someplace called Doghouse. I've never been able to find it on a map, but wherever it is, it must truly be dreadful. He never seems to have a good time."

Sarah giggled as she overheard the young king's hushed remarks, "Oh, Mikal. You're married. You'll learn soon enough."

Sarah and Lissa shared a conspiratorial look before each looked away, smiling profusely.

Once the safe was opened, Mikal withdrew the pewter box—which held the castle's portal keys—and opened the container. A brown crystal key was selected and presented to Pheron.

"Go, Captain. Find those pirates. You need to stop them, at all costs. I cannot let my parents know that we were attacked by pirates during one of their absences."

"Consider it done, Your Majesty."

"We'll meet you there, buddy," Steve told the captain.

Pheron nodded and strode out of the room.

"Are we ready to go?" Sarah asked, as she rose to her feet.

Steve nodded. "I think so. Let me double check with Pravara."

You're sure the ship is just outside of Donlari? You can see it?

No.

No? Earlier, you said that you had found the ship.

Aye. I believe I have found the ship.

Yet you don't see it?

Correct. Flinn must be using the Stone. I cannot see any traces of the ship anywhere.

So, how can you be so certain that you've found it? Especially when you can't even see it?

Because I can smell it.

Oh, come on. I know pirates don't smell the greatest, but they can't be that bad.

Allow me to explain. Aye, you're correct. I cannot see the ship. The Stone is masking the ship much too effectively for me to be able to see it. Thankfully, that works in our favor.

How so?

The Stone only hides the ship. I may not be able to see it, or smell it, but I can detect where the ship has been.

How?

By smell. I can smell disturbed aquatic life. Disturbed algae, agitated fish, and even frightened kytes are all signs that something large passed by not long ago. When many creatures are in distress, they exude pheromones in an effort to stave off predators. That's what I am detecting now.

You're telling me that a disturbed plant gives off a scent that you can smell?

In essence. One pontal, no. But dozens upon dozens of pontal? Aye. Something large disturbed the surface of the river and remains in the area.

Okay, you've convinced me. Sarah and I are on our way.

Just then, Steve felt a surge of excitement ripple through Pravara. He gasped with surprise. Sarah immediately turned to him with concern evident in her eyes.

"What? What is it?"

"I'm not sure. Something just excited Pravara. I think she might have seen something."

I have just made a discovery which validated my earlier supposition!

Say again?

I have located the human bandits. I knew I was right to trust my instincts. Father has said many times that the sense of smell is a wyverian's strongest ally. It pains me to admit he was right after all this time. Oh, well.

Umm, I'm not sure how to respond to that.

Then don't. I had believed the bandits to be on the vessel, only that isn't the case. They are ashore. I am watching them now.

You are? That's great! So, where are they now?

Hiding amongst the trees south of the human village.
What are they doing?
They appear to be arguing amongst themselves.
That's them, no doubt about it. Can you hear what they're saying?
Not at this distance, no. I will try to get closer.
Stay hidden. We'll be there in the blink of an eye.

"Pravara has located the pirates," Steve relayed. Mikal and Lissa gasped with surprise. "They're south of Donlari, hiding in the trees."

They appear to be traveling south. Why, I cannot say.

"They're moving south," Steve relayed. "Pravara doesn't know why yet."

Sarah looked at the young king and queen and smiled. She held out a hand and waited for Steve to notice.

"We'll be back when we can. Now, if you'll excuse us, we have an oskorlisk fang to recover."

"Good luck," Mikal told them.

"Be safe," Lissa added.

"We'll contact you once we ascertain where the second Stone is hiding," Balthor told the husband and wife team. "Fear not. My son and I will find it, regardless of locale."

"How can you be so sure?" Steve wanted to know. "How do you know where to look?"

"Because I've been searching for the Stone ever since Mephlas disclosed the location of the *Essence* to your Captain Flinn," Balthor explained. "Worry about that later. Go. You must recover that fang."

A look of grim resolved appeared on Steve's face.

"You got it. That fang is as good as ours. Flinn already lost. He just doesn't know it yet."

Sarah gave a quiet moan, made sure Steve wasn't watching, and then promptly rolled her eyes.

* * *

"Have you figured out what they're doing yet?" Steve whispered, as he parted the branches of the tree they were hiding behind to study the bickering pirates. "I'd sure like to know what they're up to."

They appear to be bickering. Still.

"Yeah, I know they're bickering, Pravara. You've been watching them for a while now. Do we know what they're doing?"

They search for something.

"Thanks, Einstein. We already know this."

Sarah cuffed him on the backside of his head. "Hey, that was uncalled for. Play nice. Pravara is helping us, remember?"

Steve rubbed the welt that was forming, "Right. Sorry. What I meant was … hey! Wait a minute! Can you hear Pravara, too?"

Sarah nodded. "Yes. I asked her if she'd include me when communicating, so you wouldn't have to repeat everything she says."

"Smart," Steve decided.

"I know. I have my moments."

They're finally on the move.

"What's up?" Steve asked. "Where are they off to?"

They have split into four groups, each consisting of four humans. I have heard a few of the humans whisper something about an item they wish to procure.

"We know this already," Steve pointed out. "They're looking for the second Alchos Stone. We're looking for it, too, remember?"

No. They do not seek the Stone. They seek … They seek…

"What?" Sarah asked. "What're they looking for?"

Tools. I've heard several of the humans reference tools.

"They must think they have to dig to find the Stone," Steve decided. "That could work in our favor. It can buy us some time."

"Time to do what?" Sarah wanted to know.

"Time for us to find it first."

It will also provide a welcome distraction when we launch our assault.

"Our assault?" Steve and Sarah echoed together.

Aye. It is clear these humans will not willingly return

the fang. Therefore, it must be taken by force.

Steve cleared his throat and raised a hand. "I feel it important to point out that our own force is significantly outnumbered. We're good, Pravara, but we're not that good. They're going to be expecting some type of attack."

"Pheron is on the way with three squadrons," Sarah reminded him. "That ought to level the playing field."

Steve nodded. "True. However, they're not here yet."

"So? We'll wait for them."

"But right now we have the advantage!" Steve protested.

"Flinn is down there," Sarah pointed out. "As is Mr. Steroids, as you call him. We're going to wait until reinforcements arrive."

Perhaps you won't have to wait too long?

"What was that?" Steve asked. When there was no forthcoming reply from the dragon, he turned to his wife and tapped her on the shoulder. "What did she say?"

"Just now? Pravara said, 'perhaps you won't have to wait too long'. I wonder what she meant by that."

"That makes two of us."

A commotion sounded from somewhere behind the husband and wife duo. Steve, suspecting the worst, ignited his hands and whirled around to confront the disturbance head on. A few moments later, both hands were snuffed out as twin identical heads rose slowly from behind a large clump of bushes. Both heads swiveled until they were looking at the two of them. Recognizing what he was looking at, Steve grinned, held a finger to his lips, and hurried over to the newcomer.

"Syrreth, Ferreth, it's good to see you guys again."

The two-headed dragon nodded and gingerly stepped forward. The bulk of its body became visible as it moved away from the trees. Zweigelan dragons were smaller than their winged cousins, had long, sinewy bodies—like the Chinese dragons Steve had seen so many pictures of—and tended to speak about themselves in the third person. This one happened to be the first two-headed dragon he had ever encountered. If it hadn't been for Syrreth and Ferreth's help, they might not have ever broken the curse cast on the dragons several years ago.

Now, Syrreth and Ferreth had become trusted members of the Wyverian Collective and were frequently consulted regarding activity in the southern part of the kingdom. The dragons, Steve knew, predominantly lived in the northern Bohani Mountains, and only a select few lived in the southern Selekais. Syrreth and Ferreth were one of the few who lived in the south. Kahvel must have called for aid, and the friendly zweigelan had answered the call.

"What business have you here, Fire Thrower?" the left head quietly asked. Ferreth's question had almost come out as a hiss as he tried to lower his voice.

"Asleep, we were," Syrreth added. "There are bad humans nearby?"

Sarah, still holding her finger to her lips, pointed at the pirates' hiding place nearly a hundred feet away. The pirates had still not noticed their arrival and continued to bicker as the four groups prepared to go their separate ways. The twin zweigelan heads froze as they spotted the humans. The two-headed dragon's body gently undulated, like a snake, and it was suddenly standing between husband and wife. The tip of its long, supple tail coiled around a nearby tree and held it firmly in place.

"Are we to attack?" Syrreth hopefully asked. "Terrorizing humans is a favorite pastime of ours."

"Been too long, it has," Ferreth added.

"There's something you need to know about those humans," Sarah quietly told the dragon. "They're pirates. They may not look like much, but they all have fairly powerful jhorun. Especially the one in the black hat. Do you see him?"

Both dragon heads nodded.

"That's Flinn," Sarah continued. "He's the one I'm most concerned about."

"Why?" Syrreth asked as he bared his teeth.

"He's an Air Elemental. He can summon the wind and make it do his bidding."

"Afraid of a breeze, we are not," Ferreth haughtily informed them. "Strike now while the advantage is ours, we should!"

"Cool your jets, Sparky," Sarah automatically replied. She placed a friendly hand on Syrreth's snout before anything could be said. "Flinn was able to keep Pryllan out of her nest and prevent the rest of the dragons from attacking."

A look of surprise washed over both zweigelan heads. Syrreth's jaws fell open. "Oh. Unfortunate, that is."

"We only have to wait a few moments more," Pravara's voice suddenly said.

Steve sighed, shook his head, and then turned to look behind him. The huge dark green dragon was standing less than a dozen feet behind them, studying them intently. Pravara gave a slight nod of her head to the zweigelan, who both promptly nodded back. Pravara, Steve knew, was the first wyverian to actively call this particular zweigelan *friend*. While he was certain they would both deny it, Syrreth and Ferreth were quite fond of the Dragon Lord's daughter and wouldn't hesitate to come to her aid, which was precisely what had happened.

"Are we waiting for someone else?" Steve curiously asked.

Pravara nodded. "Aye."

"More help?" Sarah added.

"Aye."

"Another dragon?" Steve hopefully asked.

Pravara nodded. "Aye."

Steve's eyes automatically shifted upwards to scan the skies. Sarah nudged his shoulder. When he looked, he was surprised to see his wife looking back at Pravara with a quizzical look on her face. The dragon was staring at the ground, alternating her gaze between two different locations nearly a dozen feet apart. To Steve, it looked as though Pravara was watching an invisible game of tennis between two players. The dragon's gaze suddenly fixated on the point closest to the pirates and stayed there, unwavering. Confused, Steve looked back at Sarah, who only shrugged.

The ground exploded upward, sending plumes of dirt and vegetation high into the sky. The two humans and two dragons stared at the crater that had appeared. Something was moving within the dust cloud. Something huge.

The pirates let out uncharacteristic screams and

immediately fled the scene. Four groups of pirates, four separate directions. Pravara groaned with dismay, eyed Steve, and immediately took to the air. Syrreth and Ferreth followed suit.

"What's going on?" Sarah nervously asked. "Do we need to leave, too? I'll teleport us back to the castle in a heartbeat. Don't think I won't do it."

"Pheron and his men are on their way here," Steve reminded her as they ran to hide behind the stump of a recently broken tree. "We can't let them encounter whatever it is that's down there."

Then they heard it: a loud growl. It was deep, feral, and sent chills down both of their spines. Whatever was coming up from the ground sounded *mean*. Steve grasped Sarah's hand and pulled her away from the huge crater. They were nearly a hundred feet away from the disturbance when Steve heard something that brought the two of them to an immediate stop.

"All right. It took a while, far longer than I would have liked, but I'm here. And … now I'm talking to myself. What the blazes is this? My instructions were clear. If I've come all this way for nothing, then there will be hell to pay."

"Who's there?" Steve nervously called out.

"Where are you?" the deep, stern voice snapped. "I hear you, and I smell you, but I do not see you. Reveal yourself."

Keeping Sarah firmly behind him, Steve retraced the steps back to the crater. Both he and Sarah fanned the air, waiting for it to clear. Once the dust and dirt had settled, they finally saw the owner of the voice.

Steve's eyes widened. It wasn't a dragon. Or, more specifically, it wasn't a dragon he was familiar with.

Something was pulling itself out of the center of the crater. It was a dull charcoal gray color, with a few flecks of black visible along its narrow back. The creature was covered with thick scales, had an elongated snout, and was without horns. Its body was squat, heavily muscled, and sported thick, chipped talons on each of its claws.

Steve nodded. Yes, this was a digger, all right. Was it some type of dragon? If so, he had never seen one like it before.

There were no discernible ears, or horns, or protruding fangs. Yet, as soon as the creature spoke, Steve could see that it had jaws full of razor-sharp teeth.

The creature snorted with surprise the moment it saw Steve.

"You? You are who I smelled? What are you doing here? How do I know you're not one of the humans I am supposed to deal with?"

"What are you?" Steve asked. "And you're here to help us? Prove it!"

"Why else would I leave the sanctity of my burrow?" the creature countered. "And I am a creeg, thank you very much."

"A what?" Steve asked, certain he had misheard.

"A land dragon!" Pravara's voice said from behind his shoulder.

Sure enough, their large wyverian friend had approached in stealth once more. Steve blinked with surprise as he stared at the creature.

"You're a land dragon? Wow. You don't look anything like I expected."

"Perhaps you were expecting a winged wyverian?" the creeg sourly asked as it twisted in place to look straight at Steve.

"Well, yeah. I guess. Sorry."

The creeg extricated the rest of its body from the earth and stood up on its ... Steve blinked with surprise. Yes, he saw that right. The creeg was standing up on its two hind legs. Steve's eyes widened with surprise. The Lentarian land dragons loosely resembled the overall body shape of a Tyrannosaurus Rex, only instead of useless vestigial forearms, the creeg's arms were directly proportional with the rest of its body. It also couldn't hurt to mention that the creeg's forearms were heavily muscled as well. Clearly, this was a creature that was used to digging.

"You're here to help us?" Sarah timidly asked the creeg. "What can we call you?"

"You may call me by my name," the creeg promptly informed her.

"And that is...?" Steve asked, trailing off as he waited for the Creeg to answer.

"You may call me Chusk."

Sarah gave the land dragon a tiny curtsy, "We're pleased to meet you, Chusk."

Chusk snorted, but elected not to say anything else. Stretching himself up to his fullest potential, the creeg scanned the area. He sniffed the air a few times before allowing himself to sink back down on his two powerful hind legs.

"I sense no other humans in this area."

"That's because you just scared the hell outta them," Steve informed the creeg. "We were in the process of sneaking up on them when you arrived. They scattered, like the wind."

Chusk comically cocked his head, much like a dog would do when it heard a strange noise.

"Then what am I hearing?"

Startled, both husband and wife also listened intently. Sure enough, the sounds of a distant battle appeared to be raging. Sarah groaned while Steve cursed.

"Damn!" Steve swore. He took Sarah's hand and hurried through the forest, following his ears. "Pheron and his men must have arrived just as the pirates were passing by. We're missing the fun!"

"Fighting pirates is *not* fun," Sarah sternly corrected. "Syrreth, Ferreth, are you following us?"

"We are here," Syrreth's voice confirmed.

"And Chusk?" Steve called, without turning to look behind him. "Are you there, too?"

The crack of broken trees sounded alarmingly close. The ground swelled up nearly a dozen feet on Sarah's left. Within moments, a new section of earth was pushed upward hundreds of feet away to the north. The pirates must have tried to flee back to their ship. Another section of the ground was pushed upward nearly a quarter of a mile away. Was Chusk digging his way through the ground? If so, then he was digging faster than they could run! That was impressive!

They emerged from the forest just in time to see a section of ground near the river explode upward, in much the same fashion as before. Chusk appeared in the center of the huge cloud of dirt and debris. He roared a challenge and advanced on the closest group of humans, who unfortunately, happened to be one of Pheron's squad of soldiers.

Steve paled. The soldiers scattered at the sight of Chusk thundering toward them, walking upright on his two back legs. Steve actually caught sight of several pirates leering evilly as they were easily able to slip away in the confusion.

"Pravara!"

No answer.

Pravara!

Yes?

Where are you?

I am trying to avoid the gusts of wind your pirate captain has created. I have almost been caught by several of them, and if that happens, then I'm certain to be pushed all the way past Lentari's southern borders. Why do you ask?

Contact Chusk and tell him not to harm the Lentarian soldiers. He's going after the wrong people!

Oh! A moment, if you please.

Steve noticed they had been spotted by several pirates. Brandishing their cutlasses, they advanced. Steve laid a hand on his wife's shoulders before she could do anything.

"I do believe it's my turn."

Sarah nodded and blew him a kiss. Steve faced the two pirates, ignited both of his hands, and generated two chasers. He eyed the two pirates, who had just halted their advance. Both of their smug smiles had vanished.

"There's only one way you're going to make it out of this alive," Steve told the pirates. "Make it to the river and throw yourselves in."

"We'll do no such thing, mate," one of the pirates sneered. "I don' care if you stick your hand in a fire and not be burned. There's no way you can ... Saints preserve us! Run! Run!"

Both pirates took off, as though they had each been shot out of a cannon. The two chasers could have easily caught them, only Steve deliberately slowed the two burning fireballs so that the pirates had a chance to make it safely to the river.

A wall of air slammed into him, knocking him off his feet. Momentarily knocked senseless, Steve remained motionless on the ground, tasting blood. After a few moments, he gingerly touched the side of his nose. His finger came away with a dark red smear. That damn captain had sucker punched him when he hadn't been paying attention!

Steve painfully rose to his feet. Sarah! What had happened to Sarah?

He heard several shouts of alarm and just then, two pirates went sailing over his head. Sarah then materialized some distance away, bent down to see to an injured soldier, and then both she and the soldier vanished. Steve nodded. Sarah could clearly take care of herself.

He wiped the blood that was threatening to trickle down his chin. Where was Flinn? It was time for a little payback.

"Get moving, ye blasted bilge rats. We don' have the time to dally. Now move or so help me, I'll leave the blessed lot of ye behind. Do ye understand?"

Steve's brow furrowed. There was Flinn, near the river's edge. He was trying to load tightly wrapped bundles onto a tiny skiff that bobbed on the choppy water. The captain and his men had their hands full as they hurriedly dealt with the packages.

Steve's curiosity was piqued. What was in the packages? Was Flinn trying to load or unload them? A few moments of observation gave him his answer. They were trying to move the bundles from the shore to the ship. Well, not if he had anything to say in the matter.

Steve hurried over to the river's edge. Thankfully, the rest of the pirates were still engaged with what was left of Pheron's soldiers, with the vast majority of them trying to distract Chusk. Pravara and the zweigelan, in the meantime, were blasting shot after shot at the river, in an attempt to get the *Emberbrand* to reveal itself. After nearly two dozen shots from each dragon had been fired, the dragons switched tactics and decided to try and keep the disguised ship from leaving. Trees were uprooted and dropped into the river, creating quite the log jam.

Steve heard Flinn curse and watched the captain begin

gesturing with his hands. One of his trademark gale-force winds appeared. It was directed at the two dragons, in an attempt to drive them off.

That left the tiny skiff unprotected!

Steve ignited his hand, pumped enough jhorun to make an impressive blast, but refrained from giving the fire jet a target. Instead, one of his seldom used "fire whips" appeared. He raised his hand, swirled the whip above his head a few times, and then slammed the burning jet of fire down, effectively cutting the skiff neatly in two.

The nearby pirates gave a collective groan of dismay. Alerted by the destruction of the tiny skiff, Flinn cursed with disgust as he saw who was responsible. Steve approached, let the fire jet extinguish, but left both hands ignited.

"You're not done with me, pal. Let's see how well you do when I'm paying attention."

"Gladly, Fire Thrower," Flinn sneered.

He redirected the fierce wind away from the dragons and aimed it at Steve.

"Ye cannot defeat me, mate," Flinn began as the jets of air strengthened. "I thought I had proved that by now. This be senseless. Let us leave and we will go."

"The plus side of that is … you cannot defeat me, either."

Flinn gave him a lecherous grin and a small bow. "Perhaps not. But I can certainly keep ye distracted, don' ye think?"

Steve was ready for just such an answer. He smiled, which wiped the smug grin from Flinn's face. He brought both of his burning hands up and clapped.

"As can I, *amigo*. In fact, watch this."

Steve generated a chaser, stretched it out until it was about three times the size of a normal fireball, and held it up for Flinn to see.

"Can you guess what I'm going to do with this?"

"I can tell you what *I* would like to do with it," Flinn sneered. "Besides, it'll take more than that to stop me, Fire Thrower."

Steve nodded. "Then, I guess I'd better put it in a good place, right?"

He lobbed the chaser toward the river, where it exploded

the moment it hit the surface. Flames raced outward, as though someone had dumped oil or gasoline on the surface. Neither growing nor diminishing in size, the flames continued to spread out, almost as if they were looking for something, which was exactly what they were doing.

Flinn suddenly realized what was about to happen. "Don't even think about it, Fire Thrower! If ye so much as *touch* my *Emberbrand*, then I will personally…"

Right at that time, the flames discovered the disguised pirate ship. Within moments, everyone could see the spreading fire suddenly change course and start burning upwards. The shimmering outline of the ship became visible as the fire rapidly spread. Seconds later, the cries of alarm switched to screams of terror.

"Call it off, Fire Thrower!" Flinn raged. "Call it off now or so help me…"

"Will you shut the hell up?" Steve suddenly snapped. "You want me to call off those flames? Fine. I'll do it. That'll be one oskorlisk fang, please."

Flinn's eyes narrowed and, Steve was certain, and internal debate began to rage.

"I wouldn't wait too long," Steve idly suggested. "I assume you'd like to be able to use your ship again. If you wait too much longer, then there will be nothing left but a piece of charcoal. Your choice."

"I can extinguish those flames," Flinn decided. "I've done it before."

"Think about your men," Steve urged. "Look over there. The vast majority of them are dealing with the creeg. How long do you think it'll be before Chusk there grows tiresome of the pests he calls humans? Trust me, pal. Your time is running out. Cut your losses and leave, which you'll be allowed to do *only* if you surrender the fang."

"Very well. You've won this battle, Fire Thrower. Rest assured, there will be others."

"Not on Lentarian soil there won't," Steve promised.

Flinn put two fingers to his lips and whistled three times. The *Emberbrand* suddenly appeared, mostly ablaze. Unbeknownst to the captain, Steve had ordered his jhorun to refrain from burning anything. Put on a show, sure, but do not allow the ship to burn. As much as he'd like to sink the brigantine, he wouldn't dare, not when there were probably a dozen or so pirates still on board. Thankfully, the pirates hadn't caught on to his bluff. Yet.

"We be leavin', Q. Prepare the ship!"

Rusty's head appeared over the gunwale. "The ship is on fire, Captain! You have to put it out!"

"Do it," Flinn ordered. "Extinguish those flames. Do not harm my ship."

Steve held out a hand, "As I said before, that'll cost you one fang."

Flinn scowled, pulled the fang from his belt, and slapped it into Steve's hand. In response, Steve glanced up at the burning ship, held out his right hand with his palm facing out, and gave the order to absorb the fires off the ship.

As if a giant vacuum had appeared, sucking the flames off the ship, the fires all leapt off the *Emberbrand* and sailed across the river to his outstretched hand.

"I gotta hand it to ye, Fire Thrower. I have never met a worthier adversary than the likes of ye. I hope we don't meet again. Ye seem a decent chap. I would hate to have to kill ye."

"And if I see you again, I will personally sink that ship of yours," Steve vowed. He tucked the fang into his own belt. "Be gone, pirate. Don't ever come back."

Flinn gave two short whistles, one long whistle, and then two more short whistles. The pirates fighting on land immediately abandoned their fights and sprinted for the ship. A blur of motion over his head had Steve looking up at the sky.

Pravara?

Aye. I am here.

Call off the attack. The pirates are leaving.

I know. I overheard. Do you really think you can hold the pirates to their word?

Of course not. Now that we know what Flinn wants, we know full well that he'd never leave without that second Alchos Stone. This is just to buy us some time to try and find that damn second Stone before they do.

Observe. The vessel is leaving.
That's a relief.
Your mate is signaling you.
She is?

Steve turned to see Sarah at the river's edge. She was beckoning him over. Pheron was there, looking none the worse for wear. The tall Lentarian captain had sliced open one of the bundles and was gently rifling through it.

"You did a great job with that chaser," Sarah told him as soon as he arrived by her side. "I didn't realize you could make the surface of the water burn."

"I didn't, actually," Steve corrected. "I instructed the chaser to only burn wood. Just the wood, mind you. It's an idea I thought of when Pravara told me she was tracking the ship by smelling disturbed algae. I knew I had to come up with some other means of finding that damn ship."

"Well, it worked," Sarah agreed.

"Yep. Now, what do we have here?"

"Take a look at this, Sir Steve," Pheron began, unwrapping the first bundle.

A selection of tools met his eyes. Hammers, picks, and bundles of tightly wrapped rope were laid out before them. Several small leather sacks caught Steve's attention. He pointed at one of them, intent on asking what it was, when Sarah leaned over, untied the drawstring, and upended the bag.

An impressive selection of glittering jewels fell to the ground. Surprised, Pheron opened the other two sacks and discovered more gemstones. Within moments, a veritable fortune in loose gems was spread out amongst the tools. Diamonds, emeralds, rubies, and sapphires—albeit tiny when compared to the jewels typically found within dragon nests— sparkled enticingly in the sun.

"What do you think they were planning on using this for?" Pheron asked in a bewildered voice.

Steve slid a hammer out of its holder and hefted it appraisingly. He fingered several of the picks and then studied the bundles of rope. He wordlessly pointed at the other trussed up bundles. More tools were revealed, as well as candles, lanterns, and a large supply of dried meat and fruit.

"If I didn't know any better," Steve began, "then I'd say they were preparing to go spelunking."

"I'm not familiar with that term," Pravara said.

"Nor am I," Pheron admitted.

"It means cave exploring," Sarah helpfully supplied.

Pheron frowned. "Cave exploring? As in, underground?"

"They have caves above ground," Steve argued.

Sarah studied the assortment of tools and supplies and suddenly groaned. "Pheron, you're right. I think they were planning on going down below."

"For what purpose?" Pheron asked.

Sarah picked up one of the emeralds and gazed admiringly at it a few moments before replacing it on the ground.

"I'd say they were on their way to the dwarves. Does anyone else think this looks like a bribe?"

"I don't care what it is," Steve decided. "We've won, they lost. They left, and we're still here. That's all that matters, right?"

"Did you get back the fang?" Sarah asked.

Steve let out a victorious grunt, pulled the fang from his belt, and held it triumphantly up for everyone to see.

"Why, yes, ma'am. I did."

Sarah clapped excitedly, took the fang, and pulled Steve in for a hug. "Great job, honey! I am so glad you got it back!"

"You and me both. Do me a favor, would you? Would you send that to the castle? Perhaps in the Antechamber? I really don't want to lose it again."

Sarah shrugged, looked at the fang sitting on her open palm, and decided to drop it on the king's desk inside the Antechamber.

"So, what now? Do you think we need to... oh, no!"

Steve ignited both hands and instantly pushed Sarah behind him. "What? What is it?"

Sarah wordlessly walked out from behind him and stopped directly in front of him. Looking straight into his eyes, she held out a hand and teleported the fang back. She groaned holding the fang up to her eyes for a closer look.

"What are you doing?" Steve complained. "Why'd you

bring that thing back out here?"

Sarah held the fang up and waggled it in front of his eyes, as though that alone would explain she was upset. "Since when I could I teleport this thing?"

Steve frowned as he stared at the giant serpent tooth. "What are you saying?"

"Honey, we've already proved that I can't teleport the fang, or that stone. Do you remember us talking about it?"

He gave her a noncommittal grunt.

"Steve, do you remember what Pedr told us? About his jhorun? Now we know why Flinn recruited him. Honey, this thing is a fake!"

Epilogue

This is only a setback. The loss of our supplies bothers me not. Stop yer frettin', Q. If this doesn't bother me, then it should not bother the likes of you, either."

"I'm sorry, Captain. I fail to see how you aren't concerned."

"I told ye before, Q. They have one of the fakes the cabin boy made."

"We still haven't located Pedr, Captain."

"While unfortunate, it isn't detrimental to the mission, Q. Now still yer tongue."

"But our supplies, Captain. We need them for the next phase of the plan!"

"We can get more supplies back in that village, Q. We'll steal them if we have to, but I would prefer if we didn't. The Fire Thrower be stronger than I care to admit. I do not want to alert them of our presence here."

"Where are we headed, Captain?"

"North."

"North? Blast it all, Captain. Why did we take the

Emberbrand down that river? That was nothing but a waste of time."

"Are ye challenging my orders, Q? Are ye suggestin' that I don' know what I'm doing?"

"Of course not, Captain. It's just that … well … never mind."

"I do not have to explain myself to the likes of you, Q," Captain Flinn warned, with a dangerous glint in his eye. "However, just this once, I will tell ye a bit more about phase two. Ye know we need to go underground next, right?"

Rusty nodded.

"What we seek next belongs to the dwarves."

"I know that, Captain."

"However, the dwarves we seek reside in the northern mountains."

"Far be it for me to question you, Captain, but are you sure?"

"So sayeth my mysterious benefactor from last year, Q."

"What do we seek from the dwarves, Captain? More jewels?"

"Jewels do not interest me, Q."

"Er, what does, Captain?"

"A hammer, Q. We're goin' after a special type o' hammer."

TO BE CONTINUED

Steve and the gang will return in
The Hammer is Strong with This One

Author's Note

Okay, what's next? Well, for me, I'm presently working on the 4th novel in the Corgi Case Files series. Thankfully, those cozy mysteries are much shorter, and can therefore be written much quicker. I'm anticipating I'll be done writing it by the end of the month. Then I'll be returning to Lentari to continue the adventures of Flinn and his band of pirates. Has Steve finally met his match? Will our favorite fire thrower be able to wipe the smug smile off of Captain Flinn's face? Only time will tell. :)

I'd like to close this with another passionate plea to ask for your help. Did you enjoy the book? Hated it? Please consider leaving a review wherever you purchased the book. We authors love reviews! They're one of the few things that can help us become more easily discovered by other readers. They do help.

Finally, if you want to make sure you never miss another announcement, or would like to sign up for my newsletter (I won't ever share your contact info with anyone else), then you can do so here: https://mailchi.mp/892eb3929891/authorjmpoole. Happy reading!

J.
July, 2017

ABOUT THE AUTHOR

Jeffrey M. Poole is a professional writer who writes in both the fantasy and mystery genres. His series are listed below. Jeffrey lives in picturesque Southern Oregon, with his wife, Giliane, and their Welsh Corgi, Kinsey. His interests include archery, astronomy, archaeology, scuba diving, collecting movies, collecting swords, and tinkering with any electronic gadget he can get his hands on.

In March, 2015, Jeffrey became a proud member of SFWA, the Science Fiction & Fantasy Writers of America! Jeffrey encourages readers to connect with him on Facebook (facebook.com/bakkianchronicles). Fans can also follow him online at: www.AuthorJMPoole.com.

BOOKS BY JEFFREY POOLE

Epic Fantasy
BAKKIAN CHRONICLES
The Prophecy
Insurrection
Amulet of Aria
Disneyland Debacle (short story)
Winter Wonderland (short story)

TALES OF LENTARI
Lost City
Something Wyverian This Way Comes
A Portal for Your Thoughts
Thoughts for A Portal
Wizard in the Woods
Close Encounters of the Magical Kind
The Hunt for Red Oskorlisk (short story)
May the Fang Be With You (Pirates trilogy #1)
The Hammer is Strong with This One (Pirates #2)
These are Not the Stones You're Looking For (Pirates #3)
Blast from the Past

DRAGONS OF ANDELA
Harness the Fire
Strike the Spark
Clear the Water*

Mystery
CORGI CASE FILES
Case of the One-Eyed Tiger
Case of the Fleet-Footed Mummy
Case of the Holiday Hijinks
Case of the Pilfered Pooches
Case of the Muffin Murders
Case of the Chatty Roadrunner
Case of the Highland House Haunting
Case of the Ostentatious Otters
Case of the Dysfunctional Daredevils
Case of the Abandoned Bones
Case of the Great Cranberry Caper
Case of the Shady Shamrock
Case of the Ragin' Cajun
Case of the Missing Marine
Case of the Stuttering Parrot
Case of the Rusty Sword
Case of the Secret Staircase (short story)
Case of the Unlucky Emperor
Case of the Ice Cream Crime

Scan the QR code to sign up for Jeffrey's
free newsletter!

www.ingramcontent.com/pod-product-compliance
Lightning Source LLC
Chambersburg PA
CBHW050132120726
47903CB00002B/319